THE
Lake
House

THE
Lake
House

MARCI NAULT

GALLERY BOOKS

New York *London* *Toronto* *Sydney* *New Delhi*

G

Gallery Books
A Division of Simon & Schuster, Inc.
1230 Avenue of the Americas
New York, NY 10020

First Gallery Books trade paperback edition May 2013

GALLERY BOOKS and colophon are registered trademarks of Simon & Schuster, Inc.

For information about special discounts for bulk purchases, please contact Simon & Schuster Special Sales at 1-866-506-1949 or business@simonandschuster.com.

The Simon & Schuster Speakers Bureau can bring authors to your live event. For more information or to book an event contact the Simon & Schuster Speakers Bureau at 1-866-248-3049 or visit our website at www.simonspeakers.com.

Designed by Jaime Putorti

Manufactured in the United States of America

10 9 8 7 6 5 4 3 2 1

Library of Congress Cataloging-in-Publication Data

Nault, Marci.
    The lake house / by Marci Nault.—1st Gallery Books trade paperback ed.
        p. cm.
    Gallery original fiction trade.
    1. Homecoming—Fiction. 2. Life change events—Fiction. 3. Neighborhoods—Fiction. 4. Self-realization—Fiction. 5. Boston (Mass.)—Fiction. 6. Domestic fiction. I. Title.
PS3614.A88L35   2012
813'.6—dc22

                                                                    2012025863

ISBN: 978-1-4516-8672-2
ISBN: 978-1-4516-8681-4 (ebook)

For my mother, Elaine Marie,
who taught me to dream.

CHAPTER 1

The last few snowflakes drifted to the ground. The nor'eastah, as they called it in New England, had passed; its brutal wake of snow and ice transformed the landscape into a winter wonderland. Downy blankets covered the tree branches, and silver moonlight reflected off the ice-hardened snow. The earth bowed its head in quiet prayer, and the stars awakened from under dark clouds. The wind died to a thick silence that Victoria Rose felt she could almost touch.

She walked along Nagog's paved road in black high-heeled boots. Cold seeped through the thin soles as salt pellets rolled and crunched under her feet. She'd left Nagog in her late teens, and except for two winters, her visits had been restricted to a few weeks here and there or the summer months. For the past fifty-five years, she'd lived mostly in Southern California's warmth. There, boots were only an accessory, and there was no need for heavy sweaters underneath a thick, cumbersome jacket. At the moment, a hideous bright blue parka, a loaner from her child-hood friend Molly Jacobs, covered her upper body and made her feel like the Michelin Man.

When Victoria had landed at Boston's Logan Airport earlier that afternoon, the heavy winds whipped the snow into furious spirals, and she realized she was unprepared to face the cold of her childhood home. When Molly met her at the baggage claim, her friend's pillow-like body had encased her in a hug and her white hair pressed against Victoria's chest. "You're home," she said, as fellow passengers bumped past them. Molly lifted her head and her blue eyes brimmed with tears. Molly was brown sugar, cinnamon, and vanilla. She was homemade bread cooling on the kitchen windowsill. Warm, doughy hands smooshed Victoria's angular cheekbones, and Victoria could hear Molly's thoughts—this day had been too long in coming.

"You're holding up traffic," Molly's husband, Bill, barked as he moved the women away from the escalator.

In the five years since Victoria had seen Bill, his girth had ballooned and the rock-hard fat, so detrimental to an older man's health, pressed against his pant seams.

"Traffic was awful," he said. "Billions of taxpayers' dollars for new tunnels, and the ceiling collapses. They closed the roads and we got stuck in gridlock. I tell ya, no one knows how to build things anymore."

Victoria slid her arm around his belly, kissed his cheek, and tousled his thin, salt-and-pepper hair. The crinkles around his eyes turned up and reminded her of the little boy who liked to drop spiders in girls' laps.

Three rose-embroidered suitcases fell onto the conveyor belt, and Bill motioned for the porter. As they walked toward the parking garage, Molly pulled the blue parka from a shopping bag and took Victoria's red cashmere coat.

"Fashion might work on fifty-degree nights in Malibu, but not here." She held out the sleeve as if Victoria were one of Molly's five great-grandchildren. She zipped the front and pulled the hood over Victoria's head, tying the strings tight. The shiny fabric crushed her short blond waves. Molly stripped the silk scarf from the red coat and wrapped it around Victoria's neck and mouth.

"Now you're ready for winter," she announced.

Victoria continued to walk as she looked at the snow-covered neighborhood illuminated by the moonlight and the metal lanterns that dotted the street. It was a scene straight from a Thomas Kinkade painting.

The community had been built in the early 1920s by Victoria's parents and their friends—factory owners and businessmen from the Boston area. Nagog Drive was a quarter-of-a-mile half loop with nine Craftsman bungalows surrounded by thick, knotted oaks, pines, and maples. The five homes across the street from the beach shared a large circular backyard. The other four homes were tucked into the woods along the lake—two on either side of the beach. Every house had a view of the water.

Nagog had been meant as a summer residence, but in 1930, four months after Black Tuesday, the community settled in permanently. The families banded together, determined to keep their factories open as the American economy fell apart; what one neighbor had, everyone shared. It allowed them a lifestyle of private schooling for their children and protection from the outside world's strife.

Victoria's boot slipped on a patch of black ice, and she tightened her stiff muscles to stop the fall. With small steps she skated until her feet found traction against the snow on the side of the road. *A broken hip wouldn't be a good homecoming,* she thought.

Throughout the small lakeside community, most of the houses were dark.

The cold tickled her back, and a shiver pulsed up her spine. She pushed her gloved hands deep into her pockets and looked toward Molly and Bill's place nestled on the side of the beach, behind bare hundred-year-old maples. Smoke plumes rose from the brick chimney and the light was still on in the kitchen. The brown clapboards and snow-covered pitched roof reminded her of the gingerbread houses she'd created with her granddaughter, Annabelle.

It was too dark to see the tree house in the big oak behind their home. An architect had designed it with two rooms and a wrap-around porch. When she was little, Victoria and her girlfriends would play tea party while the boys played cowboys and Indians. On hot summer nights, the porch became their stage as Victoria directed her friends in shows performed for their parents.

Victoria shivered, breathing in air that froze her lungs and reminded her of a snowflake's taste. As children, she and her friends would lie in the snow with wings outlined around their shoulders as they closed their eyes, opened their mouths, and waited for that one special crystal to touch the tip of their warm tongues. Those were the days when it felt like fairies sprinkled golden dust on Victoria's path so that her feet never had to touch ordinary ground. Days when the sun broke through the clouds, as if an angel's light reached out from heaven, a sign that every-thing that sparkled and shined was meant for her.

Time had passed too quickly, Victoria thought. Three genera-tions of Nagog children had played in that tree fort since those days. At seventy-four, how much time did she have—another fifteen or twenty years?

The year of her daughter, Melissa's, birth, Victoria woke one morning and saw a crease next to her eye. For years, she'd checked daily to ensure that its appearance hadn't deepened. Thick moisturizing creams were lathered and hundreds of dollars paid to Hollywood salons that promised everlasting youth.

There came a point, after she became a grandmother, when she saw a stranger in the mirror who didn't match the woman inside. Now her cheeks were smooth, but her eyebrows drooped. Her neck had a thin wattle, and she couldn't find that first line in the wrinkled fan around her eyes.

Still, she looked better than most women her age. Years of exercise and good nutrition kept her willowy figure firm, and she was proud to say that her abdominals were rock hard. There were teenagers who couldn't boast the same.

But at this stage of life, what was left? In society's eyes, living was for the young.

Victoria's heel broke through the icy snow and her calf sunk into the white drift as she made her way across the beach. With each step she fell deeper, the snow covering her boots as she walked to the picnic table next to the lake. She used her sleeve to hack and push at the white mound until she cleared the seat. The cold stung her backside. Plumes of steam encircled her gloves as she blew to warm her numb fingers.

The full moon reached its highest point, illuminating the expanse of shimmering snow that covered the lake. In her mind, she could see the blue-gray water and the gritty sand the color of maple sugar crystals hidden under the snow.

She'd learned to ice-skate on this lake. Each winter the fathers of the neighborhood would shovel off a large square, and the girls would put on white skates and glide across the ice. Victoria and her friend Sarah would hold hands and spin in circles, laughing as they went faster and faster. The boys chased pucks with hockey sticks while the fathers went farther out on the lake and cut holes in the ice to fish.

Victoria looked to the edge of the beach where the sand met the woods. The raft that had been pulled in from the water for the winter months was covered with snow. Victoria smiled as her memory wandered back to the hours she'd spent on that raft with her childhood friends.

〰⃝〰

Five bubbles of pink gum grew as the circle of teenage girls in bathing suits lay on their stomachs and blew as hard as they could. Nagog Lake's waves danced and slapped against the rusted steel drums that held up the wooden platform they floated upon. Muffling giggles, they blew harder, their faces turning red in the bright sunlight. The gum smelled like cotton candy and its aroma filled the air. The sticky material stretched thin and they leaned their heads closer to one another, their eyes wide and smiling as the sides of their bubbles touched. A horsefly buzzed around their heads, and they tried to shake it away without breaking the delicate pink circles.

Victoria closed her lips. From deep within her throat she vibrated the count of three. On three, the girls pressed their faces closer together, trying to pop the bubbles. When the bubbles finally burst against the girls' cheeks and chins, laughter erupted, and they peeled the candy from their skin.

Victoria pulled a sticky piece from her long, wavy, golden hair. "Bubblegum is one of the world's best inventions." When her father had brought her to the World's Fair last fall, he'd bought her the biggest jar of bubblegum she'd ever seen. She rationed the candy throughout the year, sharing it with her inner circle of friends.

The five girls rolled onto their backs, their heads in a circle, and watched the fluffy clouds sail across the blue sky. Victoria snapped and popped her gum, knowing that her mother couldn't hear her being unladylike this far out on the lake. She adjusted the strap of her red bathing suit. Unlike the other girls, whose suits covered their stomachs, Victoria had four inches of bare skin above her waist. Though her mother hated the suit, her father had allowed it.

Molly pointed her finger toward the sky. "I see a heart."

The hot breath of summer air flowed over Victoria's skin. The day felt like late August instead of the end of May. "You always see hearts," Victoria said. "It's because you're in love with Bill." Victoria poked Molly's side and her friend batted Victoria's hand away.

Born two and a half weeks apart, she and Molly lived next door to one another and roomed together at Dana Hall, an exclusive all-girls' school in Wellesley, Massachusetts.

Molly sat up and watched the boys of the neighborhood playing volleyball on the beach. She pulled at the top of her bathing suit, trying to cover the new curves that had blossomed on her petite body during freshman year, and fluffed the short skirt of her blue suit over her thighs. Victoria watched Molly stare at Bill. The rosy color that naturally tinted her cheeks blushed brighter. When they'd returned from boarding school last week, Bill had noticed the change in Molly's body, and instead of pulling her black hair the way he had since early childhood, he now stared at her royal-blue eyes and stumbled over his words when he spoke to her.

"Victoria, let me braid your hair," Sarah said. She sat up in her plain green suit and nudged Victoria to move.

Victoria sat at the edge of the raft and dangled her feet and calves in the cold water. Sarah knelt behind her and gently combed through Victoria's knotted hair with her piano-player fingers.

Sarah, Victoria's other roommate, loved to play with Victoria's hair, and many nights were spent with Sarah brushing Victoria's long locks. The two were often mistaken for sisters—both tall and thin, with pale skin and blond hair. They shared the same classes and danced in the school ballet. It wasn't uncommon for them to exchange makeup and clothing, and from a distance it was hard to tell them apart.

"I see a dog in that cloud," Evelyn said. She rolled over onto her stomach and crossed her tiny feet behind her thighs. Her short blond hair had dried into fairy curls around her forehead.

Sarah finished the braids and leaned her chin onto Victoria's shoulder as they watched the boys play volleyball. Victoria pulled Sarah's arms around her and stared across the lake. Bill, Carl, Joseph, and James were as inseparable as the girls.

"Do you think Carl is cute?" Sarah asked.

"He's annoying," Victoria said. Carl was the shortest of the boys and she could already tell at sixteen that he would be as bald as his father.

"I think he's funny," Sarah said. She tugged on one of Victoria's braids. "You just don't like him because he called you Frog Face when we were little."

"I socked him in the stomach more than once for calling me that name and he doubled over. Who would want a man who'd been beat up by a girl?" Victoria teased.

"I don't think you could still beat him up," Sarah said. "And who else am I going to choose? Molly's in love with Bill, Evelyn with James, and we all know at some point you'll stop pushing Joseph away. The two of you are meant to be together. Or are you going to let Maryland have Joseph?"

Maryland stared up at the clouds and didn't respond to Sarah's words. The boys had never paid her much attention. Considered a plain Jane, everything about her was average. She was shy and quiet, always following along with whatever anyone wanted to do. But she was also the first to give a hug if she saw that you were sad, the first to take a barrette from her hair to replace the one you'd lost.

When they were little, Joseph Anderson had followed Victoria around, saving her from the other boys' pranks. His blue eyes had been too big for his thin face and he had a cowlick even the best hair oil couldn't tame. He'd brought her flowers and chocolate candies and the other kids made kissing noises to tease her. He'd been annoying.

But over the last few years he'd grown into his features. As he jumped up to spike the ball, Victoria noticed the definition in his bare chest, sending butterflies to her stomach. "You know there are men outside of Nagog we could marry."

"But then we might not be together," Molly said as she moved closer to Sarah and Victoria. She leaned her head on Victoria's shoulder and dangled her feet in the water.

Victoria squeezed her friends' hands. "We'll always be together. And no matter where life takes us, we'll always come back and spend the summers here."

"And when we're old like our parents, we'll live here with our children," Molly said.

"Friends forever," Sarah whispered.

The memory faded. Victoria looked across the lake into the empty night. As a child there'd been a silver dock built as a protective barrier from the deep end of the lake. The marker for adulthood had been the day you were allowed to run down the dock and dive into the water. When you could swim out to the raft you were no longer considered a baby. The dock had been removed years ago.

How did this world of childhood fond memories become the place where her worst nightmares had happened? There were nights when Victoria awoke from dreams with her breath caught in her rib cage and the dry, bitter taste of regret poisoning her mouth. She feared that she'd never find release from her sorrow. Guilt, which started as a small grain of sand in the gut, had grown to a boulder that shackled her movement. Worst of all was the feeling of loss—a black hole that sucked life's vibrancy into its vacuum.

Tears froze on Victoria's cheeks and she brushed away the new ones that fell. She should retire to bed, but in her family's home, the place she'd known her entire life, the silence echoed with voices from the past like a child's imaginary monster when the lights go out.

It was in that house, nineteen years ago, that she'd said goodbye to Melissa and watched her daughter return to God. And it was here on this beach that she'd cradled her granddaughter, Annabelle, in her arms and screamed for help, knowing her angel had barely any breath left in her body.

On the other side of the beach, a light went on in Joseph's home. Through the bare trees she could see his body move around the sunroom. Her frozen legs were hard to control as she crunched through the snow; more than once she almost fell before she reached the road. Joseph looked out the window and she waved. He returned the gesture and turned off the light.

Behind Joseph's dark house was a path that led to a secluded beach where the two of them had once shared the most intimate of moments. Images from the past played like a movie in her mind, with big band music as the sound track.

Under the thin tablecloth, cool sand had formed curved beds for their half-naked teenage bodies. Beyond the trees she could see the party lights on the patio and hear the music. Had anyone noticed they'd slipped away?

"I love you, Victoria," Joseph whispered in her ear.

Though he'd once driven her crazy as he followed her around, now her heart craved him when they were apart. The past year of school had been torture—months went by with only letters to fill the distance between them. She'd thought they'd marry as soon as she graduated, but now he was going to war, and it would be years before she could touch him again.

Joseph swirled his tongue in delicious patterns over her neck. Warm sensations flowed through her veins like powerful energy currents and pooled between her hips. Every cell in her body burst with happiness as his hands moved over her thighs. She tried not to jump when he touched the soft, warm mound, but lightning struck her body.

He pulled away.

No one had explained sex to Victoria. Her heart was split between fear and her desire to seal their relationship before he left for the war.

"Please, it's okay." She caressed the dimple in his cheek; her finger fit the indent like a puzzle piece. The little boy with the thin face had grown into a man with chiseled cheekbones and broad shoulders.

He gently covered her body with his as he kissed her—her heart skipped as her body begged with a need she didn't understand. Pain stabbed through her lower abdomen. Her body tightened and she pulled back from his kiss, biting her bottom lip and focusing on the sensation in her mouth.

His hand swept her jaw and he nuzzled her neck. His warm breath tickled her ear, sending shivers across her arms. "Relax. I'll wait."

He drew hearts on her cheeks and placed kisses on her forehead. His fingers combed through her hair. Her muscles unwound. She felt the thickness of his body entwined with hers. The lake's small waves lapped against the shore and he moved in slow circles to its rhythm. Joseph's masculine fingers stroked her sides. Her eyes widened at the pleasurable sparks firing in her belly.

Giggles broke free. "I'm sorry I'm laughing. It feels wonderful," she said.

"You're beautiful," he said.

His tongue teased her lips as she began to move with him. Deep hunger grabbed her. Her nails dug into his back. Her thighs tightened around his waist. Explosive, joyous waves shook every muscle. Sunlight blazed through her. Her body went limp, the world went dark, and she floated in peace.

Joseph moaned. "Victoria," he called out through quick breaths.

She felt him move deeper within her. Their lips pressed, merging together. His orgasm flowed through her, pleasure not of her flesh but of his.

He rolled onto his back and she laid her head against his chest.

The breeze tickled her skin. She touched her body, so different to her now: a pleasurable world to discover.

"Again," she'd said, tracing his stomach. "Again."

Victoria shivered as the wind picked up. She closed her eyes and placed her hands across her heart. Her toes felt like icicles and burned with pain. Part of her wanted to walk that path behind Joseph's house and turn back time to when he belonged to her and not to his wife.

She stared at the quaint neighborhood with its gabled snow-covered roofs, bay windows, columned porches, and decks. The community didn't seem real. Purity, innocence, and old-fashioned values were safe here, as if a protective bubble hovered over the circle of homes and kept them isolated from the outside world.

Most of her childhood friends had moved to Boston during their working years, but they visited Nagog on the weekends, stayed during the summer months, and celebrated every holiday together. When they retired, they returned, as promised, to live once again in the Nagog homes that had been passed down to them. Victoria had been the only one to walk away and live another life.

In the eyes of many in the community, she'd fallen from grace—and no one had pushed her. As Lucifer had done, she'd made choices that barred her from Heaven.

Had she come home to let her demons take her into death or had she returned to Nagog to find the whisper of wind that swirled between the trees and floated over the lake—the call of a little girl who once believed in magic? In this place where the past had been kept alive, she was afraid to pray for forgiveness. But the truth was that Nagog and her childhood friends were all she had left.

CHAPTER 2

The last thirty hours hung heavily on Heather Bregman's shoulders. The knot of pain at the base of her neck radiated to her forehead as the airport noise vibrated behind her eyes. Two days of flying in coach had left her exhausted. Yesterday, the man next to her had snored his way from Johannesburg to London with his large thigh pressed against her hip and his elbow dug into her waist. *Whoever had decided that a human could be stuffed into a box with only a ten-degree recline should spend the rest of eternity folded in half,* she thought.

The herd of passengers made its way to the baggage claim. Logan International Airport had the ambiance of a prison: dingy gray walls met grimy floors; fluorescent lights hung next to exposed heating ducts, bundled wires, and falling insulation. The airport had been under renovation since the late nineties, with no marked improvement.

A fur coat bumped against Heather's arm. The owner flashed an apology as she ran past. Her thick, red hair flowed in long waves and her pearly skin radiated like a bright spring day. She threw herself into the waiting arms of a beau. The man kissed her lips, her eyes, and her cheeks.

It must be nice, Heather thought, while she waited for her luggage. Maybe on the other side of the automatic doors she'd find her fiancé, Charlie, waiting with a warm car. She didn't need to feel precious or missed; at this point, a ride home would be romantic.

She thought of the hours she'd spent trying to decide on an outfit to wear before finally picking a red velvet jacket and designer jeans. The strappy shoes she'd bought in London sparkled around her fresh pedicure. For the last month she'd worn beige zip-off pants, tanks, and hiking boots on her African safari. Most days she'd felt like a dusty, sweaty mess. When she'd tried on the clothing she felt like a girl again, but for all her primping, she should've worn sweats. Charlie wasn't coming and she knew it.

She twisted her engagement ring. The decision she'd made over the last month felt like a dumbbell pressed against her chest. She pulled the ring off and looked at her hand without the sparkling diamond against her tan skin. A white line marked the place. *Great,* she thought. *I wonder how long it will take to fade.*

Her black suitcase fell onto the conveyor belt. She placed the ring back on her hand and pushed through the crowd. She tried to balance in the tight space on her three-inch heels, and almost fell over when she lifted the sixty-pound bag.

As she waited for her duffel, the clock seemed to tick at half speed. For the twelfth time, the security announcement came over the loudspeaker. *We get it already. Don't leave our bags unattended.*

An elderly couple stood beside her, their eyes puffy with fatigue. They leaned on each other, the woman tucked under the man's arm. An ancient leather suitcase drifted along the conveyor belt. The man wasn't quick enough to grab it, and Heather rushed forward. The awkward bag bumped against her leg as she hauled it to the couple.

"Thank you, dear." The old woman placed her hand on Heather's arm. The skin on the lady's fingers looked like rice paper, blue veins showing through.

What was it like to be old? Heather wondered. Everything over. Mistakes known. Accomplishments checked off. No need to work. To have a home that showed years of wear and tear but exuded love from a lifetime of family memories. When you were old, no one cared how you looked. Sags and wrinkles were expected.

If Heather didn't need to keep her frame in a size 6, she would eat chocolate and ice cream without guilt, and instead of exercising every day, she'd settle onto her couch and read. If career—and relationship—didn't seem to hinge precariously on her looks, she wouldn't have to spend hours curling or straightening her long, brown, highlighted hair just to pay hundreds of dollars to fix the heat damage, and she'd wear glasses instead of the contacts that irritated her brown eyes.

Settled. Comfortable. It seemed an eternity away.

At twenty-eight, she was struggling to build her career. Newspaper syndicates around the country had dropped her column, "Solo Female Traveler." She needed that book deal, the cable show, and the sought-after television interviews.

The conveyor belt stopped. Empty. She dropped her head in disgust and trudged to the customer service counter. Just her luck: the bag with her coat, boots, and gloves hadn't arrived. The click of her heels echoed in the near-empty airport. It took fifteen minutes to file a lost luggage claim, then she made her way to the taxi stand. Cold air cut through her thin jacket, and she hugged herself for warmth.

The traffic lanes usually congested with taxis, shuttles, and cars were now empty. Heather stood alone, surrounded by concrete, silence seeping in with the cold. She longed to lean her head against a warm body.

A security officer sat on his stool, his chin curled into his navy winter coat.

"Where are the cabs?" she asked.

"They headed out. There aren't any more flights tonight. The hotel shuttle's across the street. Last one'll be by in a few minutes or you can catch the last T."

The snow that had delayed her flight had turned to gray slush on the road. She cringed as she looked from the sloppy mess to her strappy heels, which she'd never intended to wear in the snow.

The suitcase wheels stuck in the slushy muck. She tried to hop to the driest spots, but ice and sand squished between her toes. At the bus stop, ten minutes passed. Her feet and hands turned to red and then yellow ice cubes as she sat on the plastic bench.

Spent. That's how she felt. Exhausted to her marrow, as if she couldn't take another step.

The blue-and-yellow shuttle pulled to the curb. The driver stepped down and grabbed her luggage. "Where ya headed?"

"Back Bay."

"I've got four stops before ya. It might take a while," he said as he pulled her bag onto the van.

The T would've been quicker, but it was after midnight and she'd missed her chance. She climbed onto the van, found a seat, and leaned her aching head against the icy window.

A rainbow of lights flashed around her as the bus made its way along the slippery streets: the blue-and-orange clock face in the Custom House Tower; the glow of street lanterns made to resemble colonial candles flickering in glass.

Forty minutes passed and the van pulled in front of a row of brick townhomes. She dragged her suitcase up the stone steps that had been smoothed by hundreds of years of use and were now slippery with ice. The large mahogany door was heavy as she maneuvered her suitcase into the foyer and then through another door into the lobby.

Her heels clicking against the marble-tiled floor, she walked to the elevator, only to find that it was out of service. She sighed, picked up her suitcase with both hands, braced it against her thigh, and hauled it up the thirty-five stairs to the third floor, the bag banging against her leg.

A dark kitchen greeted Heather when she opened the door to the apartment. She turned on the overhead light and sat at the square metal table to peel off her shoes. The black-and-white ceramic floor tiles were cold and she pulled her toes under her thighs to warm them. The shoes dangled from her fingers, and she glared at the fiery red straps. "For how much I spent, these should make my legs look great *and* be comfortable."

Exhaustion weighing heavily on her eyelids, Heather longed for a hot bath with bubbles up to her neck. She wanted to slide into a soft bed with down comforters fluffed over her and curl into warm, protective arms.

With paper towels, she wiped the slush track her suitcase had left on the tile, then she crammed the bag into a small closet.

Snorts of contented sleep greeted her when she creaked open the bedroom door. Charlie lay in the center of the bed splayed in all four directions. He turned onto his back, his six-pack exposed above his underwear. With his thick black hair and dark Italian eyes, he could grace the cover of a magazine.

Three short snores vibrated his throat. She looked at the stray piece of hair that fell over his eye. In their first years together, she'd tuck the strand into place and kiss his cheek. It had been a long time since she'd played with his hair. What had happened to them? There'd been a time when Charlie's love had made her feel safe, secure, and happy.

Heather had spent the last six years on planes, in hotels, and exploring the world while Charlie worked as her agent, building her career. When Charlie looked at her, she felt he saw a columnist—another client in the string of people he'd made into products.

A burp of morning breath escaped Charlie's lips when she leaned over him.

"Charlie, I'm home," she whispered.

With his eyes closed, he reached for her waist and pulled her onto his body. His free hand moved under her jacket. "Good trip?"

"Yeah."

Stubble chafed her upper lip, and she tried to keep her mouth closed to avoid his sour taste. He pulled at the jacket's buttons.

"Charlie, I'm tired."

"What's new?" He rolled her away and turned his back to her.

A silk chemise hung on the bedpost. She removed her clothes and slipped into the cold garment. Goose bumps dotted her skin. She curled into the fetal position, the thin blanket pulled to her chin. Hot-blooded Charlie couldn't sleep with a comforter.

The first night she'd spent in this apartment, Charlie had

leaned against the headboard, her back against his chest and his legs wrapped around her waist, as they ate Thai food. He'd kissed her hair, nuzzled her neck, and told her she was beautiful. Now he couldn't bother to meet her at the airport.

She turned toward Charlie and looked at his back. Heather had been away for a month, yet as she lay in bed next to her fiancé, her heart still cried with the need for home.

⁓◦◦⁓

"Rise and shine!" Charlie threw open the green curtains behind their bed. The sun illuminated the darkened room with blinding brightness. Heather tried to cover her eyes with the pillow, but he grabbed it away, so she buried her face in the blanket. Charlie jumped on the bed, bouncing the mattress with his large frame.

"Why do you insist on doing this?" she snapped. They'd always kept different hours. He insisted on opening the curtains while he dressed for work. Sunlight put him in the right mood for the day. It made Heather pray for rainy mornings. She reached for the eye mask on the end table. The smooth material slipped between her fingers and fell to the floor. Charlie grabbed her wrist and rolled her to him, entwining their bodies. The sunshine pierced her retinas.

"If you don't want weeks of jet lag, you have to get back on East Coast time." He bounded from bed. "Want to join me in the shower?"

"You haven't even showered?" He didn't answer. She looked at the red LED lights on his nightstand—7:35.

Charlie's baritone voice drifted over the water's sound as he sang in Italian. She shuffled to the kitchen, pulled out the industrial-strength coffee she'd bought in Costa Rica, and leaned against the counter, waiting for the miraculous liquid to be ready.

The overhead track lighting blinked on, and Charlie walked into the room. The coffee began to drip into the pot, and she bent over the coffeemaker to take in the aroma. Covered by only a white towel, Charlie's erection pressed into her backside. He wrapped his arms around her waist and leaned until her ribs pressed painfully into the granite counter.

"Want to go back to bed?" He nuzzled her neck.

No.

"I've missed you," he said as he nipped her ear.

"I'm tired." She shifted her weight away from the counter and ducked out from under him.

"I've heard that one before." He grabbed the pot and emptied it into the cup she'd taken from the cupboard for herself.

"Do you mind leaving some for the person who barely slept last night?" Heather fumed.

"You mean the one who just spent a month lounging around in safari camps? The one who doesn't have to go into the office today? God, you're grumpy this morning." Charlie slurped from the cup and walked away.

Four aromatic ounces had collected in the pot. Heather poured them into Charlie's Harvard Law mug and walked the short distance through the living room and into their bedroom.

The large closet housed Charlie's elaborate collection of suits. He pulled a navy blue ensemble from the dry-cleaner bag and laid it on the bed. Then he inspected a pressed shirt. Always the same routine: lay out the suit, check for rogue stains or wrinkles, get dressed, fluff his hair in the mirror. His shoes were kept in the front closet. When he came home at night, he buffed them, inserted shoe trees, then stored them in cotton bags inside their original boxes.

Heather placed her mug on top of the bureau, knowing it would drive him crazy as he thought about water marks on the wood.

Like clockwork he looked at the cup and then glared at her. "I'm not in the mood for one of your tantrums. If you're trying to pick a fight, I don't have time."

"I've heard that one before," she said, mimicking his earlier comment.

He belted his pants and sat on the bed to put on his socks.

She tapped her foot, trying to control what was about to blow, knowing she should stop. She needed to have a conversation that was gentle and kind, but anger took over. "Maybe if someone had bothered to pick me up from the airport, I wouldn't be so tired and grumpy this morning."

"That's what you're pissed about?" He buttoned his jacket and looked in the mirror. "You got in close to midnight. I have an important meeting this morning—about *your* career. Did you want me to stay up all night waiting for you at Logan?"

"You were plenty awake for sex."

"Excuse me for wanting to be with my fiancé after she'd been away for a month." He returned to the bathroom and she could see him putting gel in his hair. He came out and grabbed a tie from the closet. "You know, sometimes you seriously act like a spoiled princess."

"Oh, I'm a princess?"

"You get to travel the world because of me. Yet you come home and bitch because I don't allow you to sleep all day. If the shoe fits."

"And *I* have nothing to do with my success." Her anger festered. He wasn't listening to her. She tried to calm down, but the uncontrollable fury from feeling invisible forced the words out, "You know what, Charlie, I can't do this anymore." She took a shaky breath. "I think we need to take some time apart."

The muscles in his jaw cranked with tension as he tucked a blue silk tie under the collar. He walked toward her and leaned his face within inches of hers. "You might want to be careful with what you say, or your life could change drastically. I'm going to work. We have an important networking event at the end of the week. Get over your damn tantrum and get it together." He walked to the kitchen and she could hear him putting on his shoes. The chair scraped against the tile and then the door slammed.

A stifled scream rumbled in her lungs. She climbed onto the stiff mattress and tugged at the window covers. *Damn curtains that shut out the light when he wants to sleep and brighten his day when he goes to work. Doesn't matter that I fell asleep at 3 a.m.* With the curtains closed and the room dark, Heather grabbed her coffee and slumped onto the bed. She created a cocoon around her body with the blanket as she cradled her mug.

"You don't even pay attention when I try to break up with you," she mumbled.

Heather curled the blankets closer and sipped the coffee. She longed for the coffee she drank in Africa. She let her thoughts wander back to her trip as she tried to calm her nerves.

Every morning at five o'clock, Manal, her guide in Botswana, would sing out her name. Hot coffee prepared with sugar, a splash of brandy, and heavy cream awaited her on the table outside her tent. Porridge, covered in more cream and brown sugar, greeted her when she took her place around the morning campfire. As the Okavango Delta's cool dark waters gave birth to the blood-orange sun and monkeys tried to steal her silverware, she savored breakfast. Mid-morning, Manal would set up a table and camp chairs next to the open Land Rover and Heather feasted on scones and biscuits dipped in hot chocolate and watched giraffes nibble on the sausage tree's long fruits. At night, while the kitchen staff sang, their cadences joined by hippo grunts and deep-throated lion calls, she and the other guests would stare at the stars and sip Amarula, the sweet, creamy liqueur of the marula tree.

Charlie was right. She'd spent a month living her dream of traveling and writing, and he'd helped her to achieve it. But that couldn't mean that for the rest of her life she had to feel indebted to him . . . and invisible in their relationship.

A car horn honked. The rush-hour traffic on Storrow Drive motored past her apartment. Someone slammed a door and three car alarms screeched. As the city awoke outside her window, Heather longed for quiet.

From her overstuffed drawers, she grabbed a baggy sweatshirt and pink M&M's flannel pajamas—which Charlie never saw—and threw on her glasses. In the kitchen she raised the thermostat from 60 to 75 and filled her coffee cup.

The refrigerator door hit against the table as she grabbed ingredients for a protein shake. She dug in the cabinets for the blender, but realized the glass pitcher was dirty in the dishwasher. Frustrated, she returned to the bedroom to get dressed and head out for breakfast. She opened the door to her tiny closet jammed with clothing and then closed it.

There wasn't room for her in this apartment. Charlie used three-quarters of the storage space, citing the fact that she traveled most of the year and only needed access to her things on the rare occasion she was home.

Charlie's black leather couch felt stiff and uncomfortable as she sat with her laptop. A website with lakeside houses for sale appeared on her screen. On nights when insomnia left her awake, she spent hours on the Internet taking virtual tours of the homes on the site. From her Favorites folder she clicked on a picture of a blue Craftsman bungalow. The bungalow had come on the market almost two months ago. To lull herself to sleep she fantasized about owning it and having cookouts with friends, parties with dancing, sunny days on the beach.

As a young child, Heather had lived in a rented lake house with her grandmother and mother. Heather tried to remember her grandmother's face, but it was like catching a dream. She had glimpses of memories: the gold chain that hung from her glasses, gray and black hair that tickled Heather's neck when they hugged, and sticking out blue tongues at each other when they sat in the blueberry bushes eating berries. Heather remembered sun-warmed towels after a dip in the lake.

Their five-room house had shelves filled with knickknacks of blown glass animals and porcelain figurines. Pink crocheted cozies covered tissue boxes on end tables. In the living room her grandmother or mother would rock her to sleep to the sounds of a crackling fire and the women's soft voices.

What Heather remembered best were the sweet smells of homemade bread and ginger cookies. Her grandmother loved to bake. The scent of molasses permeated the brown paneled walls and green carpets. Almost every afternoon, her grandmother would take down the yellow Bisquick box and measure out the water and flour mix. She'd roll it out on the table with Heather sitting in a chair next to her. Then, with a juice glass, Heather cut out perfect circles for biscuits. She'd sneak little corners of the dough and she still recalled the slight metallic taste of baking soda and salt.

When Heather was five, her grandmother passed away, and Heather's mother tried to pay the rent on the lake house, but after two years she'd put herself so far into debt, they were forced to move.

Heather closed the laptop and placed it on the coffee table. Charlie had paid for the apartment and their living expenses for the last six years; he opened her Visa and American Express statements before she saw them, and he allowed her a budget for luxury clothing as a business investment. She didn't see her own paychecks; they were deposited directly into their joint account. He said all this was necessary because she spent so much time on the road and he felt she couldn't be trusted with her own finances.

She looked around the ten-by-ten living room. The brick wall held a sixty-inch flatscreen TV that overpowered her senses when it was on. *Sports Illustrated* magazines had been neatly piled on the glass coffee table. The leather couch squeaked as she stood. Nothing about this place felt like home to her.

Charlie had threatened her career if she left. In everyone else's eyes she had the perfect life, but . . .

Before she could change her mind, she picked up her cell phone and dialed Information. "Littleton, Massachusetts," she said. "RE/MAX Realty." Whether or not she could buy the house, it was time to make a change.

CHAPTER 3

Victoria awoke to the smell of pancakes and the sound of hail hitting the roof. From under the pillow she grabbed a tissue and blew her nose. The delicate skin felt raw. Five rainy, icy days, along with the flu, had kept her in bed.

Each day, lost in memories of her granddaughter, she stared at her sage bedroom walls in the room her parents once occupied and listened to the fire crackling in the fireplace. Seven years ago, Victoria had renovated the house in anticipation of Annabelle's marriage to Tommy Woodward, a grandson of Nagog. She thought about all the plans she and Annabelle had dreamt up when they discussed the future: making ice cream on the porch, pushing baby strollers around the neighborhood, and, as Annabelle had put it, putting down roots secured in Massachusetts granite.

Those dreams had been lost when Annabelle died. After Victoria buried her granddaughter, she left Nagog—run away, as she had many times throughout her life. Now she was home to try to reconcile with the only family she had left—to find forgiveness and to come home somehow. There had to be more to life than loss and grief, and Victoria hoped that this place could help her to heal.

Molly came into the room and placed a wicker tray on the ottoman. "I have fresh-squeezed orange juice, coffee, eggs, and blueberry pancakes. It's time for you to eat." Molly's plump body, clad in a jogging suit, bustled around the queen-size bed. Her soft hands tucked the Egyptian cotton sheets into the mattress. With one swift movement, she fluffed the brown duvet over Victoria.

"Not hungry." Victoria rolled onto her back and stared at the cherry ceiling beams. Molly forced Victoria to sit up.

"Feed a cold, starve a fever. And you no longer have a fever. I still can't believe you stayed out in that weather and made yourself sick." She placed the tray over Victoria's lap. "Sooner or later you have to get up. You can't hide forever." She placed a glass of juice in Victoria's hand. "I'll be downstairs cleaning if you decide to move."

The orange juice no longer stung Victoria's throat, and she gulped the sweet, pulpy liquid. Her stomach awakened and growled for more. The pancakes oozed cooked blueberries as she cut through the three thick layers. She could feel herself salivating as she sank into the first forkful.

Soul food. That's what the people from the South called it. If only Molly's cooking could lift the emotional boulder currently weighing on her shoulders. Instead it would likely just add pounds to her hips.

Downstairs, Molly turned on the vacuum cleaner. Molly had already washed the linens and cleaned the bathrooms in preparation for Victoria's arrival. She'd vacuumed the soft carpet. The oak bureau, nightstands, and vanity table that had once been her parents' bedroom set had been dusted and polished. But the rest of the two thousand-square-foot house needed attention. It had sat empty for five years, and sheets that Molly had draped over much of the furniture after Victoria's sudden departure still remained. The built-in woodwork customary to an Arts and Crafts bungalow needed to be treated with kindness. Though Victoria had thought about hiring a service, she knew Molly would insist on doing it herself.

Boxes had been delivered weeks before from the home she sold in Malibu, and they still needed to be unpacked. It was time for Victoria to stop hiding and make this her home again. Yesterday she'd felt well enough to get out of bed but had decided against it. She'd been acting like a child afraid to go to school after the boys had seen her underpants.

As she stood, she knocked over the glass of water on the nightstand. Water splashed onto the brass lamp and the curtains. The glass rolled under the bed and the water soaked into the carpet. Too stiff to bend, she left the mess.

In the master bathroom, she looked at the unused jetted tub. It had been meant for dirty, giggling great-grandchildren to play in with bubbly euphoria.

She disrobed and opened the glass shower door. Hot water pulsed onto her back as she leaned against the stone tile. Steam filled the room and fogged the metal-framed mirror. She turned off the taps and wrapped her body in a fluffy purple towel.

For the last week, Victoria had kept everything in her suitcases, as if she were in a hotel. Part of her feared moving forward uncertain of what her life would be now that she'd returned. She grabbed underwear from the smallest case, along with a pair of tailored slacks and a fitted green button-down shirt. Then she pulled out a curling iron from the vanity's wooden drawer.

With quick, practiced skill she curled her hair into soft waves, not allowing the heat to scorch her fragile locks. In her youth, she'd worried about wrinkles, gray hairs, and hormonal fluctuations, but it wasn't until her late sixties that the texture and thickness of her hair became soft and fine. Aging, she thought, was not for the weak of heart.

From her makeup case, she pulled out bottles and jars. She applied moisturizer and a thin layer of foundation and blush. With a light hand she swept soft blue powder across her lids and then applied mascara. As Victoria took up her favorite soft berry lipstick, she remembered her mother saying that a lady never forgot to wear lipstick, even around the house.

Back in the bedroom, she lifted the largest suitcase and placed it on the bed. She unzipped the garment bag's sides, unfolded the heavy case, and opened the middle zipper. She removed the items that were already on hangers and placed them in the closet: designer silk blouses in a myriad of colors, tailored pantsuits, and cocktail dresses. All had been bought in fancy boutiques in Beverly Hills, London, and New York. Now she wondered if she'd have a reason to wear the fancy clothing here.

She pulled out a quilted leather box from the small suitcase and walked to the vanity. Her hand ran along the smoothness of her mother's antique rosewood jewelry box inlaid with mother-of-pearl. She lifted the lid and filled the empty box with her jewelry: five pairs of diamond earrings; the diamond necklace her ex-husband, Devon, had given her for their anniversary; the tennis bracelet from her father; gold hoop earrings, chains, and assorted pieces she'd collected over the years when she traveled.

She opened the secret compartment in the bottom of the travel jewelry box. Inside was a pearl ring Annabelle had given her. She slid it onto her finger and rubbed the white gold that swirled around the smooth pink pearl.

Annabelle had curly, golden locks that flowed over her shoulders and down her back. Her high cheekbones curved under bright, blue eyes. Always lost in her imagination, the girl would twirl the hair strand behind her ear until it became a tight ringlet. Victoria had always commanded men's attention in the past, but when she walked next to Annabelle, she knew it was her granddaughter who caused men to stumble over trash cans and walk into doorways, unable to take their eyes off of her.

Victoria continued to unpack, placing items in drawers that contained articles she'd left behind when she fled Nagog after Annabelle's death. The way she'd run from the community five years ago hadn't been so different from the first time she'd left home—she'd barely packed a bag.

Downstairs, the smell of coffee filled the kitchen. Victoria placed the breakfast tray on the wooden butcher-block counter of the island. Through the glass panels in the whitewashed cabinets she could see the dozens of plates and bowls that filled the cupboards ready for the meals she'd planned to fix her family. One cabinet contained wineglasses that now looked smoky with years of disuse. Each one would need to be washed.

She pulled a dusty red mug from the cabinet and turned on the tap to clean it. Once it dried, she filled it with coffee and curled it to her chest, pulling in its warmth as she looked out the window above the sink. By now there should've been Sunday dinners here, children playing in the sunroom. Victoria would've stood at this sink, its white porcelain front against her waist as she peeled carrots and chatted with Annabelle.

Victoria knew that an apron that read *World's Greatest Grand-*

mother hung inside the pantry door. Unopened cookbooks lined the shelves. Victoria wasn't a great cook, but she'd thought she might spend her golden years learning the skill. After dinner the children would've curled up on the old couches in the sunroom and watched movies, their heavy eyes trying to stay awake past their bedtimes.

Outside the window, black-and-white chickadees landed in the empty bird feeder and searched for food, then flew to the melted snow piles and pecked at the fallen pine needles. Snowstorms were for children: cold red noses peeking out from between scarves and hats; bright-colored snowsuits wrapped around small legs like pillows; saucers and sleds careening down hills while the children screamed in excitement.

Tommy and Annabelle would've had children by now. They'd planned to have a "truckload of kids," as Tommy had put it. Victoria could almost see the bright blond hair sticking up and the aqua eyes of their father sparkling with excitement while the children told Grandma stories of ice-skating on the pond and she made them hot chocolate.

Annabelle had wanted these things, the winters that she hadn't experienced growing up in Malibu. Victoria had taken her granddaughter on ski trips to Tahoe and Aspen, but it wasn't the same as having school canceled because the sky had dumped a winter playground on your front lawn.

The vacuum cleaner hum went silent and then restarted farther down the hall. Victoria took her coffee into the front sitting room. The furniture was still covered with sheets and the carpets needed to be cleaned, but other than that, this room hadn't changed since the day Victoria had left for California when she was nineteen. This was her mother's space. While the rest of the house had a modern flair, this room had been decorated similarly to the Boston residence where they'd lived when Victoria was a toddler.

Familiar pictures hung on the walls. Victoria scanned the frames: a black-and-white photo of the family, ancestors' portraits dating back to the 1800s, and in the middle, above the fireplace, the largest portrait of all—her thirteen-year-old face captured by a painter.

Victoria turned on the Tiffany lamps and the light created a soft glow that illuminated the dust as she removed a sheet from the furniture. She could almost see her mother in the high-backed chair. A crisp shirt and a pencil skirt had been her mother's favorite outfit, lipstick and a touch of rouge her only makeup. She kept her curly blond hair short, and tucked it behind her ear whenever she read. The epitome of grace and decorum, she never raised her voice over a speaking tone. She didn't need to—one improper move by Victoria and her mother could impose wrath with the "look." Victoria hated the "look," and she'd received it often as a child.

She walked to the window and watched the raindrops dance in the puddles on the road. She tried not to look across the beach to Joseph's home, but her heart defied her mind as she gazed at the warm light coming from his study.

⟳

The day after Victoria and Joseph made love for the first time, he became a sailor. That year, the women of Nagog had endured World War II together as the men of the community fought in Europe. Seventeen-year-old Victoria waited for the postman, always hoping for a letter. Sometimes they came daily; at other times, weeks would pass without word. She tended the victory gardens and collected tin for the drives. Then she walked the country road, under the green-leafed canopy, to the small white Episcopal church where she sat in the pew alone and prayed, "Please God, bring him home to me."

When she finished her prayer, she stood and walked to the alcove in the back of the church. The sun came through the stained glass and the colorful prism light reflected across Victoria's skin as she lit a candle and pressed her hands together. From her heart she sang, performing for God so he might hear her prayer over the millions of other women who asked for their loves' safety.

At night, she, Molly, and their friends Evelyn, Maryland, and Sarah curled under a mountain of lace in Victoria's canopy bed. They pretended to sleep, but their minds were active, recounting the news and searching for hidden messages that the war would end.

During the second summer of Joseph's absence, the heat blistered the porch paint and burned the grass tips. The temperature reached 100 degrees, and Victoria found solace in the lake. Diving deep below the surface, darkness enveloped her as she swirled her body like a mermaid. Over and over she plunged and surfaced until she gave way to fatigue. She lay in the sand, moisture evaporating from her suit as the sun melted her muscles.

Images of Joseph flashed behind her eyelids: the sunlight illuminating golden flecks in his blond hair, his infectious smile, the dimples that framed his mouth. The way he'd encircle his face with his hand and point to her—his secret sign to tell her she was beautiful.

The sounds of Molly's mother preparing dinner interrupted Victoria's thoughts. She knew it was time to go in and help her own mother with supper. Reluctantly, she stood and was walking across the beach when a scream came from Maryland's house.

Doors banged and women ran across their front yards. When Victoria reached the house, Maryland was curled in her mother's arms and they were both crying. Victoria turned to Evelyn, who stood by the staircase, a letter in her hand as she stared at the sobbing women. Victoria's circulation slowed as her blood solidified. She felt like a china cabinet suffering an earthquake, her strength breaking into tiny prismatic shards that reflected like the church's stained glass. Something had happened to Maryland's brother, James. Victoria looked at the tiny diamond on Evelyn's hand, the promise ring James had given her before he left for the war.

"What happened?" Victoria asked as she put her arm around Evelyn. More women entered the room and they turned and waited for the response.

Evelyn continued to stare out the window unable to speak.

Maryland's mother wiped her tears and said, "James's platoon came under heavy fire. He's missing in action."

Victoria knew how hard Evelyn and Maryland had prayed and still James might not come home. The protective bubble of Nagog hadn't been able to save him, and the security Victoria had felt during her whole life was crumbling.

Something changed in Victoria that day. She stopped going to church every afternoon to pray and only went on Sundays, when the community attended the Church of the Good Shepherd. The vigil she'd kept for Joseph became harder to endure, knowing that any day a letter could arrive stating he'd suffered the same fate as James. Movies became her respite. For the rest of the summer, on Thursdays and Saturdays, she rode her bike the four miles to Littleton's town center. With popcorn in hand, she lost herself in other worlds. The silver screen opened a window to life outside of Nagog, which had begun to feel like a prison—a world in which waiting for news from the war front seemed every woman's sole occupation. Instead, the women on the big screen wore sequined tops, bared their bellies, traveled. They could live the way they chose without ties to community or expectations from parents.

Everything in Victoria's life had been planned: She would attend Wellesley College this fall, marry Joseph upon his return, and have babies. Her father's plastics company would be combined with Joseph's family's textile factory. She and Joseph would summer in Nagog and uphold tradition. Parties would be thrown and social calendars kept. She would live her mother's life.

And if Joseph didn't come home from the war, a different husband would be chosen from her parents' circle.

In the dark theater, a secret hunger grew. Though she still wrote Joseph letters and tended the gardens like a good Nagog woman, she longed to be like Ingrid Bergman: known and loved by everyone in the world, not just by a long-absent soldier. She wanted to wear gowns and attend fabulous parties on Humphrey Bogart's arm.

As the years passed and she was forced to sit with the neighborhood women and sew clothing, Victoria found herself unable to join the conversations. The women read *Ladies' Home Journal* and discussed the latest recipes created to help the modern woman create tasty meals without the use of butter.

Victoria's mother snubbed her nose at the government's ads of Rosie the Riveter. "A proper woman doesn't wear coveralls and a handkerchief over her hair while flexing her muscles," her mother said. "What is this country coming to if we start treating our young women like boys?" All the ladies nodded in agreement.

Their snobbery angered Victoria. They were hypocrites. Victoria knew that her father had hired women to work in his factory. The safe life of Nagog was kept alive by the muscles in the arms of those women who were willing to work. "What's wrong with a woman working in a factory?"

Her mother gave her the "look," and Victoria went silent as she seethed inside—her spirit slammed against the cage Nagog had become.

The entire community was determined to live enclosed in their tiny bubble. Victoria felt as if she'd never be part of the outside world. She hid her *Motion Picture* magazines from her family, sharing them only with Molly. "Look at the women's dresses," she'd say as she admired the actresses' photos. "They're so glamorous. I want their life."

"They're beautiful, but who would want to live in Hollywood?"

"I would," Victoria said. She looked at her best friend and confided her secrets. "I want to become an actress. I want to live in Hollywood and be like Ingrid Bergman."

Molly patted her hand. "You miss Joseph. Once he comes home you'll forget all about Hollywood. The two of you are meant to be together."

Victoria turned away. No one understood or even dreamt of a life bigger than Nagog. And what if Molly was right? Once Joseph returned, would Victoria forget about her dreams and simply give in to the life she'd been handed? She'd be nothing more than a wife and a mother, never finding out who she could become if given the freedom to find out. The need for escape burned in her.

~§~

Victoria looked away from Joseph's home and stared at the wrinkles in her hands as she spoke to the empty sitting room. "When you're a child, you think you have control over your future. You don't realize how unforeseen events can change the trajectory of your life." She picked up a silver frame from one of the shelves by the fireplace. In the picture, her mother stood erect, a posed smile on her face, while Victoria held her arms wide as if to say, *Look at me*. Her mother's speeches had been a part of life. Victoria remembered sitting in this room by the fireplace as she listened to her mother's voice.

"I will allow you one month to accompany your father on his business trip to California," her mother said. "You will behave like a proper young lady and not socialize with the sailors home on leave or attend their raucous parties. When you return I will expect your help with my charity events until you begin college in the fall. You will not waste this summer in a movie theater."

San Diego had been a sparkling new world: the bright sun against the blue ocean; the stucco buildings with red terra-cotta roofs; the glamorous businesswomen sporting suits and hats. When she and her father went to dinner, she'd watch the women drink martinis at the bar without escorts. She wanted to be like them.

Victoria became her father's secretarial assistant as he sold plastics to large corporations. For the first time she had a job that earned her money instead of an allowance controlled by her mother, and she dreamt of what it would be like to get a paycheck as a working actress.

Her father's business took them for a week to Hollywood, where they stayed in a hotel with a pool on the roof. At night she'd look at the city lights and imagine her life as an actress. During that week, she spoke to the concierge, who was also trying to become an actor. He showed her the newspapers that announced casting calls and allowed her to tag along while he auditioned. The hunger grew, but Victoria didn't know how to make her dreams come true.

One month in San Diego turned into two, and after three months of Victoria sweet-talking her daddy, her mother realized Victoria's intentions.

The telegram read: *Return immediately. Stop. My daughter will not flaunt herself on a screen. Stop.*

Her father put her on the first plane home.

Victoria placed the picture back on the shelf and sat on the hearth, remembering how she'd returned to Nagog from San Diego determined to break away, no matter the consequences.

After a few minutes lost in thought, she went into the kitchen. From under the sink she collected cleaning supplies and cloths. Back in the sitting room she dusted the mantel and the picture frames on the shelves. She removed the sheets that covered the tables and the other two chairs.

A Tale of Two Cities, her mother's favorite book, lay on the marble end table, and she picked it up. The hardbound cover had the smoothness of her mother's ivory hands. She lifted the book to her face; the pages, tipped in gold, held a faint smell of Chanel perfume.

"Mother, I hope you and Father are watching over my girls in Heaven. I miss all of you." She placed the book back on the table and adjusted it to the same angle as her mother had left it.

Victoria turned and left the room. She could hear Molly cleaning in the study. Victoria walked down the narrow hallway between the sitting room and the kitchen and entered her father's study.

It was still raining and the gloom of the day made the room dark. Floor-to-ceiling built-in bookcases lined the walls. Across the room was the window seat where, as a little girl, she would curl up and read by the window, her back against the bookcase.

She walked around the room, tracing her fingers along the gold-embossed titles of the books that filled the shelves. The room had a musty scent from being closed for five years, but it didn't take away the smell of her father. Tobacco smoke from long ago was in the walls, and his spicy cologne in the leather-bound books. She could almost see him behind the big maple desk, his pipe touched to his lip as he read the *Littleton Town News*.

Molly was dusting the books and whistling a tune from *Mary Poppins,* and Victoria wrapped her arms around her friend from behind. "You don't need to clean everything. I can handle it."

Molly turned and put her hand on Victoria's arm. "Like you would know how."

Victoria leaned her cheek against Molly's soft hair, and breathed in the scent of lavender shampoo and pine cleaner. Molly was her home. More than this house or the lake, no matter where Victoria had been in the world or what had happened in her life, Molly was the place where her heart could rest.

"I think we need a shopping trip to stock your cupboards. I'd do it myself, but I know you'll want healthier food than I would buy. Plus, you need to get out for a bit."

"The weather is horrible. Are you sure you want to drive in this mess?"

"*Channel Five News* said it would clear by this afternoon. We'll just wait until it does." Molly squeezed Victoria closer.

It would be good to get out, Victoria thought. It was time to settle into life here in Massachusetts. As long as she had Molly, everything would be okay.

⤮

By noon the weather looked like it was going to clear, but then the sky turned a depressing gray and clouds moved in. White crystals hit against the windowpanes, and for three hours the wind whipped around the house. A large plow sent sparks along the road, blasting the street with sand. Three men jumped from the truck, shovels in hand. They spread out and attacked the walkways.

Then, as is typical of New England winter weather, the storm blew away just as quickly as it had come in.

Molly and Victoria decided to venture out, and Molly declared that a drive through the countryside of Littleton to see the fields and farms covered in snow was the perfect way to get to know Nagog all over again. The pavement was wet with packed snow. Worried that the back wheels of her car would skid and slide, Molly took her time. As they came over Nagog Hill, the fields around the McAffees' red barn came into view, revealing miles of bare fruit orchards, which produced peaches, nectarines, pears, and apples in summer and fall. Molly drove to the barn and parked in the plowed gravel area out front. "I thought we'd get some fresh milk and eggs," she said, stepping out of the car.

A man dressed in coveralls and a flannel down jacket greeted them with a smile. "Didn't think anyone would be coming by today," he said.

Molly did the introductions. "Shawn Patrick, this is my friend Victoria. She's one of us originals down in Nagog, but she's been living in California for some time. She moved back this past week." Molly turned to Victoria. "Shawn bought the farm two years ago, and somehow he's gotten the peach and apple orchards to produce the sweetest fruit I've ever tasted."

"Well, when my fruit is going into one of your incredible pies, it has to be the best." He smiled at Molly as he worked a wad of chewing tobacco.

"Isn't that the truth," Victoria said. "It's nice to meet you, Shawn."

"We need two quarts of milk and two dozen eggs," Molly said.

Shawn went into the barn and came back with a box. They paid him, and Molly promised to bring him homemade bread the following week.

They made their way along the narrow road on the opposite side of the lake from Nagog. Houses had never been built on this side of the water. Nagog owners had bought the land after the war to ensure that the view across the lake from their homes would always be a thick wooded area that turned bright red, yellow, and orange during the fall. When Molly and her friends took over the residences, they donated the land to conservation. Now hiking paths led to a dock where teenagers sometimes congregated on hot days, but because the trees couldn't be cleared to create a road down to the lake, it remained mostly unused.

Molly glanced at Victoria. Her friend was quiet as she watched the scenery pass. She could tell from Victoria's face that her thoughts were buried in the past. Molly wished she could reach in and pull Victoria to the present. She wanted her friend to be filled with everything this little town still had to offer.

Molly had never wanted to live anywhere but Nagog and was one of the few who'd never resided outside the community; her parents had given her their home as a wedding gift and then moved to a winter place down South. Molly enjoyed traveling with her husband, Bill, every few years to Europe, and family trips to Disney World and the Grand Canyon had given her special memories. But for Molly, nothing was sweeter than baking in her kitchen and being surrounded by family and friends. The community had given her everything she needed: a safe place to grow up, close friends, and the prettiest neighborhood she could imagine, just outside her window.

As a little girl, love embraced her like a down comforter fluffed over her body. Her life had been a cradle of hugs, kisses, and bedtime stories. Even when she got chicken pox, her parents told her she was beautiful. Her brothers and sisters, who had either passed on in the last few years or had moved south, had given her security. There had always been someone who looked out for her.

But most of all, Nagog had given her Bill. Molly never had to wait for her prince to come. She knew him from birth.

When Bill had gone to war, her mother held her in her arms and said, "Don't pray for God to make your life perfect. Instead, ask for the humor and courage to get you through." Molly had lived by those words.

As they drove through the commercial area of Littleton, Molly noticed how much had changed over the last fifty years. As a girl, she'd ride her bike the four miles along a dirt road to the candy store in Littleton town center. Now busy streets, apartment complexes, strip malls, and gas stations had replaced the large, green yards of yesterday.

"Before we get groceries, I want to make one stop," Molly said as she pulled into a lot in front of a small blue building. She smiled as she looked at the bay windows of the coffee shop. A hand-painted sign read *Daisy Dots.* The windows were decorated with painted purple, blue, pink, and green daisies.

"What a surprise, you want to get a coffee and some dessert," Victoria said as she climbed out of the car.

"You and I haven't been able to do such mundane things in a long time. I thought it would be nice," Molly said as she opened the glass door and a bell rang. The smell of coffee and chocolate greeted her along with the sound of milk being steamed and the buzz of conversation. Each table had a yellow linen cloth and a blue vase that looked like something out of Dr. Seuss, filled with yellow daisies.

People sat in overstuffed purple chairs and on couches near the fireplace. A long line of people stood waiting at the case of colorful baked goods glazed with fruits and chocolates.

"Grandma," Molly's granddaughter, Stacy, called out as she bounded from behind the counter. At twenty-seven, Stacy was the spitting image of Molly at that age: all feminine curves on a short frame. She wrapped her arms around her grandmother. "I didn't expect to see you today."

"Well, I had to show Victoria what incredible entrepreneurs my daughter and granddaughter have become." Molly turned to Victoria. "You remember my granddaughter Stacy?"

Victoria smiled and nodded. "Of course." She embraced the girl. "This place is adorable. When did you and your mother open it?"

"A year ago," Stacy said, as she beamed with pride. "All the baked goods are Grandma's recipes."

Molly watched Victoria force a smile. What had she done? How could she have been so inconsiderate? Victoria had just come home to the place where Annabelle had died and here Molly was showing off her very alive granddaughter. She should've waited.

Before she could rectify her mistake, Molly turned and saw her neighbors Sarah and Carl Dragone walking through the front door. Molly folded her hands together and squeezed. She closed her eyes and said a silent prayer, asking that this first encounter between Victoria and Sarah be served with love.

Sarah and Carl made their way to a table near the fireplace. Carl stood behind Sarah and helped her to remove her wool coat. Sarah was almost three inches taller than Carl and he had to reach up to help her. Carl wore a navy baseball cap with the embroidered red *B* on the front. No one but Sarah had seen Carl without a cap since 1977, when the last of his black hair had fallen out. When Sarah complained that a hat wasn't appropriate in church, he quit attending.

They walked toward the line of customers. In a white cardigan, black turtleneck, and dark green pants, Sarah carried herself like a schoolmarm. A large golden crucifix hung between her small breasts. Carl, dressed in jeans and a Patriots sweatshirt, looked and moved like a bowling ball. They'd always been opposites. Sarah believed in proper etiquette. Carl spent years perfecting armpit farts. When Sarah miscarried for the third time, she left the Episcopalian church and converted to Catholicism, saying it was a stricter faith. Carl spent his Sundays yelling obscenities at sports teams.

Sarah Dragone's lips pinched together when she saw Molly and Victoria. Her hair had been pulled back into a tight bun that accentuated the anger in her hazel eyes.

Please God, let this go well, Molly prayed again.

"Sarah, Carl, I didn't expect you would be out today," Molly said. "Victoria and I are doing a little shopping to get her place habitable."

"Why bother? I'm certain she won't be staying long," Sarah said, extending her arms to Molly's granddaughter while refusing to look at Victoria. "How's my beautiful girl?" she asked as she enveloped the young woman in a hug.

"I'm good," she said, "but I need to get back to work. Why don't you take a seat together, and I'll bring you something decadent." Stacy ran behind the counter and began putting together the orders for customers.

"Hello, Sarah," Victoria said. "Carl, it's nice to see you."

Carl went to give Victoria a hug, but his wife cleared her throat and instead he stepped back and nodded. "Nice to see you too. I bet the house is full of bugs and spiders after you've been gone so long. Maybe even some frogs." He winked at her.

"No, it seems I'm pest free. You and your henchmen must have left me out of your usual pranks," Victoria said with a smile. "I sincerely thank you for that."

"Don't know what you're talking about, Frog Face. I would never do any such thing," he said with a mischievous grin.

Molly smiled and let out a long breath. Carl and Bill had always been known for their pranks as children. More than once houses became infested with garden snakes, ants, or frogs as a practical joke.

"Better watch out or I'll sock you in the stomach the way I did when we were kids." Victoria raised her fist in pretend fight. "Would the two of you like to join us? We could catch up."

She's trying, Molly thought. Another good sign.

"I'm sorry, I'm not in the mood to hear stories of your life in California or your travels." Sarah looked to the counter and caught Stacy's attention. "We'll just get two decaf coffees to go, please."

"Sarah, please," Molly said. She wanted to grab both her friends and force them to hug. These were the women who spent every night of their school days braiding each other's hair and reading books under the covers with flashlights after lights-out was called. They'd been like sisters and now they couldn't look at one another.

Sarah turned to Carl. "I'm going to wait in the car. I'll talk to you later, Molly." She walked away and grabbed her coat.

Carl shrugged his shoulders. "Women. I swear, if you just fought it out in a boxing match it would be less painful than what you do to each other. And quicker too." He kissed Molly on the cheek and patted Victoria on the arm. "Give it time." Then he moved to the counter and paid for the two coffees.

Victoria wrapped her arms around her chest in a protective stance. "Let's get some coffee and dessert. The aroma in here is making me crave something decadent." Victoria walked to the end of the line and refused to look outside where Carl and Sarah were getting into their car.

Molly sighed. How was she going to bring them back together? A rushing noise came from behind her eardrums. Her eyes squeezed shut as blue lights swam behind her eyelids.

She felt her knees go weak and she grabbed the back of a chair to steady her. As soon as the feeling came, it was gone. Molly looked to Victoria and saw that she was focused on the specials written on the chalkboard. She hadn't noticed. *It was nothing,* Molly thought. *Just a silly head rush.* But a sense of panic fluttered through her.

CHAPTER 4

ॐ

T hrough the floor-to-ceiling windows of the Bay Towers'
penthouse restaurant, Heather could see the moonlight
reflect off Boston Harbor. Large party boats, with lights strung
across their railings, glided across the water. She leaned close to
the windowpane to see the street thirty floors below, where a
Clydesdale horse pulled a white carriage back to Quincy Market.

Crystal glasses clinking together brought Heather's attention
back to the party. The elegant room buzzed with the chatter of
hundreds of people dressed in formal wear as businessmen net-
worked over after-dinner drinks. A few couples waltzed in the
center of the room.

No matter how many events Heather attended on Charlie's
arm, or how beautiful and expensive the clothing she wore, she
never felt comfortable or that she belonged.

Heather had grown up fifty miles from Boston, but as a child
she never saw the city. When her sixth-grade class went on field
trips to the aquarium and the Museum of Science, she sat alone
reading in the library. Ten dollars for a field trip had been too
much for her mother's budget.

Boston became her Emerald City. Saturday afternoons she
scanned magazines for pictures: cobblestone streets, brick ornate

row houses, Harvard University. She cut perfect squares around the images and taped them, like wallpaper, to the smoke-stained wall behind her bed. Under her pillow she kept two pictures: Quincy Market's illuminated tree-lined walkway and a harbor view of the Boston skyline.

The day after graduation, she left her mother's dirty two-bedroom apartment with five hundred dollars in her savings account, a new credit card, and an envelope filled with the magazine clippings. In her backpack, she carried a toothbrush and five clothing changes. Her mother dropped Heather at the train station, hugged her good-bye and said, "Good luck." Then she lit a cigarette, got in her car, and drove away without looking back.

As the train pulled away from the platform, Heather looked out the scratched window. The liquor store and pizza shop disappeared behind the abandoned factories. Streets lined with apartment houses, rented by slumlords, flew past. The trees thickened and then gave way to affluent towns with boutique shops and colonial architecture.

Her every nerve felt frayed as she stepped from the train at North Station. The boardinghouse address, folded in a pocket, was her only plan. Without a map, she followed the throng of people through Haymarket Square, where the smell of fish, meat, and produce assaulted her senses. Around the corner she came to Quincy Market, where bubbled lampposts lined the cobbled path between buildings. Heather pretended to tie her sneaker as her hand brushed the smooth stones. It was real. She was here.

That first summer, she spent her afternoons in the Boston Public Garden. She'd sit under the giant weeping willow, next to the pond, the *Globe* open to the "Arts and Leisure" section. Begonias and roses scented the breeze that swayed the tree's umbrella of branches. Children played on the bronze ducks, their diaper-covered bums bouncing on the statues. Heather stretched across her blanket and watched the swan boats glide under the bridge.

Those first months were like Disney World to a five-year-old—innocent and exciting. She didn't care that she lived in a basement studio apartment that smelled like wet concrete or that she worked as a waitress. She had a real life for the first time.

Now, ten years later, she was a successful columnist for the *Globe* who traveled the world. But at events like this, a part of her still couldn't help feeling like an outsider looking in.

Heather glanced at her reflection in the window of the Bay Towers. Everyone saw glamour and sophistication. In her purple silk dress, the curve of Heather's collarbone accentuated her graceful neck. Her stomach had a soft bump of femininity, and her hip bone curved into long legs, but years ago Heather had lost the ability to see her beauty. It seemed every other woman wore her body with ease. In her eyes, her breasts were too small, so she wore padded bras to hide the perceived flaw. She caught the reflection of her rear end as she turned away from the window. The muscles never perked, no matter how many squats she did. Though Charlie never specifically said her backside disappointed him, she saw how he tilted his head and widened his eyes to catch a better look whenever a woman with a great ass walked by.

Heather looked toward the bar, where Charlie had gone to get her a drink. Three perfect women sat on the stools, oozing confidence as they laughed together. They were younger, prettier, and thinner than Heather. One showcased her augmented chest and disdain for a bra in a low-cut, backless dress. For the last fifteen minutes, Charlie had laughed and joked with them, sometimes touching them on the arm or the back.

She'd confronted him about his flirting and the way he looked at other women. He responded that every guy looked and at least he didn't hide it from her. As for the flirting, it was part of his business to network.

She looked at the woman with breast implants. More than once Charlie had suggested that Heather have augmentation to help her land a television show. Even her body was a product he could rearrange to better suit his marketing plan. For the past week he'd continued to ignore her insistence that they take a break. Time apart wasn't part of his plan, so it didn't exist.

Charlie turned and smiled. In the past, butterflies had danced in her belly when Charlie looked at her in that special way; his smile had made her feel she was the only woman in the room, and she couldn't believe that this handsome man loved her. But that feeling had left long ago.

A blond man joined Charlie and they walked toward her. "This is Heather Bregman, the one and only Solo Female Traveler," Charlie said. "Heather, this is Steven Radley. He works for the Travel Channel."

Heather extended her hand. "Nice to meet you, Steven."

Steven kissed both her cheeks in greeting and held her chin in his hands. "You're gorgeous. Why isn't your face across billboards and magazine covers? You should be on television."

"I think Solo Female Traveler is exactly what your network needs," Charlie said.

Steven stepped back and let his eyes roam her body. Heather shifted uncomfortably under his gaze. He looked like a golden boy who'd done everything right in life. He had a way to him, like one who had never had to work for his achievements, a slickness covered with flirtation that she found sexually attractive and unnerving at the same time.

"So do you live in Los Angeles?" Heather asked.

"No, I'm here in Boston. Most of our shows are shot on location, so I get to live in my favorite city and travel the globe. I guess you and I have that in common."

"Yes," Heather said, "we're very lucky people."

"Why don't we set up a meeting next week to discuss my idea for a *Solo Female Traveler* show?" Charlie suggested.

"Only if you let me dance with this beautiful woman first," Steven said as he took Heather's hand and moved her onto the dance floor.

He pulled her close and led her in a waltz, lifting her arm with fluid movements and twirling her in circles, then brought her back to his chest and pulled her tight around her waist.

"Impressive dancing skills," she said as she leaned back to create distance between them.

"I took lessons for four years," he said. "A man who can lead always gets the woman."

Heather tilted her head back and laughed. "And I'm certain you've had terrible troubles in that department."

"I think you're reading me wrong, Ms. Bregman," he said with a flirtatious smile. "I'm actually quite shy and reserved."

She laughed again as he twirled her around the floor, making her feel as if her feet floated above the ground.

"Now, as for you," he said, "I sense intense shyness."

Heather blushed and let her hair fall over her face.

"Exactly," he said. "It's incredibly charming to men, but for the camera you would need to overcome it. Could you?"

The honest answer would be that she didn't know. It terrified her to think of cameras picking up her every flaw and people across America watching her on television. As a writer, she could hide behind her computer screen and speak from her heart.

But the key to long-term success was taking the next step. The *Globe* executives were pushing her to broaden her brand. They wanted a star, as Charlie had promised them six years ago, not just a local woman who traveled. She summoned her confidence and looked directly at Steven. "I've traveled the world solo. I've met people from every culture and experienced things most only dream about. I can show your viewers adventures that will make them salivate and inspire them to get off their couches and sign up for trips that your advertisers promote. Give me a chance, and I'll make you money."

The song ended and he led her off the dance floor. He handed her his card. "Maybe you do have what it takes. Give me a call, Heather Bregman, and we'll talk."

She took the card and slipped it into her clutch. "Thank you for the dance. I look forward to discussing the possibility of working together."

Charlie was back at the bar, flirting. After tonight she might need to take her career into her own hands. Snapping her purse closed, she decided not to share with him that she had Steven's information.

On the cab ride home, Heather gazed at Charlie and once again questioned her decision. Was asking him to take a break the right thing to do?

On their first date, Charlie had taken her to Café Bella Vita on Charles Street in Boston. They sat by the window at a small table with candles flickering in the centerpiece. They indulged in lobster ravioli, drank expensive red wine, lingered over soft layers of tiramisu while she stared into Charlie's dark, Italian eyes.

He held her hand, caressed her thumb, and said, "Right now I'm at the bottom, an agent's assistant. But my plan is to take the average Joe, like a personal trainer or a financial adviser, and make them into a household name. I would move that person into a column, a book, a self-help video, and his own television series. I just have to find the right client to develop."

She didn't care about his career. She'd never seen anyone so beautiful.

After dinner, they strolled along the sidewalk, peeking into Beacon Hill's art galleries and antiques shops. At Pinckney Street, he grabbed her hand and hurried up the steep hill lined with brick colonial row houses. At the top, they reached a tiny park with two small trees. Before she could catch her breath, he kissed her, his tongue ravaging her mouth.

He pulled away. Stunned, she looked at him. This godlike man had kissed her. Desired her.

Charlie pointed to a row house. "This is where I'm going to live someday."

Ornate white metal circles decorated the windows that surrounded a bright red door. Through the glass she could see a carpeted spiral staircase reminiscent of an old movie set.

"Do you want to live here someday?" he asked.

The ability to speak was locked up in her throat. She worked two shifts as a waitress and still couldn't make ends meet. Bills were piled up on her kitchen table. When she'd moved to Boston, she'd maxed out her Visa with a cash advance to pay the two months' security deposit and first month's rent on her apartment.

In the last three years, she'd opened a MasterCard, a Discover, and another Visa, which she maxed out paying rent and buying groceries when tips were low. She had student loans from the year she'd been able to attend college. But here was Prince Charming, and it almost felt like he was asking her to live with him in a mansion on Beacon Hill.

She couldn't tell him that she didn't have time for ambitions or dreams; she was too worried about becoming homeless. For one moment, she allowed her fantasy to emerge, though she felt like a four-year-old saying what she wanted to be when she grew up: "I want to be a travel writer for a magazine or newspaper."

"I have a friend at the *Globe*. If you write an article, I'll help you publish it," he'd said.

Charlie had helped her to make her biggest dream come true. Meeting him had changed her life. And now she was going to end their relationship.

The closer the cab came to their apartment, the less Heather could feel her body. Her arms and legs felt invisible, or detached. Charlie paid the driver as the car came to a stop in front of their building. A spinning feeling began. A child's racetrack whirred in her head as her heart beat faster.

Charlie's cell phone rang and as he took the call he walked away, not even bothering to offer his arm while she stepped from the cab onto the icy pavement in four-inch heels. Charlie had already unlocked the front door and had closed it by the time she arrived at their apartment. Heather opened the door, peeled off her shoes, and walked toward the bedroom.

Before she reached the room, Charlie grabbed her around the waist. "Where are you going, my hot little columnist? Have I told you how beautiful you look tonight?"

"I think you might have forgotten to mention it. You were a little too busy flirting with the women at the bar," she said.

"Just working the room for business," he said, unzipping her dress.

"Stop!" She moved his arms away and pulled the zipper back up. "How could you think that I want to sleep with you right now?"

"What the hell is wrong with you?" The muscle in his cheek twitched and his brow furrowed, as he stared her down. "Whatever issues you're having these days, I need you to get over them and fast. We've lost another syndicate this week and I'm trying to save your career. I have twenty other clients I need to keep happy." He picked up his cell phone and began to make a call as he walked away.

She grabbed the phone. "Will you just listen for a minute?"

"Maybe I'm tired of listening." He grabbed the phone from her hand.

"What's that supposed to mean?" She folded her arms across her chest.

"I can't make you happy. I work my ass off to give you everything and all I hear about is what I haven't done."

"Well, maybe I feel invisible." Her voice came out louder than she intended.

"Invisible? You're kidding." He forcefully threw his hands in the air as he continued to yell. "Everything I do is about you and your career. I'm trying to build a life for us, yet you don't seem to care. Do you want to end up a waitress again, barely able to make ends meet?"

Heather looked at the floor and bit her lip until it swelled. In the fairy tale, "The End" never mentioned that the prince spent the rest of his life reminding Cinderella that she'd once scrubbed floors in rags. Anger fumed and she lifted her chin and looked him in the eye. "Oh, and I have nothing to do with that success? Who's done the traveling, Charlie? Who's lived out of a suitcase for the last six years? Not you. And then when I come home there isn't even room for me in this apartment. It's like I'm a guest here."

"You've gone off the deep end. I'm sick of this." He turned his back to her. "You want more room, then find your own place, because obviously what I've given you isn't enough."

Her voice became softer as she delivered the words that needed to be said. "That's my plan. I was serious when I said we needed a break. I think we should take some time apart."

The artery in his throat bulged as he turned, his face red. He came within a foot of her and loomed over with his large frame. "You leave for Europe in ten days. Make sure you have a place to live when you return, because I want you out."

She reached to touch his arm, hoping to salvage some tenderness. "Charlie, let's talk about this. We need to be able to work together. I don't want animosity between us. I just need . . ."

"I don't care what you need anymore." He pulled away and walked out of the room. She heard the front door slam.

There should've been tears, a tsunami of emotions. Instead, she felt numb and couldn't stop shaking. She grabbed her cell phone from her purse and called her friend Gina, but it went straight to voice mail. Her fingernails tapped against the metal of the phone.

She needed to talk to someone, and before she could change her mind, she dialed the number she knew better than to call. "Hi, Mom."

"Hi, Heather, are you back from your trip?" Heather heard her mother take a deep drag from her cigarette. Heather could picture her mother at the kitchen table, smoke circling her lined face—a bad habit that came with her bartending job. Her mother had been a beautiful woman. The few memories Heather had of the lake house, she could remember her mother laughing. But years of financial struggle that caused her to work nights at the bar and days in a supermarket had taken their toll. "It must be nice to be able to travel all over the world. I don't know how I'm gonna pay my taxes this year. No matter how hard I work, it still seems like Uncle Sam takes everything."

The usual guilt hit her as she thought about her mother's life compared to how she now lived. She tried to help her mother financially, but she wouldn't accept. Instead, she just kept piling guilt onto her daughter.

Heather didn't want to burden her mother with her problems, but she needed to talk to someone. "Mom, I ended my relationship with Charlie," Heather said.

"You did what?"

"I told him I needed a break."

"God, Heather, what were you thinking?"

The words were a punch to the gut that knocked the wind out of Heather. Just once, she wanted to call and feel supported. "Forget it, Mom. I'll deal with it on my own."

"Don't take that tone with me. This isn't my fault." Her mother sighed. "I'm sorry I'm not being more supportive, but Heather, I'm just tired of it all. I'm trying to get myself through the day and pay the bills. I'm trying to keep a roof over my head and food on my table. I had one good thing happening in my life, and that was that you were gonna be taken care of. Now that's gone."

Heather kicked at the floor. The story never changed. "Maybe I don't need someone to take care of me. When I was a kid, I told you that I wanted to travel the world and write, and you told me that people like us don't get those chances. I proved you wrong. Why can't you tell me that everything's going to be okay?" Heather sank onto the couch.

"You think it's easy to do it on your own? Without Prince Charming, you'd still be a waitress instead of a columnist. We'll see what happens without him. I've been alone trying to take care of you since the day my mother died. I had dreams too, Heather, but my life has been shit since that day. The only thing that ever mattered was you. And now I'm gonna see you have the same life I did."

"I can't do this right now, Mom. Life with Charlie is far from perfect."

"Oh, Heather, you don't know what a bad relationship looks like. When you tell a man you're pregnant and he walks out on you, or when a man loves his booze more than you, *then* you can tell me what a bad relationship feels like. But when he buys you a diamond, cares about your career, and gives you a home in the Back Bay, you make sure he's happy so *he* won't leave *you*."

"I have to go," Heather whispered.

"There aren't many Charlies in the world. Do whatever it takes to get him back. I just want more for you than I had."

"I know, Mom. I'll talk to you later." Heather hung up the phone.

CHAPTER 5

I t felt like winter would never end. Every morning since Victoria had returned to Nagog, she awoke to see the blue sky out her window and thought it would finally be a sunny day. But by ten in the morning, the clouds moved in and the sky turned a depressing gray. Even on days that it didn't snow or sleet, Arctic air from Canada froze her bones until she thought they'd crack.

Big red *X*s on her calendar marked the two weeks that had passed since she'd arrived home. She'd assumed spring would awaken by late March, but Mother Nature wasn't ready for flowers and green grass. For days, flakes almost the size of poppies fell like inverted parachutes, and then turned to white blasts of static so thick Victoria couldn't see her front yard. Trees crashed along the road. The power had gone out twice, and yesterday the governor had declared a state of emergency. The Nagog residents stayed huddled in their homes as the snow blocked doors and drifted halfway up the windows.

Victoria's car sat unused in her garage. No one but Molly had invited her for coffee or dinner since she'd moved home. She hadn't spoken to anyone except for her brief encounter with Sarah and Carl Dragone. Everyone had decided to hibernate through winter's fury. When Victoria complained, Molly told her to be patient.

"Things always brighten in the springtime," Molly had said.

She understood why people in California seemed happier—they had sunshine. She imagined her former home in Malibu, where she could dig her toes in the warm sand while the sunset turned the white-capped waves pink. But then her psychiatrist's words returned: "The only way out is through. You need to return to Nagog and face what you lost, without an escape route."

Tired of being cooped up, Victoria grabbed the boots Molly had left in the breezeway and zipped up the blue Michelin Man jacket. She walked the quarter-of-a-mile street from one end to the other and back for the hundredth time. Winter made her feel old. The arthritis in her left hand ached and her muscles were stiff from lack of movement.

Annabelle flashed through her thoughts. Her granddaughter's energy always made Victoria feel years younger than her age: shopping for the latest fashions, traveling throughout Europe, laughing through the night as they talked about dreams and life. Victoria enjoyed watching her granddaughter fall in love and pursue her career. Melissa and Annabelle had been the two greatest gifts of her life.

As she walked toward the beach, she pulled her hood over her head to protect her ears from the cold and tucked her gloved hands into her pockets. She burrowed into the coat like a turtle tucking its head into its shell and looked at her feet. *What a sight I must be in this outfit.* She could see the caption: "Victoria Rose, former actress, seen walking in a velvet jogging suit with big purple boots."

Almost out of habit now, she glanced at Joseph's house. As kids, he'd follow her around and rescue her from the other boys' pranks, bugs in her lap or frogs in her shoes. The girls had teased her that he was in love, and it had driven Victoria crazy. She'd told him more than once that she hated his guts. Her mother scolded her, saying that a proper lady never said things like that to a gentleman, but Victoria didn't care—she hadn't wanted his attention.

But the year she turned fifteen, everything changed. The night had been hot and sticky, and the entire neighborhood had driven to Whalom Park in the next town. People drank malts with ice cream and rode the Ferris wheel to catch a breeze. Molly and Sarah felt tired in the heat and didn't want to stand in line and wait for the Comet roller coaster, so Victoria went by herself. As she was buckling the seat restraint, Joseph leaped into the car.

"I can't allow a lady to ride alone," he said.

"If you're going to sit with me, then you have to raise your hands in the air when we go over the hills," she said.

"I don't think I'm that daring," he said and winked at her.

The car bounced around the wooden track until it clicked into the chain that carried the coaster up the hill. There was a moment, a second when the car reached the top and froze, and she could see the entire park: the band playing on center stage, boys throwing baseballs at milk containers, girls riding painted ponies on the carousel. Victoria raised her hands over her head, the car tilted, and just as her stomach jumped into her heart and the coaster began to shoot down, Joseph turned her head and kissed her full on the lips.

The drop in her stomach didn't go away when the ride ended. Victoria sat in her seat, unable to move. Joseph got out of the car and walked away, but before he left the platform, he looked back and winked. . . .

Victoria hugged her arms around the puffy blue jacket as a cold wind blew across the beach. She continued to walk, her eyes on the icy ground as she tried to push away the memories.

"Hello, Victoria."

Victoria jumped, startled by the sound of a voice so close. She looked up and saw Joseph just a few feet in front of her.

"I didn't mean to scare you," he said. "I was out walking and it seems our paths were on course to each other."

"I didn't see . . . ah . . . or hear you," she said. "I mean . . . hello, Joseph. How are you?" He looked sexier at seventy-six than Cary Grant did at thirty. In a fedora and a long wool jacket, he could've been a leading man from a 1950s film. She wondered if his white hair was still as thick as it was five years ago. She'd always loved the natural wave and how his cowlick made his hair stick up in the front.

"I'm feeling a bit cooped up with this weather," he said, looking to the sky. "I thought I would go for a walk just to remind my body that it can still move. At my age, if I sit too long, I might not get out of the chair."

"I don't think you're that old yet, but this weather certainly does remind one of former injuries. I can feel where I broke my hand when I was eight." She rubbed her right wrist.

"If I recall, you broke that hand and your wrist chasing Bill and Carl through the woods."

"Yes, I tripped over a tree root and went soaring through the air. I'm surprised I still have knees after all the times I skinned them while chasing those two for some prank they'd played."

She let her eyes drift down his body. He'd lost weight since the last time she saw him and he seemed strong and fit. Heat flushed her cheeks. She looked away, afraid he'd notice her staring. Butterflies danced in her belly that she had no right to feel. This man belonged to someone else.

Five years ago, after Annabelle's death, he'd tried to hold her—to have his friendship heal the seam in her soul that had ripped when Annabelle died, but she left without saying goodbye. He deserved to know why she'd left abruptly, but shame kept her from telling him the truth.

"I don't know where the years have gone. It seems like yesterday that we were children swimming in the lake." He turned and looked at the house directly across from the beach—Maryland's place.

"Molly told me that Maryland had a stroke and her children moved her into a nursing home. I wish I could've seen her before she left." Victoria dug her hands deeper into her pockets.

The silence stirred between them as the wind continued to shake the tree branches.

"How are your children?" Victoria asked.

"They're good," he said and he turned to her with a smile. "I'm a great-grandfather now. Emily is two years old."

"Congratulations, that's wonderful," Victoria said.

Joseph's eyes became sad and the familiar look of pity crossed his face. He couldn't return the question and ask about her family. But his pity only amplified her loss, and somehow, coming from him, it cut even deeper.

"How's Barbara? I haven't seen her around?" Victoria asked.

Joseph looked to the lake. "We divorced a few years ago."

"Joseph, I'm sorry. I didn't know. Molly never said anything."

"I asked her not to," he said without looking at her. "Well, I should be getting inside."

"Of course." She wanted to reach out and hug him, but she didn't. "I think I'll be heading in as well. My toes are getting cold standing here."

"It's nice to see you, Victoria."

"You too, Joseph."

They smiled and parted ways like acquaintances rather than two people with more than seven decades of shared history. At her driveway she turned and watched Joseph walk into his home that she realized was now empty. Emotions swirled in her body as she continued to walk toward the main road. It was sad that Joseph and Barbara had divorced and she wondered what had happened after so many years of marriage. But she couldn't contain the glee that he was single. Could there be hope for a second chance she didn't deserve? The memory of how she'd rejected him returned along with her guilt.

∽⟨Q⟩◈

The war in Europe ended May 8, 1945. By June, Bill and Carl had already returned home and proposed to Molly and Sarah. The two women were entrenched in planning their weddings. Both asked Victoria to be their maid of honor, and neither planned to return to Wellesley College for their final year as their lives became more about planning bridal showers, picking out flowers, and shopping for dresses than schoolwork. Most of their class wouldn't return as women gave up their education to become wives.

Victoria was expected to care about seating charts, party favors, and place settings. With each decision someone would mention Joseph's impending return and how she would be the next to be engaged. Joseph's letters told her that he'd be home that summer and though he hadn't asked for her hand she knew that she'd be expected to begin her life as a wife.

But she'd seen a bigger world when she was in California. Though she pretended that her girlfriends' life plans could be enough for her, she knew it wasn't true. At night, while she lay in bed, she planned her escape.

In August, one month before Molly's and Sarah's weddings, Joseph returned home. Victoria met his ship in Boston. Soldiers made their way off the boat in a flurry of excitement. Confusion swirled through Victoria. The longing all these years to see the man she loved made every moment she searched for him intolerable, while the woman who'd planned to leave the community screamed not to be forgotten.

Tears ran down her cheeks when she saw his smile from yards away. He ran to her and before she could settle on how she felt, his arms were around her, lifting her as their lips touched. The commotion around them disappeared as her body melted into the safety of his arms.

That night, a party was thrown in Nagog. Lobsters, steaks, and champagne were served. A sixteen-piece orchestra entertained two hundred guests.

Victoria and Joseph danced on the patio under the sparkling lights. Dressed in his U.S. Navy uniform, he was more dashing than when he'd left. As the night went on, she began to forget her silly dreams of becoming an actress. As he twirled her and held her close, the idea of marrying this man seemed like the perfect life.

When the song ended, Joseph joined the men for a cigar, and Victoria walked to where the women sat discussing Molly's and

Sarah's wedding plans. Someone brought up a recipe she'd found in a magazine. The familiar tug to leave Nagog returned.

Joseph crossed the dance floor, held out his hand to Victoria, and whispered, "Will you walk with me?"

The wind that precedes a rainstorm was blowing as they snuck away. Victoria looked to the sky and prayed for the storm to come. She imagined lightning striking the tree by the lake, its limbs crashing to the earth before Joseph could ask the question she knew would come.

In their private spot on the beach, he hugged her. She stiffened. His uniform smelled of cigars as he nuzzled his nose in her long locks.

"I missed your hair. I told the men on the ship that you smelled like fresh-picked strawberries," he said as he pulled her closer.

Cary Grant never told women they smelled like fruit. Women were sexy goddesses to him. They weren't housewives. They stole cars and invited handsome men to their apartments.

As Joseph knelt in the sand, he held up a hand-carved wooden box. "The light of your eyes kept me alive during the war. Your smile is all I need in life. Victoria Rose, will you marry me?"

Black velvet lined the wooden box. In its center, the diamond sparkled in the moonlight.

His blue eyes watched her. When his smile deepened the dimple in his cheek, a well of longing for him rose up inside her, and she ached to touch his face. Victoria glanced back at the party and the family she loved.

As the wind picked up and her red dress swirled wildly around her legs, she realized for the final time that she needed freedom more than Joseph's love. "No," she whispered. Tears dripped from her eyelashes. "I want more than Nagog and our families' factories. I can't marry you. I'm sorry. I don't want this life anymore." She ran from him, rushing along the path that had taken her to their special place. The high-heeled shoes sunk in the sand and she tore them off as she ran across the beach, past the music and laughter on the patio where everyone still celebrated.

In her room, the red dress was cast onto the floor as she changed into pants and a sweater. She filled a small bag with a few changes of clothing. From the bottom dresser drawer she removed her secret envelope of money and pulled out the letter she'd written earlier explaining to her parents that she was leaving and that she'd contact them in a few days. She placed this on her bed, knowing that her mother wouldn't find it until tomorrow afternoon. No one would worry about her absence until then. It would be assumed that she was at a girlfriend's house.

There was a late train to Boston that left at ten. It would take her almost half an hour to ride her bike to the station in the next town, but she might have enough time to make it if she rushed. If she was lucky, she'd be on a plane before anyone noticed she'd left.

Outside, she stood on her porch and stared at the party and her family. She shouldn't leave like this. If she went inside, changed her clothing, and returned to the party as if nothing had happened, she could finish school and be part of her friends' weddings.

If Joseph hadn't asked her tonight, she could've stayed. But now the backlash of her turning down Joseph's proposal would be unbearable. Her friends would look at her like she was a fool. Her mother would lecture that she was selfish and insist that she marry him. Worst of all, she couldn't bear to see the pain in Joseph's eyes.

"Know that I love you," she whispered to her family and friends. "And that I'm sorry."

～⤫～

Victoria untied the hood of her jacket and walked along the main road, which, like so many in New England, didn't have a sidewalk. She walked in the ditch to give the drivers room, mud and snow soaking her boots. Cars took wide paths around her, headlights flashing in the fog. Her watch read 5:30. People were rushing home from work.

A truck pulled into the long, winding driveway across the street. Victoria could imagine the male driver opening his front door to hugs from little bodies and smiles that peeked out from messy hair.

Victoria wanted to be in that house. She was certain every Nagog resident wished the same: to be able to say grace, hold hands with their family, and hear the children recount their tales from the day. When you were old, meals with family were limited to holidays and birthday parties. If you were alone like she was, you ate soup or a sandwich in front of the television, the news anchor your only companion.

She came to the curved metal gates of the cemetery and walked to where four generations were buried: her grandparents and parents, and her daughter and granddaughter. Unable to face her angels' resting place, Victoria looked to her parents' headstone and brushed away the snow. She bent down and touched her mother's name on the cold stone.

Earlier that afternoon Victoria had noticed a smaller photo tucked behind the other frames in her mother's sitting room. When she picked it up and looked closer, she realized the picture was actually a newspaper clipping of her and her father in Hollywood on the night of her first premiere. Could her mother— the woman who resisted every reminder of the life Victoria had chosen—have framed this memento?

After she ran away to Los Angeles, she'd sent her mother a telegram letting her know she was safe, but she didn't include her address. It had taken Victoria two months to build up the courage to phone home.

"Victoria Rose, you will come home immediately," her mother said in an even tone. "How do you plan to support yourself in California?"

"I have a job as a receptionist," Victoria replied, standing erect, every muscle tight.

"You were not raised to be an office assistant," her mother said. Over a distance of twenty-six hundred miles, Victoria felt the "look."

"No, I was raised to be a wife. Why can't you understand that I want a career?"

"So you've made your decision."

"Mother, please, I need you to understand."

"Victoria, what I understand is that you're being selfish and stubborn. You belong at home with your family, not playing movie star on the other side of the country. You've hurt everyone, not just Joseph, and I'm ashamed of you. I expect you to think about what I've said and return home."

But Victoria didn't listen. She rebelled against her mother's wishes and stayed in California.

Victoria stood and placed her gloved palm against the stone, as if reaching out to her mother. "I found the frame with the picture of my premiere. I keep wondering if maybe you'd placed it on the shelf," Victoria said to her mother's memory. "Do you remember when I called to tell you that I was going to be on the silver screen for the first time and I invited you and Daddy to the premiere? It took me years of going to casting calls to get that job. I never told you, but I quit the job as a receptionist and began working as a dancer at a dinner theater to gain experience . . . something I knew would shame you to no end, so I never told you, but it didn't matter . . . you were ashamed of everything I did."

Victoria turned to the stone with her father's name. He'd always been supportive of her decision to become an actress. The first time he came to visit her small basement apartment, he took one look at the dark rooms and immediately set out to find her a new place. He moved her into an apartment in Santa Monica where she could lean out the window and see the ocean. All of which he paid for while she built her career. When he came for her premiere, he bought her a silver Dior gown with a plunging back to wear to the event. Never did she feel more elegant as she walked the red carpet on his arm. But no amount of glamour could mend her broken heart when her mother didn't come to the premiere. It effectively severed their already strained relationship.

The memory of the night she'd received the phone call telling her the news of her mother's death replayed in her mind as she caressed the headstone. It'd been almost midnight in Santa Monica when the phone rang. A man with brown eyes had been unzipping Victoria's sundress.

"Hello," Victoria answered, laughing as the man reached under her dress and tickled her waist.

"Victoria, it's Molly."

"Molly, I've missed you. Please, come visit me." The four glasses of champagne Victoria had drunk at dinner made her giddy. She playfully pushed the man away and sat on the couch. Molly sniffled and her voice trembled. "Victoria, I'm sorry to tell you this. Your mother suffered a heart attack and didn't make it. Your father is devastated. You need to come home."

Victoria didn't remember hanging up the phone. She didn't see her date close the door on his way out. In the back of her closet, behind the shoe racks, she'd hidden the rosewood box her grandmother had given her for her seventh birthday. Surrounded by gowns and silk dresses, her sundress still unzipped, she squeaked open the lid and pulled out five years of letters. With shaking hands, Victoria removed the flowered stationery and reread the last letter that had come one month earlier:

It's been six years since you've come home for the holidays. I'm asking you to join us. I've included a plane ticket and I expect you to honor my wishes.

At the airport the next day she exchanged the ticket, meant for the holidays, and flew home for her mother's funeral. The cold fall day spent clutching Molly's hand as the casket was lowered into the grave was nothing like the homecoming Victoria had imagined all those years she'd been away.

The entire Nagog community stood in black around the hole in the ground as Victoria struggled to control her tears. Her mother wouldn't have cried. She would've bottled up her emotions until she could feel them in private. In honor of her mother's style, Victoria wore a pencil skirt and a black button-down shirt under her black wool coat. In this last moment, Victoria would show everyone that she was her mother's daughter, even though she hadn't been able to live her mother's life.

Back at her childhood home, Victoria left her father's side only to search for Molly. As she approached the doorway to the sunroom, she heard Maryland, Evelyn, Agatha, and Sarah talking.

"Did you see that she didn't shed one tear?" Agatha was saying.

"I can't believe it," Evelyn said. "How do you not cry at your own mother's funeral? I'd be devastated."

"I'm not surprised," Sarah said. "She left and didn't look back. Obviously, she never cared about anyone but herself to have done what she did to her mother. I think Victoria's actions broke her mother's heart and brought on her illness."

"Sarah, that's an awful thing to say," Maryland said.

"But it's the truth," Sarah said. "Mrs. Rose was ashamed of Victoria's life and the way she treated this community. She was never the same after Victoria ran away. And then to have to see Victoria flaunt herself on billboards selling household products, it destroyed her heart."

"And from what I hear, Victoria is leaving in a few days because she has to be on a movie set," Agatha said. "You would think that she would stay and take care of her father after all he's been through. But Victoria always had to be the star, and that's what's important to her."

It was only later, in the privacy of Molly's kitchen and the comfort of her friend's embrace, that Victoria could finally sob for everything she'd lost.

She took one last look at the graves. Her father had died of a heart attack two years after her mother's death. Everyone in the community said he'd died of a broken heart from missing her mother. Once again Victoria returned to her childhood home to bury a parent. The lawyers explained that her father had left her a sizable estate, including his factories, which he'd placed in a trust in her name. The men of Nagog oversaw the sale of the business. She closed up the Nagog house and returned to Santa Monica.

Snow had begun to fall again and Victoria knew she needed to leave the cemetery. She looked to the sky. "I thought I'd have more time, Mother. That's been my problem my whole life. I've always felt that there would be time to make amends, but now I'm an old woman talking to ghosts because I don't know how to heal things with the family I have left."

❧

Heather mentally cursed Charlie for not taking the time to clean off her car while she'd been in Africa. An icy sheet had covered Heather's car, already encased in snow. The plows had pushed three feet of snow up against her car blocking her in. With a scraper she hacked at the inch-thick layer frozen onto the windshield. It had snowed or rained almost every day in the week and a half since she'd been home, which made the car that much harder to shovel out. A slushy mound dropped from a tree branch onto her head, and she let out a muffled scream of frustration.

Finally she was able to ease the car forward, and then with a jolt, she moved into traffic and headed for the main highway, where her small car hydroplaned in the big puddles that flooded the road. A truck sprayed her windshield with a brown wave that obstructed her vision. When the water cleared, she found herself inches from hitting the guardrail. She screamed and swerved, nearly smashing into the car in the travel lane. The muscles in her arms shook as she grabbed the wheel tighter and regained control over the vehicle. Air escaped her lips in fast gasps as she remembered to breathe.

At the Concord rotary, she almost turned back, deciding that she shouldn't risk her life to see a house she probably wouldn't buy. But she was only a few miles from Littleton and it would take at least an hour to drive back to Boston in the bad weather. More than anything she wanted to be out of her car. She crept along the winding roads and ducked her head to look through the one clear area on the windshield. Her muscles remained clenched until she pulled into Nagog Drive.

She turned off the car and placed her head on the steering wheel. Her hands continued to shake as she took in gulps of air. She hadn't entered a church since her grandmother's funeral. No one had taught her to pray, so she faked it.

"Whoever just kept me alive during that drive, thank you."

Heather opened her umbrella and stepped from the car. She tucked her hair behind her ear and looked at the house. Even through the cold drizzle, the place looked warm and inviting, and the sight of it calmed her nerves. Heather had studied architecture during her travels. Her columns tended to include descriptions of neighborhood homes—she felt it brought her readers closer to a location. Or maybe it was her own desperate need to find a place to call home.

Fresh paint, colonial blue, coated the wooden clapboards of the house. Whereas the other homes in the neighborhood had front porches with wood or stucco pedestals or columns, this one had a small deck with white rails. Heather assumed that it originally had a porch, but someone had chosen to remove it during renovation to get a better view of the lake. Instead of heavy wooden doors typical of the time period, there were glass French doors.

Though the house was clearly a Craftsman bungalow, with thick wood casings around the windows and a front gabled roof, there were also Victorian accents like bay windows with diamond patterns and scrolled patterns on the rafters. Whoever had built this place hadn't been ready to fully embrace the modern architecture of that time.

A man with curly salt-and-pepper hair ran toward her in the rain. He extended a gloved hand. "I'm Aaron. You must be Heather."

"Nice to meet you," she said as he ushered her onto the deck.

Aaron wiped moisture from his forehead and dug in his jacket pocket for the keys. "The house is over one hundred years old, but everything has been updated. My wife's family has owned it since it was built. It has a fieldstone foundation."

"Yes, I noticed that," Heather said.

"They don't build foundations like these anymore." Aaron continued to look for the keys in his other pockets. "I'm sorry this is taking so long. I just flew in this afternoon and I'm a little frazzled. I know I put the keys somewhere."

A black car pulled into the drive. A tall woman in a beige suit and thick brown heels ran to the porch, her briefcase held over her head for protection. Aaron found his keys in his jeans and unlocked the French doors. Heather walked into the dark living room. He turned on a small table lamp and the room glowed with soft light.

"I'm Janice. I spoke with both of you on the phone." She handed them business cards imprinted with her picture and the RE/MAX logo. "This place is lovely. I don't think I've ever been through the neighborhood."

"This is the first house that's ever been on the market in this community," Aaron said. "All of the houses have been passed down through the generations."

Heather half listened as she walked around the large but cozy room. Floor-to-ceiling bookcases framed the sides of a large rectangular window that had two diamond-pattern casings. From here, Heather could have touched the large lilac bush that almost screened the entire picture window and created privacy between the houses. She imagined sitting on a couch, a book on her lap, as the scent of lilacs permeated the room. Polished maple beams had been used as molding in the recessed ceiling. She touched the rocking chair next to the hearth and it brought her back to nights being rocked to sleep to the sounds of a crackling fire.

"Why don't we move on to the rest of the house?" Aaron said. He led them past the maple staircase and down a short hall to the dining room.

Crown molding trimmed the ceiling in this room and gave it an elegant feel. Rainbow prisms danced from the small cut crystals in the light fixture. Through the two windows on the opposite side of the room, Heather could see the next-door neighbor's house, which was only about thirty feet away. Heather looked out the window and saw a detached double car garage. "Does the garage come with the property?"

"One side of it does," Aaron said. "It's a strange situation. There are actually two doors and a wall separating the space, but my wife's family and the Woodwards next door were good friends and they decided that they could get by with only one building permit if they shared the garage."

"How does that work with selling the property and clearing the title?" Janice asked.

"I'm not certain about that, since no one has ever thought about selling." Aaron began to talk faster. "In this community, it's almost like buying a townhome. The association owns the land, but the structures have individual titles. The community center across the way is also common property. But the fees are only one hundred dollars a month and they cover trash, plowing, and the use of the beach and the center."

"Why are you selling?" Heather asked as she walked to the other end of the room where a serving buffet had been built into the wall.

"These homes have been passed down for almost a century. It's time for my wife and me to give it to our sons, but they live near us, in Miami. This place needs someone to enjoy the lake and throw summer parties. It needs a youthful presence."

"So, you live in Florida," Heather replied.

"That's why the price is so low," Aaron said. "It's too hard to take care of it from such a distance. And we're willing to negotiate to make this deal happen. Are you ready to look at the kitchen?" He moved through the doorway next to the buffet and turned on the lights in the next room.

The man was driving Heather crazy. The house had a serenity about it, and he was ruining the mood with this high-speed tour.

"The cabinets are original, but the kitchen was updated with a side-by-side refrigerator, dishwasher, and new stove." He moved to the other end of the kitchen and opened a door. "Back here is a sunroom that looks out over the backyard. As you can see—"

"Do you mind if I look around on my own?" Heather interrupted.

Aaron looked to Janice, who shrugged her shoulders.

"Just let me turn on the lights upstairs." Aaron walked away.

"I'll let you look around in peace," Janice said and followed Aaron into the living room.

Heather let out a sigh of relief. The kitchen smelled of nutmeg, as if thousands of meals had been cooked in the room. Heather opened the white cabinet and saw flour dust. She could almost taste the sweet cakes and cookies baked over the years in the double oven. The cabinets had what looked like a fresh coat of paint and black knobs. The ceiling was tan with white exposed beams, and the backsplash was a soft green. The island in the center had a heavy wooden counter and two stools. Another window seat had been built in the corner and matched the big wooden table. She stood at the sink and looked out the bay window to a large backyard.

Fog was lifting between the trees. She imagined hanging a hammock near the split-rail fence. She could see herself sipping iced tea and reading a book on hot summer days.

"There are three bedrooms upstairs," Aaron said from the doorway, "but take your time."

Heather walked through the kitchen to the living room and saw Aaron looking out the window. The man was a bundle of nerves. If he was this desperate to sell, she might be able to negotiate the price. Closed double doors met her at the top of the stairs. Two bedrooms were on either side of the hallway. One looked as if it had been used as a study, with bookshelves and a desk that looked out over the side yard to the neighbor's house. Through the window she could see a bedroom with bunk beds. As she left the room she saw faded pencil marks on the doorframe indicated the growth of a little girl named Maryland. White wainscoting met floral wallpaper in the second bedroom. Not her style, but it had the charm of a Vermont inn.

In the hallway she opened the double doors to the master suite. Angles and nooks, created by the gabled roof, made the room feel expansive and cozy at the same time. The room was furnished with a queen-size cherry canopy bed, a standing oval mirror, and an antique fainting couch. Heather ran her fingers over the footboard; the carved wood felt romantic. If the bed came with the house, she'd hang sheer curtains from the canopy, and on lazy summer mornings, she'd lie in bed, the breeze shifting the material while she listened to the birds.

Through a massive window with a built-in seat, she could see the beach across the street and the slushy ice on the lake. Two wooden poles had been sunk into the sand and waited for summer when the volleyball net could be hung. A picnic table sat under the large oak tree. Heather wondered if everyone congregated in the evenings for a drink in the front yard.

She unzipped her leather boots, sank her feet into the lush carpet, and curled against the window. This was a real bedroom, a place of sanctuary where she could rest after a long trip.

She thought about her childhood home, the eight-hundred-square-foot apartment where she and her mother had moved following her grandmother's death, when they could no longer afford the lake house. The bedroom furniture from the lake house had been too big for Heather's tiny room in the apartment, so her mother had constructed a bed for her out of plywood and dowels; the mattress was a three-inch foam piece covered in vinyl.

In the winter, she stuffed the edges of her thin comforter around her body like a sleeping bag because the electric heat was too expensive to keep the room above sixty degrees. Whenever the wind blew through the plastic-covered, single-paned glass, Heather's fingers and toes froze.

Every week her mother placed a lottery ticket under the dollar-sign magnet on the refrigerator. At night, Heather would lie in bed and picture the money they might win.

They would leave the neighborhood where people fought in the middle of the night. They'd buy another lake house and she'd sleep in a canopy bed covered with pink lace ruffles. When she jumped on the mattress, fluffy blankets would poof around her. Books would fill tall shelves that lined the walls.

Heather looked out the window. The neighborhood reminded her of her daydreams, a community in which neighbors cared for one another. Heather's lifestyle didn't allow her time to form friendships, and except for her one close girlfriend, Gina, the people in Heather's life were more acquaintances.

She ran her finger over her diamond ring. She knew it was time to remove it, but it felt too final. Once the ring was gone, she knew it was over and she would actually be alone. On the night Charlie asked her to marry him, they sat in a white horse-drawn carriage, huddled under a fleece blanket, a bag of hot chestnuts between them. The horse's hooves had clip-clopped against the cobblestone of Boston as they made their way through the narrow roads. When they came to the steps of Faneuil Hall, Charlie had stepped down from the carriage, knelt on one knee, and proposed. Now it was over and time to move on.

In five days she was leaving for Europe and would be away

a month. It would be tough to buy the house. There would be contracts to sign, a formal mortgage application process, a home inspection. She was better off finding an apartment in the city, but a faint whisper came from her heart: *This is home.*

❦

Tom Woodward pushed the keyboard under his desktop and stood to stretch. Through the glass doors of his office, he could see his staff of architects focused on their computers. The clock read noon. He'd been up since four, and the morning had slipped away. He sat at his drafting table, the plan for the Watsons' five-thousand-square-foot home in front of him. "Just a few more tweaks."

His brain felt empty, as if all his thoughts had been sucked to the core of his mind, then exploded past his skull. He needed a nap, but he still had to head to Nagog this afternoon. Sarah had called yesterday, asking if he could come over and help her with some repairs. It would've been easier to call a handyman, but she was one of the women who'd raised him. Plus, he hadn't seen his grandfather in weeks, and it was time to check in.

"Thought you might need this," his assistant, Cynthia, said as she walked into the office and placed a sandwich and coffee on his desk. Cynthia had psychic abilities. She anticipated his needs: food appeared on his desk before his stomach growled; coffee came just as his fingers went to rub his eyes; the files he needed were readily available. "I have to go up to my grandfather's place this afternoon," he said. "Why don't you take the rest of the day off?"

"Thank you, but who would keep this place running?" She unwrapped the sandwich and handed it to him. "The Chartreuses are stressing about the position of the house on the lot.

They'd like you to meet them at the site tomorrow morning at ten. The address is in your PDA along with directions."

"Have I told you that this company couldn't run without you?" Tom asked.

"No, but at my next review I'm expecting deep gratitude." Cynthia smiled.

She walked to the door and leaned against the glass door. "Let me know if you need anything else. And eat something."

Tom looked at the drawings in front of him and realized his brain couldn't go any further. He grabbed the food and his jacket and headed through the lobby he'd designed in inlaid mahogany, tamarind, and redwood.

Tom took a few bites of his sandwich as the elevator opened. He pressed the button for the basement garage. As he walked to his vehicles, a few lights flickered. He'd call maintenance from his car and have them fix them.

As the owner of the large office building in Providence, Rhode Island, he tried to leave things to the management company he'd hired, but it was impossible when he saw the little things that piled up each day. He lived in a loft space on the top floor and at times he didn't leave the building for an entire week. These days, the only time he left was when he went to visit his grandfather in Littleton, Massachusetts, or to meet with clients.

He opened the door to a white rusted truck with *Woodward Architecture, Ltd.* lettered on the door and slid onto the cracked vinyl seat. Parked next to the vehicle was his new blue pickup with three thousand miles on the speedometer, and a sports car that carried him to meetings. But he only drove the white truck to visit Nagog. It had been a present from the community when he started his firm.

The rusted truck rattled down the highway as he pushed the speedometer to seventy miles per hour. Tom bounced over the potholes, the suspension similar to an all-terrain vehicle. His mechanic had tried to convince him to junk the tired vehicle, which now had 270,000 miles on it and a twice-rebuilt engine, but he couldn't do it. As the rain continued relentlessly, he prayed the weather wouldn't turn icy as he drove north.

An hour later, he pulled in front of his grandfather's house in Nagog. Two cars were parked in the drive his grandfather shared with his neighbor Maryland. Tom now cared for the house, after Maryland had been placed in a nursing home. He realized what the cars might mean, and though he didn't have time to investigate, he knew if he was right, there would be uproar in the community.

Tom walked into his grandfather's garage and removed his leather coat and button-down shirt. He pulled a sweatshirt from a laundry basket on the dryer and pulled it over his T-shirt, covering his head with the hood. He went back to his truck and grabbed his tool belt from behind the seat. The rain changed to hail and white pellets of ice bounced off the cars. Tom shielded his eyes as he looked into the upstairs window of Maryland's home. Lights had been turned on.

Every afternoon of his childhood, Tom had jumped from the yellow bus and run as fast as his legs could take him across Maryland's yard. Without knocking, he'd bang through the kitchen door, his backpack landing on the table as he fell into the padded wooden chair, a cookie already at his lips.

Maryland kept her brown hair pulled back with a barrette. She wore big glasses that fell down her nose when she kissed his head.

"How was school?" she'd ask.

"Cool. My friend Jeremy got a yellow dump truck that's remote-controlled. He let me play with it at recess."

She'd tousle his hair. "Did you learn anything?"

"Just stupid stuff." He'd open his backpack, and she'd look at his worksheets.

Maryland had been placed in a Florida nursing home by her son-in-law, Aaron. Tom had tried to stop it, but he wasn't blood. Now there were strangers in her house.

He walked into Maryland's living room and saw Aaron pacing.

Aaron looked up and walked toward him. "Tommy, I'm glad you're here. There's a shelf that seems to be buckling."

Tom crossed his arms. "Nice to see you too, Aaron. What are you doing here?"

"Maryland wants to sell the house," Aaron said.

"Really?" Tom removed his wet sweatshirt and walked to the bookshelf. Aaron wasn't worth Tom's anger. He pulled hard-bound books from the sagging wood and tried to see who was looking at the house.

"How we doing?" Aaron asked as two women walked down the stairs. "I thought you might like to meet one of the neighbors. Heather, this is Tommy Woodward."

Tom watched Heather walk toward him. He'd expected an older woman, but Heather was young and pretty, with a large diamond on her left hand. What did she want with a house in this community?

He extended his hand. "Nice to meet you. Are you and your husband looking to buy a summer place or hoping to live here year-round?"

"My husband?" Heather shook her head and stared.

Tom pointed to her ring.

"Oh." Her cheeks flushed as she tucked her hand behind her back. "Fiancé. I'm not married."

"Well, if you'd like to know anything about the house, I've done the upkeep for the last few years."

"Tommy's our neighborhood handyman." Aaron put his arm around Tom's shoulder.

He stepped away. "I have to be going. I need to fix Sarah and Carl's step."

"Everyone helps each other around here," Aaron said.

Tom snorted. "It was nice to meet you, Heather. Good luck with your home search."

As he closed the door behind him, he heard Heather say, "I'd like to make an offer." *This is going to be interesting,* he thought.

CHAPTER 6

Hail bounced against the pitched roof of the community center where Carl, Bill, Daniel, and Joseph sat around a table, piles of poker chips and cards spread in front of them. Joseph looked at his cards, two queens and a jack. It was a good hand, but the spread in front of him had a king and an ace. He looked at his pile of chips. It had dwindled to a quarter of the size of the other piles. He'd been distracted throughout the game.

"Playing poker without cigars isn't right," Bill said as he raised by two dollars. It was a twenty-dollar buy-in and Joseph had about five dollars left. "I tell ya, this whole healthy-lifestyle-phase our wives are in has to be stopped. Now we can't smoke in the community center or our own homes because it's no longer healthy. I tell ya what's unhealthy: stressing about what isn't good for ya."

"Give me bacon and eggs alongside a good steak any day and just let my heart clog up when it's ready to stop ticking. I'm going out happy," Carl said.

Daniel Littman looked at his cards and folded. He grabbed his inhaler and sucked in the medication. His breath rumbled in his chest. Joseph looked at the purple bruises beneath Daniel's skin. Someone needed to convince him to see a doctor.

Daniel hadn't grown up in the neighborhood. A Holocaust victim, he'd immigrated to the United States with his wife after the war. Bill had given him a job as an accountant in his family's factory. Daniel worked long hours and dedicated his life to the company.

Bill never asked about the concentration camp, but he had seen the numbers tattooed on the inside of Daniel's left arm. When Bill's family's house was passed down to him, he came to the community and told them his plan. He and Molly were already living in her parents' home. He'd been at Dachau the day the troops went in to free the prisoners. He'd seen the famine, the living conditions, the torture they'd endured. He wanted Daniel and his family to have a place to call home.

The community agreed that Bill could give his home to the Littmans, and Daniel became a part of the neighborhood.

"Joseph, it's your turn," Carl said. "I don't know where your head is today, but I like that you want to give me all your money." He laughed.

Joseph looked at his cards and his five chips and decided to go all in. As soon as he did, Bill flipped over a king and an ace and gathered up his winnings.

"Well, I guess that's it for me today," Joseph said as he stood. He walked across the room and into the library area. Two couches and chairs were situated around a fireplace. He hit the button on the wall and blue flames ignited the gas. He looked at the built-in bookcases and scanned the titles for a good book. Nothing caught his interest.

The community center had been built nine years ago over the patio that had held lavish parties. Now the space had a gym with Nautilus equipment, an office section with two computers—though none of his friends ever used them—and the library area. There was a small kitchen and a dining area for when parties were held. A pool table stood next to where the men played cards. Many days were spent in this room, the women playing dominoes or knitting, while the men played poker or pool. The room had warm woods, deep burgundy carpets, and soft lights for a cozy feel during the winter months.

Joseph walked across the parquet dance floor and stood by the floor-to-ceiling windows. He opened a curtain and stared at the lake. Snow covered the overgrown path that led through his yard and to the private beach.

There were thousands of little memories that Joseph enjoyed replaying: his daughter tapping her first pair of patent leather shoes on the church steps, the first time he held his son, and the night he and Victoria had made love.

Victoria's rejection had broken his spirit. Though he'd never told her, Joseph had dreamt of becoming a photographer—with Victoria by his side, they would travel the world. While away at war, he'd lie on his bunk at night and plan. He'd known that Victoria couldn't remain constrained by Nagog's lifestyle. The war had caused him to see the brutality of life, but also allowed him to see the beauty of the buildings and landscape of Europe. He imagined Victoria's eyes alight as they discovered new places.

Never in letters did he share his plans with her. He wanted to surprise her when the war was over and life could be about happiness again. Before he could share his ideas, she rejected him and ran away. Stunned by her response to his proposal, he hadn't immediately followed her. Only a half hour had passed when he went to find her, to show her what their life could be, but she was already gone. Over the months that followed, she didn't return or contact him and without her spark, and in the wake of her rejection, his dreams had died.

He'd fallen into a role: manager, then owner, of his father's textile factory, husband to the daughter of his mother's best friend, and keeper of the Nagog home. He forgot about professional photography and the world outside the community. Dreams were for teenagers. It wasn't until he became a father that his life felt fulfilled.

After his wife, Barbara, gave birth to their eldest son, Joseph began to see her as the earth goddess. Over the years, her once slim body softened as she brought another son and then their daughter into the world. Thin white stretch marks he had to squint to see lined her stomach. He enjoyed running his hand over their patterns. They were the lines of new life, the beauty marks his children had left behind. The children brightened their world with smiles and laughter. Joseph loved the way he and Barbara shared the joy of the family they created: pillow fights and stories at bedtime with the kids; private dances in the living room after the children were asleep.

Barbara had been as steady as the earth's rotation. Every day the sun came up, and every night it set, and in between there may have been clouds, but for the most part they had clear days. But then Victoria began to visit Nagog. She'd blast into the community in a flurry of glamour and excitement, usually without warning.

The first time he'd taken his daughter to the amusement park, she insisted they go on a ride called the Birthday Cake. Her small hand, sticky with cotton candy, pulled him up the metal stairs. They entered the round room and stood against the sides. The room began to spin and he felt his head press back. Faster and faster they spun until the floor dropped from beneath his feet and he stuck to the wall, unable to move.

Whenever Victoria came home to visit, Joseph felt as if he were in that cake. No matter how hard he tried to avoid her silver eyes, he felt pulled by the spirit they emanated. He didn't need to see her smile grow until her cheeks popped; he *felt* it from across the room. It had been that way since he was six.

Joseph walked past where the men played cards. He heard their voices but couldn't concentrate on their conversation. As he'd done many times since Victoria returned two weeks ago, he pulled back the curtains and peeked out the window toward her home. The porch light of the yellow house was on, but inside was dark. Had she gone out in this weather?

He looked around the neighborhood and saw lights on in Molly and Bill's place. Victoria was probably visiting with Molly. As he went to release the curtain he noticed two cars in the driveway of Maryland's home.

"Do any of you know why there are cars parked in Maryland's driveway?" Joseph asked. As he did, two women and Daniel's son Aaron walked onto the porch. Carl, Bill, and Daniel joined him at the window and watched as the women shook hands with Aaron and then walked to their cars.

"What the hell's he doing over there?" Daniel's German accent thickened as he yelled. "Damn it! Who are those people?"

"I'm certain everything's fine," Joseph said.

"Nothing's fine when it comes to my son," Daniel said as he pressed his face closer to the window.

Aaron had married Maryland's daughter, Patricia, and they lived in Florida. When Maryland had a stroke, Aaron moved her to Florida and placed her in a nursing home.

"The *chutzpah* of my son . . . He's going to sell Maryland's home."

Daniel flung the curtains closed and limped toward the coatrack. "The two of them abandoned her house. Aaron didn't even bother to board it up. Just left it for the pipes to burst and the windows to crack. If it weren't for Tommy, that house would've been destroyed." His thin arm shook as he reached for his coat.

The rain began to pound on the roof as it came down in a flash of power. "Daniel, you can't go out in this rain. You'll catch pneumonia," Bill said.

"I won't allow this. That house belongs to this community and Maryland," Daniel spat.

Carl put his hand on Daniel's shoulder. "Don't worry, we won't let him sell it."

Joseph watched as Aaron walked out of the house carrying a folder that he stuck under his rain jacket. Bill went to the door and opened it as Aaron made his way along the street to Daniel's home. Bill yelled, "Aaron, your father is over here."

Aaron turned and ran across the street and into the warm building. Water dripped from his coat and he unbuttoned it and hung it on the coatrack while he held on to the folder.

"Bill, Carl, Joseph"—he turned to his father—"Dad."

Joseph could see the shock on Aaron's face as he noticed his father's condition. His white hair jutted out to the side in desperate need of a haircut. He'd lost considerable weight and his clothing hung on him. Worse, his lungs wheezed with asthma.

"What's in your hand?" Daniel yelled without even saying hello.

"That's how you greet me?" Aaron said. "I haven't seen you in four years and you try to pick a fight the first minute I'm home?"

"I know what you're up to. You're trying to sell Maryland's home."

"Yes, I am," Aaron said. "I have a good offer and I'm taking it. Do you understand what this place is costing me? I knew if I put it on the regular market you and your men would make certain it didn't sell."

"Damn straight," Carl said. "That place belongs to Maryland and it should be passed down to your children."

"Do you think my boys want to leave Miami Beach to come and sit here all summer?"

"All you want is for us to hand over our homes so you can profit," Daniel yelled.

"This again," Aaron said and he pulled his hand through his hair. "You haven't spoken to me or come to visit me in four years because I asked you to sign papers to protect your estate. Do you realize how much you've hurt me and my family?"

Daniel slammed his fist on the table rattling the poker chips. "Maryland signed her assets over to you, and you put her in a home. She belongs here with her friends and family, not stuck in a room with an Alzheimer's patient who screams through the night. What you did to her was shameful, and you won't do it to me."

"That's great, Dad. So what happens when you can't take care of yourself like Maryland couldn't?"

"She was fine."

"She had a stroke and couldn't see out of her left eye," Aaron said.

"Then you should've come home to take care of her or hired a nurse. That's what family does. You didn't even bother to put up safety guards around the bathroom or install a Lifeline," Daniel said.

Aaron shook his head, unable to speak for a moment. "There's no talking to you. You don't understand what it's like to live in the modern world. I couldn't afford a private nurse or to move back here. Patricia and I have full-time jobs and we can't retire because money is tight. The taxes on this property are killing us. You live in this tiny community stuck in the past. The proceeds of Maryland's house would belong to the nursing home if she hadn't signed papers. When you need a care facility, they're going to bleed your estate dry. I'm trying to protect you."

Daniel slammed his fist again. "I'm not letting you put me in a home."

"And what if there's no choice? You people think that because you made a stupid promise to retire here, some magic fairy dust is going to keep you young. Look around, Dad. You're getting older. You're pretending, just like you did when I was a kid, you're not seeing the reality that could come in just another ten years."

"Pretending?" Daniel coughed and took a puff from his inhaler.

"This place was always a fantasy to you. You pretended we were like them. They're rich Episcopalians. You were their Jewish accountant who had to be given this house. Now you want to pretend that this is the paradise of the glory days. Well, what happens when you can no longer drive and you can't live alone?" Aaron asked.

Daniel forced his words through constricted airways. "So I should sign my house over to you so you can sell it and move me to a nursing home to die? What about passing down heritage and family traditions?"

"What's my heritage? Two parents rescued from concentration camps—not a house in Nagog. And when you can't take care of yourself anymore, you're going to lose this heritage because you didn't sign the papers," Aaron said. "And it's not like I haven't offered other solutions."

"To sell my home and for me to move into some retirement place in Florida. No thanks," Daniel said.

"You could be near your actual family." Aaron took a deep breath. "I can't do this right now, Dad. I didn't come here to fight with you. I'm doing what needs to be done."

Aaron moved past Daniel. Bill and Carl stood together and blocked his way to the door. "We won't let you sell her house to a stranger," Bill said. "We'll take care of the taxes and the upkeep."

"And what happens when you can't do that any longer? Are you going to bleed your children's inheritance dry? You don't understand that I'm doing this community a favor. These homes are going to be hard enough to sell because of the age of the community. Selling this house to this young woman starts the process that needs to happen. Things have to change, whether you like it or not." Aaron pointed his finger at them. "And the two of you better stay out of this. If you touch that house with any of your little pranks I will call the police. And Dad . . . I won't bail you out." He opened the door and closed it behind him.

Joseph put his hand on Daniel's shoulder. Aaron had never been comfortable in Nagog. For the other children, this community had been a place of sanctuary that created wonderful childhood memories when they visited, days of running through the sprinklers, Popsicles from the ice cream truck, and barbecues. Christmas transformed the street into a winter wonderland of lights and decorations. Parties were thrown and people danced on the patio.

For Aaron, living here hadn't been the same experience. Among the other children he'd been an outcast. While everyone else attended private school and lived in Boston, Aaron resided year-round in Nagog and received a public education. Instead of coming to the cookouts on Friday nights, he celebrated Shabbat with his parents.

The fifties were a time of anti-Semitism, and though Nagog didn't agree with the sentiments of the nation, racist jokes were common in school. Many times, Aaron became the target of the Nagog kids' ignorance. Even though he married within Nagog, he'd never wanted to stay close.

"I wonder if that young girl is trying to buy the house," Bill said as he moved back to the poker table. His girth pressed against his belt and pant seams as he sat.

"From what I could see through the rain, she had a pretty little caboose," Carl said.

"Too skinny. Women should have something to hold on to," Bill said.

"Could the two of you focus?" Daniel boomed. "We can't allow Aaron to do this. With a girl like her around, young men will follow. There'll be drinking and loud music."

"I don't think there's anything we can do," Joseph said.

Carl rubbed his bulbous nose. "We could make Nagog an over-fifty-five community. Wouldn't mind seeing that girl in a bikini this summer, but that house belongs in Maryland's family."

"Over fifty-five won't stop Aaron from selling it to someone outside the community. Plus, we can't take retroactive action if she has a signed agreement," Bill said.

"Then we take Aaron to court. We can't let our kids think they can sell our homes and put us in care facilities. I'm not spending my last years pasting macaroni to cardboard like a four-year-old."

"Daniel's right," Carl said. "My daughter's been talking about us moving to a happy retirement community that transitions to assisted living. I'm not spending the rest of my years being watched over by some nurse and being stuck with hundreds of old people."

"Yeah, my kids took me on a tour of one of those places," Bill said. "The whole damn place had pastel colors."

"I have an idea," Carl said.

Joseph knew the mischievous glint in Carl's eye. Along with admiring women's backsides, Carl had four favorite things in life: food, sports, a good cigar, and pranks. After Victoria's father's death, Carl's family had bought the Rose Plastics Company. Carl added a new line of gags like whoopee cushions, fake doo-doo, and phony vomit.

Carl winked at Bill, but Joseph worried about the plan Carl had in mind.

❧

Victoria and Molly sat around the folding table in Molly's sunroom, dominoes arranged in an elaborate pattern, while Sarah and Agatha sat on the wicker couch and knitted small pink and blue baby hats. Evelyn sat across from the women in a large white wicker chair that engulfed her tiny form. Molly's homemade brownies, cookies, and cakes lined the buffet table. Though each woman had taken a small sample of the desserts, the goodies sat untouched on their plates.

Molly tapped her domino against the table, creating noise in the silence. Victoria knew that she'd arranged this gathering in the hope that everyone would allow history to be left in the past, but the small room was thick with words unsaid.

Evelyn Price's eyes were wide with confusion, her white curls like a halo. In her pink turtleneck and sweater, she still looked like a little girl. Victoria gave her a small wave and Evelyn smiled just like when they were children: a big, radiant smile that spread to her pink cheeks. Then she looked out the window and stared at Maryland's house. Her friend's illness was another reminder that Victoria hadn't made amends in time.

Sarah cleared her throat. She lacked only a broom and a pointy hat to complete her resemblance to the Wicked Witch of the West from *The Wizard of Oz*. Her black lace collar accentuated her pinched face, and her bun pulled her hazel eyes tight as if she'd had a face-lift. Where was the teenager who'd snuck into Victoria's bed with a flashlight at night and told her dirty jokes? Molly had always followed the rules, whereas Sarah had been Victoria's partner in crime as they snuck cigarettes and alcohol.

"Sarah, how's Beatrice?" Victoria asked.

"My daughter is fine," Sarah said as she continued to knit.

"Will she be coming around?"

"She remarried and lives in Vermont. I don't see her that often," Sarah said through tight rose-tinted lips.

"Oh, congratulations."

"For what? My daughter's breaking the Lord's law and divorcing her first husband or for taking a new one without getting an annulment from the church?" Sarah looked at Victoria.

"I'm sorry, I didn't mean to bring up a sore subject."

Sarah grunted and clicked her needles together.

Agatha Lowe put down her knitting and picked up a large brownie. Agatha had grown up in the community and attended

Dana Hall School with the other girls, but she had never been part of Victoria's inner circle. She hadn't liked playing make-believe or staging tea parties. For the most part she'd kept her nose in books and only joined the other children when forced by her mother. Of course, it might have had something to do with the fact that Victoria had never made her feel welcome.

Agatha hadn't shed a tear when Victoria left—she'd celebrated. They'd never been close. When they were twelve, Agatha had auditioned for the school dance team. As captain, Victoria made certain only the most talented—and prettiest—girls made the squad. Agatha, in a black leotard and pink tights, had looked like a lumbering hippo to Victoria, whose long, graceful legs were accentuated by her own ballerina outfit. She hadn't let Agatha make the cut.

Agatha listlessly chewed on the brownie and fingered the large brace that covered her right knee. Molly had said that she'd had three surgeries on it in the last few years. She seemed to have given up on her appearance—her hair had been cut short and lay flat against her head, her breasts hung against her belly. She'd never been a beauty queen, though in the years before her husband's death, when Victoria visited in the summer, she'd seen Agatha motherly and soft, in bright sundresses, her auburn hair flowing over her shoulders. The gray sweat suit Agatha wore today reminded Victoria of that awkward teenager.

"I think we should take a trip," Molly announced. "Someplace warm like the Caribbean or the Bahamas. We'll lie on the beach and drink fruity umbrella drinks."

"Why?" Agatha asked.

Because she's trying to force us together, Victoria thought, *until we either kill each other or work things out.*

"We need an adventure. Clear out the winter stiffness and prepare for summer. We'll buy new sundresses and bathing suits. It will be a fun adventure."

"I have no interest in flying. It's too dangerous these days with terrorism and poor plane maintenance. With all the new regulations, it's too much of a hassle," Sarah said. She cut the end of her yarn and placed a blue hat on the coffee table. Then she grabbed pink yarn and began a new line of stitches.

"It's not dangerous. And life is a hassle only if you make it one," Victoria said.

Sarah didn't look up. "I did my traveling when I was younger. I'm content right where I am."

What had become of this once-vibrant group?

Only a few years ago they planned vacations, sat on boards, threw parties, and attended charity functions. They wore perfume and shopped in boutiques, went to Boston for movies and the theater. Molly had told Victoria that they'd barely left Nagog this winter. If they'd let Victoria back into their lives, she had to try to shake them up, get them out and moving again.

Sarah looked out the window toward Maryland's home. "Did you see that Aaron came to visit and he showed the house to a young woman?"

So, they were finally going to discuss the news of the day. Victoria had been in her mother's sitting area staring out the window at the rain when she saw the little blue car pull in and watched as the young woman stepped out of the car in her stylish red raincoat and high boots. Victoria's presence hadn't allowed the old friends to gossip the way they would have if she hadn't been there, but they couldn't hold it in forever.

"I saw that girl through my window, and we don't want her

kind here," Sarah said. "Tommy came over to fix our step, and you know Tommy, he won't say a harsh word about anyone, but I could tell he didn't like her either." Sarah put her knitting on the coffee table and paused for theatrical purposes. "I stopped and spoke to the men before I came over here and they say she's already made an offer to buy the house."

Molly clapped her hands together. "Maybe she's married and wants a place to raise a family. It would be nice to have a baby around."

"Mothers don't drive tiny cars," Agatha said.

Sarah's lips puckered till lines fanned around her mouth. "I think that girl is looking for a place to party."

Agatha nodded in agreement. "We don't want young people living here, they have no values. My grandkids are spoiled. They party and go on extravagant vacations. They refuse to marry and settle down, and they hop from one partner to the next." She nodded toward Victoria to emphasize the immorality.

"Well, we can't let her move in," Sarah said.

"It's a young woman, not the end of the world," Victoria said aloud before she could edit her thoughts.

The circle went silent except for the tap of Sarah's black shoes against the hardwood floor.

"Well, it's not like it matters to you. I doubt you'll be here more than a few months," Agatha said.

Molly put her hand on Victoria's arm. "She's here to stay."

"I've heard that one before," Sarah said.

"She probably wants a new playmate now that Annabelle is gone," Agatha said.

"Stop it!" Molly said. "You will not speak to her in such a painful way again. Do I make myself clear?"

Victoria looked at Sarah, trying to recall the young girl with whom she'd once shared her deepest secrets.

Sarah glared at Victoria, daring her to challenge her. "Every time you show up, someone gets hurt. Last time you came home, Joseph paid the price, and this time, if you push to have this young woman move in, we all will. You've never cared about being here, but you could at least respect that this is our home and we would like it to stay in our family."

"What do you mean, Joseph paid the price?" Victoria asked.

"He and Barbara divorced because of you," Sarah said, "but of course you were too selfish to notice what was happening around you."

Victoria stood and gathered her coat. "I don't need to listen to this nonsense." Molly tried to stop her, but Victoria shook her head. At the door she turned. "Sarah, Agatha, I'm sorry you feel the way you do, but this is my home too. And my family."

"Not like you ever acted that way," Agatha said as Victoria closed the door.

The gray twilight had turned black. The wind stung her cheeks, like when she held an ice pack too long against her skin. The cold watered her eyes and her forehead ached as she walked home trying to understand what Sarah had said about Joseph's divorce. There were things Victoria knew she'd done in her past to hurt her friends, but to be blamed for Joseph's divorce was ridiculous.

The warm air of her sunroom made her tight muscles feel like ice cubes dropped into a hot frying pan. She held her arms to her chest and shivered while her frozen body melted. The arthritic bones in her hands creaked and the joints popped with movement as she stretched the tight tendons. Upstairs, she changed into violet silk pajamas, slipped her feet into the furry slippers Molly had given her one birthday, and huddled under the covers.

Victoria filled her lungs with air, letting her ribs expand and her collarbone rise. She counted to ten. The breath released, her shoulders dropped, and she squeezed her stomach to exhale. Hours of yoga, recommended by her psychiatrist, had taught her this special way of breathing. After fifteen minutes of inhaling and exhaling she felt warm, but the sword through her gut continued to bleed memories.

❧

Two years after her father's death, Victoria returned to Nagog for a social visit—her first in twelve years besides her parents' funerals—and the community hadn't opened their arms to welcome her back.

It was 1954, but in Nagog, it might as well have been the 1940s. Orbed lanterns filled with moonlight crisscrossed over the patio. Crisp white linen covered the tables. Champagne glasses sparkled in flickering candlelight as men in brown business suits slapped each other on the back and lifted their drinks in revelry. It was déjà vu—from the waiters' black-and-white uniforms to the antique rose-patterned china—the traditional Labor Day party that had been held for thirty years.

Oppressive humidity caused the women to dab their foreheads with embroidered handkerchiefs, but their shirtwaist dresses never wrinkled. It wouldn't have been appropriate, and somehow the clothing knew it.

Victoria's three-carat diamond ring sparkled in the party lights. The dance floor was Victoria's stage. Her bright green silk halter dress made her feel as sexy as Marilyn Monroe, when her new husband, Devon Massaro, spun her in wide steps, pushing the slower couples to the sidelines.

All her childhood friends had given her quick hugs and perfunctory kisses on the cheek when she entered the party. Victoria could tell they were sick to their stomachs with envy. She'd dangled her diamond in the cluster of women. Sarah had turned her long, thin face away and pursed her lips like she'd sucked a lemon. Her friends' coy glances at her husband let Victoria know they were mesmerized by Devon's good looks. Every bored housewife in America secretly wanted to be a model and movie star, and though Victoria was only a supporting actress, she already had an Oscar award under her belt, and her face was often featured in the magazines her friends read.

As she danced, she caught glimpses of Joseph. No words had passed between them. No "congratulations on your wedding" or "you look beautiful." Something seemed to connect and also separate them. She could feel his presence, but no matter how hard she tried to cross the ten yards to reach him, he moved back the same distance she'd advanced.

A child ran up from the beach and jumped into his arms. He cradled the girl on his protruding belly and petted her hair. What had happened to the strong muscles she'd admired through long summers of watching him play volleyball and football on the beach? When had he married? She'd seen him talk to two other children down on the beach. One looked to be around eight years old. He'd attended her parents' funerals, but she didn't remember him having a family then.

The song ended. Devon kissed her ear and demanded, "It's time we leave. I can't listen to another word about plastics and textiles."

"Darling, please. It's only ten. These people are my family, and I haven't seen them for years." She ran her fingers through his thick, brown hair and combed the strays into place.

"Then stay. I'm going back to the house. We have an early flight tomorrow," Devon said.

He kissed her, his tongue exploring her mouth, his teeth biting her lips. She felt herself quiver with the quick endorphin release. He leaned back and touched her face. Then he walked away, lit a cigarette, and headed down the dirt road.

Around the patio, women whispered and nodded to one another, shocked by the audacious display of affection.

"A woman of a certain social standing is expected to show grace and dignity at all times," Victoria's mother had lectured. "As a Rose, I expect nothing less of you than to become an educated woman with elegance and poise."

All Nagog women had been brought up with the same lecture, and Victoria was certain they felt she acted with impropriety. Still, Molly had told her that they watched her movies. Each woman who now obscured her moving lips with the side of her hand would later brag in other circles that Victoria Rose was her childhood friend.

Victoria walked to the edge of the patio and looked out over the beach. Children screamed as they ran around the bonfire, their feet kicking up sand. Victoria felt the warmth of Molly's curvy body against her back.

"Devon is rather handsome," Molly said as she hugged Victoria.

Victoria held Molly's soft hands. "What's everyone saying?"

"Oh, don't bother yourself with their gossip. They're hurt you didn't invite them to your wedding, and they don't understand what's kept you away." Molly rubbed Victoria's fingers.

Victoria had wanted extraordinary, and she'd accomplished it: In the last twelve years she'd traveled to Paris, Cuba, and Rome for different roles. She'd worked in the theater in London and New York.

The band played their last song while the older people retired to bed. The waiters cleared the last of the tables as the band packed up. Her friends gathered around the tables and dealt cards.

The weather changed as they played Five Hundred rummy. The wind shook the trees in an orchestra of creaks and snaps. Napkins blew from the tables as the lake's waves lifted the rowboats tied to the dock and the wooden bodies tore at their ropes. And through the impending storm, her friends seemed focused on nothing but turning the conversation away from Victoria. Sarah laid a card on the table and picked a new one from the deck. "Did you hear that Maria is going to run for president of the PTA? Like the woman has a chance of winning. Last year she forgot to bring baked goods to the fair."

Oh no, how could she have forgotten the baked goods? Victoria thought.

"I won an Oscar for best supporting actress," Victoria tried to interject casually. "You should all come to California—"

"We know. We read about it in a magazine," Sarah snapped, as if Victoria was a three-year-old who'd interrupted the grown-up talk. "Did you know we've decided to retire here? We're going to leave Boston and move back. We plan to live out our golden years having parties and traveling together. Doesn't it sound fantastic?" Sarah placed her cards on the table. Between two fingers she lifted a long brown cigarette.

Victoria rubbed her arms, goose bumps rising in the chilly

weather. "I can't imagine living here full time. It's too cold." Her friends were quiet and she finally had the stage. "I love the warm nights in California, and it only rains a few weeks out of the year, but I don't think Devon and I will retire in the United States. We love Europe too much. We're planning to buy a home on the French Riviera. You're all invited to visit. We'll have plenty of room. Have any of you traveled to Europe?"

"Roger and I went to Paris for our honeymoon," Evelyn said.

"Ah, Paris," Victoria said, before anyone could get another word in about PTA meetings. "The food, the art, the fashion, it's just one of my favorite places. I've been there three times now. But Italy is my favorite destination. Even though the landscapes are similar to California's, I find Italy more romantic. You should see it when the sunflower fields are in bloom. It's a wave of yellow against the blue sky."

"You know, it's getting a little too cold out here," Sarah said. "I think I'll turn in."

"I will as well," Agatha said, and the two stood.

"It was nice to see you, Victoria," Sarah said without a smile as she walked away. "Safe travels."

Within a matter of minutes the other women had said quick good-byes and walked over to where the men were playing poker.

Molly sat with Victoria as she gathered the cards and placed them in a box. "Why don't you and Devon come to our house for breakfast in the morning?" Molly said.

"Our flight is at six a.m. We need to leave by four," Victoria said as she watched the rest of the community walk toward their homes.

"Well, then, I'll bring you muffins and coffee for your trip.

I need one last hug before you leave again." She stood and embraced Victoria. "Who knows how long it will be again before I get to have my arms around you?"

"I promise it won't be so long this time," Victoria said. But as she looked to the empty patio she wondered if her presence was all that welcome.

Victoria watched Bill and Molly walk home, then she headed down to the beach and the dying bonfire. Red lines of heat danced through the blackening coals. Warmth, she needed warmth. Victoria moved closer to the fire ring and bent down to get closer to the heat. The coals looked innocent, quiet and gentle, but if she were to touch the charcoal, her hands would blister black and red.

She stood and trudged along the water against the wind, the sand pooling in her shoes. The path that led to the private beach was before her, and she didn't know why, but she took the dirt path covered in pine needles.

Joseph sat on the log in the place she'd left him twelve years before. Frozen, she waited. His back was slumped in a C curve and his belly hung on his lap as his hands raked his blond hair.

A cloud moved away from the moon and silver light brightened the beach. In unison they looked to the stars. He turned. Stood. Stared. Their eyes met. She took a step forward. He moved a step back. He put his hand up to stop her from coming forward.

"Joseph," she said, and then stopped, uncertain of what to say.

"I should be getting back to my house." He began to walk toward the path and then he turned. "It's good to see you so happy, Victoria."

"You too," she said, and watched him walk away.

～◌◌◌～

Victoria took another yoga breath and removed the comforter, stood, and went downstairs. Her slippers' rubber soles brushed against the stone tile in the kitchen, breaking the silence of the house. She poured water into a blue teapot and placed it on the cast-iron stove. Exotic teas from around the world lined the second shelf of the pantry. Victoria dropped a chamomile bag into a mug with *Number 1 Grandma* hand-painted on the side.

Molly had stocked the refrigerator with salad, lasagna, and casseroles. Victoria pulled out the lasagna and picked at the crusted cheese. As a young woman, Victoria had been focused on showing her friends that she'd made the right decision when she left for Hollywood. Looking back, she realized she hadn't bothered to pay any attention to their lives. Never did she ask Evelyn about her wedding. She didn't even know how her friend had met Roger. Now it was too late to hear those stories.

In 1954 she'd come home to brag, and it took her this long to realize she'd acted like a snob. Over the years, she'd used Nagog as a vacation home or as a safe haven in times of pain. This time, Victoria had returned to face her demons, but the truth was, she also missed her friends. Her friends' anger had grown and festered over the years. Would her presence only create more pain? But a fallen angel must do her penance, and choices can't be undone because one desires them to be.

Victoria covered the lasagna and placed it in the refrigerator. She'd have to start preparing her own meals before Molly's cooking widened her waistline. She poured hot water over the chamomile tea bag and watched the yellow color seep into the mug.

She walked out of the kitchen and down the hall to her father's study. She breathed in the smell of pipe tobacco and grabbed her ratty copy of *Emma* from the low shelf next to the window. The book's corners were dented with teeth marks where her childhood beagle had chewed. She curled into the chair at her father's desk. The green lamp illuminated the wood's swirling grain. She opened the book, but the words blurred in front of her, their logical path senseless to her.

She stood and looked in the mirror that hung above the fireplace. An old, lonely woman stared back, a face sculpted by loss. A young woman believes in happily ever after. The problem with age is that you learn the truth—no matter how hard you fight to make your life perfect, the pain always finds a way in.

CHAPTER 7

‿֍‿

Heather wanted to reach out and touch the gilded frame of Renoir's life-size *Dance in the Country* painting. In middle school, she'd spent three years singing in the choir as she stared at a poster of this painting and dreamt of someday coming to Paris. Now she stood in Musée d'Orsay, three feet away from the original.

As the Solo Female Traveler, Heather had visited most of the world's greatest art museums: the Louvre, the Uffizi, London's National Art Gallery, Tokyo's National Museum of Western Art, the Vatican. Most of the art she'd seen had consisted of religious pieces or stern portraits of royalty created to display power. But the Impressionists' work was different: colorful and bright, they brought the softness of everyday life to the canvas. Instead of demanding that she see the hard lines of reality, they blurred landscapes into something serene and almost touchable, as if the world was in a constant state of peace.

Heather caught a glimpse of Monet's *Water Lilies* out of the corner of her eye, and turned from the Renoir she'd been contemplating. Monet had always been her favorite artist, and she wanted to stand before his work and allow the pastel colors to swim in her spirit. As she approached Monet's masterpiece, people rushed around her. They stood before the painting, looked around for security guards, and then snapped a quick photo of the piece before moving on to the next. Heather shook her head as she watched the tourists. They were always rushing, and not just with art. She remembered sitting at the Grand Canyon and watching people walk up to the edge, take dozens of photos, and then say, "Let's get some ice cream." The amount of time they spent actually looking at the Grand Canyon averaged about twenty minutes.

Heather weaved her way through the halls of the old train station turned museum, taking in the works of Degas, Monet, van Gogh, and Manet. Three times she walked the hall filled with Vincent van Gogh's swirls of color, stopping at *Starry Night* with each pass.

A man's voice came over the intercom and said in French and then English that the museum was closing. She walked through the central hallway, taking a last look at the statues before exiting the building.

Outside, the afternoon rain had stopped and the sun was streaming through the clouds reflecting golden light on the brick Renaissance buildings. Sometimes Paris overwhelmed Heather: the ornate buildings with sculptured facades that looked like frosting on a wedding cake; the confident Parisian women who wore clothing as if it were art; the restaurants where people savored their food until late into the night. Everything about this city spoke to opulence and class. But, during the course of four visits, Heather had found her way into a softer side of Paris. She shopped in the Latin Quarter instead of the Champs-Élysées. She turned down tiny alleys and found small restaurants visited by locals with owners who didn't mind that she dined alone.

Heather walked along the streets toward the Pont du Neuf, her favorite bridge from which to watch the sunset. Groups of friends began to congregate on the bridge with picnics of wine, bread, and cheese. Heather could hear laughter and conversation all around her.

The sky turned a dark blue and the lights of the palaces along the river reflected like candlelight. With each visit to Paris she'd stood here at night, wishing to share it with someone. It was the most romantic spot—the place she longed to have a lover wrap her in his arms and kiss her like the man kissed the woman in the Renoir painting. It wasn't a place of passion; it was a place where you felt how much you loved and were loved.

She looked down at the three half-eaten desserts that she'd bought at a corner patisserie on her way to the bridge—more than enough to share with friends. It was that time of night that Heather dreaded when she traveled; she needed to find a restaurant. Her readers wanted her dining suggestions, and though she loved French food—cheese platters covered in fig sauce, butternut squash sautéed with sticks of butter, lemon-roasted chicken—the knowledge that she'd be dining alone dampened her spirits. All around her, people would be with friends, lovers, and family—and she'd have her notebook.

She walked along the Seine until she reached the Louvre. Through the palace courtyard, past I. M. Pei's pyramids of glass, cello music floated across the air, and she stopped to listen. The deep notes brought tears to her eyes. She didn't want to go to a restaurant, but she also couldn't bear to return to another barren hotel room. She'd been traveling a month: London, Scotland, Ireland, and now France. Each night she went back to her hotel and didn't have anyone to call to let them know that she was okay.

There'd been brief conversations with other guests at a hotel during breakfast, or another tourist as she rode the train, but other than that she'd been alone. She sent her articles to her editor and conversed through e-mail. Her lawyer sent her papers to sign for the house sale in Nagog and the bank sent her mortgage documents. This was the extent of her social interactions.

She placed coins in the musician's velvet-lined case and walked into the central courtyard of the Louvre. She thought about the house on Nagog Lake with its window seats and lilac bushes. Her mind wandered to the man she'd met there, Tommy Woodward, standing in the living room wearing jeans, a tool belt, and a black shirt that accentuated a strong chest. His eyes were the color of Maui's ocean, and the dampness in the air had curled the tips of his wavy hair. His rugged cheekbones made him look like James Dean. Heather had found herself daydreaming about him more than she cared to admit. What would it be like to stand with him on the Pont du Neuf while they watched the sunset over Paris?

She reminded herself not to get too carried away; there was a good possibility that he had a girlfriend. There hadn't been a wedding ring, but she'd glimpsed a room with bunk beds in the Woodward house. Maybe he had nephews that visited. At least she hoped that was the explanation.

Tomorrow was the home inspection on the Nagog house. Heather prayed that no serious problems would be found. Everything was set for her to buy the house by the end of next week. At the last minute, the agent had once again suggested a home inspection, and Heather had finally agreed. She didn't know how to explain that no matter what, she needed this house. She didn't have anywhere else to go when she returned to Boston, but more than that, she needed to be part of a community, not just a tourist in life.

☙

Tommy pulled his truck in front of his grandfather's home. Dark gray clouds covered the moon and stars and the wind moved between the Nagog houses, rattling windows.

He saw movement between Maryland's yard and the Dragones'. He walked around the back of Grandpa's garage and saw Bill, Carl, and Daniel making their way across the yard between Carl's garage and Maryland's sun porch. Blue lights from their headlamps illuminated Maryland's once elaborate rose garden. Daniel squeaked open the screen door on the back porch at 8 Nagog Drive, and the three men entered.

What were they up to? He snuck closer to the sun porch and listened.

Carl looked at the other men. "Synchronize your watches to eight fifteen. We'll plan to meet back here in twenty minutes. Keep low and quiet. Remember the signal. I'll hoot like an owl if anyone comes round."

Bill leaned a shovel against the railing and pulled a crowbar from his black bag. "Remember, his hoot sounds like a crow squawking. I'm going to give the porch a remodel, so watch your step when you come back."

Carl turned to go into the kitchen. "Make enough damage to make the home inspector tell the girl not to buy it, but not enough to ruin Maryland's house."

Tommy covered his mouth with the back of his hand to stifle his laughter. Earlier that morning, Aaron had called Tommy asking him to check on the house before the home inspection the following day. He was worried that the men had done something to sabotage the place. Tommy had called Grandpa to say he was coming for a visit and had told him the reason. Grandpa must have leaked the information that the inspection was tomorrow.

Tom watched as Bill knelt down on his good knee and with his large body slammed the crowbar underneath the step plank and lifted out the nails. Tom knew he should stop the men, but he'd let them have their fun. They couldn't do too much damage, and he'd fix it after they left.

Tom's mother had died when he was five. A few months later, his father had left him at Grandpa's house for the summer while he worked in Switzerland. Tom spent his days with the other grandkids. They played cops and robbers, climbed trees, and practiced diving off the dock's springboard.

At night, Tom watched marshmallows turn brown and bubble over the bonfire while Bill told them stories about lake monsters. Dark shadows crossed Bill's mammoth face as he spoke, the firelight accentuating the deep creases between his bushy eyebrows. At fifty years old, Bill still acted like a big kid. "The monsters form in the mud and grow to the size of trees," he said, stretching out his large arms and lumbering around the ring of boys. "They have leech mouths covering their bodies, all starving for children's blood. They rise from the lake at night and climb through bedroom windows. Before you can scream, their mouths latch onto your skin and they suck out every last drop of blood." Bill screamed and grabbed Tom, whose marshmallow fell into the fire and exploded into flames.

The other children jumped and ran for their parents. Bill

laughed, noogied Tom's head, and then tickled his lanky body. "You're not scared of a little tale. Are ya?"

Tom shook his head no, but that night he'd climbed into Grandpa's bed.

In September, when the other children returned to their homes, Grandpa enrolled Tom in Littleton Elementary. At Thanksgiving, frost covered the grass like powdered sugar, and his father still hadn't returned. When the tree buds burst green, Tom realized his father wasn't going to return. Tom demanded that Grandpa take him to the airport. He sat on the porch, his suitcase packed, determined to go to Europe and find his father. While he was waiting, Bill walked toward him, a saw in his hand. "I need a strong man to build tables. You up for the assignment?"

Tom wanted to stand his ground about going to the airport, but the saw's sharp teeth looked cool. "Yes, sir."

Bill swung him onto his shoulders and they twirled in circles, making airplane noises all the way to the Jacobses' garage.

For hours, sawdust flew while they cut and sanded wood. Butterscotch candies melted and stuck to Tom's teeth. Molly fed him homemade whoopie pies served with whole milk from the McAffee farm. Under the garage lights, Tom brushed stain onto the wood. Hours past his bedtime, he presented the table to Molly.

"It's a masterpiece," she said.

"You keep that saw. I think I see carpentry in your future," Bill said.

Tom ran home, the prized tool in his hands. The suitcase had already been unpacked. Grandpa had drawn a bath, and Tom sat in the bubbles recapping his day.

The silly table remained in Molly and Bill's sunroom. A rock propped up the leg that Tom had cut too short. To this day, the smell of sawdust always brought with it the memory of butterscotch and chocolate.

Bill began to unscrew Maryland's screen door until it hung from the top hinge at a strange angle. Tom began to worry about how much damage the other two men might be doing.

He walked around to the front deck, careful not to turn on the automatic floodlights on Grandpa's or Maryland's house that shined on the driveway. Many nights of his youth he'd snuck in late, so he knew the exact path to take. He stood on the deck. The curtains had been left open just enough that Tommy could peek in the window without the men being able to see him. A reddish hue filled the room, and Tommy realized they'd lit flares, probably to create phony smoke damage.

Daniel, carrying a black duffel, walked into the living room and went upstairs. After his wife passed from cancer, Maryland had become Daniel's companion. Her husband had died of a heart attack just a few years before. The friendship hadn't been romantic. Neither believed marriage ended with a spouse's death. Their children had wed, and that made them family.

Whenever Tommy came to visit, the two were together. Maryland cooked Daniel dinner. In the summer, they ate on the deck and talked while they waited for the orange sun to dip behind the trees. On Friday nights, she joined him for Shabbat. When his eyes were tired, she'd read the newspaper aloud at her kitchen table while he enjoyed her cookies and coffee.

Then Maryland had a stroke. When Tommy took her flowers at the rehab center, Daniel would be there attending her physical therapy sessions. When she cried as she tried to walk, he cheered her on, "You aren't a quitter. You can do this."

When she came home, she could get around her house and even climb the stairs to her bedroom, but she couldn't walk distances. On spring and summer nights, he pushed her wheelchair around the loop. She'd lost vision in her left eye, so he described the colorful blooms bursting from the ground.

The day Aaron took Maryland to Florida, the community had tried to stand in the way. Daniel yelled at Aaron as Maryland sobbed in Sarah's arms. As Aaron packed the car with suitcases, Daniel tried to grab them and said, "She'll move in with me," but in the end, Maryland agreed to go, in order to be closer to her daughter. Everyone knew it wasn't what she wanted. No wonder Daniel didn't want someone new moving into this home.

Carl's light illuminated the dust-covered pictures on Maryland's shelves in the living room. He ran his fingers over a beige, wooden frame.

He picked up the picture and Tommy saw him speaking. He pressed his ear to the window to hear, "Hey James, you would've enjoyed this little prank. Of course, if you were alive, this wouldn't be happening, but that's life. I hope you're looking down from Heaven and watching over your sister. I'm sure she's pretty lonely in Florida." He placed the frame back. "Sorry about the damage to your house. We'll fix it once we run the girl off."

He pulled a white stuffed owl from his duffel bag, its wings stretched in flight. Tommy had heard the story of the owl many times. Young Bill, Joseph, Carl, and James had found the dead owl in the old McAffee barn on the hill. They tried to hide it in the tree house while they gutted and stuffed it, but the girls tattled. Each night they transferred the decaying bird to a different house. Neighbors noticed the stench, but before anyone could find the source, the boys changed its location. The odor became the summer's mystery.

The owl had been their mascot, its hoot their secret call. Carl's childhood lisp didn't allow him to hoot the way the others did. It always came out, "Thooth, Thooth, Thooth." When the other boys laughed, the caw of the crow became his signature, but not before they named the owl after his pathetic hoot. At his bachelor party, his friends had presented Thooth as their gift to him.

Using a broomstick, Carl pushed and twisted the bird into the fireplace. Tommy once again stifled a laugh. He almost didn't want to fix the damage, just to see the look on the home inspector's face.

Carl looked at his watch and blew out the flares. Bill came into the room and Daniel came downstairs and began to cough in the smoke-filled room. Carl took his arm and led him toward the front door. Tommy jumped over the railing and hid at the side of the house as the men stepped outside.

Daniel took a puff from his inhaler and handed Bill a margarine container.

"Are you sure about the termites? What if they spread?" Bill asked as he put the container down and began taping a piece of paper to the front door.

"There's only twenty," Daniel said.

"Is everything done?" Carl asked.

Bill shook his head. "We need to dig up the oil tank and soak the porch. Then we'll add the final touch."

Tom knew exactly what the final touch would be, and he didn't think termites were the best idea either. He also didn't want to have to fill in a hole in the ground. He ran around the house and came up on the other side causing the floodlights to illuminate the driveway. The men froze and looked at one another.

"What's up, men?" he called to them.

Carl whispered, "Tommy, we're just following our wives' advice and getting some exercise."

"Dressed in black?" Tommy crossed his arms and tried to give them the stern look he'd been given as a child.

"We thought we'd get some fresh air," Carl added.

"And do a little yard work," Bill said. "Tomorrow's the home inspection, and Maryland's house looks bad."

"Were my excuses this lame as a kid? No wonder you busted me. I think you boys are getting a little slow in your old age," Tom said.

"Don't be disrespectful," Bill said.

"This wouldn't have anything to do with a young woman moving into the neighborhood?" Tom asked. He walked onto the deck.

Daniel took a step toward Tom. "Now you hear me, Tommy Woodward. Just because you wouldn't mind having a young woman in her skivvies walking around—"

"Nah, he's gay," Carl said.

"Very funny," Tom said.

"It's okay. It's in vogue these days. Sarah doesn't condone it, but it's all over the television," Carl teased.

"Will you shut up for three seconds?" Daniel said.

The light went on in Victoria's yard, and the men stiffened.

"Is Molly visiting with Victoria? I wonder how *she* would feel about this? I think you might be in big fucking trouble," Tom teased.

"Don't swear," Bill scolded.

"I learned that word at your knee. If you don't like it, blame yourself."

"Tommy, step aside. We're doing what's best for our community," Daniel said.

"I think I will go. Molly always brings baked goods when she visits." He stepped off the deck and moved toward the road.

"Get him!" Carl yelled.

Bill and Daniel grabbed Tom's arms. It took all of Tom's willpower not to laugh. He raised his hands as far as he could without creating pressure on their hold.

"Okay, you've broken me. I won't talk if you promise me a poker game next week."

The men looked to one another, nodded, and released his arms.

Carl patted his arm. "It's always good to see you, Tommy."

The three men walked toward Carl's garage, the duffel bags clanking against the shovels. "For Pete's sake, do you want to wake up the community?" Daniel boomed.

Tom shook his head and laughed.

He walked into Grandpa's small kitchen to the sour smell of garbage and the blaring sound of the television in the living room. He turned on the fluorescent overhead light. Dish piles covered the counters and filled the sink. The refrigerator door hung open. He checked the burners on the stove. Thankfully, they were off. What had the housekeeper been doing this week?

A pile of mail had been left on the green stove. Under the AARP magazine he found a three-week-old issue of *The Providence Journal*. Someone in the community must have found the article, which meant everyone had seen it.

Tommy Woodward, owner of Woodward Architecture, Ltd., is considered one of the sexiest bachelors in Rhode Island. In a designer suit or a tool belt, this man can carry you over the threshold or build a cabana in your backyard.

Tom had known the bachelor auction for the Make-A-Wish Foundation would feel degrading. He thought the pictures, taken at the construction site and in his office, were for the auction catalog. Then the images hit the paper.

"Pretty Boy, Tommy. Will you marry me?" the guys on his construction crew catcalled.

At the office meeting, his female architects held up dollar bills. "I'll give you ten for a hot night."

"I'll pay twenty," another said.

When the men joined the fun, Tom felt his face flush. By the end of the meeting, his employees were willing to give him a hundred dollars if he'd dance like a stripper. As he opened the glass door, they began to sing, "I believe in miracles," before the door swung shut they yelled out, "You sexy thing!"

He threw the newspaper in the trash. Next time he'd write a check to the charity.

Grandpa lay asleep in the recliner. Tom turned on the lamp next to the couch and shut off the television.

"Tommy, what are you doing here on a Friday night?" Grandpa said with his eyes closed.

"It's Thursday, Grandpa." He kissed his grandfather's coarse white hair. "And I know you told the other men about the home inspection, so don't act all innocent."

"I don't know what you're talking about," Grandpa said as he rubbed his eyes.

Tom had gotten his build from Grandpa. Until fifteen years ago, Grandpa swam five miles a day and sported a Speedo to show off his muscular body. Now, at eighty-four, he walked a little bow-legged, he'd lost a few inches of height, and his face was thinner. But when he smiled, the devil could still be seen in his aqua eyes.

"You know exactly what I'm talking about. Were you the lookout, and when you realized that I came a little early, you decided to fall asleep as your alibi?"

"What are you doing here on a Thursday night anyway? You shouldn't be hanging out with an old man. You're young and vibrant. You should be out having sex."

"Yes, Grandpa." The opening conversation hadn't changed in four years. "Did the housekeeper come this week?"

"She quit," he mumbled, "I grabbed her caboose . . . told her it was an accident, but she didn't believe me."

"Grandpa!"

His grandfather began to snore.

"I'm not going to believe you're asleep again. I'm going to do your dishes, but the next housekeeper I hire is going to be a fat man with a five-o'clock shadow."

Tom looked around the living room. The gold curtains from the seventies reeked of cigar smoke. The brown shag carpet had crumbs and dirt sprinkled across the matted fibers. Dust covered his late grandmother's collection of knickknacks, Hummels and porcelain swans. The room had a moldy smell and the brown paneling peeled away from the wall. Unglued linoleum caught Tom's foot as he walked to the kitchen.

What was he going to do with this place?

Tom filled the sink with soap and water. The kitchen needed a dishwasher. He'd drawn up plans to renovate years ago and invited Grandpa to stay with him in Providence during construction.

"I don't want the hassle," Grandpa had said.

"What hassle? You stay with me for a few weeks and my crew will do the work."

"I'm old. I don't need fancy stuff."

The first time Tom asked, frustration with Grandpa's stubbornness had kept him from seeing the fear in the old man's eyes. Too many times Grandpa's friends left their homes for a simple procedure, or to visit their children, and hadn't returned. Maryland lived in a nursing home against her will. The remaining Nagog residents had to be terrified they would be next. When their adult children did visit, many times it was to try to take away a driver's license. A few had dared to bring brochures for elderly housing.

But this community wouldn't go silently. If Heather Bregman wanted to move into this neighborhood, she'd better be ready for a fight. Tom looked out the window. He'd wait until the other houses went dark, then he'd sneak over to Maryland's home and undo the damage they'd done. A part of him didn't want to—he didn't want things to change in Nagog—but then every bit of him wished he could turn back time to five years earlier, when his life had been right. When Annabelle had been alive.

CHAPTER 8

Heather tapped her pen against the desk in her tiny cubicle at *The Boston Globe,* stuffed into the corner at the back of the bullpen. Her desk was clear except for her coffee cup, a black phone, and her laptop. Pictures of her travels were pinned to the cubicle: the Tongariro Alpine Crossing in New Zealand, two mother elephants with a baby between them, all with their trunks in the air, the Great Wall of China, the Golden Temple in Kyoto, Japan, and many others.

Unlike her coworkers, Heather hadn't hung the decorations to brighten or personalize the space but to remind people at the *Globe* that she actually worked. Months went by without her entering the building, and more than once she'd come into the office to find her cubicle used as storage.

She looked at the clock on the wall. Her boss and editor at the paper, George, was running late and had said he'd get to her as soon as he could. The latest column she'd written while on the road was up on her computer screen. Most of her columns were first penned in a notebook while she traveled. Plane and train rides gave her time to type up her notes and edit the stories. Rarely did she write at home or in the office, but she felt she should look busy when she was here.

She opened her purse and took out the keys she'd picked up from her attorney that morning. The house in Nagog belonged to her. It turned out her credit history had improved since moving in with Charlie, and her steady income was enough to secure a loan. Heather never wrote a check; as seller, Aaron paid her closing costs, and the second mortgage covered her down payment. The home inspection had been clear and her attorney signed the final documents while she was in Europe.

For the first time in her life, tonight she'd go home to her own place. The clock on the wall above her cubicle ticked away the minutes. A delivery truck was bringing her new mattress between four and six o'clock, and it was already after one. She needed to leave.

"Heather," George said as he put his arm on the cubicle wall. "I'm ready for ya." George Samson always wore a navy polo shirt stretched over his belly. By ten in the morning, creamy coffee drips decorated his wiry gray-and-black beard. He was a sweetheart until your name found its way to the blacklist. Mess with his deadline, and his wrath made you feel like you were sitting in the principal's office, about to be expelled. It had happened only once to Heather in her six years on the paper. It hadn't mattered that her computer had been stolen; George lectured her for ten minutes about backing things up on the *Globe*'s servers, then sent her away with her head hanging in shame. She hadn't missed another deadline.

"Hey, boss," Heather said as she gathered her laptop and purse and followed him into his office. Unlike Heather's dark corner, light came through the large wall of windows in his office. Heather sat in front of George's desk and continued to look outside at the blue sky. The front of the building had a glass wall that created light throughout the office space. Except for Heather's cubicle and the closets there weren't many dark spots in the building.

"You know you're one of my favorite writers," George said as he sat at his desk, his back to the beautiful day outside. He picked up his coffee and drank. "You're always ahead of your deadline and your column brings in good advertising revenue, but we need to think about the future."

Her chest tightened with anxiety and she remained quiet. Heather had learned through the years to let her boss say everything on his mind before she spoke.

"Your column came up at last week's board meeting, and I know that you and I have had this conversation before, but they're worried about the syndicates you've lost in the heartland. Around the perimeter of the country you're doing fine, but even there, papers want someone more famous. By now we were expecting a book deal, a product line, and even a television program."

Heather nodded, squeezing her hands together so she wouldn't bite her lower lip, her habit when she was nervous.

"There's a former beauty queen on the Travel Channel, and there are rumors they might begin negotiations with her. It doesn't mean you're out, but it would be competition for your Sunday spot."

"I know who you're talking about," Heather said. The woman was able to travel the United States, stay in five-star hotels, go to the best spas and restaurants, and had a crew to help her. If they asked her to write the Sunday column, the woman would also acquire Heather's hard-earned fans.

"Look, I don't think she's right for the job, but she has appeal.

How's Charlie coming with the book deal and the television show? You need it to happen fast."

Heather decided to skirt the mention of Charlie. She hadn't spoken to him since their breakup, and last night she'd slept at Gina's place.

"I have a contact at the Travel Channel, Steven Radley. We're supposed to get together to talk sometime this month, and he's also coming to the party I'm throwing at my new house. I'm hoping the event will help to solidify his interest in me."

"Good. Let him see you in a fun environment. God knows, whenever you're at a formal event, you're wound pretty tight." George rubbed his temples and pinched the bridge of his nose. "It's sad how journalism has changed. Back when I was a staff writer, you could walk around with a bag over your head if you wanted. All that mattered was the news. Now you have to have a public persona."

"Tell me about it," Heather said. "So what can I do to help my popularity in the south and the middle of the country?"

"I'm thinking you need to do something a little more on the home front. Summertime in New England."

"Apple pie and Fourth of July," Heather said as she smiled. "I have the perfect idea. What about summer fun at the lake? The advertising department can sell to summer rental places. I can write about Lake Tahoe, Lake Champlain, and even lakes around Massachusetts." And she could stay home for a few months and enjoy her new place.

"Let me think about it." George scratched his beard. "It's a good idea, but I want to chew on it for a bit. Now get the hell out of my office so I can get some work done."

Heather stood. "Can I expect you and your wife at the party?

I sent an e-mail invitation last week and you haven't responded yet."

"I'll ask Debra tonight. Why the heck did you buy a place so far outside the city? Who wants to live in the burbs?"

"You'll understand when you see the place. It's my dream house," she said as she gathered her things. "Thanks, George. I promise I'll find a way to make this happen."

Heather waved to her coworkers as she made her way out of the office. "I'll see you at the party." She knew her workmates by name, and their faces were familiar, but for the most part she was the writer who breezed in once in a while and had her face on the travel page. She'd been surprised by how many had said they would come to her party.

She drove along Boston's Memorial Drive, where ancient maples lined the street in front of Harvard's brick buildings. The sun glinted off the Charles River in a flashing smile, white sailboats dotted the water, and crew boats raced past. Along the banks, young people in shorts and tank tops basked in the sun.

Magic happened this time of year. Unlike fall, when the bright red, orange, and yellow foliage brought tourists from around the world, spring couldn't be timed. In April, pink and green buds poke their heads from bare tree branches. New Englanders anticipating warm weather store their heavy coats. Then cold wind and rain return, giving the illusion that winter's bleakness will never end. The city scowls, and visitors think Bostonians rude and unfriendly. But a miracle happens in May. A seventy-degree day awakens the tree's buds. Lilacs burst into colorful waves. The city slows as people take to the outdoors.

Through the open sunroof, Heather peeked at the blue sky. She turned up the radio and sang at the top of her lungs. She was on her way to her new home, and even her conversation with George couldn't take away her happiness. The house made her feel settled, secure. These feelings tasted like the blueberries from the backyard of her grandmother's home when she was little.

She made a quick stop to buy groceries, cleaning supplies, a broom, and a mop. She stuffed her purchases in her tiny car alongside her carry-on suitcase, which had enough clothing for a few days. Later she'd need to rent a truck and go back to Boston for her things, but for now she wanted to make the place her own.

Maybe there'd be a barbecue tonight, she thought as Nagog Lake drew nearer. Heather imagined dancing on the beach, a margarita in hand, while she laughed with her new neighbors. She pictured Tommy in swim trunks, shirtless. A sight worth the money she spent on the house. She shook the fantasy from her mind—he was too good-looking to be available.

Heather soon found herself behind a blue Cadillac and had to drop her speed to ten miles per hour. She hung her head and took her hands off the wheel. The Cadillac's right blinker flashed. The next road was more than a mile away. Heather tapped her nails against the steering wheel, then decided to check her lipstick in the rearview mirror, and applied more glossy color.

With the speed of a disintegrating log, the Cadillac turned right onto Nagog Drive and rolled into the first driveway. Heather sped around it and parked outside her new home. She stepped from the car and stared at the blue bungalow. In the sunlight it looked like a dollhouse.

Between her house and her neighbor's, Heather had a clear sight of the Cadillac. An older gentleman opened the door for a woman with white, curled hair. He held her by the arm as they walked to the house. *That's nice,* she thought. The grandparents still come to visit.

Suddenly she had a quick flash of panic—what if she wasn't accepted into this close-knit community? She quickly pushed the thought aside when she noticed stacks of boxes on her porch. She bounded up the steps and saw UPS labels—her new plates, wineglasses, coffeemaker, towels, bed linens! Every free moment during her trip, she'd ordered housewares online. She knew she shouldn't have spent the money, but it wouldn't be a home without furnishings and kitchen equipment. She'd forgo new clothing until she paid off the debt—a sacrifice worth making. Finally—a home all her own.

The brass key felt warm in her palm. For a moment she held the knob, smooth and curved in her hand. The key slid into the lock and she opened the door. Light streamed through the windows in the living room, illuminating dusty shelves.

In the bright light she could see how badly the pale yellow paint on the walls needed to be freshened. The pictures had been removed, leaving black squares of dirt. She wondered if she had time to paint before the party next week. Heather had never painted, but it couldn't be hard. With all the built-in woodwork, there'd be a tremendous amount of taping, but it'd be fun to decorate her home.

With the help of a decorating magazine she'd picked up at the airport in Paris, she had an idea of what furniture she planned to buy, but first she needed to take measurements. Gina had promised to get her a discount from one of her suppliers.

Gina was also taking care of the food for the party. It was the first time Heather had hosted her own affair. It was risky to throw a party before even fully moving in, but the sooner she caught Steven Radley's attention, the better her chance of getting the Travel Channel gig. She needed to prove that she was an outgoing, confident woman who could entertain her public. Gina was bringing friends from work, and Heather planned to invite her new neighbors.

In the kitchen, she pulled out a bottle of wine and some red plastic cups and a corkscrew from one of her grocery bags. "A toast," she said to the kitchen, "to being home." The cherry tones of the wine warmed her stomach.

Where to start? She went upstairs. Aaron had included the master bedroom furniture in the purchase and she touched the footboard. She went to the window seat and sat sipping her wine and took in the view of the lake, the sun glinting off the water. Heather turned the crank on the window, opened the glass outward, and a bee buzzed at the screen, bumping against the mesh. Lilac permeated the air. She looked down at her yard and saw the elderly gentleman under the oak tree.

Was it some kind of family holiday?

Heather looked next door where Aaron had said Tommy lived. She didn't see a car in the drive and assumed he wasn't home.

She went into the bathroom to admire the beautiful tub. Tonight, before she went to bed, she'd sink into a bubble bath with wine and chocolate.

It would be at least two months before she'd have to travel again. She had four columns ready for publication and eight rough drafts. If George approved a summer series of lakeside vacations, she might even get another month before she had to board a plane. Her conversation with George flashed through her thoughts and a sick feeling dropped into her stomach. She pushed it away. The Travel Channel would be hers, and she'd find a way to sign a book deal with or without Charlie.

The dust from the windowsill had left black smudges on her fingers. When she turned on the faucet, she heard, and then saw, water cascading from the pipe below the sink. She quickly turned the handle to stop the flow and knelt down to look closer. The elbow of the pipe was missing. What the heck?

Somehow the home inspector must have missed the broken sink. A trip to the hardware store was in her immediate future. She began to make a mental list of what she'd need. Then again, she could ask her handsome neighbor for help. Aaron had said he was the neighborhood handyman and Tommy said he'd done the upkeep on the house. She could be the damsel in distress and then repay him with a glass of wine. *I really have to stop thinking about him.*

A loud knock from the front door lurched her from her daydream. She left her wine on the bathroom counter and ran to the living room to be greeted by two older women with buckets, rubber gloves, and a casserole dish. "Hello," Heather said.

The tall woman, a blonde in tailored clothing, extended the casserole. "Hello, I'm Victoria Rose. I live in the yellow house." Victoria pointed toward the woods next to the beach. "And this is Molly Jacobs. She lives in the house next to mine."

"It's so nice to meet you," said the soft, round woman with white curls. Molly dropped the bucket filled with cleaning supplies and pulled Heather into a warm hug. "Welcome to the neighborhood. We know the house is in rough shape, so we thought we'd bring reinforcements to help you clean." She stepped back and smiled.

"Aah, thanks . . . I'm Heather Bregman. It's nice to meet you." Heather shook Victoria's hand and took the casserole. "Um . . . did you say you live here?"

"Yes." Victoria smiled. "Most of the residents have been here since early childhood."

The woman in the car . . . the man under the oak? No, they couldn't be. Not residents. Aaron said it was time to pass the house down to his boys. And Tommy was Charlie's age.

"I'm sorry, I'm a little confused. Aaron told me that these houses were passed down through the generations . . ." Heather said and realized how rude she was being. "Excuse my manners. Please come in, but you don't have to help me clean."

"Nonsense," Molly said. "A young woman can't get this house in shape all by herself. It will be our pleasure." She dropped the bucket and looked around the room, her hands on her hips. In jeans and sweatshirt, she looked ready to clean. Victoria, on the other hand, might have been dressed for high tea. "Everyone who lives here grew up together, and our parents passed these homes down to us," Victoria said. "We're all young at heart."

A large delivery truck pulled up and parked on the road. Heather saw Molly pick up a rag and wood polish and, with practiced efficiency, attack the mantel.

"Have you chosen furniture for this room yet?" Victoria asked. "I know some fabulous stores in Boston. Maybe you and I can take a day and go into the city."

A deliveryman stood at her front door with a clipboard and a pen. Heather was still holding the casserole, trying to juggle it while she signed. Victoria came up behind her, quietly took the dish, and swooped elegantly into the kitchen.

"The old mattress is upstairs and I need to wipe down the bed before you put the new one on," Heather said to the man.

"I've got it," Molly said. She bustled up the stairs and motioned for the deliverymen to follow her.

Victoria returned. "Heather, where's your bedding? I'll unpack it."

Heather was spinning with everything going on around her. "It's somewhere in the boxes on the deck."

Victoria nodded, went outside, and brought two boxed lamps into the house just as the deliverymen were carrying the old mattress downstairs. Heather watched the scene, uncertain what she was supposed to do. She walked out on the deck, took a deep breath, and was watching the men unload her new mattress when she was distracted by the small woman she'd seen getting out of the Cadillac, walking up the road in her little pink sweater. When she reached Heather's mailbox, she opened it and put her arm all the way in. Her soft white hair bobbed and she had a huge smile on her face as she fished through the flyers. Then a tall woman with a large crucifix around her neck walked up to the mailbox, and Heather heard her say, "Evelyn, is there a letter today?"

"No, not today." Evelyn frowned and looked as if she might cry.

The taller woman took the mail and placed it back in the box, then guided Evelyn up the road. Heather looked to where she'd thought Tommy lived, and an old man came out of the house. He walked across the driveway and onto Heather's deck. His eyes were the color of Maui's ocean, just like Tommy's eyes.

"I'm Thomas," he said. "Aren't you just a pretty little thing. I bet we're going to be great friends."

What world had Heather moved into?

❧

Victoria sat on the porch swing, enjoying the rusted hinges' squeaking in the night. The dark sky looked like silver glitter had been tossed against black ink. The moon was only a sliver, and Victoria could see the Big Dipper between the tall pines around her home.

The lake was still tonight; she couldn't hear the waves beating against the two rowboats that had been put in the water last week. They were tied to the new wooden dock that had been built last month. It was a peaceful quiet night, the sounds of nature a meditative song. Small critters scurried in the woods behind the house. Frogs croaked in the small vernal pools.

Grass blades poked through the fertile earth, and tulip leaves held up round buds ready to burst open any day. Spring had been late in coming, but now new life bloomed around Victoria. Two cardinals built a nest in her eaves. Soon little baby birds would open their mouths and squawk for worms. The mother would feed one from her own mouth while the other babies pushed to get their share. Youth was everywhere.

The sound of bass disrupted the quiet night and Victoria looked to Maryland's place. Heather had every light on in the house and all the windows open. The girl had been quiet when she said that she'd recently broken up with her fiancé and was starting fresh but had lit with enthusiasm as she told Victoria about her career as a travel writer, and Victoria enjoyed hearing about her latest adventure while they scrubbed and straightened the kitchen together.

Earlier she'd seen Heather return from the store with paint

cans, brushes, and rollers. The child had already started to make the house her own. It was too bad she had to do it alone.

Though Victoria had spent most of her life as an independent woman, she still remembered the joy of sharing her life with Devon: buying their first home, planning vacations, making decisions together about their future.

They'd met on the set of *On the Waterfront*. She had a role as a supporting actress, and Devon was a supporting actor. Victoria tried to maintain her composure when she spoke to him, but his charisma and deep brown eyes caused her to stumble over her words whenever he smiled.

One night the cast had gone to a bar on the waterfront in Malibu. She'd tried to sneak glances at him, but he caught her. He took a long sip of his drink and raised his eyebrows, showing her in this exasperating way that he knew she found him attractive. When her face flushed red he laughed, enjoying her discomfort. She excused herself from the conversation and walked outside to the edge of the pier to calm her nerves. As she stood staring at the stars, he'd grabbed her around the waist and kissed her, and she melted instantly to his will.

When they made love for the first time, it was like choice fell away; she drowned in his touch when his large hands pulled her to him. He sucked the wind from her lips, leaving her breathless—as if he stole all her thoughts so that she could only feel what he chose: a deep bite on her shoulder made her gasp; he pinned her to the wall and traced the curve of her hip; she still remembered the fire that ignited when he entered her body so ready to embrace him.

Devon didn't bow to her as so many other men had. His confidence claimed her as his own, and a primal part of her loved being his woman. After nine years of independence and the loss of both her parents, she'd been ready for a partner and their courtship had been quick. They married at the courthouse because Victoria hadn't wanted to face a large wedding without her parents or her childhood friends.

They honeymooned in Italy, where the thin walls of their Tuscan villa couldn't muffle Victoria's cries of pleasure, but the more she tried to stifle her moans, the more Devon forced her to release them.

"Devon, we can't again," she said as he woke her from slumber with soft kisses along her spine. Through the large windows she could see the pink light of sunrise touching the terra-cotta roofs of the village below. "I'm certain we kept the whole place up last night. It's improper to wake them as well."

"I like you improper," he said as he pinched her waist. "And we're in Italy. Everyone here is enamored with sex."

Those first years with Devon had been among the most exciting of her life. They took spontaneous trips throughout California, jumping in the car and driving north to wine country or the mountains to ski. Together they attended premieres and the afterparties, and they bought the house on the beach.

This new girl, Heather, looked like her daughter, Melissa— long hair, thin face, small frame, the legs that went on forever. Deep chocolate brown eyes, just like Melissa. It had been a surprise when Victoria found out she was pregnant with her daughter. Melissa hadn't been planned. Victoria had been getting bigger roles in movies and the pregnancy put her on hiatus, ruining her momentum. But when her baby was born with fuzzy brown hair the color of Devon's, Victoria took one look at her child and her career no longer mattered as much. She didn't care about running to auditions or working long hours to rebuild her career.

Victoria could sit for hours cradling Melissa and staring into her eyes. During that time, a longing for Nagog tugged at Victoria's heart. She wanted Melissa to have lazy days playing in the sand by the lake and nights by the fire making s'mores. What once felt confining had seemed like a place to wrap her child in warmth, love, and protection.

Fathering hadn't come easily to Devon, who saw Melissa as an intrusion. His career was on the rise and he didn't have time to spend at home. He wanted to hire a nanny so that Victoria could return to work. They were supposed to be the Hollywood supercouple building their careers together, and he didn't like the changes in Victoria. In the bedroom his forceful touch no longer suited her. It began to feel like masculine bravado. She'd become maternal and wanted gentle caresses, to make love slowly. More than once her thoughts turned to that first, tender time with Joseph.

Their passion turned from lovemaking to fights. When she divorced Devon, she gave him the house and all of their material goods in exchange for full custody of Melissa. She changed her and Melissa's last name from Massaro to Victoria's family name of Rose. Victoria focused her career in the international markets and they lived all over Europe, depending on where she was filming.

Hearing music and singing coming from the blue bungalow snapped her back to the present moment. Oh, to be young again: to feel the rush of new love, to have every opportunity open to you as you dream of a bigger life.

Victoria looked over in Joseph's direction. What did he do at night now that he was alone?

In the sunroom, she touched the lighter to the starter log in

the fireplace and the paper wrapping ignited. She added small
kindling and then the big logs that Bill had brought in last
week. Around the room she lit candles. Above the mantel was
a large portrait of Annabelle at sixteen. She traced her fingers
along Annabelle's smile. On the mantel below the frame was a
golden statue. Victoria touched its shiny metal. The night she'd
won the Oscar for best supporting actress had been one of the
best of her life, but that was a lifetime ago. There'd been afterparties and a run of publicity. Victoria had felt like the belle of
the ball.

The statue didn't fit in this room, but she'd been uncertain
about where to place it in the house. The photos and framed
posters on the cream-colored wood paneling made the room
feel like the warm hug of family. The space was overstuffed
with furniture: the denim blue couch and matching chairs, the
rocking chair by the fire, a large ottoman for a coffee table, a
window seat that looked over the woods and had bookshelves
underneath covered in knickknacks and little treasures from
Victoria's travels. A thirty-six-inch television was tucked into
the wooden entertainment center by the fireplace. Beneath
it was a drawer filled with hundreds of DVDs and old VHS
tapes.

She cranked open the large windows and let in the air that
smelled of moist earth and clover. It mixed with the smell of
wood from the fire and spice from the candles.

A collage on the wall held pictures of Melissa. Victoria ran
her hand over the images. "My darling baby girl, the fun you and
I had together." In one picture, Melissa was dressed in a purple
and blue sari. "Do you remember our first time in India? You
were only eight when we went to my friend's wedding. When

the dancing started, you stood up and imitated the women's movements."

A smile played at Victoria's lips as she floated around the room, humming and moving her hands in wave patterns. She could see Melissa's tiny hips swaying and hear her laughter that started as a giggle and erupted into fits of shaking joy.

"Melissa, do you remember wearing the princess tiara all over Paris? You sang that song until I heard it in my dreams. You told me my director had given you the tiara, but you had stolen it from the set." Victoria sat in the rocking chair and opened a polished wooden box on the side table. Tiny flickers of light sparkled off the crystal stones of the tiara. Victoria placed it on her head.

"For months you wouldn't part with it. Whenever I tried to take it away, you would say, 'My jewels.' I would sneak in while you slept and try to remove it, but your little fingers would reach out through your dreams and protect your coronet . . .

"There were times I thought I should've been stricter. God knows you were a curious child. I can't count how many times you went off on your own in a big city because something caught your eye while we were shopping." Victoria could still feel the panic in her heart that she'd felt whenever Melissa disappeared and she'd feared she'd never see her again. "It was as if my insides became empty and worry became my blood and breath."

Victoria sighed. "I couldn't punish you. I tried a few times when you snuck off to the bar in Ireland to meet that boy. But how could I tell you not to be adventurous or to live by rules when our lives didn't have any?"

When Melissa came to her at seventeen, pregnant and scared, Victoria hugged her and said, "We'll do this together." Victoria knew it had been her fault that her daughter was in this position;

she hadn't given her the stern lectures or upbringing of her own childhood. But in the end, her granddaughter, Annabelle, had been one of God's greatest gifts.

Victoria saw her reflection in the glass window. She looked ridiculous wearing the tiara.

Suddenly Melissa's words came back to her. *Promise me you'll take care of Annabelle.*

Victoria had held her daughter's hand on her deathbed and nodded her head, tears clouding her vision. "I'll protect her. I'll teach her she's the most precious thing in the world."

Victoria placed the tiara in the box. Annabelle had planned to wear the crown the day she married Tommy.

Tears fell from Victoria's cheeks. "I'm sorry, Melissa. I failed you."

CHAPTER 9

∾

The small moving truck Heather had rented earlier that morning was filled with boxes from Charlie's apartment and her storage unit. The items rattled as she drove the cumbersome vehicle along Route 2. The first four days she'd lived in Nagog all she had was the suitcase that she'd carried while in Europe. Charlie had told her she could get the rest of her things from the apartment today. He'd conveniently made appointments and hadn't been able to help her move. When she'd entered the apartment she found her belongings packed in boxes: clothing, art from her travels, dishes, and personal items. A thick manila envelope had been taped to one of the boxes, holding two opened credit card statements and a standard agent-client contract stating that he owned fifteen percent of all monies made on Solo Female Traveler. They'd never signed an agreement, and now Heather needed to hire a lawyer to go over the contract—that is, if she wanted to keep him as her agent—but it was a pivotal time in her career, and she was worried about starting over with someone new.

Charlie's love of money would drive him to help her, but she wondered how dedicated he would be now that she'd left; now she was just one of his twenty clients. They still hadn't spoken since the fight. Heather had called him after she returned from her trip to tell him about her conversation with George, but his phone went to voice mail. He responded with an e-mail stating when she'd be allowed to move her things.

It had taken Heather three hours to pack up the rest of the items she felt belonged to her from the apartment and carry them down to the rental truck, then another two hours to drive to her storage unit, pack its contents into the truck, and close out her account.

As she reached Nagog, every muscle ached with exhaustion. She still needed to unload, and just the thought of it made her feel sore. After parking the truck, she immediately went up to her room and changed out of her grimy clothing and into shorts and a tank top. She pulled her windblown hair back in a ponytail and secured it with elastic.

Outside, she stood on her deck, staring at the moving truck, trying to will the boxes to march themselves into the house. She grabbed a water bottle from the cab of the truck, sat down in the grass, and drank in large gulps while the muscles in her thighs twitched. Feeling better, she reached her hands to her feet and stretched her tight hamstrings and back. A ladybug crawled on her arm, its tiny legs tickling the hairs on her skin. The last two days had been warm and bright blossoms had emerged from the fertile earth. When the breeze came through the kitchen window at night, it brought the scent of roses from the backyard.

The flowers brought with them the memory of her grandmother: trowel in hand, face smeared with dirt as she planted in the garden. Heather wondered how old her grandmother had been when she passed. She would've fit right into this community.

For the hundredth time, Heather went over the conversation with Aaron the day she saw the house. He'd said that the houses had been passed down to younger generations, and then he'd introduced Tommy as one of her neighbors. He'd swindled her into buying it, knowing full well the age of her neighbors. She realized her need for the house had led her to be impulsive and buy the place without researching first. It was finally hitting her that she was living in a retirement community, basically, and seemed to be the only resident under the age of seventy. A part of her knew if she heard this story from a friend she'd find it funny, but the realization didn't fill her with mirth. There definitely wouldn't be parties with neighbors, or margaritas on the beach.

Heather moved her legs apart and pulled her head to her left and then right knee to stretch her inner thighs. The muscles began to unwind and she leaned her chest on the soft lawn. A second ladybug flew onto her arm and chased the first one.

A woman rode her scooter along the road. A black brace stuck out from under brown cotton culottes. She had on a floral long-sleeved shirt that skimmed away from the rolls above her waist. A wide-brimmed hat fluttered as she sped nearer, then she stopped in front of Heather, and without further introduction, said, "You know the sun is dangerous. Look here. Melanoma." She pointed to a scar on her nose and then lifted up her shorts to reveal a long sunken area on the back of her thigh. "I beat it twice against the odds, but they removed large chunks of my skin, and chemotherapy nearly killed me. If you don't want to endure what I did, you should stop wearing skimpy clothing and cover up."

Heather stood and walked toward the woman with her hand outstretched. "I'm Heather. It's nice to meet you."

"Agatha Lowe. I live three doors down."

"Thank you for the advice, but I wear sunscreen, and it's after six. I don't think I have to worry."

"Every young person thinks they're unbreakable. In my day, women didn't go around wearing shorts that barely covered their cabooses and their bras as shirts. We still got skin cancer. Think about it."

"I'll keep it in mind." Heather smiled.

Agatha nodded. "Well, I'll be on my way. I see you have quite a bit of work ahead of you with that moving truck." The gravel crunched under the scooter's tires as Agatha rode off.

Heather sat back down on the grass and pulled her head to her knees. Her thighs still screamed with tightness, and she took deep breaths as her body unwound.

A breeze moved over Heather's skin, carrying with it the sour, thick scent of a cigar. No one seemed concerned that she might end up with lung cancer from the old men smoking in her front yard. Every night since she moved in, as the sun was setting over the lake, the men took up residence under her tree. The thick burnt smell of tobacco filled her house as they yelled stories about World War II to one another. She wanted to ask them to move to a different location but hesitated, trying to think of a way to avoid making her first encounter with these men a disagreeable one.

Last night, before she went to bed, she'd dragged the picnic table to a different location closer to her neighbor's house on the right. Now she looked up from her fragmented moment of yoga serenity to the astonishing sight of the four men, cigars hanging from their mouths, carrying the table back to its original location, putting it down in the ruts it had already made in the grass, and sitting down as if nothing had happened. Then the man with the Red Sox cap pulled out a deck of cards and began to shuffle.

Thomas came out of his house and made his way across her lawn.

"Evening, Heather," he said as he smacked his lips. Heather moved to stand but he put up his hand. "Oh, don't stop on my account. You just go right ahead and stretch that cute little figure of yours."

Heather blushed, stood, and tugged her small shorts down her thighs a couple of inches. Thomas took her fingers in his hand, bowed, and kissed them. "If I was a younger man, you'd be in trouble."

Heather laughed. *Dirty old man.* "I think I still have to be careful."

"Better believe it." He smiled and squeezed her hand as he led her toward the picnic table and the other men.

"Men," he said as he put his thin arm around Heather's waist. "Our new neighbor, Heather. Heather, this is Bill, Carl, Joseph, and Daniel." He pointed to each, and she tried to remember the names and faces.

Joseph stood and extended his hand toward her. "It's nice to meet you. How are you liking your new home?"

"It's lovely. It's been a lot of work to get it cleaned, but Molly and Victoria have been such a great help."

"Well, you let us know if you need anything."

"Thank you." She smiled and looked around the picnic table.

The other men grumbled under their breath and looked at their cards. The smoke began to fill her sinuses, and she sneezed and began to cough.

"Well, it was nice to meet all of you. I have to get back to work."

"Yeah, finish unpacking your stuff, but leave ours alone," Daniel said as she walked away.

She thought about turning around to say something but felt it was better to leave it alone. In time, she'd suggest that they smoke somewhere besides her front yard.

Heather opened the back of the truck and lifted the top box. She could hear Bill's booming voice as she carried the box to the deck.

"It was so cold in northern Germany that when I tried to move the scope, my skin froze to the metal. The doctors tell me the reason my fingers are swollen now is from the frostbite."

World War II stories again? Didn't they have anything else to discuss besides what she suspected were exaggerated tales from half a century ago?

"A missile missed our sub by inches!" Carl yelled. "The explosion knocked me into the radar equipment, and I thought, this is it—any moment the flames are going to blow through and we're all dead."

Apparently that missile took out most of his hearing. Heather continued to move the boxes from the truck to the deck.

"Do you need some help, Heather?" Joseph asked from the picnic table.

The thought of carrying the boxes upstairs exhausted her. She wanted to say yes, but she couldn't ask the old men to help her move. She'd be worried they'd get hurt.

"Thank you, that's a nice offer, but I've got it."

The work was heavy and dusty, and she began to sweat as she carried the contents of the truck to the deck. At least once they were on the deck they'd be halfway into her house. As she worked, a white rusted truck rattled into the driveway. Tommy stepped from the vehicle and Heather froze between the truck and the deck, a box in her arms, taking in the sight of Tommy standing in her driveway: white T-shirt and jeans, hair as if he'd just run his hands through the thick waves. For a moment she let herself stare into the ocean of his eyes, then without volition, her gaze dipped along the taut deltoids, the chestnut hairs gleaming on his forearms . . . Blood flushed her skin and her heartbeat quickened.

He waved to the old men and walked up to greet her. "Hello again."

"Hi," she said, ducked her head, and walked quickly to the deck to deposit the box. Catching her reflection in the glass door, she gasped. She looked like someone who'd been hiking in the woods all day.

"Do you need some help?" Tommy asked.

She didn't want him seeing her like this. She picked up the box she had just dropped on the porch, opened the door, and half turned toward him, keeping the door open with her no doubt grass-stained backside. "No, I'm fine. I think I hear my phone ringing. I'll see you later." Then she rushed into the house and upstairs.

In the mirror she'd hung on the closet door, Heather looked pasty white. She looked haggard with the combination of jet lag and moving stress; the ponytail elastic hadn't been able to hold Heather's mane, so frizzy strands stuck out. This is what he'd seen. In all her fantasies and daydreams of meeting him again, never was she dressed in running shorts, sweaty, frazzled, and covered in dirt.

Now she was trapped in the house because she didn't want to run into him again. It would seem strange if she showered and changed before she moved the rest of the dusty boxes. Then again, anything was better than looking the way she did. At least she'd be clean and smell better. She went into the bathroom and turned on the shower.

⤧⤨

"Tommy, what are you doing here on a Friday? You're young and vibrant. You should be out having sex, not hanging around an old man," Grandpa said as he walked away from the picnic table.

"You're more fun than any woman my age." Tom waved to the other men and then went to the back of his truck. He grabbed a large flat box and carried it into the house as Grandpa opened the door for him. "What did the doctor tell you about smoking cigars?" he said as he put the box down.

"That it's bad for my health. I think being eighty-four is a bigger problem. And the other men were the ones smoking, not me."

"Liar. I saw you when I pulled into the driveway."

The box contained a desk Tom had bought, which came in four pressed wood panels. Glue and an Allen wrench were the only tools he'd need to assemble the furniture. He'd wanted to spend a day locked in the wood shop, feeling smooth wood under his palm, but work had been too hectic to take time to create a handmade desk. He ripped open the cardboard box and spread the contents around the room.

Grandpa settled into his recliner with a bag of chocolate chip cookies. "When was your last date?" He held the bag out to Tom, who grabbed a cookie and popped it into his mouth.

"I went out with a nice young lady two days ago. Which is why I didn't come to see you."

"Was she hot?" Grandpa leaned forward.

Tom chewed absently, looking at the assembly instructions. "She was pretty."

Grandpa swished his false teeth with his tongue. "Nah, I don't want pretty. I'm an old man who lives vicariously through his grandson. I want details." He pounded on the chair with his fist. "Details. And speak up so I don't miss anything."

Tom looked at his grandfather. "She had red hair and freckles across her cheeks."

Erica had bought Tom at the Make-A-Wish bachelor auction. With the body of a Victoria's Secret model, she caused more than one wide-eyed waiter to stumble during their dinner.

As they ate, he learned that she'd grown up in Southern California and moved to New England to attend Smith College. She graduated magna cum laude, then came to Providence to work in advertising. She had a plan: three children by thirty-seven, one of them adopted from China, and a house on the ocean. When she retired, at fifty-five, she would travel the world doing charity work.

Tom had paid for dinner, kissed her on the cheek, and thanked her for her contribution to the charity.

Grandpa pushed a button, and his recliner rose to help him stand. His black pants, a size too big now, were covered in cookie crumbs that fell to the rug as he stood. Over his Oxford shirt he wore a thick wool sweater that never came off, even in August. "Cold bones," he'd say.

"How old are you again?" Grandpa asked.

"Thirty."

"At thirty you should be getting nailed every night. That's when women are hitting their sexual peak. Or better yet, you should get a wife to keep your bed warm."

"Grandpa, where did you learn the term 'nail'?" Tom asked.

"I watch television."

"They say 'nailed' on television? What kind of shows are you watching?"

"Ah, it could've been the smut I was reading. What difference does it make?" Grandpa walked to the window. "Did you see that hot young thing next door? Earlier she was stretching on her front lawn. I think she likes giving me a show . . . but if you want her, I won't use my charm."

Tom began to organize the parts of the desk according to the instructions. "You go for it, Grandpa. She's not my type. Plus, she's engaged."

"A man hasn't come 'round. She's been moving in all by herself," Grandpa said. "As for type? You're too picky. You need to go out and get the pipes cleaned."

"I'm not looking to get my pipes cleaned."

Grandpa grunted. "What kind of man isn't looking for that? I wonder if I raised you right."

Tom had heard the stories from his grandfather's conquests throughout his life. As a young man, Grandpa had been a cad. He'd been older than the other children in Nagog by at least ten years, yet he was one of the last men in the community to marry. Thomas had loved women. He didn't care about the shape, size, or age. Each one was a different flavor in an intricate buffet of gourmet foods. The way they smelled and tasted and the light that caught in their hair drew him like fish to a baited hook.

At twenty-two he managed his father's factory, and every woman at the social dances knew he would inherit the business. The Great Depression had been in full force and many people looked for relief in simple pleasures. Thomas had taken full advantage.

Then the war came—a time Tom knew his grandfather still relived in his nightmares. The tragedy he saw, the horror and death, the blood of too many people sickened him.

When he came home, he was ready to settle down. He met Tom's grandmother on the town common. She'd been sitting with her girlfriends listening to the band play in the gazebo, and her long, jet-black hair caught his attention. He asked her to dance, but she refused. Said that she knew what kind of man he was. He didn't give up. It took two years, but she finally agreed to marry him. During the thirteen years they had before she passed, Grandpa said he was a better man than at any other time in his life. That was the power of a woman.

"With those shorts Heather wears, I bet she's wild in the sack," Grandpa said.

Tom screwed two pieces of wood together. "I guess she's pretty."

"Boy, I don't understand you. Your name isn't Woodward for nothing." His grandfather looked at him. "I'm assuming you got my blood. But if your mother's genes got ahold of you . . . they were docile people . . . then you should get some of those pills they have these days. I think this whole community could use a little."

Tom banged desk parts together and held them until the wood glue dried. Grandpa hadn't been shy about the women he brought around when Tom was a boy. It didn't matter to him if the relationship lasted a year or a week, and he tended to court more than one at a time. He'd hoped his grandfather would lose interest, having had enough sex in his life for seven people, but his obsession worsened as he aged.

"Grandpa, I'm fine in that department," Tom said.

"Good, good. You should go out and find one wearing something pink, soft, and fluffy. I loved those angora sweaters your grandmother wore in the fifties, so soft to the touch when I felt her up."

Tom cringed behind the desk as he listened to Grandpa's stories of conquest while he set up the computer. Grandpa had never remarried, nor had Tom's father. It seemed the Woodward men were doomed to bachelorhood.

Tom looked out the window and saw Heather pick up a box and carry it into the house. "She's not bad, now is she?" Grandpa clapped his hand on Tom's shoulder. "Why don't you go get her?"

"Told you . . . not interested," Tom said.

Grandpa looked Tom in the eye. "I know it's hard, but at some point you have to let Annabelle go."

Tom looked away. "I'm working on it."

"You need a woman to get your blood moving. It's not good to work as much as you do and to spend your free time with an old man."

"I like hanging out with you." Tom sat Grandpa at the desk. "Now you push this button and the computer will start up. You shouldn't have to shut the computer down, but if you have to restart, I've left the instructions." He pointed to the yellow paper covered with bold black lettering that he'd taped to the desk.

"I don't see why I need a computer. I've lived eighty-four years without one." Grandpa squished his mouth together and smacked his dentures again.

"Are your teeth hurting?" Tom asked.

"My teeth don't exist. But my false ones don't seem to fit anymore. I'm fine." Grandpa waved his hand.

"I'll call the dentist and make an appointment," Tom said, making a mental note to call the doctor too. His grandfather's skin looked ashen.

"Stop fussing. There isn't much on me that doesn't need maintenance or an upgrade. I'm not complaining."

"So, on the nights I can't be here . . . Grandpa, are you watching?"

"Oh, I'm watching all right." Grandpa turned from the window to grin.

"I don't mean Heather. Look at the computer," Tom said. "If I can't visit, I'll call you. When I do, you press this icon here—this picture of the camera—and then press the key I marked with red ink. I'll do the same, and then we'll see each other through the computer."

"What's that thing you're moving?" Grandpa asked.

"It's called a mouse and it's how you control the computer," Tom explained for the third time. "Now, if you press this button, it will open the Internet." He moved the mouse to the top of the screen. "I've set up bookmarks for you. This one will allow you to order your groceries from the computer and have them delivered. They have a better selection than Swanson. I have it set to my credit card."

He was surprised at Grandpa's quiet response. Usually, the idea of Tom's handling some of the finances was cause for a fight. But Grandpa had paid for private high school and Harvard University, and Tom felt it was only right for him to take care of the man's needs now that he could afford to.

"Get out of my way. Let me play with my new toy. And go help that fine young thing. She's all fresh and showered and trying to move those boxes on her own. They look heavy." Grandpa pushed Tom aside and strained his eyes to see the computer.

Tom added the ophthalmologist to the list of appointments.

He glanced at his watch, which read eight o'clock. He needed to return to work. Construction on five projects had been delayed due to the blizzard in April, and he'd hired extra crew to finish on time. There were design details and billing, along with hiring problems to contend with. He needed to add four architects and five support staff before the end of summer if he wanted to have time to sleep. After hundred-hour weeks, he needed a break.

Tom looked out the window. Heather bumped into her door and the box fell on her foot. The women of Nagog had raised Tom to be a gentleman, and the men of the community had provided fine examples. Funny, he thought, she'd showered and changed into jeans and a nice shirt to move boxes. Didn't running shorts make more sense?

"Oh, what the hell. Grandpa, I'll be back."

"Now that's my boy."

He went out the door, crossed the drive, and walked onto her deck. The front door was open and he saw Heather as she tried to maneuver the heavy, large box up the stairs in her sandals that slipped on the polished wood. She tried to kick off the shoes, lost her grip, and the box broke open. "Damn!"

"You want help with that?" Tom asked.

She jumped and placed her hand over her heart. "Do you always just walk into people's homes?"

"Sorry, I've been coming into this house like it was my own my entire life. Next time I'll knock." He walked toward the stairs and grabbed the mangled box, along with the books and clothing that had fallen out. "Where do you want this?"

"You really don't have to help." She tried to pull the box from him but he held tight.

He looked at her, waiting.

"Thank you. It goes in my closet. I'll show you." She began to lead the way.

He moved past her. "I know where it is. Decide where you want the rest of the boxes."

Tom walked up the stairs and into the master suite. He stood at the closet doorway, thankful that Heather hadn't followed. The room brought back a flood of memories. Tom had renovated the master suite as a gift to Maryland for her sixty-fifth birthday. The closet had been created as the perfect showroom for her extensive ball gown collection, handed down from her mother and grandmother.

Now a few pairs of fancy shoes lined the racks he'd built. A sweater, some skirts, and a few shirts replaced the long full gowns made out of silk. Tom spun the revolving jewelry armoire, exposing the hidden mirror.

Tom remembered watching Annabelle in the mirror, wearing short jean cutoffs and one of his white button-down shirts tied up in a knot around her waist, while he worked on the closet.

"Hey, lover boy," Annabelle had cooed.

"I'm working right now, and I'm covered in dust." He tried not to watch her. The skimpy outfit worked better than lingerie, and it made him ache.

Small dimples framed her smile as she strutted toward him. He tried to steady the shelf as he fired the nail gun. She released her hair from the ponytail; golden locks cascaded down her back as she shook her head. With painful slowness, she unbuttoned her top.

"Don't distract a man with power tools," he'd said.

Tom dropped the box, and the thud lurched him back to the present moment. He bowed his head and held the doorframe for support. He could still remember the goose bumps on Annabelle's skin when he touched her. If only he could reverse time.

He turned and walked downstairs to collect the rest of the boxes.

Heather was leaning against the deck railing. "Thanks for your help. It's really nice of you." She smiled at him.

He looked at the boxes. "You're welcome. Where do you want the rest of these?"

"This pile here goes upstairs in the bedroom, the rest in the kitchen. I'll help you carry them."

"I've got it," he said. Heather grabbed a box at the same time he did, and they bumped against each other. Her box tumbled, and he caught it with his free hand before it hit the ground. He tried to step around her just as she tried to move out of his way. When they bumped again, she laughed and looked up at him with a sweet, radiant smile. Standing there, Heather's body so close to his, he felt something that he'd thought was long dead—a flicker of attraction to someone besides Annabelle.

"I'm not usually this klutzy," Heather said. "It must be your influence."

Heat rose from her skin, bringing with it the faint scent of floral perfume. She was flirting with him. Grandpa had been right, it'd been a long time, but Tom wasn't the kind of man who would use a woman to forget the deep ache left by the loss of the one he loved. "Heather, as far as I know, you're engaged and shouldn't be flirting with me." He turned and walked into the house without pausing for her reaction. He continued to move the boxes marked for the bedroom, while she brought the others into the kitchen. They moved in opposite paths and when the work was done, he found her on the deck, her back turned as she looked at the lake.

"Well, that looks like the last of it," he said. "I'll see you later."

She turned, her voice, quiet and hurt, caught him before he could leave. "I wasn't trying to flirt. I just didn't know where to move."

In her eyes he saw loneliness. It made him uncomfortable to realize how much he also noticed the curve of her waist and hips.

"No, I'm sorry. I was a jerk," Tom said. "I need to be going. Good luck with the unpacking." He walked off the deck and went into the garage. He knew Grandpa was right—he needed to move on. He just hadn't figured out how.

CHAPTER 10

❧

Lemon-scented suds overflowed onto the counter and covered Molly's checkered apron. She passed a sponge over the greasy pan while she stared out the window. Victoria sat alone in her sunroom. Molly had invited her over, but Victoria had declined when she realized Joseph would join them.

Excited cheers came from the living room. The Red Sox must have scored. Molly looked at the sudsy mess and turned off the water. She wiped her wet apron and the soap-covered floor with a towel. Carl, Joseph, and Bill sat around the television with bowls of homemade caramel popcorn and Chex Mix between them. Molly had invited Sarah, but she'd declined when she found out Victoria had been invited.

A bunch of children, Molly thought.

There had to be a way to bring them together. Bill had told her to leave it alone, but you didn't mind your own business when it came to family.

The phone rang and she grabbed the black receiver from the wall. "Hello?" Sarah's voice came over the line. "I think Tommy and Heather had a fight. I'm telling you, this girl is trouble. First I have to listen to her loud music while she paints, and now she's upset Tommy. He's been through enough without getting involved with the likes of this one."

"Sarah, Heather is a perfectly wonderful young woman, and if you would introduce yourself and get to know her, you would see that. And what do you mean they had a fight? About what? They don't even know each other."

"He was helping her move boxes and she was getting all flirty with him, then Tommy walked away very quickly after he moved the boxes, and Heather looked upset."

"That could be many things, and it's none of our business. Instead of being nosy, you could've been over here keeping me company while the men watched the ball game."

"I had things to do," Sarah said. "I'm creating a rule book for Heather."

"You're not!" Molly exclaimed.

"Someone has to keep things under control. And I know it won't be you and Victoria, the way you've been helping her settle in. I'm certain Victoria will be throwing parties with this young woman and creating problems while she's here. But I'm going to nip it in the bud."

Molly sighed. "Sarah, this needs to stop. At some point, either you and Victoria need to have it out, or get over it. Victoria is here to stay."

"I doubt that very much," Sarah said. "I have to go. My tea is ready." Sarah hung up.

Molly shook her head. The towel and apron went into the laundry hamper. Molly poured herself a glass of Chardonnay and retreated to the four-season porch. Through the window she watched Victoria walk outside and settle on her porch swing.

When Melissa was five, Victoria had shown up at Logan Airport, twisted and bruised. Molly watched Melissa, her eyes wide with terror, try to support Victoria as they walked through the airport. Molly had thought she'd never allow her friend to leave Nagog again.

When they arrived at the Jacobses' home, Molly tucked Victoria into their guest bed and asked, "What happened?"

Victoria stared straight ahead, her back rigid, her eyes proud, the picture of her mother's decorum as she spoke, "Devon had been drinking, spending time with friends instead of coming home to us. He woke me, wanting to be intimate, but I pushed him away, disgusted with the smell of scotch on his breath."

Molly smoothed Victoria's hair as she sat next to Victoria on the bed.

"He yelled that the first time I kissed him he was drinking scotch, and that it didn't seem to bother me then, but now it disgusted me. He yelled that I no longer liked anything about him.

"Melissa began to cry and I ran to her, but before I could reach her room, he grabbed my arm and spun me toward him."

Molly saw the shadow of bruises in the form of a handprint on her friend's upper arm and brushed it with her fingertips, trying to heal her with love.

The soft touch caused tears to form in Victoria's eyes as her strength broke. "I told him to take his hands off me . . . he yelled that's all I said anymore." Victoria shook as she held Molly's hand and whimpered in pain. "Melissa cried out for me and he blocked the door yelling that all I wanted was to be a mother and I had forgotten that I was also a wife."

"How could he be jealous of his own daughter?" Molly asked, thinking of how Bill rocked their children to sleep each night.

"Molly . . . he told me he never wanted Melissa . . . uncontrollable anger spewed from me. I grabbed him and tried to force him away from the door. He pushed back hard and I lost my balance. I tripped and hit my head against the railing. My neck wrenched as I fell backward down the stairs."

"Oh, honey." Molly gently hugged Victoria and felt her wince with pain as she leaned into Molly's embrace. "Did Devon help you when you fell?"

"He was by my side in moments, cradling and calling my name in panic, and then I blacked out . . . I woke up in the hospital with a concussion, a sprained back, along with a broken arm and wrist . . . I didn't know where else to go, so I came here."

"Of course you did. This is your home."

In the month that Victoria stayed, she hid in Molly's home, not wanting the community to see her in her bruised state. When questions were raised, the other women were told that Victoria tripped on her gown and fell down the stairs of a movie set. They were caught up in their hurt at how long she'd stayed away, happy to give her space to convalesce, so no one questioned her explanation.

As soon as her body healed, Victoria left Nagog with Melissa and headed to Paris for a movie role. Over the next eleven years, Molly received postcards from Europe, Australia, Morocco, and Italy. Once a week, Victoria called and spent an hour telling Molly grand stories of her and Melissa's adventures.

Molly worried, not just for Victoria but also for Melissa. A child needed stability: a home with dinner on the table, a bedroom to hang posters and hide diaries, and a yard to play in. Children needed schoolmates, not tutors. Victoria had bought the house in Malibu, but they never seemed to be home.

Then a phone call had come late one evening. In a frazzled voice, Victoria asked, "Can we stay with you for a few months? Nothing's wrong. Well . . . you'll understand when we arrive."

Molly was raking leaves with her own teenage daughter, Jennifer, when seventeen-year-old Melissa waddled up the walk, her hand resting over her expanded belly. She picked up a handful of bright red, orange, and yellow leaves. "Fall is so beautiful here."

Victoria scooped up the leaves and showered them over Melissa's head. The two kicked and played in the pile. Then Victoria looked at Molly and nudged Melissa. "Oops. We can get carried away. I'll rake these back into a pile once we're settled."

Molly pulled Victoria into a hug and held her tight, almost squeezing the breath from Victoria's lungs. All the fear from the last eleven years released when she could touch her friend and know she was safe. Then she turned and pulled Melissa into the same embrace. "I haven't seen you since you were five. You're beautiful." Then she looked down at Melissa's stomach. "Well, let's get you off your feet. They must be swollen after that long flight."

That evening, Victoria and Molly sat on the Adirondack chairs by the lake with iced tea between them as the sun set in purple streaks across the sky.

Victoria took Molly's hand and held it to her heart. "Thank you for this. I didn't know Melissa remembered this place; it must be the nesting thing."

"Who's the father?" Molly asked.

"A boy from Ireland. It's up to her if she wants to contact him. You can't tell her anything. The doctors told her she couldn't fly, but she insisted on coming to Nagog. You should've seen the fit she threw when I tried to stop her."

"Sounds like someone I know," Molly said.

Two weeks later, Melissa's screams curled through the open windows and sent the wood critters into their nests. The baby, determined to break into the world, was weeks early. There hadn't been time to drive to the hospital. The golden crown pushed its way through. Molly eased her hands around the baby's shoulders, slid her into the world, and the little girl announced her arrival with a howl.

Molly placed the pink, scrunched baby into Melissa's arms as the paramedics rushed into the room. Victoria cradled Melissa as they laughed, tears streaming down their cheeks. The paramedic cut the umbilical cord, checked the baby's heart and lungs, and placed her back in Melissa's arms.

"Welcome to the world, Annabelle Victoria Rose," Melissa said.

Everything will be okay now, Molly had thought.

Now, as she looked out the window of the sunroom at Victoria sitting on her porch swing, Molly placed her hand over her mouth to stop the tears that always came when she thought about Annabelle. The sweet girl had left this earth long before her time. Molly had been witness to the child's birth and death, and had a hard time trying to make sense of God's will. What happened to Annabelle had left Victoria's heart in tatters, and Molly didn't know how to sew it back together.

The men came into the room, led by Carl, saying, "I'm headed home to the wife." He kissed Molly's cheek and burped. "Ah, the sign of good food. You know, in Italy, a man's belch is the highest compliment he can give the chef."

"Yes, but with you, I know it's pure hatefulness," Molly teased. She guided him off to the side a bit with her hand on his arm, and said in a low voice, "Carl, I need you to talk to Sarah."

He put his hand up. "I'm not getting involved in womenfolk's problems. I learned a long time ago to stay out of it."

"Well, if you won't deal with the Victoria issue, will you at least get her to stop spying on your new neighbor?"

"Would that I could, but my marriage is strong because I keep my mouth shut and my head to the ground." He waved as he walked out the screen door. "See you tomorrow, men."

"Molly, thank you for a lovely meal." Joseph kissed the top of her head and pulled her into a hug.

"I'm glad you enjoyed it," Molly said. She looked at him, knowing she shouldn't say anything. He and Victoria would work things out in time, but it had been two months, without progress. "Why don't you, Bill, Victoria, and I all go out for lunch tomorrow? Maybe to a little restaurant in the North End?"

Joseph patted her shoulder. "I have plans with my daughter. Another time." He walked out the door and waved good-bye.

Bill came up behind her and encircled her in his arms. He smelled of beer and popcorn, and she relaxed into his warmth.

"I can't bear to see them hurt," Molly said.

He kissed her curls and nuzzled his chin against her head. "Come to bed. You can't fix the world tonight."

❧

Joseph chose to walk the beach to get home, the sand spilling between his shoes and socks. It had been a warm spring day, the kind where light swooping clouds filled the sky. When his children had been small, Joseph would pack the station wagon and drive to the ocean on days like this. Though it was still too cold to swim or wear bathing suits, Barbara would bundle their little bodies in sweatshirts, roll up their pant legs, and let them run. While he and the children flew bright-colored kites, she'd sit on a blanket, a book in hand, happy for a moment to herself.

"Mom, look how high the kite is!" Little Joey would yell.

Barbara would shade her eyes with her hand so she could see the kite twirling, and then smile at her family.

Joseph looked to the starry night sky. Kite-flying days were in the past. His grandchildren had traded in days with Grandpa for sports, gymnastics, dance, and school activities. Now work and their own families kept him from seeing them as much as he'd like.

He looked over at Victoria's home and saw her on the porch, swinging back and forth to the rhythm of the crickets. An owl hooted in the distance as he watched.

When Annabelle was born, the community fell in love. Everyone took turns visiting Molly and Bill, bringing presents and food in exchange for a moment holding the baby. Victoria's absence through the years was forgotten as Annabelle brought people together in the way only new life could.

Victoria, Melissa, and Annabelle moved into the Rose home. Painters and carpenters fixed the house, and Victoria made Nagog their residence through Thanksgiving and then Christmas. Ladies visited once, sometimes twice per day, unable to resist Annabelle's first smile or the little baby sounds that puckered her lips.

Joseph kept his distance. Victoria looked like the Madonna: pure, beautiful, radiant with life. Before bed, he and Barbara would sit on the porch and share a bottle of wine. He'd hear Victoria's laugh ring out from across the beach, and a place inside him that he thought he'd long forgotten began to ache.

The three Roses returned to Victoria's home in Malibu that spring, but continued to visit Nagog for the next six years. Three weeks out of every summer, their presence lit Nagog like a nuclear blast. During those times, Joseph found himself spending longer hours at work. At times he'd come home to find Victoria and Molly sitting with his wife, enjoying a glass of wine, while their children, all college age, sat around the bonfire. He'd give Barbara a quick kiss and then retreat to his study or the garage. Confusion singed his nerves. He loved his wife, but his heart continued to skip each time Victoria smiled.

It was as if magnets pulled them together, no matter how hard he tried to keep his distance. In the morning he'd be fishing on the dock, only to see Victoria emerge from the water, the curves of her body apparent in her suit. When he went for walks, they'd bump into one another. One day, as he followed a bright red hummingbird through the woods, his camera slung around his neck, he came upon Victoria and Annabelle in the tree house.

Victoria wore a white sundress with yellow flowers that left her defined shoulders bare. Her golden legs dangled off the porch and swung in the breeze as she sang a nursery rhyme.

"No, Grandma. I sing." Annabelle held up her five-year-old hand and stood. Twisted, golden curls bobbed around her shoulders, and her pink cheeks popped when she smiled. The familiar voice from his childhood came from those little lips.

Suddenly, he was eight again, sitting under the tree, watching Victoria sing and dance. Annabelle twirled and took a bow. Joseph clapped and Victoria looked down.

He looked at the two women. "It's déjà vu. She's the spitting image of you."

Annabelle ran into Victoria's arms. They rubbed noses and gave each other big smooches.

An explosion burst through his heart: the smell of Victoria's hair, the feel of her skin under his hand, the way she nipped his ear when he teased her. He hadn't been able to stop himself. The camera to his eye, he captured the love between Victoria and Annabelle: the smile on her face, the laughter between them. He'd seen in Victoria not just the sexy woman who commanded a room, but also the soft and loving grandmother.

Joseph looked away from Victoria's home and walked back to his empty house. He turned on the stove light and placed a cup of water in the microwave for tea. In the later years of his marriage, Barbara had gotten him into the habit of having chamomile tea before retiring to bed. The appliance beeped, he dunked the tea bag into the mug, and took it into the dark, empty living room. He didn't think the tea would help him sleep tonight. Too many memories were spinning.

His laptop and camera were on the coffee table. He sat on the old leather couch in the indentation that years of family time had created and connected his camera to the computer with a USB cord. The digital age had brought back the excitement of his childhood; he had a reason to play with toys again. Many nights, Joseph stayed up past midnight downloading music. His collection had grown to six thousand songs, with hits from 1940 to the present. Many of his friends thought computers were too complicated and didn't enjoy DVD players or video cameras. They were like bulls that wouldn't leave the confinement of the pen to walk to the pasture. Joseph tried to pull them into the twenty-first century by the horns, but they refused to leave the safety of the past.

The photos began to appear on the computer in fast blips. Last weekend, his family had come for a cookout. His eldest son, in his early fifties, had more white than blond in his hair. His daughter, Shelly, the spitting image of her mother, now had her own grandbaby.

The computer finished importing the pictures. Joseph looked at the images of his great-grandchild. Emily, only two years old, ran across the beach in a neon-colored bathing suit with a built-in life jacket. In another picture, she smiled as Molly let her hold a sparkler, her brown hair stuck to ice cream–smeared cheeks.

How had his heart grown so big in one lifetime? The love he felt for his family, the amazement that overwhelmed him every time he looked at his three children, seven grandchildren, and now those chubby cheeks and wonder-filled eyes of his great-grandchild—how did he deserve all of them?

Joseph touched the computer screen and traced Emily's cheeks. "Beautiful baby girl, I love you so much."

He walked to the porch and sat on the swing. As he rocked, he listened to the night sounds: raccoons scavenging around the locked trash cans, the soft breeze rustling in the leaves. Joseph breathed in the smell of the lake, which had been his serenity throughout his life. But even this couldn't calm his mind tonight; thoughts of Victoria continued to resurface.

He thought no one had known about the pictures he'd taken of Victoria and five-year-old Annabelle that day. The film, hidden in his desk drawer, had sat in its canister undeveloped.

Victoria had been asked to perform onstage in London the

fall of Annabelle's sixth year. Victoria, Melissa, and Annabelle didn't return to Nagog that next summer or for a few years after. Joseph had been relieved, but her absence created anger throughout the community as once again Victoria chose a life filled with glamour over even a short visit with her friends. Molly tacked postcards from Europe on the bulletin board and later a picture of Annabelle in her first stage performance as one of the orphans in *Annie*.

Then the three of them came home, late one night in January. Melissa had been diagnosed with stage four ovarian cancer and Victoria had brought her to Massachusetts to see the doctors at Brigham and Women's Hospital. They removed her ovaries, but the cancer had already spread.

Barbara brought casseroles and flowers. Joseph found himself visiting every day. Annabelle would sit on his lap while he helped her with her schoolwork.

"Your beard tickles," Annabelle had said when Joseph rubbed his cheek against her baby skin.

He'd scrub his face against hers until she giggled and squirmed.

Each night after dinner, Victoria and Annabelle would crawl into Melissa's bed in the den and watch movies until they fell asleep. Many mornings, when Molly brought breakfast, she'd find the television screen filled with static and the three female hands entwined.

Everyone believed that Melissa would live and that the chemotherapy would work. But as the months passed, Melissa wasted away and sometimes was too tired even to smile or watch TV with her family. On April 18, 1981, Melissa passed. For three days after the paramedics took her daughter away, Victoria refused to leave the bed. When Bill tried to carry her from the room, she thrashed against him. Screams echoed through the community, and a doctor had been called to administer a shot, and after that, Victoria just stared at the shadows that moved across the walls.

Annabelle stayed with the Jacobses while Molly made arrangements. The day of the funeral, Molly dressed Victoria in a black dress and veiled hat. The neighborhood held hands at the Rose plot. Victoria stared at her parents' graves, refusing to look at Melissa's coffin. She never spoke or acknowledged the minister or the community's condolences. She was the model of stoic resolve as she held Annabelle's little hand.

When they returned from the cemetery, the community gathered in Victoria's home. Molly and Evelyn laid out food, and people sat with china plates on their laps. People spoke, trying to enliven the silence that permeated the house. Victoria didn't see or hear them. She returned to Melissa's bed with Annabelle curled into her arms.

A week later, through a blurring rain, Joseph thought he saw a ghost—a woman running in the downpour and wearing only a nightgown. He grabbed Barbara's flowered umbrella and rushed into the rain without his slicker. He splashed through the puddles on the main road in the direction Victoria had gone, until he came to the cemetery.

Victoria stood there, staring at the grave, her hair clumped in knots. He sloshed through the mud and held the umbrella over her head. She looked at him, her silver eyes emptied of their brilliance.

"God's not supposed to take angels," she said. The cold rain had soaked the thin blue cotton nightgown and dirt splattered her calves and bare feet. He squeezed her to his chest, trying to warm her trembling body. He worried that her sanity had shattered.

The tears flowed from her eyes as hard as the rain came down around them. "I'm the sinner. I don't deserve this life. Why didn't he take me?"

The next day, Victoria and Annabelle left the community and didn't return for another eight years.

Joseph sipped his tea as he rocked on the porch swing and listened to the breeze rustle the leaves. Victoria had suffered deeply in her life. He wanted to be her friend, but he was afraid of the emotions that stirred when he looked at her. If her past behavior was any indication, it wouldn't be long before she left again, and he could go back to pretending that he didn't think about her.

CHAPTER 11

"Heather, are you here?" Gina Saducci called as she walked up the front steps and onto the deck. Heather opened the door, and Gina wrapped one arm around her. "Sorry I didn't have time to call you back last night, but I figured I was headed here today anyway." She handed Heather a cup of coffee and a white bag with *Michelangelo's* printed on the front. "My mother sent cannoli, biscotti, and mochachino lattes to fatten you up." She glanced around the living room. "Oh my God, this place is too cute. I love it, and the couch we picked out looks perfect. I'm a decorating genius even when I haven't seen the space."

"Thanks for bringing coffee. I didn't sleep last night. I was up finishing the painting in the dining room."

"You painted? I'm impressed. The pale green in this room is perfect." Gina's hand flew to her chest. "Look at these windows and the bookcases! This place is gorgeous, but we need to do more shopping to get some accent colors going, and you need curtains."

"The color's called April Mist. One of my neighbors helped me pick it out," Heather said, knowing that Gina, an interior designer, would need to see the entire house before she could focus on the party. When Gina was excited, she spoke like a hummingbird gathering nectar. She flitted from one idea to the next, barely stopping to breathe. Gina moved from room to room with a confidence that always made Heather feel overshadowed. Rather than try to hide her soft stomach and prominent curves, Gina flaunted them in fitted embellished jeans, a lace tank, and a satin short-sleeved jacket that gave her an air of sophistication and coolness. Her long black hair fell in waves to her mid-back, and with dark eyes and olive skin, her friend hardly needed to wear makeup.

As she made her way up the stairs, Gina chatted at her usual frenzied pace. "My boss is an ass. He gave our craziest client my home number. This guy works in London and he called me seven times at three this morning. I was in bed . . . with Michard, I might add. So I didn't answer."

Gina worked for one of the most prestigious interior design firms in the city, and though she claimed to love her job, Heather heard more complaints than raves.

"So at eight this morning my boss calls and screams at me for not taking care of the client's needs. So I call the guy back. And do you know what his big emergency was? A shark tank."

"What?" Heather asked as they walked upstairs toward the master bedroom.

"He wants a giant saltwater tank in the middle of his living room. Do you have any idea what kind of bracing it's going to take for an aquarium that big? When I tried to explain this to him, he became irate, telling me that he didn't want a great white, just a small nurse shark, and I was an idiot for not understanding that."

"What's the budget on this project?" Heather asked as she looked out the window and noticed four ladies—not one of them a day younger than seventy—walking toward the beach in bathing suits.

"There isn't a budget, and now the guy wants us to decorate his flat in London as well. That's why my boss wants me to deal with his every whim, even if it means staying up all night taking down notes for his crazy ideas. Oh, and speaking of work schedules, Michard can't come tonight. The backup chef at the restaurant called in sick, and since my father will kill Michard if anything goes wrong with his big dinner party, he has to work."

Heather panicked. "Gina, who's going to do the food for tonight? I have a really important guest coming."

"God, you worry too much. It's just a party. I have all the food being delivered in our catering truck in two hours. I hired two waiters to serve. I know this is your big night to wow the television guy."

Heather exhaled. She plopped down on her new mattress, and Gina lay down next to her. "This bed is so beautiful. I love antique furniture."

Before they became friends, Heather had been a waitress at Gina's family's restaurant, Michelangelo's, where she'd taken orders, cleaned tables, and prayed that people would eat fast and leave a big tip. On Wednesday nights, when Gina walked in to claim her spot at her reserved table (nicknamed the Princess Section by the staff), the energy of the whole restaurant would shift. All eyes turned to her as she spoke to regular customers, flirted with the male waitstaff, and fell into her father's embrace when he came from the offices upstairs.

After two years at Michelangelo's, Heather had been promoted to head waitress of the dinner shift. Which meant after busting her butt serving customers, she had to stay until midnight to help close the restaurant. One night, as Heather got ready to close up, Gina burst in and grabbed a bottle of Chianti.

"I've had a lousy day. You want to join me for a drink?" Gina asked.

Heather didn't know what to say. She stood in her sauce-splattered apron, feeling awkward.

Gina's tailored skirt showed off her toned legs as she slid into the booth. Heather touched her ponytail, pulled out the elastic, and tried to fluff her flat hair as she sat. Gina handed her a wine-glass. She drank; strong flavors exploded in her mouth, prickling her tongue. Gina swirled the red liquid in her glass and held it to the light. She stuck her nose in the glass and breathed deeply, then sipped and rolled the wine around her mouth. "Ah, that's good," Gina said.

Heather kept her eyes on the table, embarrassed by her lack of sophistication, as Gina talked with the speed of a Ferrari about her interior design career. She tried to keep up with what Gina was saying, but the wine was making her head feel fuzzy. Something about trying to fit an armoire through a third-story window with a crane.

"The old bat told me to park the crane across the street. How am I supposed to move an armoire through a window from across the street?" Gina asked.

"That sucks," was all Heather could think to say.

Gina sighed. "Well, enough about that. What about you? Have you ever been to Europe?"

"No."

"I spent two years studying abroad. You should go." For two hours, Gina talked about art, food, travel, and men.

Heather could only listen while she drank. She didn't have

stories to share. She spent every waking moment at work trying to keep her utilities paid. She'd had one relationship since
moving to Boston. Roger had been an engineering student
who worked in the café next door. They were both broke, so
their dates consisted of take-out dinners from their respective
restaurant jobs and rented movies. They'd been each other's
first sexual partners, and then split after six months. There
wasn't any real reason except that the relationship had run its
course.

By 4 a.m., the late hour and copious amounts of wine had
loosened Heather's tongue. "I wish I had your life. I want to
travel, and write about the places I see. I want to date the men
you talk about."

"I know just the man for you," Gina said.

"I'm not like you."

"What are you talking about? You're beautiful and independent. He'll adore you."

Lust grew, a hunger to live in Gina's world.

A week later, Gina had introduced Heather to Charlie.

"Gina, I need to tell you something," Heather said as she lay
on the bed and stared at the ceiling. "I broke up with Charlie."

Gina sat up and looked at Heather. "What?"

"Well, I thought it was just going to be a break—some time
to think about what I wanted—but we haven't spoken in over
six weeks."

"I don't understand. I talked to Charlie last night at my parents' restaurant. He came in with his family. We spoke about
tonight's party and the television show and how important this
was for your career. He said he would see me tonight."

Heather sat up and looked at her friend. "He what?"

"He's coming tonight. Didn't you know?"

"No." Heather had given him her address on the contracts she signed, but she hadn't told him that she'd contacted Steven and invited him to the party.

"What's the problem? He's still your agent, right?"

"Yes, but I went behind his back to invite the television producer. He's going to think that I want to break ties completely, and I don't. I just couldn't face him tonight. We haven't dealt with the breakup or had closure. He must be pissed to know that I invited Steven behind his back."

"Since when did you get a backbone?" Gina laughed as she put her arm around Heather's shoulder. "I'm proud of you. I might have to make you an honorary Italian after all. It's about time you told Charlie to shove it up his arse."

"Seriously?"

"Look, Charlie's been ruling your life for six years. This is a wake-up call for him. The fact that he didn't tell me that you broke up says he's thinking about what he needs to do to get you back. Maybe he's coming tonight to make amends."

Maybe Gina was right and Charlie was willing to make some changes now that he'd lost her. But was that what she wanted? "There's one more problem," Heather said.

"What?"

Heather stood, moved Gina to the window, and pointed to the beach. "That."

"You have a few older neighbors who like to sit on the beach in bathing suits. So?"

"Not a few. All."

Gina's head fell back as she burst into laughter. "You moved into a retirement community. Did you know when you bought the house?"

"What do you think?" Heather said. "I met this young, gorgeous guy when I looked at the place."

"Naughty girl. You bought a house because of some nice booty and instead got Grandpa as a neighbor. Shame, shame. That's what you get for thinking with your hormones." Gina continued to giggle.

"I didn't buy the house because of the guy, and I'm glad you find this so funny." Heather told her about the blue book she'd found on her railing that morning. The cover read *Nagog Community Rules and Regulations*. A bookmark, imprinted with a cross, marked a page: "Quiet hours: 9:00 p.m. to 7:00 a.m."

"The party doesn't start till six, and Steven isn't coming until after eight thirty. I'm supposed to show him the fun, confident Solo Female Traveler. How am I going to do that when quiet hours start at nine?"

"Oh, lighten up." Gina looked out the window. "From what I can see, I don't think your neighbors will be able to hear anything. You need to relax. It's going to be okay."

Paper lanterns swung in the breeze as people stood around the lawn with margarita glasses and beer bottles, talking and laughing, while music played in the background. For the most part, the party was a success, but Steven still hadn't arrived.

Molly waved as she walked along the street with Sarah, Joseph, Bill and Carl, and Agatha on her scooter. Heather smiled and returned the gesture. When she'd realized her neighbors' ages,

Heather had decided not to invite them to the party, thinking they wouldn't want to come. Now she realized how rude she'd been.

Molly walked toward the house, motioning for the others to follow. Heather's guests turned and watched as the older woman embraced Heather in a hug. "We don't want to interrupt, but I just wanted to tell you that the food smells wonderful and the decorations look great." Molly held her at arm's length. "And that blue dress looks stunning on you."

"Thank you," Heather said. "And thank you for all your help this week. My house wouldn't have been ready if it weren't for you."

"That's what neighbors do," Molly said. "You've met everyone." She gestured to the rest of the group.

"For the most part." Heather extended her hand toward the woman who wore the crucifix. "But we haven't met yet. I've seen you around, but I haven't gotten the chance to say, 'hello.'"

"This is Sarah Dragone, Carl's wife," Molly said as she guided Sarah in front of her.

"It's quite the gathering," Sarah said as she looked at the groups of people.

"It's just some friends and coworkers. There's plenty of food. You're more than welcome to make a plate. We have stuffed peppers—"

"Peppers give me gas," Agatha said. "I'll be rolled in a ball all night. I'm in enough pain from my prolapsed bladder." She turned to Sarah. "Did I tell you that the doctor wants me to have surgery again? They had to sew it back three times. I tell you, those babies are worth it, but it's hell on the body. I told them just close up that hoochy-coo. It's not like I'm going to use it anymore."

Heather's eyes widened. Bill, Carl, and Joseph moved toward a group of Gina's male friends.

"I assume you saw the rule book I left you on your railing. I hope you know that we won't tolerate music or loud noise after nine," Sarah said, her face pinched.

She'd hoped they'd give her a little leeway tonight. "I promise we'll keep it down."

Victoria walked up behind Heather. "Don't worry about it. Have fun. This is your first party in your new home." She placed her arm around Molly's shoulder. "Why don't we let this young woman enjoy her friends? Bill, ready to go?"

Heather moved over to the group where the men were now engaged in a conversation about volleyball. "It's all in the motion. You have to swing through and not up, then the ball will go straight down," Bill said.

"Well, first they'd have to be able to jump. They don't look like they can get up too high," Carl razzed the guys. "In my day, men didn't have a problem getting over the net. We worked hard and stayed in shape."

"He's selling you a bunch of baloney," Bill said. "He was always too short to hit on anything higher than a woman's net."

"I think your wives are walking away without you," Heather said, trying to move the men along. "Would you like some food before you go?"

"Thank you, Heather, but we've already eaten," Bill said.

Joseph put his hand on Heather's shoulder. "I put wood in the fire pit. Bonfires are a tradition at Nagog parties, and since you're now a resident, I thought I'd pass the torch to you."

"Thank you. That's sweet," Heather said.

"Have fun," he said as the men walked away.

"What did he want?" Gina asked. "Are we in trouble from the grannies for being too loud?"

Gina's breath smelled like tequila and she passed Heather a margarita.

"No, he was being nice."

"Well that's cool. See? Living with ten grandparents won't be so bad." She giggled until she almost fell down. "Think about it, for your birthday and Christmas, you'll get at least ten bucks if each one gives you a check for a dollar."

"Funny," Heather said as she looked to the road, and then at her watch. It was almost 8:30, the time she'd given Steven. Her nerves made her feel like she'd drunk six cups of coffee. Charlie hadn't shown yet either, and she wondered if he'd decided to stay away.

As darkness came and alcohol loosened inhibitions, her guests began to dance. Heather had almost given up on Steven when lights finally flashed onto the road. Her heart jumped. She walked to the silver Mercedes as Steven stepped from the car.

"There's my hot new star." He came up and kissed her on both cheeks. "Where's your man? Let me get the business talk out of the way so I can enjoy the party. I know Charlie will want to discuss our ideas for a travel show."

"I'm not certain he's coming tonight," Heather said. "And I didn't invite you to talk business. It's a night to celebrate with good friends, food, and my associates." Heather knew she lied, but he didn't have to know. Tonight she'd show him a fun, confident woman, no matter how much her hands were shaking.

"Well, then, get me a drink," he said, looking Heather up and down.

"What's your pleasure?" she asked.

"Ah, that's a dangerous question to a man when you look this good, but a beer will do just fine," he said.

Heather grabbed a bottle from the table on the deck, hiding

her flushed cheeks. She handed him the beer. "Are you ready to dance? Or do you first need alcohol to be as smooth as you were that night at the Bay Towers?" she challenged.

"I don't know. I'm seeing a whole new side to you," he said. "I might not be able to keep up."

She put her drink down and grabbed his hand. "Let's find out."

The music pulsed through Heather's body. Sweaty bodies bumped against her as she moved to the beat. Steven knew how to dance and she found herself smiling. The alcohol from her first drink began to take effect and the buzz released her worry. She leaned on Steven, his nose brushing against her cheek. His mouth came close to hers and she turned her head away.

"So sexy," he whispered.

She stepped back. "You, sir, are dangerous."

"It's just a dance," he whispered in her ear. "Charlie's not here. What's the problem?" He pulled her to him.

She leaned her head back and laughed. It felt good to flirt and to be in control. "I think I'll check on the rest of my guests while I let you cool off." She stepped back and winked at him.

"Point taken, but you can't blame a guy for trying when a woman is as gorgeous as you."

Heather turned and flashed him a smile as she walked to the back porch. She opened the screen door and made her way into the kitchen. She was smiling until she saw Charlie at the table.

"How long have you been here?" she asked, walking toward him.

"Long enough." He glared at her.

"Why didn't you come find me?"

"Didn't look like I was missed. In fact, I wasn't even invited," he said.

"Charlie, you haven't returned any of my calls or acknowledged that I sent you the representation contract. How was I supposed to invite you?"

"You changed the direct deposit on your check and wiped out your savings account. I looked up your credit cards online. You spent five thousand dollars on stuff for this place," he said.

Heather bit her lip. "That's none of your business. You only own fifteen percent of my rights, and as long as you get that, my finances aren't your concern any longer."

Charlie paced. "What do you know about finances? Without me you'd still be a broke waitress. You wouldn't be traveling the world."

"Maybe you're right," Heather yelled. "But if you haven't noticed, *I* write the columns."

Someone turned up the music outside and she realized her guests could hear them fighting. Charlie loomed over her. "You almost ended up homeless last time you dealt with finances. Or don't you remember?"

"How could I forget? You never stop bringing it up."

"I don't know you anymore."

Heather looked into his eyes. "Maybe because you don't bother to listen."

A muscle in his cheek twitched. "Here we go. All the ways I've failed you. When have I not been there? I helped you out of debt. I gave you a place to live. I built your career. What do you want, Heather?"

"To be happy."

"Funny, I thought we were." He stared at her, his jaw locked with tension.

She didn't know how to explain it to him. Why couldn't he

see that she needed more than an agent—she needed a soft place to land and a man who loved her enough to pick her up at the damn airport.

He looked out the window. "So you used me to get your column. Are you going to sleep with Steven for a television show?"

"How could you even think that?"

"I don't know, Heather. You go behind my back and invite him to a party at your new house, and from what I saw of the two of you dancing, it looks like you're acting like a whore."

Anger brewed, and she turned away in an attempt to calm down. She walked through the living room and onto the deck to avoid a bigger scene. The music blared in the front yard and everyone was dancing. For a moment she thought about her neighbors and how she needed to turn down the volume.

Then Charlie was behind her, forcing her to face him. His hands clamped onto her biceps. "All I've done is care about your needs. You have your dream job. You travel the world. You wear nice clothes. I bought you a diamond and asked you to marry me. Oh, that's right . . . you cared so much you took it off and left it on my bureau when you moved out." His hands gripped harder and she yelped with pain as he pulled her to him, his lips close to her ear. "But with how bad you are in bed, I doubt Steven will keep you for long. I'm done, Heather. Maybe *I* want something more."

"Charlie. You're hurting me." Tears welled in her eyes.

Gina ran onto the deck and pushed Charlie away. "What the hell are you doing?"

Charlie shot her a look of disgust and walked away. Heather looked down at the red marks on her arms, then glanced toward the yard. Her guests had turned away, pretending they hadn't witnessed the scene. From Sarah and Carl's home she saw curtains close. Had they been privy to the fight too? She felt naked, like she stood in the middle of a three-ring circus with the spotlights pointed right at her inadequacies.

Her body vibrated like a jackhammer breaking concrete. Her biceps ached as if she'd been stoned. Gina gently took her arm and led her into the house. She sat Heather on the couch and went to the kitchen. When she returned, she placed a shot of tequila in Heather's hand.

"I'm going to send everyone home, and then I'll come back," Gina said.

Heather tilted her head back and downed the drink. "Gina, wait." Heather stopped her friend before she could end the party. She couldn't hide now, or all Steven would remember would be the fight. If this was the way Charlie was going to act, their work relationship needed to end, and she would need Steven even more. "I'm fine. I'll be out there in a minute."

"You sure?" Gina asked with a look of concern.

Heather nodded. Her career was what was important now.

CHAPTER 12

❧

Heather's swollen brain pressed against her skull. The beaded throw pillow on her bed had imprinted its design onto her face. She rolled over and covered her eyes from the sunlight that streamed through her bedroom window. She'd only had two drinks last night, but they'd left an impression on her body.

Through travel she'd learned to appreciate wine and enjoyed a glass or two, but she'd never taken to hard alcohol. Last night, nerves had caused her to avoid food. She'd had the margarita and the extra shot to calm her nerves, but hadn't been drunk. The party had run until almost one in the morning and Heather realized that her headache could have more to do with exhaustion than alcohol.

Her life had been a blur since her last trip: buying the house, moving in, decorating, planning the party . . . there hadn't been time to feel or think. A blue jay swooped into the oak tree outside her window, and three little beaks peaked out of the nest to be fed. *When had the nest been built?* Heather wondered. She hadn't noticed it before. Every morning she'd awoken and immediately started working.

She pulled back the down comforter and stretched in the sunlight as she walked to the window. The lake looked like glass in the morning light. Its stillness calmed Heather, reminding her to breathe deeply. Through her open window she could smell bacon and eggs coming from one of her neighbors' homes.

In the walk-in closet, she caught her reflection in the mirror. She wore a pink tank top that left her biceps exposed. Faint purple bruises had formed where Charlie had grabbed her. They didn't hurt physically, but her mind couldn't wrap around the fact that he'd grabbed her so hard. She pulled a sweatshirt over her shoulders to hide the marks.

Downstairs, paper plates and cups had been left on end tables, the mantel, and all over the deck. Gina walked in from the kitchen, handed her a cup of coffee and biscotti. A box of baked goods sat open on the coffee table. "How are you feeling?" Gina asked.

"Headache, exhausted, and like I want to curl up and sleep for a few days," Heather said as she plopped onto her couch.

"The aftereffects of stress," Gina said, curling up in the oversized chair. "Eat. It'll make you feel better."

Heather dipped the biscotti in the coffee and bit into the cookie. The sugar began to revive her. "I've missed your mother's baking. You know your family's food could be considered one of the deadly sins."

Gina raised her eyebrows. "That's our secret. My great-great-grandfather actually signed a pact with the devil. In exchange for the women in our family being beautiful and the men rich, we have promised to lure good Christians to gluttony and thick waistlines."

"Are you the Siren created to make men feel lust?"

"You know it." Gina bit into a cannoli and licked the cream from the side of her lips.

"I keep wondering if what happened with Charlie is my fault," Gina said as she looked at Heather. "If I hadn't told him about the party, he wouldn't have shown up."

Heather ran her finger over the cup's rim. "It's not your fault. If I'd handled our breakup better or told him about the party, then last night wouldn't have happened. I've been too reactionary. Not thinking very clearly."

"Still, he's a prick for the way he acted."

"Well, *that* I'll agree with," Heather said. She looked out the window to the lilac bush. The tiny purple flowers had bloomed in large bunches. Heather put her coffee down and opened the window to let in the sweet perfume. The scent eased her headache. Two squirrels chased each other around the side yard running up and down the trees. *Twitterpated,* she thought, recalling the term for falling-in-spring-love from *Bambi.* Heather's friend had the hint of a smile on her face, and she knew where Gina's thoughts had gone. "What's it like between you and Michard?"

Eight months ago, Michard had moved from Italy to become the head chef at Michelangelo's. Gina, who'd always been too independent and focused on her career to be bothered with long-term relationships, now blushed with giddiness every time she spoke about him. When Michard and Gina looked at each other from across a room, their gaze was so intimate, it embarrassed Heather.

Gina squirmed in her seat. "You sure you want to hear about this right now?"

"Yeah," Heather said as she pulled a pillow across her lap.

"It's hot. He feeds me chocolate cake and with each bite he kisses me deeply. He tastes my body as if I were as decadent as one of the dishes he creates." Her skin flushed. "It's crazy how much I crave him."

"Wow."

Gina looked at Heather with sad eyes. "You know, it's not all perfect. He's incredibly jealous and freaks out if I talk to other men. He's a hot-blooded Italian and so am I. Put the two of us together and sure, there's great passion, but we fight. You know how relationships go."

"Yeah."

"You never really told me why you left Charlie."

Heather played with the button on the pillow's center. "Because I need to be more than his client."

Gina stood up and sat next to Heather with her arm around her. "Charlie loves you. He wouldn't have been that insane last night if he didn't."

"Maybe, but I can't excuse his behavior." Heather leaned her head on Gina's shoulder. "Just promise me that we're still going to be friends even though I'm no longer with him."

"Of course." Gina petted Heather's hair.

"I can't lose you too."

"You're stuck with me forever." Gina paused and looked at Heather. "I hate to do this to you, but I have to get going. The stupid shark tank client keeps calling and I need to go into the office. Do you want help picking up? The waitstaff cleaned the serving trays and the kitchen before they left, but there's still a lot of stuff left over from the end of the night."

"I'm fine. You go."

"I have a date with Michard tonight, but I can cancel if you need me." Gina began to gather her purse and put on her shoes.

Heather stood and walked her friend to the door. "You enjoy

your night with Michard. I have a huge bathtub and a gorgeous lake right outside my door. I'm going to spoil myself today and relax."

"Okay. Love ya." Gina kissed Heather's cheek and gave her a hug.

When the door closed, Heather looked around the living room. Now what? She wasn't ready to deal with the mess in her house. She went upstairs and poured a bath.

The fatigue from the night before evaporated from her pores as she sat in her tub trying to relax. Bubbles spilled over the side of the bath and pooled onto the floor, but Heather didn't care, the swirling water and hyacinth scent were soft and calming, at least to her body.

She tried to still her mind, but thoughts continued to flash through it: the fight with Charlie, Steven and the Travel Channel, the fact that she'd bought a house in a retirement community. Plus, would Charlie remain her agent, and if not, how would she go about building her career? Could she dump Charlie altogether and go it alone? Relaxation evaded her, and she gave up on the bath.

Downstairs she threw away the plastic cups that had accumulated on the counter and began to unload the dishwasher. When she opened the silverware drawer, she was startled to see a line of ants march out and onto the counter. She opened the other drawers. Teams of little red bodies swarmed her phone book. An infestation had taken over the kitchen. Under the sink, she found a bright red can of soda and a puddle of sticky liquid swarming with insects. What the heck? Who spilled a soda under the sink?

The ants crawled on her arm as she tried to wipe up the soda with a rag. She screamed and shook her hands to get rid of them.

With her shoe, she smashed the bugs until they were dead. She'd need to get ant traps from the store.

With a trash bag in hand, she gathered the rest of the cups from the living room and the deck. Standing on her deck and looking out at the neighborhood, she wasn't certain what to do next. When she lived in Boston she'd go shopping, to a museum, or out for coffee on a Sunday afternoon. When she thought about buying this place, she'd imagined having people her age to hang out with on the beach, but now she was uncertain what to do with her afternoon.

"Excuse me, Heather," Thomas called from next door through his open window, "could you help me with something?"

Heather walked down the three steps and crossed their shared driveway. She opened his side screen door and walked into his kitchen, where dishes were piled in the sink. As she walked into the living room, she saw Thomas sitting at a new desk in front of a large computer that looked out of place next to the old paneling and worn rug. Knickknacks covered the shelves along with pictures of Tommy.

Thomas was squinting at the screen as he peered over his bifocals.

"Is this new?" Heather asked, pointing to the computer.

"You betcha. My grandson decided to bring me into the modern age with this contraption, but I can't seem to get the hang of it." He wore a nice suit jacket and a shirt and tie, even though the day was summery.

She put her hand on his shoulder. "You're still in your Sunday best. Did you just get back from church?"

"Nope," he said as he clicked his mouse impatiently. "I haven't been in years. Sarah's always trying to convert me, but I've been a happy sinner most of my life."

"What are you trying to do?" she said as she looked at the screen.

"Open that dang Internet thing."

"May I?" she asked and pointed to the mouse. He lifted his hand away and she leaned around him. He smiled up at her and winked. She stifled a laugh. This old man was too much. She clicked on his browser and the screen came to life.

"What website are you looking to get on?"

"That dating one I see on the television," he said. "I started filling out the forms the other night after Tommy left, but now I can't remember how to get back in. And I need to take a picture with the computer and somehow get it up where it can be seen by the ladies."

"What?" Heather stepped back and looked at him. The sport coat and tie now made sense. "You want me to put you on an Internet dating site?"

"Yep," he said. "How else am I going to find a new lady? Everyone around here is like family. Over at the Amvets dinners they're all a bunch of old farts, and I can't go looking in the nursing homes, because I don't live there. Turns out they frown upon nonresidents coming in just to find dates. And I've been kicked out of most of the bereavement groups because I dated too many of the widows and they all talk."

Heather tried not to giggle, and her eyes watered as she stifled her laugh. "Thomas, you dog."

"I'm just looking for a little love in this big lonely world." She opened a few different dating sites until she found the one that Thomas recognized. He couldn't remember his password or username, so she created a new one and wrote it down on a sticky note that he stuck under the desk so no one would see it. Then they took a picture with the computer's camera and posted it. "I'm not certain how many ladies in their eighties are going to be looking on this site," Heather said.

"Who said I wanted someone my own age?" Thomas said. "I like 'em young and frisky. Someone in her early seventies or even sixties would be good, unless *you* want to have a go with me?" He smiled and she saw the devil in his eyes.

"I think you might be a little too much for me," she said.

He pinched her bottom and her mouth dropped in shock. "Thomas!"

"What? I didn't do anything. These old hands just do what they want."

"I'm going to leave you to your search. If you need more help, just let me know, but next time I'll slap that hand if it gets too fresh."

He smacked his gums and smiled at her. "Thank you, Heather." She shook her finger at him and then walked away.

Tommy's rusted white truck pulled into the driveway just as Heather was walking up her deck stairs. Thomas had put a smile on her face and she turned to Tommy as he got out of the vehicle. He slammed the door and walked toward her.

"Hi," she said, and then noticed his aqua eyes were brewing with anger.

He stepped onto her deck. "We need to talk."

Heather's mind flashed to how Charlie loomed over her with his hands squeezing her biceps. Instinctively, she took a step back and crossed her arms over her body.

"You had a party last night," he said.

"More like a gathering. Why?"

"From what I understand, the music kept getting louder long after dark, and then a fight broke out because everyone was drunk. This is an elderly community, what were you thinking?"

He didn't yell, but the harsh tone he used was too much for Heather's current state of mind. "I think you got your facts wrong."

"Oh, really, because Sarah and Agatha called me last night and this morning with the same story."

"Yes, I had a party. There was music until about eleven and people stayed until around one. Victoria said that it would be okay."

"And what about the fight?"

Heather blushed. "Not that it's any of your business, but yes, a small argument broke out. It was over quickly and it wasn't due to alcohol."

"Do you understand that you live in an elderly community and that one night of missed sleep could cause an illness? You live next door to my grandfather, and I won't put up with this."

"Look, I'm sorry. I didn't mean to cause any problems, but Victoria had said it would be okay to play the music past quiet hours. And by the way, you don't have any right to come onto my property and start yelling at me." She pushed past him and walked off her deck. At the end of the driveway she turned back. "You know, you could take a few lessons from your grandfather on how to treat a lady. So far, you've been a class-act jerk." She stormed off without giving him a chance to speak.

❧

The cool evening air smelled like roses as Victoria clipped the flower bushes in her front yard. The sun had begun to set and the sky over the lake looked as if it had been washed in purple and pink watercolors. Victoria watched as Heather walked out of her house and across the street with her head down, kicking at the sand as she walked toward the shoreline.

Victoria went inside, brewed coffee, and poured it into a thermos, and grabbed a bag of chocolates from the pantry. She gathered a blanket from the sunroom and walked out to the beach. Heather sat in the sand, her jeans rolled to her knees, her bare arms curled around her calves. Victoria saw that the girl was creating holes with her feet.

"Digging to China?" Victoria asked.

Heather jumped at the sound of Victoria's voice. "Thinking that if I dig a pit deep enough, I can crawl in and hide."

"Things that bad?" Victoria asked as she looked at the water and listened to the small waves lap against the beach and the rowboats bump against the wooden dock. This time of night the lake held such peace, and Victoria breathed in the scene.

"Actually, I'm pretending I'm in Belize," Heather said. "Do you know that when the wind blows through the long pointed leaves of the palm trees, it sounds like rain?"

"I didn't know that. I've never been to Belize."

"A tropical island would be perfect right now: a hammock, a piña colada, and the ocean waves crashing. I feel like my life has become a strange vacation and any minute I'm going to take a flight back to Boston."

"Well, I own a hammock and if you want, we could string it between the trees along the shore. I know how to make a rather good piña colada, and I think we could find the sound of rain on a meditation tape. We could re-create Belize right here in Nagog."

Heather smiled. "Thank you. That helped."

"I didn't mean to interrupt your thoughts, but you looked like you might need some company." She extended the thermos to Heather.

"Got anything stronger than caffeine?" Heather asked as she stood and walked to the picnic table.

"Sorry, it's decaf. If I drink caffeine in the evening I'm up all night. Chronic insomniac."

Heather looked at Victoria and then sat at the table. "I'm sorry if the music kept you up last night. I realize that you probably had church early this morning."

"You were having fun. A woman your age is supposed to play loud music. And everyone got off to church just fine this morning, but personally, I slept in." Victoria placed the cups on the picnic table and poured the rich, dark roast into the mugs. They watched the sunlight fade, the steam rising from their cups. Heather faced the lake. Mosquitoes began to buzz around them and Heather smacked at a few that landed on her skin. A small black shadow flew over them. "What was that?"

"A bat. They live in the old McAffee barn up on the hill, and they come here because the bugs make their nests around the water. They're harmless and they eat the mosquitoes."

"Too bad they don't eat ants. I found a whole family under my sink this morning."

"Put a paper plate of honey near your foundation. The ants will be attracted to the sugar and then they get stuck. That's what my father used to do."

"Thanks, I'll do that. Of course, if someone hadn't spilled a Coke under my sink, I wouldn't have had the problem."

Victoria looked at her with concern. Soda under the sink sounded a little too familiar. She'd have to keep an eye on the men of the neighborhood.

The air turned cool and Victoria placed the fleece blanket around Heather's shoulders. The girl had yet to take a sip of her coffee; she simply stared at the lake. Victoria wrapped her arm around the child. "Drink. It'll make you feel better."

"I don't think coffee is going to solve my problems." Heather gave in and gulped the warm liquid. "Now, if only you had chocolate . . ." She held out the cup for a refill.

Victoria poured more coffee into the mug. A handful of Hershey's Kisses appeared from under the pashmina.

Heather looked at her questioningly.

"I'm a woman, a mother, and a grandmother," Victoria said.

Heather smiled weakly. "Thank you." She peeled the silver foil and popped the candy in her mouth.

"I hear you had a fight last night with a young man," Victoria said.

"Did you hear it all the way at your house?" Heather pulled a wrapper off another chocolate.

"No, but Sarah next door to you did, which means everyone knows by now." Victoria patted Heather's shoulder. "There aren't many secrets around here. We've known each other since the beginning of time. You're fresh blood, so you make for interesting dinner conversation."

"Great." Heather swirled the chocolate in her mouth and looked at the stars that emerged in the darkening sky. "Have you ever felt safe?"

Surprised by the question, Victoria didn't answer. Heather peeled the chocolate and pulled the blanket closer. A breeze brought the scent of Molly baking cherry pies.

Victoria looked toward the tree house. "As a child, I thought my daddy ruled the world. How could anything go wrong with him in charge? It wasn't until the war that I even understood fear. After that, safety felt confining. I think a part of me loved excitement and the unknown."

"At least you felt it once." Heather looked at her hands. "Got any more chocolate?"

Victoria handed Heather the bag. "My metabolism isn't what it used to be." Victoria looked at the chocolate. "But a few won't hurt the waistline."

Heather grabbed a handful of candy and returned the bag.

"Haven't you felt safe in your life?" Victoria asked.

"I don't know. Maybe when I was first with my fiancé." Heather sighed. "I mean my ex-fiancé."

"I'm sorry," Victoria said. "Was that what the fight was about last night?"

Heather nodded. "And I don't know if he actually made me feel safe. He helped me to make my dreams come true. But I felt . . . I don't know. Any woman would have killed for my life, but I felt as if any misstep could make it all fall out from under me. All I needed was to follow his plan and make certain I didn't leave my luggage around. I didn't even have to think about money, but then I started to let a bunch of little things bother me and I handled everything all wrong. God, I fucked up! Sorry, didn't mean to say that in front of you."

Victoria laughed. "I've heard worse. Said it too."

The blanket fell from Heather's shoulder and Victoria tucked it back.

"I'm worried I'm going to lose my career without him," Heather said.

"Why? Does he do the writing? Does he do the traveling?"

"No, but he's my agent, and when I'm stuck and can't write, he's great at talking it out with me. And I'm at a pivotal point in my career. I need him to get me to the next level. I don't know where to start and I thought I had a handle on things, but I don't know how to negotiate with a television studio or how to get a book deal. He's always handled those things. I thought we could still work together, but the way he acted last night . . . I don't know. I'm not certain I can do it without him."

"Did he tell you that?" Victoria asked.

Heather's hands began to shake. "It's true. He went to Harvard. I never finished college."

"Marriage is about unconditional love and acceptance. It's the place where you're beautiful whether you're wearing a dress or sitting around in a bathrobe. It's about a life of laughter and holding each other up through heartache. If that's not what your relationship was going to be, then you did the right thing by leaving," Victoria said.

Heather laughed. "I'm sorry, but that's your generation. Fairy tales and happily ever after don't exist anymore. Success—financial security—is the only way I'll feel safe."

"Heather, take it from an old woman, success doesn't create safety."

Heather handed Victoria the cup and blanket. "Thanks for the coffee and chocolate, but I need to go. You can't understand." She walked to her house, closed the door, and shut off the lights.

Victoria looked at Heather's house and thought, *The question, Heather, is how do I make you understand?*

~⚬~

The ocean waves crashed against Newport's shore as Tom walked in the sand, his jeans rolled to his knees, his feet frozen from the icy Atlantic and a bottle of Patrón in one hand.

Tom sat on the sand and opened the bottle of tequila. The smooth, clear liquid burned his throat. He lay back; the sand mixed into his hair and scratched his scalp as he listened to the ocean's steady rhythm. For the last five years since Annabelle's death, he'd come to the beach to find a way to be closer to her.

The memory of Annabelle's teenage voice came back to him. "You're a jerk," she'd yelled as they sat on the dock in Nagog. "I've been nice to you all summer and you've treated me like I'm a pest."

Swing music filled the air as the community celebrated the annual Labor Day bash. Tom was drinking a cold beer, taking in the last moments of freedom before he started his junior year at Harvard. The bonfire popped and hissed behind him, the smell of pine sap in the air.

"You're sixteen. I'm not interested in babies," he said.

"Fine, then kiss me. Prove you don't have feelings for me."

He stood. Her lip trembled when he put his arm around her waist and leaned close. Her breath smelled of apple pie and her blue eyes stared at him, reflecting both fear and longing. He felt her heart beating fast against his chest. With one arm he picked her up and threw her into the lake. The sound of the splash didn't cover her scream.

"That will cool you off." He laughed.

As she climbed from the water, blond hair stuck to her cheeks, the pink shirt clung to her breasts and he could see her white lace bra. She stormed off the dock swearing, her wet white shorts revealing lacy underwear.

Another memory quickly came: the year he graduated from Harvard; he went to the Memorial Day party in Nagog to put in his time. He'd planned to leave by ten to meet his college roommate at a bar in Boston. He was on the patio visiting with Molly when Annabelle appeared. Her yellow dress flowed over her hips and the low-cut neckline followed the lines of her cleavage. Tasteful, elegant, and the sexiest thing he'd ever seen.

She walked up to him and extended her delicate hand. "Dance with me, Tommy."

Mesmerized, he followed her to the dance floor. This time his hands trembled when he placed them around her curved waist. He stumbled and stepped on her toes. She didn't flinch, but led him into a slow waltz. He found the pattern Maryland had taught him. Together they glided across the floor.

"I hear you're graduating next week," Annabelle said.

"I am." He stared at her blue eyes. "I have a job in Boston working for a design build company. It will take me a few years to earn my architecture license and then I'm hoping to start my own firm."

"Woodward Architecture . . . it has a nice ring to it. You'll do it. I believe in you."

She smiled at him. A strange feeling began to build in his stomach, the need to bring that look to her face.

"I was just accepted into Juilliard's drama and dance program," she said. "I start summer workshop in two weeks. I want to be a dancer and have the lead role in a London musical. Ever since Grandma worked at Queens Theatre I've wanted to be on that stage."

He watched her eyes light with her dreams and her passion for theater. "Why do you love it so much?"

"There's something that happens when I dance. Thoughts cease to exist and I get lost in the movement and the energy from the audience. It's a rush like nothing else."

"Well, you've always had a knack for the dramatic," he teased her.

She punched his arm with mock anger. "What's that supposed to mean?"

"You've been walking around in tiaras pretending the world was a stage since you were little. I still remember how many times you bugged me, when you came to visit in the summer, to play movie star with you."

Annabelle's skin flushed red. "You remember that?"

He leaned into her, his lips brushing against her hair as he whispered in her ear, "I remember a lot of things, including the night I threw you in the lake. Do you still want to kiss me, Annabelle Rose?" He felt her quiver in his arms as electricity danced between them.

"I don't know, Tommy, maybe you're the one who needs to cool off tonight." She pulled back and sauntered toward the beach, her hips sending an invitation to join her. He followed, and when she reached the dock, he took a moment and stared at her in the moonlight: the curve of her shoulder, the gold of her hair, the seductive smile as she pretended not to notice his approach.

His hand went around her waist. With his other hand he lifted her fingers and brushed the inside of her wrist with his lips. Her breath caught and she turned toward him. He looked into her eyes and no longer saw the little girl or the teenager who'd come and gone from Nagog throughout his life. For the first time, he saw a woman he desired.

The cold ocean water washed over his bare feet. He could let the coming tide lift his body and carry him out past the large waves. Under the stars he could drift, the salt water buoying his body. Tonight was the seven-year anniversary of his proposal.

It was Annabelle's twenty-first birthday, and she and Victoria had flown in from London so she could celebrate with Tommy. For one year she'd been performing onstage as a dancer, limiting their time together. On the morning of her birthday, she'd awoken in her bedroom in the Rose home to dozens of gardenias, her favorite flower, and a large dress box. Victoria's silver Dior gown and Melissa's tiara had been tucked inside. A limousine had driven Annabelle to this spot at the ocean. The light from the moon reflected off her skin as she walked toward him, and the ocean breeze blew soft tendrils around her face as he greeted her with a kiss. Candlelight flickered on the table he'd set for dinner.

"May I have this dance?" He pulled her into a slow waltz, the cold sand squishing between their toes.

Once again his feet faltered from nerves. She took the lead until he could find his balance, but his legs buckled under him. He bent to one knee and took her hands in his.

"I want to spend my life kissing, fighting, laughing, loving, and growing old with you. You okay with that?" he asked.

"Since I was sixteen. What took you so long?" she said.

He took another drink of Patrón. The stars twinkled and he closed his eyes. He pictured Annabelle's smile. His lips moved in a repeated pattern as he whispered, "I miss you."

❧

Tom unlocked the door to his loft and threw the keys on the coffee table. It was two in the morning, he'd let the effects of Patrón wear off before driving home. He rubbed his eyes and entered the black-and-silver kitchen.

When Tom bought the abandoned warehouse on Providence harbor, the building had four floors filled with concrete, bricks, and dust. Round poles supported exposed steel beams. Dirt smudged the large windows and plywood covered the floors. Now the first level held seven retail shops; the second, an accounting firm; and the top levels, his office and home.

From the refrigerator he took out some milk and walked to the windows that overlooked the bay. The boats' lights reflected on the water. Teenagers walked along the harbor, playfully pushing and bumping into each other. He tilted back the container and chugged.

Tom sat on the leather couch and turned on the television, letting blue light illuminate his dark cave. Actors' voices chattered and he saw movement but couldn't focus. Memories continued to play.

He remembered the day six months after he proposed, when he'd awoken in the small one bedroom flat Annabelle had rented in London. He reached for her soft skin, but she wasn't in bed. He untangled the sheets and pulled on his shorts. In the morning light he watched her stretch her leg in an arabesque as she worked at her ballet bar in the living room. "Come back to bed," he said as he watched her leg quake with effort to hold the pose.

"Just a few more minutes. I can't get this right," Annabelle said as she arched her back farther, the small muscles in her back rippling with the exertion.

The woman didn't know how to quit. It didn't matter what

she tried to accomplish—from a new song to a dance move, she couldn't let it go until she achieved perfection.

"Just a little longer," Annabelle said.

"I thought you didn't like ballet," Tom said as he grabbed a bagel from the paper bag on the counter.

"I hate it. It's too slow, but the only way to be a great stage dancer is to practice ballet."

"You know, there is something called overtraining. Try not to practice yourself to death," he said.

It was Annabelle's motto in life—push through until you accomplished what you desired. The term "type-A personality" didn't seem strong enough to describe Annabelle's determination.

Her leg came down and she pliéd, then rose back onto her toes for another arabesque with the other leg. Her leg warmer shifted around her ankle and he saw the Ace bandage.

"It's not about practice this morning. I'm stiff from rehearsals and I need to move."

He came up behind her and wrapped his arms around her waist, interrupting her movements. "It *is* about practice, and it's because you want to be the best. Don't think I don't know how driven you are. It's one of the things I love about you."

She turned and kissed him. "It's not always going to be like this. It's just that right now there are so many opportunities, and if I can make my mark, then I have a chance at my dream."

"One of these days you should realize that you're already living your dream."

"I want the leading role just once. To have that perfect performance in front of a huge crowd."

"And I will be in the front row cheering you on, but remember you have people who think you're amazing just the way you are." He spun her slight figure around the room until they fell onto the couch with her on his lap. He cradled her in his arms and pinned her to him so that she couldn't get up.

"When did you hurt yourself?" he asked as he lifted the leg warmer.

She tried to squirm away, but he held her tight and looked into her eyes.

"It ached a bit when I was running this morning. I'm just being careful," she said.

"You've already gone running? How long have you been awake?"

"An hour or two."

He placed her on the couch and sat on the floor. He wrapped his hands around her ankle as if he could heal it with his touch. He unwrapped the bandage and saw the swollen tissue. "Annabelle, this is bad."

"It's just a strain." She smiled at him. "I've danced on worse."

"Promise me you will take at least a few days off." He climbed onto the couch and pulled her body over his. He cupped her chin. "I love this body and I would like to keep it safe and healthy for an entire lifetime. You're pushing too hard." He tickled her and she jumped away in laughter and then curled closer.

"I'll be more careful."

When he brought Annabelle to see the warehouse in Providence, she'd danced around the dusty space. "It's perfect. I can't believe you bought this for us. Can we build a loft for our bedroom? The ceilings are high enough. It will be like sleeping in a fort every night. Oh, and a dance studio. Will you build me a place to dance?"

She ran to the dirty square windows, the sunlight illuminating her pale skin. "We need at least five bedrooms for all the kids we'll have, but we should keep most of the space open for parties. And with your office right downstairs, I can pounce on you every time you decide to work late."

It took him a year to design and craft this place. The kitchen and living area took up a third of the space. Water cascaded down a ridged glass wall that separated the kitchen from the entertainment area, while giving the illusion of an open room. A wooden spiral staircase led to the bedroom he designed like a tree house. He used planks on the ceiling to create a warm log cabin feel. In the bathroom, he'd installed a tub under the large window so Annabelle could relax and stare at the harbor. It was their dream home.

Tom put the milk carton back in the refrigerator. He walked past the three bedrooms he'd built for their future children—empty now as they'd always been. The dance studio down the hall had never been used. He opened the door to the guest suite. Still dressed, he fell onto the bed and pulled the blanket over his legs. The city lights illuminated the room through the wall of windows.

Grandpa was right. He needed to move on. It had been five years since her death. His business, this place, all of it had been to provide the life he wanted to give Annabelle. After she passed, he continued to work nonstop in order to block out his loss. He'd achieved success in business, but it wasn't much of a life.

He thought about Heather and how her scent had affected him when they were moving boxes. He'd been a jerk that night and then again this afternoon. He hadn't meant to pick a fight with her. The poor woman was getting the worst of his personality, and he needed to make amends. There was something about her that brought out the worst in him. Or was it that she awakened in him a need, a desire that he thought had died along with Annabelle?

Memories couldn't touch his skin or make him laugh spontaneously. Pictures of his beloved didn't give him someone to share a meal or build a family with. At the end of a day, longing didn't create conversations or fights. Pushing away every woman in the world wouldn't bring Annabelle back, and holding on to the past didn't give real answers to why she'd died.

Heather was sassy, fiery, and sweet all at the same time. Her smile was cute and sexy. That afternoon on the deck he'd seen loneliness in her eyes and it had stirred something in him. He realized that thinking about her had forced him to begin to feel again.

CHAPTER 13

～❦～

The smell of apple cinnamon buns and fresh-baked bread filled the kitchen. Molly beat six eggs in a ceramic bowl, her belly pressed against the counter. In the cast-iron pan, bacon sizzled. Victoria sat at the round table sucking on a strawberry. The jacket of her jogging suit hung on the white chair. Her tank top showed off her muscular arms.

"It's such a good day," Molly said. She loved this time of year. During their morning walk, two bluebirds had chased each other from tree to tree. The bulbs she'd planted in the fall had bloomed in purples, reds, and yellows across her yard. Roses graced her entrance, their fragrance filled her living room.

Victoria twisted the green top off a strawberry. "Why don't we bring Heather some muffins and brownies? Maybe convince her to go shopping?"

"Hmmm." Molly knew Bill worried about Heather's impact on the community. And it was more than residual resentment from the party—there was a fear among her friends that their reign was ending.

Molly knew her children worried about her and Bill living on their own. Last year, her eldest son had even taken them on a tour of a senior housing facility. How could she explain to her children that she and Bill were fine, when this past winter had been so brutal? It seemed every month there'd been a funeral of an old acquaintance or a distant cousin. But that was life at this age—she couldn't afford to focus on mortality. Aside from a rare dizzy spell, she felt healthy.

Molly looked out the window to Heather's empty deck. The girl seemed lonely. There'd been no one to help her unpack her things or prepare her house. There'd been plenty of people at her party, but Molly hadn't seen anyone visit since that night. Victoria had told Molly about their conversation on the beach. From what Molly could see, this child needed the family Nagog could provide.

Molly placed the bacon on paper towels and poured the eggs into the pan. "We should buy her a housewarming gift. The consignment shop has a beautiful patio set."

"Who're you buying furniture for? One of the kids?" Bill limped into the kitchen, leaning on his cane.

Molly put her hands on his lower back and shoulder. "Hurting this morning? Sit. I'll get your arthritis medication."

The chair creaked under his weight. She kissed his forehead. The dark mole looked bigger. She'd have to make an appointment with the dermatologist; God knew Bill wouldn't bother unless she forced his hand. She opened the cabinet next to the refrigerator and sorted through the rows of orange bottles. She'd already placed his other medication next to his plate, but Bill didn't always need the anti-inflammatory.

"Here you go." She handed him a glass of fresh-squeezed orange juice along with the pill. "And the deck furniture is for Heather." Her hand went up before he could comment. "I know how you feel and that's not going to stop me." The eggs popped and she returned to the stove.

"I suppose this is your suggestion?" Bill said to Victoria as he shifted his weight and groaned. "And don't you have a kitchen of your own? Oh, that's right, you only know how to burn things."

"At least I know how to use a computer. You know, the box with the screen?" Victoria said.

"Play nice or I'll separate the two of you. And I won't feed you breakfast," Molly added to Victoria.

Victoria stuck out her tongue; Bill retaliated with a shaking fist. Molly placed the eggs, cinnamon rolls, butter, and bacon on the table. She smiled as she looked at the two of them. They'd been like brother and sister as kids, Bill's teasing had been Victoria's constant frustration. It hurt Bill more than he'd let on that Victoria hadn't been a part of their wedding, and his anger toward her for hurting Joseph only exacerbated that resentment. It took Joseph's marrying Barbara—and Molly's continued loyalty to Victoria—for Bill to come around and forgive her.

"You know, that furniture is going to encourage her to throw more parties." He picked up his paper and began to read the sports section.

Molly sat. She buttered a thick piece of homemade bread until the oil melted through. "Friendship is the answer. If she cares about the community, she won't disrupt it. And the party wasn't *that* bad. I remember you tying on a few in your younger years."

The sunroom door creaked open. "I was on the beach and I smelled bacon," Joseph said as he walked into the room. He stopped and stared at Victoria.

Molly looked at her friend. Her back had straightened and her cheeks were flushed. Electric static filled the air. "Joseph, come on in and sit." Molly stood and grabbed a plate. She placed it next to Victoria at the table.

"Good morning, Joseph," Victoria said and she picked up her coffee mug and sipped.

"Morning, Victoria." Joseph didn't take his eyes from her as he sat, but then he turned to Bill. "So how 'bout those Sox last night."

"Ridiculous game," Bill said. "Damn Sox had better get it together this season or it's going to be over before it even starts."

Molly watched Joseph and Victoria. They looked like two middle-schoolers at the lunch table, afraid to talk but aware of the close proximity. Yes, she thought again, friendship could heal any rift.

❧

The sound of knocking woke Heather. The soft warm cave of her bed enticed her to ignore whoever was at her front door. Insomnia had been her companion for the last week. George had approved her summer lake series, but she was finding it hard to write in her home office. It seemed that ideas came to her only at night, when she tried to sleep.

"I'm coming," she yelled, realizing she didn't have time to change out of the tank top and shorts she had slept in.

Victoria and Molly stood on her deck, smiling and waving. Molly held up a basket and Victoria followed with a thermos. "Heather, we have baked goods and coffee," Molly called. Heather shuffled to the door, squinting in the sunlight.

"I brought scones, cinnamon buns, and muffins," Molly chirped as she bustled into the room, set the basket on the coffee table and unfolded the white linen. "Oh, and I brought you brownies for later. A little sin from me to you." Her soft figure fell into the rocking chair, sending it swinging.

"This is Venezuelan dark roast, caffeinated this time, and I grabbed your paper." Victoria's hand shook, and the paper fell to the floor. "Sorry about that. Silly arthritis, but you don't want to hear about our maladies."

Heather looked away from Victoria's flushed skin. She gathered the loose newspaper sections from the floor. At the bottom of the pile she found a manila envelope without an address.

"Let me get some cups and plates," Heather said.

"Take your time. We know we barged in," Molly said.

In the kitchen, she ripped open the manila envelope and pulled out a church's bulletin with areas highlighted for Heather to read: Bible study hours; singles activities; and classes for conversion to Catholicism. *Sarah,* she thought. The woman wouldn't speak to Heather, but she was willing to save her soul.

Heather gathered plates, napkins, silverware, mugs, and milk, and returned to the living room. "I'm sorry, I don't buy butter or cream," Heather said as she put everything on the coffee table.

"That's all right, dear. Victoria would make us feel guilty for eating it." Molly put her hand over her mouth and whispered, "She's a health nut."

Victoria grabbed a muffin, broke off a piece, and popped it into her mouth as she sat in the overstuffed chair. "I eat butter now. I believe in whole foods. I've gotten away from processed products. Margarine is no better than eating plastic. I read—"

"Told you," Molly interrupted.

Victoria rolled her eyes.

"Is any of this considered healthy?" Heather asked as she sat on the couch.

Victoria laughed. "Molly doesn't know the meaning."

Molly huffed.

"I'm not saying you're fat. You're a wonderful baker who doesn't sacrifice taste for the waistline," Victoria said.

"Call me fat if you'd like, my husband loves my body. And no, dear, every bite is filled with love and at least five hundred calories. So eat up and enjoy, for tomorrow you can diet again. Victoria has managed to be my friend her entire life, and my cooking hasn't affected her skinny rear," Molly said.

Heather bit into a blueberry muffin, the warm, soft sugar waking her taste buds and bringing back safe memories of her grandmother's home: warm linens, brushed hair after a long bath, and delicious baked goods.

"I've never tasted a muffin this good. Please, don't tell me what you put in this," Heather said.

Molly's face brightened. She handed Heather coffee. "Victoria and I were noticing you don't have furniture for your deck."

"We'd like to take you shopping," Victoria said.

"I'd love to, but money's tight after everything I spent on furnishing this house."

"Well, that's fine, because it's a housewarming gift," Molly said.

Heather was taken aback. "I can't let you do that."

"Of course you can," Victoria said.

"It's too much. You barely know me," Heather said with a slight flutter to her voice as she choked on emotions. These women had cleaned her home, helped her paint, and now they wanted to buy her furniture.

"You're part of the Nagog family now, and I hate to tell you, but it's a life sentence." Molly laughed. "Just ask Victoria."

Heather put the muffin down and ran a hand through her knotted hair, suddenly embarrassed by her unkempt appearance. "I still need to take a shower and—"

"Go ahead. We'll wait, and we won't take no for an answer," Victoria said.

"And I would love a ride in your cute little car," Molly said.

Heather went upstairs and turned on the shower. The sounds of Molly and Victoria talking downstairs gave her a feeling of comfort. Being mothered for the first time since early childhood felt strange but good. Heather stripped down and stepped into the shower, then a scream ripped from her lips, she fumbled against the door, and stepped out soaking wet.

"Heather, are you okay?" Victoria called from the stairwell.

"Yes, but I think there might be something wrong with my water heater," she yelled. The shower dial was turned to hot, but the water was ice cold. She wrapped her body in a fluffy white towel and then fiddled with the shower knob trying to force hot water from the showerhead.

"I'll have Molly get Bill to come take a look. It probably needs to be reset. It hasn't been used in years," Victoria said from the hallway.

"Thank you," Heather said. What more could go wrong? She was beginning to feel like her house was haunted or that someone was sabotaging her living space. But both ideas were ridiculous.

❧

The Mobil station on the corner looked out of place, its blue-and-red fiberglass sign an intrusion on the colonial ambiance of Littleton town center. The church bell rang out as Heather waited at a stoplight. In the park, children played tag around the white gazebo while their mothers sat on the park bench socializing. The old hotel with the wraparound porch had been converted to apartments and retail stores. The proprietors sat on the front steps sipping Cokes out of the can while they fanned their faces. *It's like I've gone back to the 1950s,* Heather thought.

The women directed Heather to the consignment shop and she pulled into the driveway. The Victorian home had been painted dark purple, green, and blue to accentuate its architectural details. Deck furniture, an old wishing well, weather vanes, and a spinning wheel dotted the front lawn.

"Over here." Molly motioned to the side yard as they got out of the car. "Isn't it in beautiful condition?"

Six teak chairs with armrests surrounded the beautiful wooden table. A blue umbrella protected the smooth red wood from the sun. Heather ran her fingers along the curve of the chair. She picked up the price tag and her throat constricted. "I thought this was a consignment shop."

"Oh, don't look at that." Molly took the tag.

Heather punched her heels into the soft earth. "I can't let you buy this. It's too much."

"Nonsense. Think of it as our investment in Nagog's beautification. During our evening walks we'll get to look at it," Molly said.

"Do you like it?" Victoria asked.

The furniture looked like it belonged on the cover of a home magazine. The two women waited for her response with anticipated smiles.

"It's gorgeous."

Molly bounced with excitement to the front door of the shop. "I'll have them deliver it this week. You'll have to plan a dinner party to christen it."

Victoria put her arm around Heather and steered her to follow.

"Victoria, I can't . . ."

"Darling, when someone gives you a gift, it's best just to say thank you," Victoria said. "We're trying to make you happy, not uncomfortable."

Heather smiled. "Okay. From the bottom of my heart, thank you. I love it."

When they returned to Nagog Drive, Agatha and Sarah were at the picnic table in the front yard knitting and they scowled as the women stepped from Heather's car.

Heather turned to Molly and Victoria. "Would you like to come in for a brownie? I have skim milk. It has to cancel out some of the calories."

"Skim milk won't do. I'll be right back," Molly said, and headed for her house.

Victoria and Heather went inside and Heather curled onto the couch, the big white pillow across her lap. "So what's the deal between you and the knitters?"

"Deal?" Victoria looked around. "You really did a lovely job on this room. The pale green is perfect and the furnishings are great, but I do think you need some accents. I have three full boxes of decorations from my old house that I can't use. You're welcome to look through and pick out anything you like."

"That would be great. Thank you," Heather said. "And did you notice that I thanked you instead of protesting? I did listen to your wisdom."

Victoria smiled as she looked out the window to where Sarah and Agatha were gathering their things.

"Do I need to get out the Hershey's Kisses and decaffeinated coffee to get you to answer my question?" Heather asked.

Victoria sat in the overstuffed chair. "Jealousy is a powerful emotion. Same with anger and resentment. All three combined can't be undone."

"Are they jealous of you?" Heather asked.

"I know it's hard to believe, but there was a time when people admired my life. I thought I had years to make amends, but some mistakes are too big."

"And some people can't accept those who stand out," Molly finished, walking into the room, a glass bottle from the farm up the road in hand. "Let's dig in."

Molly passed Heather a thick brownie and a cup. The milk tasted like cream, and the gooey dessert melted in her mouth. "Molly, we can't be friends. Your baking is going to cost me too many dress sizes."

"Better to have sweet friendships and big thighs than be skinny and never taste the goodness of life. That's what my mother always told me," Molly said.

"So, Victoria, why are the knitters jealous?" Heather asked.

Victoria focused on the brownie, nibbling the corners. "I left Nagog to try my hand at becoming an actress and I didn't come home very often."

"Were you famous?" Heather leaned forward.

"Like Ingrid Bergman," Molly said.

"Really? Like *Casablanca*?" Heather asked.

"Something like that," Victoria said.

"Were you in that movie?" Heather asked.

"*Casablanca* came out when I was a teenager," Victoria said. "If you're going to hang with us cool old ladies, you're going to have to learn about the classics. I'll make you a deal. I'll teach you about movies if you tell me where you shop. Those shoes are exquisite."

"Deal. I can't believe you were a movie star. What was it like?"

"In my time, it was all about the glamour. Life was sequins and diamonds, and extravagant parties with gowns and tuxedoes," Victoria said.

"Tell me everything," Heather said as she took another bite of the brownie. "How did you break into the movie business?"

"Hard work," Victoria said. "My first apartment was a dump. I worked as a receptionist, which drove my mother to complete heartache. Of course, she never knew about the years I danced at a dinner theater. She would've thought I was a whore dancing for money, but the place was classy and elegant."

"How long did it take you to make it big?" Heather asked.

"I don't know that I ever made it 'big.' I spent years going to casting calls and dance tryouts competing against hundreds of other hungry actresses, but it was modeling that gave me my break."

"Really?"

"It hadn't been my dream, but the first time I saw my picture larger than life on a billboard, I stopped my car and simply stared for hours, shocked that everyone that passed it would see my face."

"You had your own billboard?"

"For Coca-Cola."

"Wow," Heather said. "So when did you start doing movies?"

"I got my first role five years after I moved to Hollywood. It was three lines and a main dance number that took about a minute. Of course, the filming of that dance took two days to get it perfect. Patience is the one thing you learn when you're an actress. With the lighting changes, the cameramen not getting the right angle, the director feeling that someone in the background cast a shadow somewhere that wasn't flattering, people tripping . . . we did thousands of takes. I think that's why they stopped making movies as musicals—it was too much work to get the stages set.

"But back then, the studio sets were romantic and elegant. The costumes were handmade works of art. After a long day of filming, we would hit the bars and drink until three in the morning. It was a fun time in my life. What I wouldn't give to do it all again."

"How many movies were you in?" Heather leaned forward entranced by Victoria's past.

"Hundreds. As a dancer I could be cast in different projects at the same time and I would race from one studio to the next for rehearsal and costume fittings. When movies began to feature fewer musical numbers, I traveled all over the world doing lower budget films with starring roles. But my biggest films were always as the supporting actress."

"But she always stole the show," Molly said. "*And* she won an Oscar! It was so much fun to see her movies at the theater."

Heather nibbled at her brownie. "Wow, an Oscar? When did you stop performing?"

"I stopped filming after my granddaughter was born. I missed the dancing and singing, so I switched to theater and performed in London for a few years. When my daughter passed away from cancer, I stopped working to take care of my granddaughter."

"Victoria, I'm sorry. I didn't realize you'd lost your daughter."

Victoria waved her hand to ward off the conversation and they moved on to other subjects. The sky turned dark and Heather turned on the floor lamps to illuminate the room. They ordered pizza and Heather opened a bottle of wine. Soon all three women were sharing.

"You're a young woman, a new generation," Victoria said. "Much more open, more liberal. I thought . . . I thought you might have some advice on how to spice up a sex life."

The wineglass knocked against Heather's front tooth. She choked and the wine caught in her windpipe.

"Victoria, you're embarrassing the girl." Molly jumped up and patted Heather's back. "Put your arms over your head, dear."

"We're all women," Victoria said.

"We're old enough to be her grandmothers," Molly said.

"Well, she has to know you don't give up sex as you age. Are we so repulsive you can't imagine us being intimate? You know, ugly people of all ages do it too. It's not just for the pretty ones like you," Victoria said. "How do you think we *became* grand-mothers?"

"Victoria, do you remember how repressed our mothers were? No one discussed money, never mind sex," Molly said.

"Oh, I have a good story for you," Victoria said. "I'm not certain which of the girls told Sarah this, but she came to our room at school and asked me if I wanted to know how a woman became pregnant. Well, of course I said yes."

"What did she tell you?" Molly asked.

"We were curled up in bed, and she whispered, 'The man takes a razor and cuts the woman's belly open. Then he places a seed inside and sews her up.' That's when Sarah and I decided we would never have children."

"How old were you?" Heather asked as she caught her breath.

"Fifteen," Victoria said.

Heather's mouth fell open.

"Honey, you have to remember we thought *War of the Worlds* was a news broadcast," Victoria said.

"Oh yes, people were jumping out of windows, killing themselves just like the day the stock market crashed," Molly said.

"So how did you find out the truth?" Heather took another sip of wine to soothe her throat after coughing.

"When you met the man you were going to marry, he usually explained it on your wedding night," Molly said. "They talked to other men, read books, and I think their anatomy has a homing device. It knows how to find its way.

"I remember the first time Bill asked me . . . to, you know . . . down there." Molly motioned to her lap.

Heather shook her head in disbelief.

"I believe you kids call them 'blow jobs' these days," Victoria said. "And yes, some older people still enjoy it . . . they just have to ensure their dentures are secured properly. Or not in at all."

Heather covered her face with the pillow and sank to the floor. "Oh, God, don't tell me these things. I'm very visual."

"So, Molly, what were you saying about the first time you gave Bill a—"

"Don't say it again," Heather cried out in a muffled plea from under the pillow.

"All right, we'll call it fellatio. Go on, Molly."

Heather dug her face into the couch.

"Well, I'm not as good of a girl as I come across. I always

wanted to please Bill, and he was a wild one. When we started dating at fifteen—"

"You dated him at fifteen?" Heather said.

"Well, courtship. He was always trying to sneak kisses and hold my hand. Of course, we never did anything serious that would get us good little Episcopalians in trouble. Well, most of us didn't, but Victoria was wearing lipstick by twelve. And for your information, Heather, wearing lipstick or your father's shirt tied up around your midriff was a sign of being loose."

"A shirt and lipstick. You're kidding? I was wearing short shorts and half shirts by age nine." Heather looked at Victoria. "Wild woman. Was it red lipstick?"

Molly answered for her. "I could tell you some stories about her time in Los Angeles, or her European adventures. If she ever gets on your case about the men you date, let me know and I'll give you plenty of ammunition to fight back."

"You were telling us about Bill asking you for a certain something?" Victoria said.

"Oh, yes. It was our first anniversary, and Bill told me that if I kissed him down there it would help me to get pregnant."

Heather lay on the couch and threw the blanket over her head. "It's a wonder your whole generation reproduced."

"Are you kidding? The Pill didn't become available until the sixties. All I can say is, thank God for small miracles. I love every one of my children, but having babies until I was fifty, like my mother, was unappealing. And I enjoy my marital bed.

"So, getting back to my first anniversary. I didn't know what to do. Bill told me to treat it like an ice cream cone. I was young and pretty and had a curvy, tight little body. Don't I miss that figure."

"You're sidetracking, dear." Victoria placed a hand on Molly's arm.

"Yes, well, I decided a little ice cream might help my nerves and give me something to focus on. It worked for me, but poor Bill. It was years before he asked again. That ice cream nearly gave him frostbite."

Heather threw off the blanket and sat up. "What will make you stop?"

"Give us your best tip," Victoria said.

Could Heather tell them what was going through her mind? It was the one sex secret Gina had shared, and she wasn't sure it was for the elderly. "Fine. But we never discuss this again."

CHAPTER 14

Early-morning dew soaked through her sandals, the scent of sap filled the crisp air, as Victoria made her way toward the beach. She stepped onto the dock. The lake was still. At this hour the community was silent, and no lights had been turned on in her friends' homes.

She knew better than to dip her toe in the water, the cold temperature would convince her to turn back. Once, when she was a teenager, she'd tried to walk slowly into the water at this time of morning but never got past her thighs. Morning swims had to be done with one quick plunge. She unzipped her velvet sweatshirt and matching pants, exposing her torso in the yellow one-piece suit, and left her clothes in a folded pile on the dock. Before she could change her mind, she dove into the cold water, her lungs constricting with the frigid temperature.

Victoria surfaced and treaded water moving her muscles to warm them. She looked to Maryland's, now Heather's home, and stared at the upstairs window where she knew the girl slept. The thought of Heather tucked under a soft blanket brought her comfort.

The previous day with Heather had given Victoria the strength to return to life. The company had brought laughter and memories without pain, and she realized she was tired of being a woman locked in the past, barely living.

It had been months since she'd exercised. With years of practice she pumped her legs and swept her arms in graceful arcs, water droplets falling from her skin as she swam away from the dock. With her face in the water the world around her sounded tinny. She could hear her heart beating faster with the exertion. At first her muscles screamed in protest and her bones creaked and groaned after months of disuse. She fought, knowing that the only way through the discomfort was to keep going.

The sun rose overhead and illuminated the fog with golden light. In the middle of the lake she floated and caught her breath. With her hands overhead and her toes pointed to the lake bottom she sank into the dark water, then with a quick burst of movement, rose and came back to the surface. She laughed, then repeated it, falling and rising in the water, feeling weightless as she twirled in the darkness and light. The rhythmic dance of her youth made her feel alive.

For a quick second the question flashed through her mind. *What right do I have to feel joy?* She stilled the voice in her head. *Not today. Let me have one day without my grief.*

The fog began to lift and she could see the other side of the lake. The distance between Nagog's beach and the woods on the other side of the water was approximately forty laps in a pool. Victoria floated on her back, staring at the blue sky through the last of the low clouds. Her mind brought her back to the summer she and Annabelle had spent in Nagog when her granddaughter was a teenager.

Victoria was sixty-three when Annabelle turned sixteen, and raising her alone in Southern California had been challenging. The child had become obsessed with boys, clothing, socializing, and rushing ahead to adulthood. Victoria worried about the tiny outfits and the boy she'd seen Annabelle necking with on the couch when Victoria came home early one day. Instead of letting her spend the summer with her friends, Victoria had packed up the infuriated Annabelle and headed to Nagog.

"I can't believe you're doing this to me. I'm going to lose an entire summer of theater and dance classes," Annabelle yelled in the first-class cabin. "How am I going to get into Juilliard if I can't practice?"

"You're being obstinate. A proper lady acts with dignity and grace," Victoria said through clenched teeth as she pulled her seat belt tight.

"Well, I don't want to be a proper lady. I want to be a performer," Annabelle said, and placed her headphones over her ears. They had arrived in Nagog in silent fury. Annabelle put on her string bikini, the forbidden one, and smiled at Victoria, daring her to restart the fight. When she returned for dinner, her eyes were distant and dreamy. "So, Tommy Woodward, does he have a girlfriend?" she'd asked.

Annabelle changed that summer in a way Victoria hadn't expected. Away from the drama of Southern California, the teenager spent her days on the beach with the other Nagog grandchildren. For once, her life was about roasting marshmallows around the bonfire, parties on the patio, swimming in the lake, and shopping trips with Victoria in Boston. They visited museums and went to the theater. A childish innocence pinked in Annabelle's cheeks.

A flock of geese flew over her bringing Victoria back to the present. She turned and swam hard toward the opposite side of the lake. She arrived and climbed up the rickety ladder on the poorly built dock and sat on the rotting wood. A white crane stood on a log off to her right, its graceful neck curved. It reminded her of a ballerina, of Annabelle. It was as if Victoria's mind was a record player on skip and she couldn't move the needle out of the groove. No part of her wanted to forget, but in order to move forward, she knew she had to find a way to listen to the rest of the album.

⁓◦⁓

Joseph walked along the stained wooden dock; its rails creaking under his weight. He came to the end and noticed the large purple towel. The fog had lifted and he saw the smooth ripples of movement in the water. He turned to walk away, but then changed his mind and placed his tackle box on the dock. The fishing pole in hand, he readied the hook as he watched Victoria swim, her arms moving like a graceful dancer.

Victoria had stayed away from Nagog for eight years after Melissa's death. From then on, Victoria's visits became more frequent. At least three times per year, they'd grace the community with their presence on their way to Europe or on trips to prospective colleges and drama schools. When Annabelle moved to London after attending Juilliard, Victoria floated in and out of the community between visits to see Annabelle in London and trips home to Malibu. Whenever Annabelle came to Nagog to spend time with Tommy, Victoria also returned. Five years passed as Joseph's heart felt tortured, never knowing when she would show up or how long she would stay.

But then Tommy and Annabelle announced their engagement and Victoria decided to renovate the Rose home and take up permanent residence in Nagog. Maybe she'd been oblivious to her friends' resentment as she danced around the community talking about Annabelle's success as an actress and the wedding plans, but if she noticed she gave no heed to her neighbors' emotions.

At that time, Joseph decided it was in his best interest to let his feelings go. Victoria forced a friendship holding him in lengthy conversations when they bumped into each other on walks. Whenever he fished in the morning, she'd swim up to the dock and her laughter filled the air as she teased him about not actually catching any fish. As the year passed, he felt he'd finally let go of his attraction to her.

Then one night, at the annual Memorial Day party, two months before Annabelle and Tommy's wedding, he realized he'd been a fool to think his feelings had changed. He'd set up a studio to take pictures of the grandchildren, and Victoria had watched as he'd taken Annabelle's portrait. Joseph didn't need to direct her poses as she flashed her big baby blues and tossed her hair.

"I'm going to grab Tommy," Annabelle said, jumped off the stool, and ran outside.

"I can't imagine where she gets all that flair," Joseph teased Victoria. They laughed, and memories of when they'd been teenagers danced between them.

In the small studio space he found he couldn't breathe with her so close. He turned his back to her and organized his camera equipment. A soft touch against his arm made him look up. Memories moved between them like electrical currents jumping from metal: he could hear her laughter as he threw her in the lake the summer before he'd left for the war, the closeness of their lips at the dance when they hadn't noticed the music had stopped.

Joseph looked away, shame flushing his skin. Barbara stood in the doorway, hurt apparent on her face. Victoria walked past her, head hung low to avoid her gaze.

That night he went to the beach where he'd proposed. Victoria was already sitting on the log, throwing stones. He listened to the plunk each rock made as it hit the water. He loved his wife and cherished his children. He was wrong to be here.

"I can't leave her," he said when she looked up and saw him standing behind her. "She's the mother of my children and the woman I built my life around. But why can't I let you go?"

Victoria walked to him. She tried to apologize, but he stopped her. Their heads bowed together. Shock waves of teenage love singed his nerves.

Victoria took his hand and placed it on her heart. No outsider would've considered it infidelity, but Joseph knew better. After that, they avoided each other again.

Two months later, Annabelle died. After the funeral, he found Victoria at their private beach. The emptiness in her eyes as she stared at the water broke his heart. All the light, the exuberance that was Victoria had left. Without hesitation, he wrapped her in his arms and held her tight, hoping she'd cry and release the pain. Not even a whimper came from her lips.

For the next week, about the time of day Annabelle had collapsed on the beach, Joseph would see Victoria walk across his backyard and knew where she was headed. He followed, not wanting her to face her grief alone.

One day, as he walked back with Victoria's hand in his, Barbara stood on the path. Victoria let go of his fingers and moved past Barbara without a word.

"You're in love with her," Barbara said. She'd stood, her white hair pulled back in a barrette, a yellow Kodak envelope shaking in her grasp.

"No. She's an old friend in pain, and I'm just trying to comfort her."

Barbara's lip quivered. "I can't do this anymore. All these years I felt plain and ugly whenever she was near. When she came home that first time, I couldn't believe that I was going to meet Victoria Rose, the model and actress. When you didn't introduce us, I thought you were ashamed of me, and that's why you looked so sullen."

"Barbara . . ."

She put her hand up. "No, I've waited too long to say these things. Whenever she came around, you retreated. I would look at you across the dinner table and you'd be lost in a daydream. You don't think I knew where your mind took you? I couldn't compete with a movie star, but she was more than that to you."

"I love you and our family. I didn't know you felt this way," Joseph said.

Barbara held up the envelope. "Fifteen years ago I found a canister of film you'd hidden. I knew what it might be, but I never developed it. But now . . . after Victoria renovated her home and took up residence to be closer to Annabelle and Tommy . . . after she danced around this community singing the wonders of their wedding plans, and now that her pain has taken over this community like she's the only person that has ever suffered loss . . ." She drew a shaky breath.

"I've watched you sneak off to be with her, pretending that you're going for a walk. I tell myself I shouldn't be jealous of a woman who's lost so much . . . but something snapped in me. So I developed the film."

From the envelope she grabbed the images of Victoria and Annabelle in the tree house and threw them at his feet.

"I was following a hummingbird when I came upon them," Joseph said. "It was a moment, that's all."

"And what about Memorial Day?" Barbara asked.

He shook his head. "Old friends remembering."

"No. Those are the lies I told myself. You were ashamed to develop those pictures and we both know why."

He placed his hand on Barbara's arm.

"Please, don't." She moved away, her hands creating a wall between them. "Times were different when we married. People didn't get divorced. We've had a decent life, and I've loved you more than my words can express. You gave me my children and you were a good father. But I won't spend my last years being a burden to someone."

The next day, his children had come to gather their mother's things.

At the time, Joseph knew he should've stopped Barbara, but he turned his focus to Victoria instead, hoping his love could break through her grief. Days later she left without saying good-bye.

He pulled in his fishing line as Victoria swam toward him. The ripples in the water came closer and his heart beat faster. With a trained hand, he cast his line off to the side of the dock away from Victoria. The bobber plunked into the lake and then there was nothing to do but wait.

She emerged in a bright yellow suit, her shoulders strong and firm, her legs dripping with water. "Morning," she said as she grabbed her towel and wrapped it around her body.

"Morning. Good swim?" The bobber floated toward him and he reeled in the line and recast.

"It was refreshing. Made me feel alive again. Like you said

last winter, at this age, if we don't keep moving we might not be able to start again."

"It was a brutal winter." He tried to keep his back to her as she toweled off, but the bobber kept floating toward shore, and he needed to cast the line into the deep of the lake. With the line reeled in again, he turned and saw her leaning over to pull on her sweatpants. The long lines of her body still made him feel like that young man who'd watched her his entire childhood.

"In March I thought I'd die of hypothermia without ever feeling sunlight again." She laughed and then looked up and caught him staring.

"That's your California blood," he said as he focused on his fishing pole and line. "You're going to need to toughen up if you plan to stay this time." The air between them thickened. He hadn't meant his words to be harsh. He knew the talk that went through the community—that she wasn't here to stay—and now he'd told her that he had the same opinion. He changed the subject. "It's going to be interesting having a young woman living here. I have to admit, the way they danced shocked me. In our day, I was happy if my hand slid to your waist for a second."

Victoria nodded. "It started when the movie *Dirty Dancing* came out. I believe they call it grinding or grooving now . . . something like that. Hollywood has changed. I think it's trying to convince young women to act like strippers."

Joseph smiled. "I remember a time when the press said your Coca-Cola advertisements were immoral."

Victoria laughed and covered her face. "If only they knew that just a few decades later the thong would be invented."

The fishing line was finally where he wanted it. He knelt onto the dock and sat, his bare feet dangling over the edge. He expected her to leave so she could change into dry clothing, but instead she sat next to him.

"Do you mind?" she asked. "It's such a beautiful morning."

"No, I don't mind," he said.

The lake returned to stillness and he could hear the sound of her breathing. He looked to the trees next to his home. The sun illuminated the last of the mist evaporating from the ground and created a mystical glow.

"Joseph," Victoria said. "I'm here to stay this time. I know you don't have any reason to believe me, but I sold my home in Malibu. I'm not going anywhere."

"Victoria, we both know that your spirit has always been too big for this place. It's okay if you need to leave again."

She placed a hand on his arm. "I'm sorry I didn't say good-bye after Annabelle's death."

"Victoria, it's water under the bridge."

Victoria looked to the Dragone home. "Not according to Sarah."

"When did you start caring about what other people think?"

"You tried to take care of me. I don't know if you'll ever understand how much that meant." A tear moved down her cheek. Instinctively, his hand came up and brushed it away. "You've been the one to wipe away so many of my tears, and for that I'm truly grateful . . . I'll let you fish in peace. Thank you for listening." She stood and walked away.

Though he tried to focus his attention on the bobber, he turned and watched her leave. It was something he'd done before, and no matter what she promised, he was almost certain she'd leave again.

Victoria stood in the lobby of Tommy's office and marveled at the beautiful mixture of polished woods that fanned out in a circle on the floor. Through a glass wall she could see a dozen architects on stools as they worked at drafting tables and on computers. The pretty young receptionist picked up the phone and dialed an extension. "Mr. Woodward, I'm sorry to bother you, but Victoria Rose is here to see you."

The door to the left of the receptionist burst open. Panicked, Tommy raced forward. "What's wrong?"

She placed her hands on his shoulders to calm him. "Everyone's okay. I should've called. Thomas is fine."

A sigh of relief came from his lips as he hugged her into his large frame. She leaned back and placed her hand on his face. For the first time since she'd returned to Nagog, she took a close look at him. There were fine lines of pain around his eyes that hadn't been there when she left five years ago. The last few months, she'd hidden in her home when she saw his truck, justifying it by thinking that a visit would intrude on Tommy's time with his grandfather. It had taken her too long to make this trip.

"Come into my office. Cynthia, could you get us some coffee?"

"Of course."

Victoria looked around Tommy's office. Fine woodwork curled around the room like delicate art. "This craftsmanship belongs in a museum."

"Thank you. Let me take your jacket."

"I'm fine." Victoria walked around the room, touching the carved wood. Large glossy prints of the homes Tommy had designed lined the walls. To anyone else's eye, the bright images would have detracted from the small frames on the shelves, but Annabelle's smile had a magnetic power over Victoria's heart.

She held a picture. Tom couldn't have been more than ten. He stood at his workbench with hammer in hand, tongue stuck out in concentration. Six-year-old Annabelle wore a tiara and boa as she watched him work. Victoria petted the frame. "I remember how she drove you crazy."

"In more ways than one." Tommy sat on the couch, his arms spread across the back of the furniture, his legs crossed.

Victoria looked at him, so handsome and successful. He had the kindest heart of anyone she knew. "How have you been?"

"I'm good," he said. "Work is crazy, but it's better than the alternative."

"You eat, and take care of yourself?" she asked.

Cynthia walked in carrying a tray with coffee mugs and cream and sugar. She placed it on the table and moved away. "There are muffins, but would you like me to run out for something else?"

Tommy looked to Victoria to answer. "No, thank you, but it's very sweet of you to offer."

"It's my pleasure," she said as she walked to the door. "Mr. Woodward, would you like me to hold your calls?"

"Yes, please."

"She's very young," Victoria said.

"And I'd be lost without her," he said as he poured her coffee and added a splash of milk remembering how she took it. "Most days she's the reason I remember to eat."

Victoria took the cup. "I know your grandfather is very proud of you, but also worried."

"I'm fine," he said as he sipped at his black coffee.

"You work too hard, kind of like someone I once knew," Victoria said.

"I guess we had that in common," he said.

"Or is it because you fell in love with her and wanted to give her everything her heart desired? I know part of the reason you bought this building was to give her a good life." He was silent and she took his large hand in both of hers. Annabelle had said the scars on his fingers from years of woodwork were like splashes of paint on an artist's skin. "How are you really?"

"I miss her," he said.

"She'd want you to be happy and to move on."

"Are we talking about the same Annabelle?" he laughed.

Victoria smiled. "Okay, maybe she was selfish, she spent most of your relationship in another state or across the ocean, but she loved you. And though she might find a way to throw arrows from the other side at the women you date, I know she wouldn't want you to spend the rest of your life alone."

"And what about you, Victoria?" he asked as he looked into her eyes. "Can you move on?"

"This isn't about me." She patted his hand. "I'm old and I've lived my life. I have time to lick my wounds, but you've done that long enough. Molly tells me that Thomas says you don't date and all you do is work."

"I have a company to run. There isn't much time for a social life."

"Well, I just happen to know a lovely young woman who lives right next door to your grandfather."

"So this is a setup?"

"Don't think of it like that. I'm just saying that Heather's talented, beautiful, and a travel writer for the *Globe*. Right now she's single and, from what I can tell, a little lonely." Victoria was surprised at the boldness of her words. Who was she to speak of moving on, when she herself had such a hard time facing the future without Annabelle?

"From what I see, Heather has a great life with lots of friends and parties. She doesn't need me."

"You're wrong. Most nights she sits alone working in her office." She looked at him as if to say, *Like you*. "I'm just asking you to check in on her when you visit Thomas."

"I'll think about it."

Victoria sipped her coffee to allow her time to form her next words. "I'm sorry I didn't say good-bye five years ago. I was a coward."

"Victoria, I understood. You were hurting."

"As were you," she said. "I miss seeing you."

"I've wanted to visit, but I didn't know—"

"—if it would be too painful when we both miss her so deeply. I know." She smiled. "You're always welcome in my home. I hope you know that. I promise I'll have Molly cook so you don't have to endure my food."

With that he laughed and she squeezed his hand. She hoped he'd be okay, that they both would.

❧

Tom tried to focus on his work after Victoria left, but memories plagued him. He picked up the picture of Annabelle from his desk, one he'd taken during a walk in Hyde Park in the spring-time. In the photo she laughed as the wind whipped her dress. She never strolled; she bounced—a springy skip as she looked at the world in wonder. She loved to spin with her arms out to the side feeling the cool air on her skin.

He placed the photo on his desk. It was his fault that Annabelle wasn't with him. The day he took the picture he'd known something was wrong. He'd tried to keep her inside, bribing her with movies so she'd rest. She'd performed in three shows the days before, but sitting still wasn't her strength. It was a sunny day, and she'd felt the urge to explore.

When she suddenly stopped, mid-bounce, and covered her eyes with her palms while shaking her head, he reached out to hold her steady. "You okay?"

"Yeah, just a head rush." She took a deep breath. "I think it passed. I'm fine."

Her skin looked as pale as her hair. "Why don't we go home and relax?"

"But you promised we'd go to the National Gallery." She wrapped her hands around his arm and smiled. "And I have a craving for a cupcake from Covent Garden. I feel fine."

He lived for her smile and he couldn't deny her what she desired. He'd been so busy trying to give her the perfect life and make her happy that he hadn't seen what was right in front of him.

But Victoria wanted him to move on. Everyone did.

He looked at the work on his desk and the exhaustion grew. The thought of sitting on the beach in Nagog stargazing made him think of Heather.

He opened his browser, searched for the *Globe*'s website, and clicked on "Solo Female Traveler." A picture of Heather in a black dress appeared at the top of the page. He scrolled down and began to read.

While visiting Africa I learned a little about the mating customs of monkeys. One day while sitting by the pool reading a book at Mfuwe Lodge in Zambia, a monkey came down from the tree and sat in the chair next to me. I was frightened by the close proximity, but he looked at me with gentleness and stared as he rubbed his hands. I tried to ignore his presence, assuming he'd return to his tree, but instead he settled on the chair, crossed his legs mimicking my posture, and pretended to read a book. As I turned pages, he copied my actions.

Another monkey jumped onto the chair and tried to usurp my first suitor's territory. The two battled, screaming at one another until the second monkey retreated.

My suitor turned his attention to me and puffed up his chest in pride. I guess he decided that he'd won my love because he moved toward my chair. I backed away, my muscles tightening as I put my arms up in defense.

In the end, I'd hurt his feelings and he turned away. From up in the tree I heard the sad sounds of rejection coming from my sweet monkey.

Tom laughed as he read the column. He could picture Heather sunning in her little shorts as the monkey tried to woo her. He continued to read back copies of her column, getting caught up in her adventures. Her childlike wonder at the places she described reminded him of Annabelle in a small way. He'd been avoiding Nagog and Heather, but now he wanted to hear her stories in person. Maybe Victoria was right: it was time to move on, if only to make a new friend.

CHAPTER 15

The gears on Heather's small car screamed as she tried to downshift and missed the notch. The road to Nagog was dark and she clicked on the high beams, wiping tears from her cheeks. It had been a grueling day. First, Charlie had been at her meeting with George at the *Globe,* where the two men had discussed her career as if she weren't even in the room. It had been the first encounter with Charlie since their blowout at the party.

George had left early that night and hadn't been privy to their fight, but Heather was certain he'd heard about it from coworkers. The office was thick with tension as Charlie told George that it would be at least another year before anything on the Travel Channel would even start to be in motion. Then he discussed a book deal that he was working on with a publisher in New York, which was news to Heather. Last, George turned to Heather and told her he wanted the four columns about vacationing close to home at a lake by the end of next week—a nearly impossible request.

As they left the office, Charlie told her that he needed the first one hundred pages of her new book ready and edited in twenty-one days, a book that, so far, had only a sample chapter written. Then he walked away without an apology for humiliating her the night of the party, or further comments on her career. She'd wanted to fire him on the spot, but the chance of a book deal meant she was stuck with him.

Feeling overloaded emotionally and mentally, Heather called Gina to meet for drinks. As soon as Heather walked into the bar in the North End, she knew it was going to be a bad night. Gina was with Michard, and the two couldn't keep their hands off each other as they nuzzled. Heather felt like the third wheel while she suffered through a glass of wine and finally excused herself.

As she pulled into her driveway, her shoulders ached with stress. She needed a good, cleansing breakdown to lift the tension, but it wouldn't come. Afraid of waking Thomas, she gently opened and closed her car door, then walked onto her lit deck.

"Hi," Tom said.

Heather jumped and held her heart.

He sat at the far end of her deck. "Sorry, didn't mean to scare you. I was enjoying your new furniture and stargazing."

"Glad you like it." With her head down, she walked into the house.

Heather changed out of her black dress and into shorts and T-shirt, then sat on her window seat and brushed her hair. Tom wore his usual jeans and T-shirt. He reclined on her deck chair, his muscular arms around his head as he stared at the sky.

He grabbed a beer from his cooler and looked up to her window. "Want to join me?"

"What are you doing here?" she asked.

"Come down and have a drink with me," he said.

She didn't need more drama tonight, but the loneliness she'd felt at the bar stirred in her heart. She gave in and went downstairs. The night air felt warm and thick as she stepped outside. Mosquitoes flew around a bug lamp in Sarah and Carl's yard.

"You looked fantastic in that dress. Party tonight?" He handed her an opened beer.

She took it without question, sat and took a sip, shocked at the sweetness in the bottle. "This is root beer."

His grin deepened the cleft in his chin. From the cooler, he grabbed two frosty mugs filled with vanilla ice cream. "I had a craving." He placed a straw in the pink cup and pushed it across the table.

"Why are you doing this?" she asked.

"Sucking up for forgiveness. I took something out on you, and I don't play the jerk well," he said.

"So you thought you'd wait for me on my deck, not knowing when I might be home or who I'd be with?"

"Your deck has the best view of the stars besides the beach." He pulled his hand through his hair. "If you walked in with someone then I would've looked the fool . . . the way I know I made you feel the night I helped you move boxes. If you were alone I'd get a chance to apologize. Either way, my conscience might leave me alone."

The lake looked like glass, and an owl hooted in the woods. She took a deep breath filled with the scent of roses and let the serenity of the scene seep into her frayed nerves.

"I'm sorry I yelled at you the day after your party," Tommy went on. "I can be protective when it comes to my family."

"Thanks, I really am sorry for what happened. I didn't mean to disrupt anyone's night."

"Good to know," he said. "Do you mind turning off the lights? It'll give us a better view. I can't see the stars in Providence."

Heather flipped the switch. The Milky Way's river of light illuminated the black sky. She plopped into the chair and leaned her bare feet against the deck railing. "My root beer float is at the perfect marker."

"I didn't know there was a perfect marker."

"When there's still enough ice cream to eat with the spoon, but some has melted, making the soda creamy. That's the perfect marker."

"I wasn't certain you'd be a root beer float kind of girl. I was thinking martinis, but that's not my style," he said.

"You know, for someone who doesn't know anything about me, you seem to have formed a lot of opinions."

"I guess you're right. Sorry."

The silence stretched over them while Heather sucked at her float. "One summer my mother dated this guy who always brought us root beer floats on Wednesday nights. The three of us would watch the sunset from the front stoop, and I could have as much as I wanted." She shrugged. "It's a good memory."

Tom looked to the lake. "I have lots of memories like that. Fishing with Grandpa and Bill. Roasting marshmallows. Eating Molly's brownie sundaes."

"Oh, those brownies smothered in chocolate sauce and ice cream. Thanks for ruining any chance I have of saying no to her baking this week."

He pulled his chair next to her and rested his legs on the railing.

Heather licked the ice cream off the straw. "So let me ask you something. The first day we met . . . why didn't you tell me what I was getting into?"

"I didn't like you," he said.

"You didn't know me."

"You looked at me like I was a piece of meat."

"Well, aren't we stuck on ourselves?"

He sucked at his float. "Maryland was like a mother to me. I didn't want you in her home."

"So, I'm a martini-style girl who doesn't know how to be a good neighbor and you wished I'd never moved in. Oh, and let's not forget that I'm a flirt who only wants you for your body. Tell me how you really feel."

"Slam dunk on being an ass." He fidgeted in his seat and then looked at her. "Sorry, my attitude has nothing to do with you."

"Why didn't you get rid of me by telling the truth about who lives here? You know, this is your fault," she said.

"Interesting perspective. One that I've wondered about."

"And your grandfather's a dirty old man."

Tom's laugh echoed across the lake.

"Every time I stretch on my front lawn or sit on the beach, he makes an excuse to come talk to me, and when I helped him with his computer, he pinched my butt. There are way too many horny old people around here."

Tom turned to her. "You might not want to wear those shorts in front of him. He's a Casanova."

Heather rolled her eyes. "In his mind."

"His last girlfriend passed away two years ago. He's prowling for another. But I warn you. There hasn't been a woman who's been able to keep up. No matter how young she was. And thank you for helping him with his computer. It means a lot to me. Of course, he might have been using that as excuse to hit on you."

"Oh, I don't think that's why he wanted my help." Heather smiled as she wondered how Thomas was doing with his online dating adventures. He hadn't needed her help lately.

"What's that grin for?" Tom asked. "What aren't you telling me?"

"None of your business." She giggled and sucked at her drink. Tom shook his head and stared at the sky, a deep, contented grin on his face. He looked peaceful, like the world was this safe place filled with love and happiness. His large muscles made him look solid. Secure. Sparks of energy fired along her nerves as she stared. He was certainly pretty, but "ass" was also a good description.

"So, since you're being brutally honest, are you gay? I never see you with a woman, and you don't like it when someone flirts with you."

"Carl's trying to start that rumor to razz me, but I think you know I'm not gay." He looked at the sexy way she'd angled her legs.

Heather uncrossed the leg she'd pointed at him and curled her feet under her thighs.

"Just a guess," he said.

Silence, strained and uncomfortable, followed.

"Point three on being a jerk." He put his root beer on the arm of the chair. "I should probably leave before you completely hate me."

She stabbed her straw into the slush. "Don't worry, I already do. So you might as well stay."

"At least I brought you ice cream to enjoy," he said.

"Yes, that makes up for you treating me like an unworthy vixen after your hot body." She sucked on her straw. "Nope, doesn't taste that good."

"So you do think I'm hot." He smiled and raised his eyebrows, making her laugh.

"I think I'll just start calling you Conceited Ass instead of Tommy."

"Fair enough."

They were silent as they looked at the stars and listened to the lake lap against the shore.

"Do you see the Big Dipper?" Tommy asked.

Heather looked up at the constellation while she sipped her float. "Have you ever been to Africa?"

"No," Tommy said.

"I was there in March. My guide took me to the middle of the field one night. We sat in the Land Rover drinking hot chocolate and listening to the lions call to one another from either side of the delta. The sky had more stars than blackness. I wanted to make that moment last forever."

"It sounds incredible." He leaned his head against the back of the chair.

"It was amazing. I saw a lioness with two baby cubs. They looked like stuffed animals you could cuddle, but they strutted as if to say, 'I know I'm the king.' Actually, they acted kind of like you," she teased.

He looked at her and laughed. "Touché." They smiled at one another for a moment and then he looked back to the stars. "Tell me more about Africa."

"I slept in a tree house that overlooked a watering hole. Every day, Frank, the resident elephant, would hang out in the early evening and eat leaves from the tree. I could see his eyelashes."

"You're kidding?"

"No. He was so close that he would take his trunk and reach it over my railing and sniff me like a dog."

"I'd love to go to Africa someday."

"It was great, but everyone around me had someone to share it with. Wherever I looked, there were families—the people, the animals. I felt pathetic. They assigned guides to eat dinner with me. I love to travel, but I hate being alone all the time."

"I can understand how that could be tough."

She looked at him. "Please, you have this big family, and I'm sure you have plenty of women to take on vacation."

He shrugged. "Except for Grandpa, I don't have anyone to take to Africa." He looked down at his empty mug. "So how do you like your new home? Are you settling in?"

"The house is beautiful. I still can't believe I own it. There's something about waking up every morning and smelling the lake air, watching the geese land on the water . . . and I've probably taken too many days on the beach reading books than I should have. I'm rather swamped with work right now."

"It sounds like the Nagog life suits you."

"I don't know about that. It's not exactly what I expected. Instead of barbecues and parties every night, I listen to the frogs. And home ownership is more work than I thought."

"What do you mean?"

"I guess I should've expected there'd be problems with a home this old, but between the ants under my sink and plumbing issues, it's been a little stressful."

"Is there anything you want me to take a look at?"

She turned and smiled at him. "Thank you. That's sweet, but not right now. Molly has had Bill fix everything."

"That's good. Well, I should get going. I have an early day tomorrow." He stood and gathered the cooler and went to his truck. Heather walked to the edge of the deck as he returned and handed her a piece of paper with his number. "Just in case anything else goes wrong in your house."

Their hands touched, and when she looked at his aqua eyes, she felt the same electricity that had been there the night they'd moved her boxes. "Thank you. It's rather neighborly of you."

"It's the least this conceited ass can do." He smiled and then turned. The engine in the old truck revved to life and he drove away.

Heather went back to the deck and sipped the last of her float as she stared at the stars. The empty seat next to her made her feel even lonelier. She listened to the night sounds: crickets chirped, a loose screen door banged against the neighbor's house, and the wind started to blow.

Heather saw a light on in Victoria's sunroom. Three times she turned back before finally making her way to Victoria's stoop and ringing the doorbell.

∽◌∾

Victoria had been in the sunroom in a red silk robe and pajamas, perusing her drawer of movies, when she heard the bell ring. Concerned, she ran and whipped the door open and was surprised to see the girl on her front porch.

"Heather? Is something wrong?"

"I know it's late, but since you're up, I was wondering if you wanted company?"

She looked uncomfortable asking and Victoria opened the door wider. She wrapped her arm around Heather's shoulder and ushered her into the house. "Of course. Are you okay?"

"Yeah. Just . . ."

Victoria smiled and pulled her into the kitchen. "Is it the strange sounds in your house? It takes time to acclimate to your home's song, especially one as old as yours: the squeaks and the creaks. My guest room is always open. I was about to watch a movie, would you like to join me?"

Heather took a deep breath. "Yeah, that'd be great."

Victoria led her into the sunroom. "Is the fire too warm?" Victoria asked. "My California blood is a little cold tonight, but the fresh air is nice so I have the windows open."

"No, it's fine." Heather looked at the large portrait that hung above the mantel. "Is this your granddaughter?"

Victoria touched the frame. "Yes, that's Annabelle."

"She's gorgeous," Heather said, her eyes scanning the room.

"Oh my God," Heather said. She pointed to the golden statuette. "Is that what I think it is?"

"Yes," Victoria said. "You can touch it."

Heather tentatively reached out her fingers as if it were a magic lamp that made wishes come true. "I've never seen an Oscar in person."

Victoria looked away and busied herself by opening a large drawer filled with DVDs. "What would you like to watch? I have everything."

"How about one of your movies?" Heather said.

"Why don't we save that for another night? I'm in the mood to watch something fun, with a handsome leading man. How about *Singin' in the Rain*? Gene Kelly's finest moment."

"Never seen it," Heather said as she turned and looked at a collage on the wall behind the rocking chair.

Victoria placed her hand over her heart. "Pure sin. We have

so much work to do. I'm going to make hot chocolate and pop-corn. I say we watch movies until we can't stay awake."

Victoria went to the kitchen and left Heather to scan the pic-tures around the room. When she returned with two blue mugs with sunflowers painted on the sides and a large bowl over-flowing with white popped kernels, she saw Heather looking at a large photograph hung on the wall above the shelves. She placed the tray on the ottoman and stood behind Heather who was studying the women in bright-colored dresses standing in the windows of an abandoned brick building. The picture had been signed: *Ormond Gigli 1960.*

"Do you like it?"

"It's incredible," Heather said.

"Look at the second row from the top, the girl in the white dress."

Heather's eyes widened. "Is that you?"

"It is. The picture is called *Girls in the Window,* and it graced the cover of *Ladies' Home Journal.*"

"You wore pointy shoes back then?" Heather asked.

"You think you're the first generation to realize they elongate the leg? You'd be surprised how much us old folks influenced fashion."

Heather leaned closer to the picture. "You all look so sexy and powerful."

"And we're covered up. Not wearing bikinis for clothing. Back then, women were in touch with the sensual pride of the femi-nine spirit." Victoria brushed Heather's hair from her face. "These days I think girls are ashamed of how they come out of the womb. They're determined to stuff themselves into a perfect mold."

"Determined? More like forced." Heather looked at a framed movie poster. "Is that you in the background?"

"Yes. I won the Oscar with that film," Victoria said.

"I know this picture. Where do I know it from?" Heather asked. "Oh my God, I remember. My grandmother. We watched this together when I was little. She *loved* this movie. You really were famous."

Victoria waved Heather's words away as she walked toward the television. "You're the famous one these days. I've been reading your column, you're a wonderful writer."

"I think my writing is a far cry from an Academy Award, but I might have a chance at a travel show."

Victoria smiled with excitement. "Let me know if you need any tips on how to work the camera. I'd love to share all my secrets with you. We'll have such fun. But for now, let's watch our movie."

Heather sat on the couch and pulled a throw pillow across her lap. The black-and-white MGM lion roared on the television. Heather grabbed a mug and a handful of popcorn. "That's Gene Kelly? He was hot."

"And he could kiss," Victoria said as she sat.

"Okay, I'm jealous," Heather said as she sipped her hot cocoa. "Victoria, can I ask you something?"

"Anything."

"I was wondering about your husband since I assume you were married, but if it's none of my business . . ."

"I was married for eight years to a man named Devon. He was an actor."

"What happened?"

"Devon and I were two fast-burning flames. He'd touch me

and it was like thought ceased to exist and I drowned in a current of passion."

"Oh, God, are you going to talk about sex again?"

"I'll spare you the details."

"Thank you," Heather said. "So what happened?"

"I changed and Devon didn't." Victoria took a handful of popcorn and passed the bowl.

"So, what you said about marriage being the place where you're beautiful whether or not you're wearing a fancy dress or a bathrobe—was that from being with Devon?" Heather popped the puffed kernels into her mouth.

"Well, it's nice to know my advice didn't fall on deaf ears, but sadly, no. Just consider that advice from a woman who's lived a long life and knows a thing or two about love because of her experiences."

"Did you remarry?"

"No, I spent many years dating and being an independent woman."

A sad look came over Heather's face. "Were you lonely?"

"Oh, I'm certain at times I was, but I was caught up in my adventures. The world is such an incredible place, and I had my daughter and granddaughter."

"What about now?" Heather said. "Joseph seems rather eligible? Have you thought of asking him out?"

Victoria choked on a popcorn kernel and Heather patted her back as Victoria put her hands over her heart.

"I'll take that as a yes," Heather said when Victoria caught her breath and took a sip of her hot chocolate.

"Why don't we watch the movie," Victoria said.

Heather nodded and with a smile she turned to the television.

"I think you should go for it. He's kind of the Sean Connery of Nagog."

"I'm ignoring you now."

"Fine." Heather sipped her cocoa and watched the movie as she munched on the popcorn.

A tug of guilt played at Victoria's conscience. She hadn't been completely honest. If she told Heather the truth about leaving Devon, she would've needed to explain that life had been lonely after they split. She missed the passion and the companionship. He'd been her friend as well as her lover, and she knew she'd left him without fighting for their relationship—their marriage hadn't matched the perfect picture of what she'd thought it should be. But the real truth was that once Melissa had been born, Devon no longer lived up to the feelings she'd had for Joseph.

The rhythmic breath of sleep came from Heather's lips as the movie finished. Victoria looked at the sleeping girl and placed a blanket over her before turning off the television, then retired to her own bed.

❧

Hundreds of dragonflies in vivid colors of blue, red, and green flapped their wings in a dizzying circle around Victoria's face. She could see Annabelle; the moonlight reflected off the silver gown that clung to the girl's curves as she twirled three feet above the patio. "Dance with me, Tommy," Annabelle said.

Tommy tried to hold her, but she slipped away and floated higher.

Annabelle laughed as she ascended, blissful in her weightless freedom. Her hands reached for the high tree branches. Victoria tried to yell, to stop her baby from going higher, but nothing came out. She willed her feet to move, but they sank in the sand, her calves disappearing into the earth. The dragonflies hit at her face, but she didn't swat them away. She didn't want to harm their elegant bodies.

Victoria struggled to free her legs, but the beach became quicksand, and the more she moved, the deeper she sank. Annabelle twirled higher and Victoria could see the stars all around her granddaughter. Annabelle smiled at Tommy and blew him a kiss.

Victoria shook awake, the top of her pajamas soaked with sweat. Outside, the moon was still high in the sky; Victoria looked to the clock and saw that it was only three in the morning. She'd been asleep only a few hours. In the closet she stripped off the nightshirt and replaced it with a white tank top and zip-up sweatshirt. Adrenaline surged through her body and she couldn't return to bed.

Downstairs the darkness of her memories called to her. The cool tiles of the kitchen floor led her feet to the counter with the butcher's block of knives. Sarah believed that Victoria left after Annabelle's death because she wanted to go play in Malibu and forget what had happened. Joseph thought that she ran away without a thought to the kindness he'd shown her. No one knew the truth of what she'd almost done.

Victoria sunk to the floor. Moonlight came through the window and reflected off the pale skin of her wrist. This had been the place Victoria had reached five years ago, a week after Annabelle's funeral.

She'd sat on this floor ready to end her own life. But grace had come from an unseen touch on the wrist—a breeze, perhaps. Victoria felt a presence lift her from the ground, and she'd put the knife away. That night, in the window over the sink, she'd seen someone else in her reflection, a sick woman who needed help.

Ashamed of what she'd almost done, she'd flown back to Malibu early in the morning and checked herself into a hospital. She still hadn't told anyone, not even Molly, what had happened or that she'd been institutionalized for severe depression.

In the sunroom, Heather slept in contented peace. The crickets and peepers had gone silent and the night air had cooled. Victoria closed the windows as she looked around the neighborhood. Everything looked safe. She tried to hug the secure feeling into her body, to infuse her soul with Nagog's peace.

CHAPTER 16

❧

C arl, Daniel, Bill, and Joseph carried the picnic table across the yard and set it down under Heather's oak tree in the original ruts.

"Damn girl, how is she moving this thing on her own?" Carl yelled.

Joseph looked at the tracks of matted grass. "I think she drags it. Maybe we should simply leave it closer to your home, since this is the fifth time she's moved it. I think the smoke bothers her."

"So we just let her decide that our meeting place needs to change because she's sensitive to smoke?" Bill said. "Bad enough I have to go in and fix the problems we caused because Molly's befriended her, but you want me to give up my tree as well?"

"I'm just saying that we could try to be a little more courteous to our new neighbor," Joseph said.

"You mean the neighbor who threw a party and played loud music until all hours of the night?" Carl said.

"That was almost two months ago. I think it's time to forgive," Joseph said as the men sat and started dealing the cards around the table.

"I bet there's going to be more parties real soon," Daniel said. "Why else would she have bought a place out here?"

The men lit their cigars and changed the subject to their usual conversation. From the open second-floor window, Joseph heard Heather scream in frustration. Her feet stomped on the wood floors and then the window slammed shut.

Carl laughed. "I think we upset her."

"Good, maybe she'll leave," Bill said.

"Why do you want her to move?" Joseph asked.

"Because our kids can't think they can come in here and move us into homes and sell our places," Daniel said.

Sarah, who was passing by on a walk with Evelyn, came up to the table and added, "The girl is rude and unfriendly to everyone but Victoria and Molly. What a surprise, Victoria has a new playmate and is ignoring the rest of the community."

Evelyn pulled her pink sweater around her shoulders. It was over eighty degrees and Joseph knew that Roger had probably tried to change her into something lighter but then gave up. He barely joined the men anymore. Every moment was spent looking after Evelyn, making certain that she didn't get hurt and her needs were met.

Heather came out of the house just as Evelyn opened the mailbox. "Hello, Evelyn," the girl called. "Can I help you find something?"

"I'm just looking to see if a letter came," Evelyn said, smiling at Heather.

Heather pulled the mail from the box and sifted through. "Nothing for you today."

Sarah raced to Evelyn's side. "Dear, why don't we walk back to your house and we'll check back later."

"Good afternoon, Sarah," Heather said with a touch of sarcasm. "How are you today? Did you have a nice time at church?"

"I've noticed you don't bother to attend, but the Lord might look favorably if you found your way into one sometime."

"I'm certain the Lord also looks favorably on forgiveness and I don't see a whole lot of that going on around here."

"I don't know what you are speaking about and I find your tone of voice rude."

"Oh, I think you know exactly what I'm talking about," Heather said, waving to Victoria as she came out of her house and headed to the beach. Heather turned to the men. "Excuse me, gentlemen, I really need to ask you a favor."

"What do you want?" Daniel asked.

"We seem to be at an impasse with the picnic table location. I move it over there, and you bring it back. I was hoping we could find a compromise since your cigar smoke is coming right into my house."

"This picnic table has been here for fifty years," Bill said.

"Well, then, maybe it's ready for a different view?" Heather asked.

"Nope," Carl said and blew out a thick puff of smoke.

"Please?" Heather asked again.

"Nope," Bill said. They turned to their cards and ignored her.

She looked to Joseph for help and he shrugged his shoulders. A lifetime of friendship had taught him that nothing he could say would change their minds.

Heather had walked away and headed to the beach to join Victoria when Joseph heard the phone ringing in his house. "I'm going to try to grab that." The men barely looked up as he left.

The caller had hung up by the time he reached his phone. He had one new message and the caller ID showed his daughter's phone number. He decided to call her back without listening to the message first.

"Hi, Dad," Joseph's daughter, Shelly, said.

"Hi, baby. How's your day going?"

"It's fine." In a sullen voice, the same tone she'd used when she'd admitted wrongdoings as a child, she said, "I need to tell you something. Mom met someone and she's getting married."

Joseph sat down at the table. His wife was remarrying and his fifty-one-year-old daughter had to tell him. Divorce was such a strange thing for children to face, no matter the age. "That's good news. I want your mother to be happy."

"Dad, I know this must be hard on you."

"Baby, I understand." Joseph wanted to pull his daughter into a hug and stroke her hair. She was a grandmother now, but in his mind she'd always be that little girl who placed her feet on top of his shoes when they danced. The divorce had hurt her, and he knew that this marriage must be painful as well.

"Mom's the one that walked out, not you," she said.

"There were circumstances and I don't blame your mother." He could hear his daughter scuffing her foot against the floor.

"I want you to be happy," she said.

"I am."

"Dad, Mom told me why she left. I saw Victoria the day we came for lunch. I know she's back. If you really love her, then why aren't you with her?"

Joseph paused. "There are circumstances that I don't want to get into."

"Dad, do they really matter all that much? For a long time I hated her for breaking up your marriage, but it's been five years, and if you love her, then you need to do something about it."

"I'll think about it. Let's change the subject. How's our little Emily?"

"I'm babysitting her next week and I was thinking of bringing her for lunch. I know how much she loves her great-grandpa," she said.

"That would be nice," he said, realizing that his eyes had misted over.

"I love you, Daddy."

"Love you too, baby."

Joseph hung up. He went to the bedroom and lay down. The last time he'd spoken with his wife was in a law office. Joseph had offered the house, but Barbara said she couldn't bear to live in Nagog. In her mind, she'd always be the outsider. Joseph had set up accounts to take care of her financial needs and that had been the end of his marriage. Now his ex-wife was with another man. Someone else would touch the white stretch marks created by his babies.

Joseph went into the study, where the spicy smell of pipe tobacco, smoked thirty years before, impregnated the thick drapes and antique carpets. This was Joseph's father's study and now his sanctuary.

He looked out the window to Barbara's overgrown flower garden. The patio had been designed to look like a European bistro, complete with café chairs and a fountain that once played a soft trickling medley. The wineglasses that hung from the outdoor baker's rack had gone dirty with years of dust. Joseph didn't have his ex-wife's green thumb. Weeds had broken through the brick walk and vines choked the flowers, siphoning off their nutrients.

It was a beautiful day outside. He stretched his limbs and walked into the garden. Four months ago, when he saw Victoria in the snow the night she'd returned, he didn't believe he could open his heart again. She said she was here to stay, but if he let her in again, would he only be left heartbroken once more?

∽⟨§⟩∽

The barista called out coffee orders as people stood around the café waiting for their drinks, buzzing with chatter. Heather sat off to the corner in a blue armchair, sipping her latte as she stared at her computer screen. She'd hoped that a change of scenery would help her write, but it hadn't.

Horror stories about writer's block were taboo in the *Globe*'s office. No one wanted to say the words for dread of the writer's virus spreading. Until this moment, Heather had never experienced any of the symptoms: hours of staring at the computer without progress; days of cleaning and laundry to avoid work or, worse, when the block completely took over, endless hours of television without the desire to move. The problem wasn't the column—she'd sent off the four articles to George about lakeside vacations, but the hundred pages Charlie needed for the book publisher had become her nemesis. In her brief conversation with Charlie yesterday, she'd asked for the name of the publishing house or editor and he responded, "Are you asking so that you can go behind my back and invite them to a party?"

The man was a child. Of course, in some ways she deserved said blame for that.

She stared at the computer screen. Fear blocked every thought in her mind. Instead of writing, she read her e-mail. Steven had written. His correspondences were all the same: his producers loved the Solo Female Traveler show idea and he was meeting with top executives and would be in touch with her and Charlie soon. The first few e-mails had sent her into euphoric excitement as she dreamt about staying in luxury hotels and being able to eat dinner in fancy restaurants with her film crew. But after hearing what Charlie had said to George at their meeting at the *Globe,* she realized that it was a long shot at best.

She scrubbed her face with her hands. *Just type anything that comes to mind, even if it's horrible.* She looked out the window for inspiration. A rusted white truck with *Woodward Architecture, Ltd.* printed on the side pulled into the parking lot. Her stomach did a little flip as Tommy stepped from the vehicle. She hadn't seen him since they'd stargazed, and though she hated to admit it, at night she sat on her deck hoping he would come to visit Thomas.

He walked into the shop and went to the counter. A blond woman, Heather's age, came from behind the register. She wrapped her arms around his neck and gave him a quick kiss on the mouth. Heather couldn't hear what they were saying, but a pang of jealousy crept through her body. Was the blonde his girlfriend?

An older woman brought him a coffee to go. She kissed him on the cheek and held him close, inspecting him in a motherly way. *He's loved,* Heather thought.

As he made his way to the door, he noticed Heather. She smiled at him and gave a shy wave and he walked over.

"Hiding from my grandfather?"

"His Casanova ways are too much for me to resist. I had to escape before he carried me off," she joked.

He laughed and sat down. "I told you, be careful. No woman has outlived him."

"I might need to call on you for a rescue," she said. "But really, he's fine." Heather looked at the young woman at the cash register, expecting her to be watching Heather's interaction with Tommy, but she didn't seem to care. Maybe she wasn't his girlfriend after all. "So what brings you to town so early in the day? You usually only come at night and on weekends."

"Keeping track of me?" He smiled at her.

She blushed and then said with as much cool as she could muster, "No, I could care less about your comings and goings, but I'm a writer so I notice things."

"I heard a rumor about your writing. I assume that's why you went to Africa?"

"Yeah. I travel solo and write a column for the *Globe*," she said with a touch of pride.

"Not a bad gig. So, if you don't mind me asking, why the house in Nagog?"

Heather sighed and shook her head. "Momentary fall into insanity."

"Okay?"

"Actually, I spent the first years of my life living on a lake. When I saw the house it reminded me of a time when everything felt safe. It probably sounds stupid."

"No, it's the same for me, but of course I grew up here. Whenever I drive in I'm transported back to when days were lazy and I could spend my afternoon fishing or playing in the woods," he said.

"That's nice. Of course, I've ended up with men blowing cigar smoke into my house and Victoria and Molly asking me for sex tips."

"They didn't?" He laughed.

"Oh yeah, the girl talk has gotten a little personal."

"Just remember that around Sarah you're still a virgin or she'll try to bring you to church with her."

"She's already trying." Heather rolled her eyes. "What's her story?"

"What do you mean?"

"She's cold to Victoria. And she leaves me flyers about church but refuses to have a real conversation. The woman hates me even though she doesn't know me."

"Sarah's a good person. She's been through tremendous heartache and her faith has helped her survive. I think if she's trying to get you to church, it's her odd way of being a neighbor. As for Victoria, they have things that go back to childhood that were never worked out."

The blonde came up and put her hand on Tommy's shoulder and handed him a white bag. "A little gift for the drive home. They just came out of the oven."

Tommy opened the bag and the smell of warm chocolate chip cookies filled the air. "Thanks. Stacy, I'd like you to meet Heather. She owns Maryland's house."

"Oh, you're the one." She smiled with a touch of a fun laugh. "I've been dying to see what you look like. I'm a little disappointed. I thought there'd be horns sprouting from your head, from the way Sarah and Carl talk about you." She rubbed a circle on Tommy's back. "I wish I could stay and chat but I have to get back, the line is getting long. See you later, Tommy."

Heather looked at him, waiting for an explanation, but none came. "Okay, you're going to make me ask. Who was that?"

"You don't know?"

Heather shook her head.

"Molly's daughter owns this cafe. Stacy's Molly's granddaughter. I stopped in thinking that the gang would be here."

"So with all the cafés in town, *of course* I picked my neighbors' local haunt." Heather rolled her eyes. She couldn't escape. He laughed at her, and she responded by gently kicking his calf. "Shut up."

He smiled and for a moment they looked at one another in playful teasing. "Speaking of the devils," Tom said. Bill, Molly, Joseph, and Victoria walked through the door. Molly ran up to him and wrapped her arms around his shoulders. "How's my handsome man?"

"Better now," he said. He stood and folded Molly's soft body into his large form. He greeted Bill and Joseph but paused when he came to Victoria. She pushed back the hair near his eyes and then pulled him close.

"I'm sorry I can't stay. I'm already late getting back to work," Tom said as they pulled away.

Victoria touched his face. "It's okay. We'll visit soon."

Tom looked at Heather. "Thanks for the company. Sorry if I disrupted your brilliant writing."

"Yeah, sure, show up, throw me off my deadline, and then leave me with these women who I'm sure will stuff me full of dessert." She shook her head in mock frustration. "You are definitely a pain in the you-know-what."

"I guess I owe you another root beer float night." He winked and then waved good-bye.

Bill and Joseph went to the counter to order as Molly and Victoria commandeered the table next to Heather. "What did he say about a root beer float night?" Molly asked.

"It's nothing," Heather said as she watched the truck pull away. But she realized her cheeks hurt from smiling. She turned to Victoria expecting a comment, but Victoria stared out the window, looking forlorn. Heather wanted to reach out to her, but Molly placed her hand on Victoria's shoulder and the moment passed.

"Well, that looked like a nice visit with Tommy," Victoria said. "I didn't realize the two of you had become friends."

"I don't know about friends. He stopped over the other night when he was visiting his grandfather and we bumped into each other today. It wasn't a date or anything."

"No one said it was, dear." Victoria raised her eyebrows and smiled.

Joseph returned and handed Victoria a cup of coffee and a scone. He sat down next to her and Heather saw a flush of red on Victoria's cheeks when she looked at the man. Heather noticed that Victoria was in a pair of designer jeans today with a red silk short-sleeve blouse and had taken extra care with her hair.

"So, Joseph, have you caught any fish? I see you out on the dock almost every morning," Heather said.

"They haven't been biting much."

"I guess Victoria's swimming keeps them at a distance." Heather knew her comment would make Victoria uncomfortable, but if she was going to tease her about Tommy, then Joseph was fair game.

"Well, it's going to be interrupted again this week," Molly said. "The Red Hat Society from church is going to be coming three days a week to do aerobics on the beach. Heather, you should join us. Victoria is going to lead the class."

"What time?"

"Six in the morning," Molly said.

Heather's eyes widened. They would be right outside Heather's bedroom window early in the morning. Maybe cigar smoke was the least of her worries.

CHAPTER 17

~⚬~

Victoria could hear children running and playing on the beach through the community center's open window. Roger and Evelyn's kids and grandkids had come for a barbecue, and the smell of roasting meat and charcoal floated on the air. There was something special about the sound of young children playing that made the world feel right.

She placed three kings in front of her while she looked around the table: Molly and Bill, Sarah and Carl, Agatha, Daniel, Thomas, and Joseph. It had taken time, but they were all together, playing a game of Five Hundred rummy. Molly and Bill had sassed each other all afternoon in playful competition just as they'd done when they were teenagers. At this moment, Victoria wanted for nothing. A warm breeze came through the windows and carried music from Heather's living room. Victoria had invited the girl, but she declined, stating that she had too much work to do.

"Life is good," she said as she picked up her glass of iced tea and sipped.

"It'd be better if we could get rid of that girl," Sarah said as she chose a card from the deck.

"Sarah, I don't understand why you have a problem with Heather," Victoria said.

"Of course you don't. You like having a new playmate. Well, personally, I have to listen to her music all day long."

Molly put her hand on Sarah's arm. "I have some great news. The Red Hat Society from church is going to come to Nagog three days a week to teach aerobics here. Isn't that wonderful? We'll all get in shape this summer."

"That sounds wonderful," Sarah said. "I'll look forward to it."

"And Victoria is going to lead," Molly said.

Agatha huffed and Sarah's face pinched.

"Be careful, Sarah," Thomas said, "your face is starting to freeze in that position. You don't want to walk around looking like you're sucking on a lemon drop. And I think I might join you ladies in the morning."

"Thomas, I think that's a wonderful idea. How about the rest of you men?" Victoria asked.

"Thomas just wants to watch all those ladies shake their cabooses," Bill said. "I've got my woman at home every night." He tickled Molly's side and she smacked at his hand.

"You know, Bill, it would do you some good to get some exercise," Victoria said.

"Yes, because you know what's best for everyone," Sarah said. "Of course, once it's cold again I'm certain you'll be jetting off to the Riviera or back to California. Isn't that where you'd planned to retire with Devon?"

Agatha piped in, "The only reason you're here is because you have no one left."

"Agatha, Sarah, stop!" Joseph said.

Victoria put her hand on Joseph's arm. "No, if they have something to say, why don't we get it out in the open? I'm tired of tiptoeing around and dealing with snide comments. I'm here to stay. So let's deal with this," she challenged Sarah.

Sarah's lips pinched as she dug her nails into her palms. "You left. You cared about no one but yourself. You were supposed to be my maid of honor, but you didn't have the decency to tell me that you wouldn't be there. I miscarried three times, and where was my friend when I needed her? You were gallivanting around the world having a grand time. You didn't even call. You waltzed in when you needed comfort or used this place like a summer home."

"I didn't know you miscarried," Victoria said in a softer voice.

"Of course not. And that's not your fault. Just like Joseph and Barbara's divorce. You broke up my friend's marriage. I don't see her anymore. She can't bear to be around anyone in Nagog because it reminds her of you."

The room went silent as the two women glared at one another. Tears filled Sarah's eyes. "You waltzed in wearing fancy clothes, displaying your movie star husband, so you could dazzle every-one. You didn't care what was going on in our lives. Did you ever think it was all a lie? You were nothing more than a supporting actress and model, but you acted like you were this big star—a life Annabelle killed herself trying to obtain." Sarah glowered, her body shaking. "And now I see you with Heather. You care more about playing with her than making amends with any of us."

"You hate me so much you insist on continuing to bring up my worst pain?" Victoria stood and pointed to the cross around Sarah's neck. "How Christian of you."

Sarah stood so suddenly the table rocked. "Don't you dare preach to me about being a good Christian."

They stood in silence, their eyes piercing one another.

"Selfish is what you are," Agatha said.

Bill hit his fist against the table. "That's enough."

Agatha glared at him. "You and Molly are just as much to blame. If it wasn't for you bowing down every time she came around—"

"I said it's over," Bill boomed.

Molly stood and placed her hand on Victoria's back.

Agatha's breath came like a bull ready to fight. She scowled, picked up her cane, and guided Sarah to the door.

"Agatha," Victoria said.

She turned.

"I made a mistake when I was a teenager. I said horrible things that hurt your feelings and for that I'm sorry. But I was a young girl. If after sixty years you can't find it in your heart to forgive, then that's *your* problem."

"Well, I never," Agatha said.

"Oh, you have so," Victoria said, tears welling in her eyes as she looked at Agatha and then at Sarah. "Bringing up Annabelle that day at Molly's . . . blaming me again today for what happened . . . that's more hurtful than anything I ever said to you."

Sarah turned. "The difference, Victoria, is that she speaks the truth. You were just cruel." They turned and left.

Molly grabbed Victoria's hand. "I'm sorry. I pushed too hard for everyone to get along."

Victoria felt her breath catch in her chest. "I need some air. I'm okay." She patted Molly's arm and walked across the community center dance floor toward the back door.

"Well, that's the closest thing to a boxing match I think they're going to have," Carl said as Victoria opened the door and walked through. "Maybe now they can move on."

The sun was beginning to set and Evelyn and Roger's kids were rounding up their children, trying to get them into the car. Hugs and kisses were given and Evelyn smiled, even though Victoria knew she was confused by the activity.

The beach felt too exposed, so she walked along the grass next to Joseph's home. Near the water she stood in a circle of birch trees; the white bark marked with black lines had always reminded Annabelle of zebras. The tears came hot on her cheeks and she gasped for breath.

"Victoria," Joseph said behind her, "Sarah and Agatha were wrong to say those things."

Victoria wiped the tears and tried to regain her composure. She crossed her arms over her chest and stared at the water. The breeze blew her long yellow skirt and it fluttered against her legs. "Everything she said was true. I left. I didn't call or check in. I waltzed back in years later to brag about my life. I hurt you and everyone else."

"We both know that your life wasn't here in Nagog. You did nothing wrong. Following your dreams wasn't a sin. Nor was doing what was right for you."

He put his hands on her bare upper arms and turned her toward him. He looked down with his beautiful blue eyes. With one hand he swept her hair away from her face. "You've suffered so deeply and lived fuller than anyone I know. Not one of us ever left the safety of this place. When someone lives as brightly as you, it's hard for all of us in the shadows, because it reminds us of the dreams and chances we didn't take. That's where the real anger lies."

"Stop it," she said. "For once will you tell me what you really feel? Why does Sarah keep saying that I broke up your marriage?"

"Victoria, it doesn't matter."

"Yes it does." She stared at him willing him to answer.

Joseph stepped away. "I don't know where to start, Victoria."

"The beginning is always good. I rejected you and I left without saying goodbye the night you returned from the war. The letters I sent while you were a sailor never gave you any indication that I wanted a different life than the one you could provide—"

In a quiet voice he interrupted, "And you didn't stay long enough to know that the war had changed me too . . . that I wanted something different as well. I could've gone with you. I wanted to travel, to be a photographer. I didn't want to stay in Nagog."

"What?" She shook her head in confusion.

"I went after you to tell you, but you were already gone."

Victoria stared at him unable to speak.

"You didn't have to run away, but I understood that you didn't love me the way I loved you."

Victoria shook her head. "No, that's not true."

"You didn't call or write, and I gave up hope that you'd return. I moved on, and I was fine the years that you stayed away. I loved Barbara, and we had a good life with our children, but every time you came home the old feelings would return."

"That's why you kept your distance. I believed you hated me for what I'd done."

"Victoria, I only wished I could've hated you. Then I wouldn't have hurt Barbara the way I did."

Memories returned from five years earlier: the brief interlude she'd shared with Joseph on the beach after he'd taken Annabelle's photograph on Memorial Day; his arms around her after the funeral. Grief from her loss had caused deep depression and Victoria barely remembered the weeks after Annabelle's death. When she was hospitalized, she lived under the sedation of heavy antidepressants, but now the blurry memories became clear. Barbara had seen them holding hands.

"You lost your marriage because of the comfort you tried to give me."

"It wasn't your fault. It was mine."

"You held me in my darkest hour and it cost you everything. And then I left again and I didn't say good-bye. Joseph, I'm so sorry." Tentatively she reached for his hand. Their fingers intertwined. "If I had known, I wouldn't have let you comfort me."

Joseph turned to her. "It was my choice. Just as it was my decision not to find you when I knew you were in Los Angeles. Like I said before, I would never have been enough for you."

Victoria squeezed his hand and looked into his eyes. "Joseph, I didn't leave because I didn't want you. I loved you so much I was scared I'd give up my dreams and become only what your love could fill. But I need you to know that I've never forgotten what we shared."

CHAPTER 18

࿇

L oud music shook Heather's office windows and jolted her from
sleep. Through half-open eyes she saw that her cheek had
typed *jkkkkkkkkkk* across her computer screen. The clock read 6:00.

"What the hell?"

"Are we ready, ladies?" Victoria's voice boomed over a sound
system.

"No!" Heather said as she realized what was happening.

The sunlight blinded her when she opened the curtains in her
bedroom. After her pupils adjusted, the scene on the beach became
clear. Women in pink, brown, purple, and teal jogging suits moved
across the sand, lifting their knees and pumping their arms. Short
styled hair was pulled back with colorful sweatbands. Many of the
ladies wore red baseball hats with purple flowers pinned to the
front. Heather stood, mouth agape, wishing the vision away.

Victoria noticed her and waved. "Come join us!" She wore a
microphone headset and blue velvet jogging pants with a fuchsia
tank top.

"What's with the sound system?" Heather yelled.

"What?" Victoria began a set of jumping jacks. The other
women copied with side toe-taps. "The sand is a natural resis-
tance workout. It's great for the buns."

"Honey, my buns disappeared after my third child," a woman in a yellow suit yelled.

"It's all in building the muscle. That will give you a strong, firm derrière," Victoria said.

"Bill likes my derrière soft and grabbable," Molly said. "So I'll just wiggle mine to make my heart stronger."

The ladies laughed. It was a bouncy pep squad.

"Do you think you could turn it down?" Heather yelled.

Victoria jogged to Heather's deck. "Sorry, I can't hear you down here. The sound system is based in the community center. We turned it up to get the full dance effect. If you look at the eaves of the building you'll see our outdoor speakers."

"Where did you get the mike?" Heather asked.

"Do you like it? I feel like Madonna when I use it. Joseph helped Molly buy it."

Heather wanted to rip the mike set off her head and throw it into the lake, but instead she smiled and said, "It's great. How often did you say you're going to do this?"

"Three days a week, Monday, Wednesday, and Friday, if the weather's good. I'm hoping to get the ladies to go a little wild and do water aerobics. It keeps the circulation moving. You should plan to join us. I'll post my classes at the community center."

The women had begun to stand around and chat. "Ladies, keep moving!

"Also, if you'd like to join me, I'm going to lift weights on Tuesday, Thursday, and Friday. Keeps me young," Victoria said.

Heather continued to force a smile as she thought about how many horrible mornings were in her future. "Do you think you could turn the music down? I was up late working."

"Oh, sorry. I think the winter storms knocked the speakers

around and they might be facing your house. I'll have someone come take a look."

"That would be great," Heather said as she closed the window.

"Let's move it, ladies. Whooo!" Victoria yelled.

For the last week, sleep had eluded Heather as she'd tried to meet Charlie's deadline. The bed looked soft and cozy and she wanted to curl under the covers, but the music was too loud. In her closet, she tried to make a bed on the floor with a blanket and pillow, but she could still hear Victoria's voice.

"Oh, what the heck," she said. She pulled on shorts and a tank top and went outside. Outside, Frank Sinatra's voice boomed as Victoria did high kicks and the women followed with low ones.

"Okay, Victoria, you win," Heather yelled. "Let's do this. But you owe me breakfast when we're done."

"Better yet, I'll have Molly cook it and then I'll take you for a spa day," Victoria said doing grapevines across the sand. Heather couldn't help but laugh and follow along.

∞

A bottle of Muscat sat on the wooden table, along with two wineglasses, cheese, and bread. Molly leaned across the double Adirondack chair and linked hands with Bill. Her head rested on his shoulder as they watched the sunset.

This time of day had been Molly's favorite when her children were small. Bath time came at six o'clock. The boys, covered in sap and dirt, climbed into fragrant bubbles. With a soapy washcloth Molly revealed pink skin under the grime. Then she brushed the girls' silky hair and planted kisses on their cheeks.

When everyone had on his or her thin summer jammies, they grabbed frozen juice pops and ran to this spot.

She and Bill would enjoy a glass of wine while the children lay in the cool grass watching for the first star. After the sun slipped behind the trees and the moonlight covered her babies with iridescent radiance, the lightning bugs blinked around the yard. Bill told bedtime stories as eyelids became heavy. Whenever his tales turned to dragons and monsters, Molly placed her hand on his arm, her sign that his stories would create nightmares.

Molly missed her babies. She was proud of her grown children, but she still longed for footie pajamas and bubble baths.

The intense humidity dampened her clothing and made the pressure behind her eyes intolerable. She wondered if it was time to call the doctor, but she didn't want to worry anyone.

"Well, I need to get the dinner dishes cleaned," Molly said as she stood.

"I can help you with those if you like," Bill said.

They walked up to the house. In the kitchen he set the wine and cheese on the counter. His arms went around her waist. "You feeling all right?"

His blue eyes had worry in them. "Just a little headache. I'll take some aspirin." She touched his cheek. "Thank you for your offer to help, but I know you want to watch the game. I'm fine."

Molly was finishing up when Victoria and Heather exploded through the sunroom door with loads of packages in their hands from their day in Boston. Victoria blocked Heather's entrance into the kitchen. "Molly, I would like to introduce you to the new and improved rising star in travel writing—Miss Heather Bregman." Victoria moved aside and Heather came through the door with her hands in the air.

The girl glowed with excitement. Her hair had been colored a deep auburn and cut shoulder-length at a chic angle. She twirled to show off her new fitted black dress, cinched at the waist with a thin red belt.

"Well, don't you look stunning," Molly said as she pulled her into a hug. "But then again, you're always beautiful."

"Thank you, Molly," Heather said with a big smile. "Victoria brought me to this incredible salon on Newbury Street and then we shopped all day. It was so much fun. You should've joined us."

"I don't know that I could've kept up with the two of you," Molly said. "Plus, I needed to bake for the church. I have meat loaf and mashed potatoes I can warm up if you're hungry."

"No thanks," Heather said. "We went out for sushi at my favorite place on Charles Street. I haven't been there in months."

"Molly, we have to take you. This place actually rivaled the restaurants in California."

Molly took down the cookie jar from the top of the fridge and made up a plate of desserts. "Hot chocolate or port?" Molly asked.

"Port," Victoria said.

"For me too, please," Heather said.

Molly gathered glasses and napkins and moved them out to the sun porch. Heather curled onto the couch next to Victoria. "So, Molly, I need your opinion on something."

"Okay." Molly handed a glass to Heather along with a dark chocolate fudge cookie.

"I think that Victoria should ask Joseph on a date."

"Not this again," Victoria said. "She's been at it all day."

"She says that she's not interested, but I know she's lying. The two of them are like magnets for each other." Heather sipped the wine and bit into the cookie. "Oh, God, this is orgasmic."

"I'm glad you like it that much, dear," Molly said.

"Sorry about that. I guess after all our sex talks I've gotten comfortable with the two of you," Heather said. "Anyway, back to Victoria. Joseph lives on the left side of the beach, Victoria on the right, and I'm smack in the middle. I swear I can feel the tension between the two of them as they sit in their houses. There has to be some kind of history, but she won't tell me anything."

"They were in love as teenagers," Molly said.

"Hah, I knew you liked one another."

"Thank you, Molly. Now she's never going to stop."

"Well, Victoria, maybe she's right. And as for you, Heather, I think it's time for you to have some friends over to your house or maybe invite Tommy for another night of root beer floats. It's not good for you to be stuck with us old biddies all the time."

"See what you started?" Victoria said. "Now she's going to meddle in your life too."

As they spoke, Molly laughed. The two made her feel like a teenager at a slumber party. The pressure behind her eyes began to ease as the aspirin and wine took effect. Two hours later they left and she decided to turn in.

Bill, in a white sleeveless undershirt and striped boxer shorts, leaned against the brass headboard with pillows supporting his lower back, his bifocals balanced on the bridge of his nose as he read. Deep into his story, he didn't look up. Molly stood in the doorway and regarded her husband of fifty-five years.

There were times in her youth when good-looking men had

flirted with her. No woman minded that kind of attention. Some asked for dates, but her heart had always belonged to Bill. She loved this man: the comfort of his touch, the security of his large build, and his playful spirit. A lifetime felt too short to spend with him.

"Are you feeling all right, hon?" she asked as she kissed his forehead. He wasn't warm. "Nine is early for you to be in bed."

He didn't look up. "I was bored. The game ended and you were playing with that young thing. So I figured I'd get comfortable and enjoy my book."

"Good idea. You fall asleep when you read in the recliner, and you're a bear to carry." She patted his shoulder and smoothed his hair.

As she entered the bathroom to begin her nightly routine, she hummed a lullaby. Her hair pinned into curls against her head, she washed her face with a soapy cloth. She rubbed Pond's cold cream into her skin. Angel kisses, her mother had called the rosy coloring of her cheeks that graced Molly's skin since birth.

Her mother's body had been a cloud of bosom and belly, a never-ending warm embrace. Love had been unconditional and freely expressed. Molly had tried to pass this example on to her own babies.

She thought about Heather and Victoria and the possibility of love in their lives. They needed good men to care for them, to hold them at night. And Joseph and Tommy had been alone for too long.

It seemed like forever since she and Bill had shared the intimacy of their marriage bed. Tired and grumpy from being left alone, she was certain Bill was upset about her friendship with Heather. But he would cave. After a lifetime together, she knew every secret spot that made the man tick.

She undid the bobby pins and wiped the cold cream from her face. She slipped into the silk bathrobe Victoria had given her for her birthday. The material felt soft on her skin. She allowed the robe to flow open to showcase her beautiful body: soft rolls, curved thighs that created a big lap for small bodies, large breasts for tired babies to lay their heads on.

She turned off the light and walked to the bedroom. The room spun. Her eyes forced shut as the blood swooshed in her ears with loud ringing. She grabbed the doorway and sank to the floor before darkness called to her. Blue lights flashed behind her eyes. Bill was by her side in an instant, cradling her shoulders with his strong hands.

"I'm going to hit Lifeline. Just lie still," he said.

Her lungs filled with air. The room came into focus. She shook her head to force out the cobweb feeling. "No, I'm fine. I had port tonight with the girls. You know me, I could never handle heavy wines." She placed a hand on his arm. "I promise I'm okay. Can you help me to bed?"

With her arms around his neck, he pulled her to her feet and helped her to bed. Pillows cradled her head as he tucked the blanket around her.

"You look pale again. I think we should go to the hospital." He traced her cheek with his fingers.

In the back of her mind she felt the tug of fear, but she pushed it away. It was the wine and nothing more. She'd call the doctor if it happened again. "I'm fine. Let's go to sleep and we'll see how I feel in the morning."

CHAPTER 19

~⌒o⌒~

Joseph took shaky steps along the overgrown path through the trees that led to the private beach. He ripped ferns from the earth to clear the path as he walked and placed torches in the sand. It took five trips back and forth from his house to create the scene. A circle of white light crackled around the linen-covered table. Crystal candlesticks held glowing tapers, and two silver serving trays were flanked by champagne flutes. Satisfied with the setup, he returned to his house to shower and change.

Earlier that morning, he'd sat on the dock fishing when Heather had appeared beside him, jeans rolled up to her calves and her hair pulled into a ponytail. "I need to talk to you," she said.

"Okay," he said. "Would you like to try your hand at fishing while we have this discussion?"

"Sure." He handed her the rod and she swung her bare feet over the dock's edge as she held the line he'd already cast. With the proficiency of someone who'd taught many children how to fish, he showed her how to reel in her hook, place her hands in the right position, and then recast.

"Nicely done," he said on her third try.

"Thank you," she said. "Now, on to our discussion. I don't normally meddle in other people's business, but something needs to be said. And I don't mean to be disrespectful or to tell you what to do, but I think you should ask Victoria on a date."

Joseph laughed at the girl's conviction.

"I'm serious. I don't see you with anyone, and she's alone. I saw the two of you in the coffee shop. You were sneaking looks at her every chance you had."

"Heather . . ."

"No, just let me say this. Victoria barely shuts up, but when she's around you she can't speak. All she does is blush. Feelings like that are rare."

"I guess you're right," Joseph said.

"Well, good. We agree," Heather said. "Now are you going to do something about it?"

By noon, Heather's words still rung in his ears, and he'd decided it was time. He tacked an invitation to dinner on Victoria's door, and spent the next few hours pacing, watching her house. Finally, the car pulled into her driveway and Victoria emerged. She walked to the front door and Joseph watched her. She read the note, looked to his home, and saw him staring. With a nod she accepted his invitation.

It felt like hours until he heard her footsteps on the path leading to the private beach. He straightened his suit jacket as she came into the clearing. In the soft blue dress she looked breathtaking. Holding a bouquet of lilies, he greeted her. "For you."

"Thank you." She bowed her head into the fragrance of the flowers and he saw her flaming cheeks.

"You look stunning."

She smiled and looked into his eyes with the same soft look

that had made his teenage heart burst with love. He extended his arm and escorted her to her seat.

The champagne cork popped and icy smoke wafted from the bottle. He poured them each a glass and lifted his hand in a toast. "To you, Victoria."

She lifted her glass as he sat. "To you, Joseph, for making a woman feel incredibly special."

As they drank, the sultry voice of Billie Holiday playing in the background, Joseph tried to find words or whit, urging his lips to move, but nothing came out. Finally he pulled the ornate silver covers from the plates that lay before them. "Shall we eat?"

Victoria picked at the food. "I can taste the hint of sherry in the lobster ravioli, Molly's secret ingredient. I promise to give compliments to the chef."

The lake's small waves lapped against the beach, bringing with it the memory of the night they'd made love on this spot. Warmth flushed his face as he stole glances at her. She looked uncomfortable as she barely touched her food. A blue jay swooped over the table and grabbed a piece of bread.

"He certainly knows what he wants," Victoria said.

Joseph looked at the downturned angle of her mouth and his heart sank. "Victoria, have I made you uncomfortable tonight?"

Victoria looked at her food. "I don't know what to say. I'm surprised . . . and . . . speechless." She pushed the ravioli with her fork. "With all that I've done, you plan this night for me?"

Joseph placed his hand on hers and laid her fork on the table. "I wanted to." He'd wanted to give her Cary Grant tonight. Instead, he was a lovesick old man who felt like a twelve-year-old boy on his first date. Joseph lifted her chin and stared into her silver eyes. "Victoria, I'm seventy-six years old. I'm far from being Cary Grant. I'm just a man who has loved a girl since he was a boy, and I'm asking her for one last shot at being with her."

"Have you ever thought that you were a fool for loving me?"

"Yes." He laughed. "I spent my entire childhood being told that you hated my guts."

Tears glistened her eyes, but this time they came from laughter. "I was so mean to you, and yet you kept saving me from the other boys."

"You had so much sass. You were loud and a leader and unlike any other girl. I didn't have a choice but to love you. Not much has changed."

She laughed harder. "You poor man." Victoria stood and walked to him. She knelt in the sand and placed her head on his thigh. Joseph touched her soft hair, then pulled her to sit on his lap. Her finger caressed the dimple in his cheek; it fit the indent like a puzzle piece locking with its mate. The softness of her lips brushed against his cheek. "Do you remember the night we made love?" she asked.

"It's imprinted on my heart."

"Can we here?"

Would she find him attractive? His old body and slackened skin. "I'm nervous," he said.

"Relax." She kissed his forehead and traced hearts on his cheeks. "I'll wait for you."

CHAPTER 20

Heather sat in her office waiting for Charlie's phone call. Three days earlier she'd submitted pages for him to review before he sent it to his publishing contact in New York. Outside her living room window she could hear Sarah and Agatha at the picnic table talking about health problems. Agatha had exchanged her scooter for a cane but complained of the swelling in her knee due to the humidity.

Heather needed to have fun. Molly had asked several times why she didn't invite friends over for a dinner party, but Heather had been too busy with work. She picked up the phone.

"Hey," Gina answered, "I was just thinking about you. The city is sweltering. Can I come out to your place tonight? Maybe bring some people?"

"You read my mind, let's make it a party. Say about seven o'clock."

"I'll bring food and wine."

"Don't bother with dessert. My neighbor Molly has loaded me down with cakes and brownies that I need to share before I can no longer fit into my jeans."

"Sounds good. I'll see you in a few hours."

Heather looked at the piece of paper on her desk with Tommy's number on it. Should she call him and invite him over tonight? He'd given her the number for house emergencies, not personal invitations. Reading him was impossible. Their conversations felt flirtatious, but then he'd become distant. She needed guts. Maybe she'd find confidence after she spoke with Charlie and he told her he loved the pages.

The day was hot and she changed into her red bikini and a pair of shorts. Outside, a book had been left on her deck railing. "A Bible. I wonder who brought me this," Heather said with sarcasm, loud enough that Sarah could hear her. A note fell from the pages.

Heather, the Lord is always there, awaiting our return to his love.

"Can he get me a television show or a publishing contract?" she asked Sarah.

"If the Lord sees it as his will, it shall be done," Sarah replied, then she and Agatha stood and walked away.

"Heather," Thomas called from inside his house, "could you help me with something?"

"Of course," she said as she walked across the driveway, opened his door, and went inside. "Problems with your computer?"

"No, I think I'm getting the hang of it." He looked up from the screen and smacked his lips. "Now that's a bathing suit. You should enter one of those beauty pageants. I'm sure you'd win the swimsuit competition."

"Thank you, Thomas, but I don't think you're right," she said as she walked to the desk and stood beside him. "And if you grab my behind I'm going to smack that hand of yours. You hear me?"

"Don't know what you're talking about," he said as he handed her a tape measure. "I need to buy a new suit and I found some good deals on the computer, but I need to know my measurements. Now, don't worry, I won't have you doing my inseam or anything. I know that one." He winked at her. "I just need across the shoulders and down the arms and back. And no getting fresh with me while you're doing it."

"I'll try to contain myself." She pulled the tape across his shoulders. "Wouldn't it be better to go to a store? I'm sure Joseph or Bill would take you."

"Nah, that would take six weeks. If I order one online I'll have it by the end of next week."

"What's the rush?" she teased as she placed the tape on his left shoulder and brought it to his wrist, then wrote down the number.

"I have an event to attend," he said.

"It wouldn't have anything to do with an Internet site I helped you join?"

"None of your business." He smacked his gums and smiled.

She finished the measurements and turned to the screen; tabs were open for limo companies, flowers, and take-out menus, along with a menswear store. It hadn't taken Thomas long to get the hang of the Internet. She wondered if Tommy knew what his grandfather was up to.

Her cell phone rang and Charlie's number came up on the screen. "Sorry, Thomas, I have to take this. If you need any more help, just let me know."

Outside, she flipped open the phone as she noticed the men situating themselves at the picnic table with a deck of cards. In minutes her house would be filled with smoke. She looked at the picnic table on the beach and willed them to move away from her house, but it didn't work.

"Hi, Charlie. What's up?"

"Are you trying to ruin your career?"

"Excuse me?"

"I don't know where to start, Heather," he said. "First of all, I can't use these pages you sent me."

"Why not?" Heather said in a sharp tone that made the men look up from their cards. "I've worked almost every day and night for the last three weeks to get you what you wanted—what's wrong with them?"

"They don't have any edge. It's just more of the same stuff you put in your columns. The whole point of the book is to give your fans more insight into your life and travels. The sad thing is that I'm not surprised. I've read your columns lately and they're boring."

"Really, because George loved them," Heather said.

"You're writing about vacationing on a lake and relaxing in a hammock as you read a book. Where's the adventure? The sexiness?"

"I'm appealing to middle America. It's Americana, Norman Rockwell, the Fourth of July. It's what George asked for," Heather said.

"Well, that's great. I'm sure Steven has been reading your articles too, realizing that he can't sell this boring crap to his producers. Get on the damn road, find something sexy, and do it before you destroy the career I built for you."

He hung up the phone and Heather stood on the deck fuming.

"The waves in the Arctic were so big that the ship would rock to a forty-five-degree angle," Carl yelled from under the oak tree. "If you didn't hold on, you'd go straight over the side."

Heather groaned as she went inside, closed all her windows, and turned on the air-conditioning. *The career he built.*

She'd bled her soul into those pages, but it wasn't right. Charlie and Steven wanted sexy, not shy. Television was filled with bleached blondes with big breasts partying around the world. And Heather was the woman who'd realized she liked eating brownie sundaes on Molly's screened porch while chatting with two seventy-year-olds.

No wonder her voice had become dull. Well, tonight she'd change that. She'd loosen up and remember what it's like to party, to be young and carefree and adventurous—even sexy.

～⦿～

Victoria stood in front of her mirror, applying moisturizer and a lifting-serum to her skin. She fluffed her hair and applied the makeup she'd bought at the spa. She wanted to look beautiful for Joseph. Slipping into a blue sleeveless dress with a white belt that cinched her waist and black nylons with a seam up the back, she wondered if her outfit might be a bit too racy. But then again, she was entertaining a sexy gentleman later. Victoria stared at her reflection. If only she could reclaim the radiance of youth for one night.

In the kitchen, she hummed as she chopped carrots on the wooden butcher's block. Her mind wandered to their date the previous night.

Joseph had cradled her in his arms, removing her clothing with a gentle caress. They watched each other as they touched, exploring the bodies that were different from the ones they'd adored when their love had been fresh.

His warm mouth on her neck sent waves of shivers through her body. Tears glistened on her cheeks as his strong hands softly pushed back her hair and he looked into her eyes. When their bodies joined, she realized that the wetness against her cheeks hadn't been her tears alone.

The pain, the loss, the need for so many years came together in a sweet rhythm that melded with the wind and the sound of the lake against the shore. The longing to connect, to merge their bodies and hearts, filled her and her peak came as a shock that rolled through her body releasing all the years of missing him. After making love, she'd curled into the crook of his arm, their clothing beneath their bare bodies. She finally understood that he was her soul mate, her other half, and no matter how far the distance between them, their love had never been a choice. In the early morning, they'd gone to his house and curled into his bed making love again.

Joseph's knock on the front door jolted her from her daydream. When she opened the door and saw him in jeans and a white button-down shirt, desire ignited. "Hello beautiful lady," he said as he handed her pink roses.

"Thank you." They smiled as he took a moment to stare. Red flushed her cheeks as youthful hormones flushed her body. She turned and led him into the kitchen, gathering a vase as her nerves made words impossible. Goose bumps prickled her skin when he kissed the back of her neck. She leaned into his embrace and wrapped an arm around his neck. "You smell delicious," he said.

"Really? Is it the Burberry perfume or the muscle rub? My neck was hurting earlier from sleeping on the beach."

"As I recall, we didn't sleep very much." He placed her arm by her side and rubbed the taut muscles. "Hmm, it's all menthol, with a little sexy lady mixed in. For an old man, the smell of muscular relief is exciting."

She turned and bopped him with a towel. "You're not an old man."

"Ah, let's see, I'm seventy-six. I'd say that's pretty old."

"Not in my book." She turned and kissed him, letting her body melt against his chest. They'd made love again that afternoon at his place. "For two very old people, we seem to be having sex more than most thirty-year-olds."

He ran his fingers over her bare shoulders. "We have more time."

"You want to move this to the bedroom?" Victoria whispered.

"I would love to, but I think we might need some nourishment first." He kissed her cheek and then pulled away. He selected a CD and The Starlight Orchestra came over the speakers in the kitchen. Joseph danced across the tiles, slipped his arms around Victoria's waist, and moved her into a waltz.

"What's for dinner?"

"I came up with minted carrots and chicken of some sort," Victoria said. "I'm cutting the carrots, but I thought it would be safer if you cooked the rest."

"Don't expect me to make it healthy." He twirled her and finished the dance with a dip.

"Try and find junk food in this kitchen," she said, reaching up to kiss him. From the refrigerator, she handed him two small chicken breasts denuded of fat.

"I miss dark meat," he said. "I'm sure there will be hell to pay if I cover this poultry in a thick batter and throw it in a deep fryer. We should've gone to Molly's for dinner, then we would've had a meal filled with delicious grease."

He looked in the refrigerator and grabbed tomatoes, onions, garlic, and olive oil and placed them on the counter next to the stove. Victoria coated a pan with cooking spray and threw the carrots in with the chopped mint.

Joseph walked by and kissed her on the cheek. "You know, a little butter and brown sugar would make that dish delicious. Let's give up being healthy and enjoy being old enough not to care."

"I may be in my mid-seventies, but I have a long life ahead of me that includes you by my side. And I don't intend to have a pooch around my belly."

"I like a little pooch." He grabbed her midsection. She swatted him, and he pulled her into a long, slow kiss.

The phone rang. Victoria leaned back and grabbed the receiver.

"Victoria's Kitchen, how may I help you?"

Daniel's voice came over the other end of the line. "Did you see that your little friend has guests tonight?"

"Actually, Daniel, I didn't." Victoria hadn't had time to check on Heather today. "I don't see the problem. The girl is allowed to have guests."

"I don't want to have to listen to music and loud noise all night. I expect you to put an end to this. She's your friend." Daniel's voice became louder.

Victoria handed Joseph the phone. "You talk to him. No one will listen to me. There's no reason for them to get their panties all twisted over nothing. *Oh no,* Heather's having a dinner party. Call the fun police before someone enjoys themselves."

They ate dinner on the sun porch as they watched the sky turn inky black. Loud music came from the beach as she and Joseph talked and sipped wine. He pulled her into his arms and played with her hair as she curled into his warmth. They spoke of his children and grandchildren. They reminisced about childhood and playing in the tree house. She told him about Hollywood. They found words they hadn't been able to speak through the years and it seemed they needed another lifetime to catch up with everything they'd missed.

Victoria heard squeals coming from the beach as Heather and her friends splashed in the water, a roaring bonfire illuminating the waterfront where the girls danced. It was good to see Heather come to life with people her own age. Heather had blossomed over the summer, from a quiet, embarrassed child who seemed apologetic in the face of kindness from her and Molly into a confident young woman who knew what she wanted from life and was ready to make it happen. Victoria began to drift to sleep in Joseph's arms as he softly snored. Through her dreams she heard someone yelling for the music to be turned off and then the slam of car doors. Contentment continued to flow over her and then suddenly she was awake, panic in her heart. Something was wrong.

She went to the window and saw Heather walking toward the water in a drunken stupor, a wine bottle in her hand. She tripped over the sidewalk and landed on the pavement, then stood, regained her balance, and stepped onto the sand, swaying. Suddenly, her head fell and her body followed.

"Oh, God. Not again." Victoria banged the screen door as she ran across the beach. Her little girl was in trouble. She had to fix her. Had to help her before it was too late. "Heather!" she screamed. "Heather!"

Heather lay in the sand, her hair covering her face. Victoria dragged her into her lap and held the dead weight of the girl in the crook of her arm. With her ear to Heather's mouth, Victoria could hear the girl's soft inhales and exhales. "Thank you, God," Victoria whispered.

Joseph stumbled from the house and Molly ran from her place in her nightdress, her hair in pin curlers. Victoria brushed the sand from Heather's cheeks. "She's okay. She's unconscious, but she's breathing. I think we should take her to the hospital."

"No. She's just had too much to drink. Let's put her to bed and watch her." Joseph lifted Heather and carried her across the sand. The girl's head rolled back and her arms fell open.

Victoria stood as Bill joined them. Sarah stood at her door along with Carl and watched Joseph carry Heather into her place.

"Why don't you go home?" Molly said to Bill.

"This girl's a menace," Bill said.

"Not now," Molly said as she patted his arm. "Come on, Victoria, let's help Joseph."

They walked across the road, Victoria's hands shaking as Molly waved Sarah and Carl to return to their house.

At Heather's, the sour smell of vomit invaded the upstairs hall, and a yellow puddle had pooled in front of the master bedroom.

In the guest bathroom, Heather coughed over the toilet as Joseph held her hair back. Victoria soaked a washcloth in cold water and placed it on the back of Heather's neck. Molly wet towels, grabbed soap, and worked on the vile spot in the hallway.

Victoria went into Heather's office and saw piles of paper covered with red slash marks. On the front of a manila folder were five written lines:

1. Be a better columnist so I don't lose my job.
2. Get a television deal.
3. Lose weight so they will want me on a television show.
4. Sign a book deal and make it onto *New York Times* best-seller list.
5. Become a popular travel star.

"Victoria?" Molly placed her hand between her friend's shoulder blades.

"Look at this." Victoria's hand shook as she handed her the folder.

"This is private," Molly said.

"She's been pushing herself too hard. That's why she got drunk," Victoria said. "I didn't pay attention to how much stress she was under. I need to do something. She could kill herself trying to obtain all of this."

"She's not Annabelle," Molly said in a quiet voice.

"I know that," Victoria said.

Joseph stood at the door. "Heather's sleeping. I think we should go."

"I'm not leaving her," Victoria said.

Joseph looked to Molly. "You go, Joseph. We'll stay with her."

"Why can't she see that she has everything? That she doesn't have to push this hard?" Victoria sunk to the chair and her body shook as she cried.

Molly leaned over Victoria and wrapped her arms around her friend.

Victoria whimpered. "She has everything: opportunity, beauty, and success. Why isn't that enough?"

"I know, honey. I know." Molly swayed and almost fell. Victoria stood and grabbed her friend. "Are you okay? What happened?"

"Just a little dizzy spell is all," Molly said. "It's from being woken so abruptly and then running across the beach. A little too much excitement."

"Why don't you go back to bed? I'll stay with her."

"No. I'm not leaving you alone tonight."

⌒⌒

The breeze fluttered the curtains around Heather's bed as she curled into a fetal position. A sour taste covered her swollen tongue. It should've been raining: a big, dark storm with ominous clouds that bent the trees and stirred the lake. Weather to match her life. She wore her M&M's pajamas, but couldn't remember changing her clothes. Her mind reached for memories from the night before.

The evening had started out wonderfully. Gina had invited over a few friends, and they'd sat on the deck drinking wine and eating Michard's tortellini primavera with heirloom tomatoes. The conversation turned to travel and Heather took the spotlight as she gave out tips and told stories from her adventures. For a few hours, she felt normal, young, and part of a crowd. Then worries about her conversation with Charlie had crept in and she drank her wine a little faster than usual. She recalled swimming and a bonfire . . . and Carl, then Daniel, yelling at her to be quiet.

The rest of the night was a blur. When everyone left, she wanted the carefree feeling to continue and poured another glass of wine. The last thing she remembered was walking toward the beach thinking that she should take a dip in the lake.

How could I have been so stupid?

Heather roused herself and stood. The room swirled and the migraine felt like a bomb exploding in her head, with the pain radiating up her neck and mushrooming into her skull. Her stomach felt like it had been sucked dry, and she returned to her curled-up position on top of the covers. A platter with blueberry muffins and an insulated coffee mug sat on the nightstand. Molly had visited. Was she the one who had changed Heather into her pajamas?

The screech of circular saws and the old men yelling came through the window. Heather looked and saw Victoria, asleep on the chaise. The memory of Joseph holding her hair while she vomited returned. "Oh, God," she moaned in embarrassment.

"Well, good morning," Victoria said, stretching. "How are you feeling?"

"Like death," Heather responded.

Victoria moved over to the bed and sat with her back against the headboard, she reached out and combed her hand through Heather's hair. "I can't imagine what they're building out there, but they're making quite the racket."

"I think they're probably trying to torture me for keeping them up last night," Heather said. "I'm kind of mortified by the way I acted."

"Oh, darling," Victoria murmured, "we've all had those moments in life. I'm just a little worried about what caused it. You said you weren't a big drinker."

"It was a rough day, and with the stress of late I needed to blow off steam."

"What happened?" Victoria asked as she continued to pet Heather's head.

Heather pulled the sheet closer. "Charlie called and said he couldn't use any of the pages I sent him for the book proposal . . . they weren't sexy enough."

"That man again?" Victoria said. "For someone who is supposed to be supporting your career, he seems to tear you down more than build you up."

"Without him I wouldn't have my career, and I need him to take me the rest of the way," Heather said.

"You're already a successful columnist. Why do you need to accomplish more?"

"They want someone famous and I'm not." Heather looked up at Victoria. "I'm not like you. When you showed me your modeling photos and movies, I could see how confident and sexy you were. When a camera is on me, I'm uncomfortable in my own skin." She bit her bottom lip. "I might lose my column. They told me last spring that I was in danger of being replaced."

"Oh, Heather, I didn't realize what you'd been going through."

Heather sat up with her back against the headboard. "Tell me what's going on with you and Joseph. I saw him walk over to your house last night."

"Is that your delicate way of saying you don't want to talk about your career anymore?" Victoria asked.

"Yep. Plus, you've been a little busy the last couple of days," Heather said as she watched Victoria's face flush.

"Well, would you like all the dirty details?" Victoria teased. "I was actually thinking of using that tip you gave me."

"My stomach can't handle that right now. I'm still a little queasy." Heather put her arm around her midsection.

Victoria laughed. "Let's just say that life can surprise you with the way things work out. Who would've thought that after all these years we'd share this love?"

"Victoria, that's wonderful. I'm happy for you." Heather

stood. "I'll be right back." A horrid stench assaulted her nose in the bathroom. She walked into the hallway and the smell burned her eyes as she came to the top of the stairs.

Victoria came up behind her with a coffee mug in hand.

"Does my house smell like garbage and rotten eggs to you?" Heather asked.

"I think your septic tank's sewage line might be backed up," Victoria said as she covered her mouth and nose.

"Great, another thing I need to deal with today."

CHAPTER 21

⤜⤛

It had been the kind of day that made Tom long to be a kid again. The temperature stayed in the high seventies, and the lack of rain in the past month made the humidity tolerable. It reminded him of summer days when he lay on the beach, his mouth smudged with chocolate ice cream, creating pictures out of shifting cumulous clouds as the sun reflected off the lake, making wavy light patterns on the leaves.

It had been weeks since he'd visited Nagog, and he felt homesick. He needed a day to fish with Bill and Carl while they told him their crazy stories. The thought of a meal at Molly's made him salivate. He'd eaten too many meals in restaurants and at his desk lately. He wanted to lie on the beach, take an afternoon nap, and then have a beer with his grandfather and Bill around the campfire. The last time he'd spent a full weekend in Nagog had been before Annabelle died. Since then, he hadn't made time for lazy days with his family.

Tom loosened his tie and pulled it from under the collar. Instead of sitting in the grass enjoying the beautiful day, he'd spent ten hours in meetings that concluded with a three-hour dinner with the developer from the West Coast, who had high-lighted hair and manicured nails, sucking down oysters and telling Tom he wanted twenty distinctive home designs with all the bells and whistles.

It had been hard to turn down hundreds of thousands of dollars in design fees and the chance to create homes across the western seaboard, but Tom didn't want his name associated with cookie-cutter homes stuffed together with only three feet of yard between them. Those kinds of communities didn't leave room for family barbecues in the backyard, and they created emotional distance between neighbors.

He switched the radio station to heavy metal rock and drummed his hand against the steering wheel. Up ahead he saw the exit for Route 93. He could be home in half an hour. Then what? More work?

He needed to check on Grandpa. Tom had lied to himself, pretending work had kept him too busy to visit Nagog the last couple of weeks. He knew that he was avoiding Heather. His mind had wandered to her more often than he wanted to admit. At night, before sleep came, Heather's laugh or her story about Africa replaced his memories of Annabelle. Though he hated to admit it, the thought of opening his heart again scared him.

When he pulled onto Nagog Drive, he saw a limo parked in Grandpa and Heather's shared driveway. Tom assumed the fiancé had come to make amends or Heather had met someone new. Either way, it didn't matter. It was better this way, but his disappointment surprised him. He hadn't realized how much he'd been hoping to see her tonight. The memory of her sitting on the deck with her legs angled toward him made him wish that there'd be more nights of flirting or possibly even dinner out, but it looked like he was too late. He backed up and parked his car on the other side of his grandfather's house and walked around to the front door.

The house was dark. Tom unlocked the door and heard the sound of a saxophone coming from the stereo in the living room. Red roses had been placed in his grandmother's crystal vase and he saw two plates with half-eaten dinners on the table. Tom walked into the living room, where Grandpa was dancing with a short woman in a purple dress, a flower tucked in her white hair. When the two smiled and leaned in to kiss, Tom cleared his throat.

"I don't mean to interrupt."

The couple broke apart like teenagers caught necking. Grandpa looked up. "Oh, Tommy. I thought you said you had meetings tonight."

"I did." He moved toward the woman and extended his hand. "I'm Tommy, the grandson."

"Nice to meet you, dear. Your grandfather has told me so much about you. He's very proud."

"Grandpa, could I speak with you?" Tom led his grandfather into the kitchen. "Who's that?"

"That's Geraldine," he said. "She's eighty-two. Quite a hottie, don't you think?"

"Where did you meet her? And how did she get here?" Tom asked.

"I sent the limo for her. Neither of us can drive, and I wanted to show my lady some class." Grandpa winked at him. "Heather helped me sign up for an online dating site. We met on it about a month ago. And that camera let her know she was getting a hunk. I even ordered my suit on the computer." He pulled the jacket's lapels and puffed his chest in pride. "You're not hanging around here tonight, are you?"

"I was thinking about sleeping over and doing some fishing tomorrow. Is that okay?" Tom teased.

"Sure, Molly and Bill would love to have you." Grandpa pushed him toward the door. "You say hello for me."

"Hey, you don't have to shove. I was just kidding. I wouldn't want to get in the way of your hot date. Just make sure you use protection."

"Yeah, yeah, you little wiseass," he said. "And Tommy, I think it's time to renovate. Give the house some sprucing. What do you think?"

"Will you be staying with me during construction?" Tom asked.

"Not if I'm lucky." He poked Tom in the ribs. "Now get lost. Go visit that young hot thing next door. She's had a rough week."

Tom walked outside and looked to Heather's house. Nerves held him back for a moment. Was he ready to pursue this?

As he stepped onto her deck, putrid fumes made his eyes water and dozens of toads jumped across the wood. He walked to the open front door and rapped on the doorframe.

"What?" Heather said without looking up from her book.

"Got some new pets?" he asked, as one of the toads hopped into her living room.

She looked up. "Oh, it's you." She studied his clothing and then turned back to the book. "Have you come to yell at me? Or maybe to read the Bible aloud? Because if you have, you're too late. It's been done."

Heather wore pink pajamas with green M&M's and a tank top, and her hair was in pigtails. He was surprised to see her in glasses, and through the tank top he could see that the cleavage she normally wore wasn't her own. "Little early for bed. You sick?"

"Please, I'm not in the mood. I've had a crappy week," she said without looking up.

He stifled a laugh. "Speaking of crap, is it garbage day?"

The book slammed. "Very funny. No, it's not garbage day. For the last week, a horrendous stench has permeated my house." She stood and paced, her arms flailing. "I can't get rid of it. If I sit by the water to get some fresh air, the men blow cigar smoke at me." She confronted him close up. "They seem to be following me—in the bookstore, the coffee shop, the goddamn grocery store. So I'm stuck working with the smell of sewage and listening to them reminisce about the war outside my window."

"Are the toads some kind of old-man repellent?" He covered his mouth to hide his smirk.

She paced again. "No, they just showed up the day my screen went missing. If I close the door to keep the toads out, I choke on the nauseating smell. I'm tired of chasing the buggers out, so I've let them move in."

They stared at one another.

"Boy, do you bring out the life in them." He chuckled.

"I'm glad you're finding entertainment in this." She hurled the book at his head.

He caught the paperback before it hit his face. "*Memoir Writing for Dummies*. I thought you were a famous writer for the *Globe*."

"Screw you! I'm having difficulty writing in this environment."

Tom liked seeing her like this—frazzled, unraveled, and passionate as hell.

"Have you tried talking to Victoria or Molly?"

"No—" Heather stopped. "I see the way Sarah and Agatha treat Victoria. If I say something, it might start a fight, and I don't want to cause her any problems. Plus, she's been busy with Joseph this last week."

"What about Molly?"

"No. She's hasn't been feeling well and I don't want to bother her. Will you stop staring at me like I'm crazy?" She grabbed the book from him and sat on the couch.

"How about this? You stay here and I'll get rid of the smell. I think I know what's causing it."

"How? I don't even know what the problem is. I called a repairman and he said a bad septic system wouldn't smell like rotten eggs and dog poop."

"Do you have a flashlight?" Tom asked.

She shot him an incredulous look. He put his hands up and backed away. "I'll get one out of my car."

For Tom's tenth birthday, Carl had bought him a chemistry set and taught him to make stink bombs. Tom went to his car, took off his dress shirt and grabbed the flashlight. In Grandpa's garage he found a rake and garbage pail. He searched the yard and listened for buzzing flies. He removed the grating under the back porch and found the smelly culprits. Using the rake, he fished out yellow boxes and brown bags of dog feces. The smell made his eyes burn. Flies swarmed his face as he sealed the offensive items in the trash.

As he dug out clothes from his car and changed, he had to laugh. God, he loved these old men. The dog poop was a nice touch. He wondered where they'd gotten it, since no one in the neighborhood had a pet. Still, this latest prank was exceptionally cruel. He'd need to talk to them.

He went inside and walked past Heather on his way to the kitchen. She kept her eyes on her book. After washing his hands, he stood in the doorway to the living room and watched her. Heather's ponytails reminded him of his first love, Stacy Sisilack, whose short brown pigtails were always tied in ribbons that coordinated with her dress. One afternoon, he'd found a robin's egg that matched the light blue of Stacy's ribbons. When he gave her the gift, she agreed to join their desks together during art time. It had been the best afternoon of his first grade year.

"Have you eaten?" he asked.

"I went for Thai food. Daniel and Carl joined me, uninvited. They talked about the Depression, World War II, concentration camps, and how our generation is a bunch of spoiled brats who don't know the meaning of hard work," she said.

"Go throw on some clothes. And you might want to grab a sweatshirt."

"Why?" she asked.

"Well, you have two choices: stay in here and deal with the smell or come with me. I'll be your shield against the elderly. But only if you keep the pigtails. They're cute."

She stormed up the stairs. "I'm not going out in pigtails. I haven't lost that much dignity."

"Okay," he yelled after her, "but I don't think the trees care about your dignity. I thought we'd sit on the beach and have a glass of wine."

❧

Tom walked to the fire pit and threw another log on the flames. He poked the embers with a large stick and then laid it in the sand.

"So, were you able to fix the problem?" Heather asked.

"Let's just say that in a few hours, the smell should be gone. Keeping it away might be another story." He sat down next to her in the sand with his back against a large log.

"Do I need to call some kind of repairman?"

Tom smirked. "More like a garbage man."

Heather shook her head. "I don't understand."

"Your neighbors are putting stink bombs under your house."

"What?" The wine splashed onto her jeans and the sand. "Why would they do that?"

"I don't know. Did something happen between you and them?"

Heather looked down at her wine and pulled her hands around the glass. "I guess you don't know that I had a few people over again last week, and the music was loud. I figured you had showed up to yell at me again."

"They didn't call me. I guess they decided to take matters into their own hands." He stood. "I'll be right back."

"Whatever." She waved him away as she thought about all the mysterious things that had happened in her house: the ants, the missing pipe, the lack of hot water, the horrendous smell . . .

Tommy walked toward the Jacobses' home, and Heather groaned, worried he was going to ask Molly to join them. Still embarrassed by her drunken behavior, she'd found ways to avoid her, Victoria, and Joseph with the excuse that she was overloaded with work, which hadn't been a lie. Charlie had called every day with suggestions for her writing and the upcoming travel she needed to arrange. Between him and her neighbors, she was on the verge of a breakdown. So much for lakeside tranquility.

Tom returned with marshmallows, graham crackers, and chocolate bars. He sat next to her and placed a white candy puff each on two long sticks with carved points. "You can't have a fire without s'mores." He handed her a stick. Heather watched him place his marshmallow near the fire, careful not to get too close to the flames, expertly rotating his stick.

"I've never done this before."

"You're kidding. Not as a Girl Scout or at camp?" he asked.

Heather avoided his eyes and dug her feet in the sand. "I never did those things."

"Well, the trick is to find good black coals on the fringe of the fire. You need to rotate your hand until the marshmallow begins to smoke and turns brown. Or you can catch the sugar on fire and pick off the black crust when the flame goes out." He pulled the cooked marshmallow from the embers. It melted off the stick and fell into the sand. "I'm out of practice. It takes time to perfect the roasting technique. Give it a try. I'll get the crackers and chocolate ready."

Heather moved closer to the flames, the heat reddening her cheeks until she felt the blood vessels would burst. She kept her eyes on the end of the stick, watching for the smoke. "Where did you get this stuff?"

"Cabinet in the Jacobses' garage." He ripped open the cellophane packaging of the graham crackers.

"Are Molly and Bill awake?" she asked.

"No." He squatted next to her, put his hand over hers and rotated her wrist. "Go a little slower and you'll start to get the browning."

The closeness made her skin flush. "So you walked in, took the food, and didn't ask?"

"Didn't need to. Everyone does it. It's been that way for a hundred years. In the last twenty years they've started locking the doors at night, but we all have keys."

"What do you mean everyone has keys?"

"You should have a set in your garage, or maybe someone took them before you moved in."

"So everyone in this neighborhood has a key to my house." She smacked her forehead. "Well, now it all makes sense. They've been sabotaging my home since I moved in."

"Yeah, I've been kind of wondering about that since you mentioned the ants and the water heater," he said as he pulled his hand away from hers.

"Those little brats," she said through clenched teeth. "Why would they do this?"

Tom turned to her with a concerned look. "I should've done something about it sooner."

"Ah, conceited ass—I can tell you find your buddies' pranks hilarious," she said as she shook her head in disgust.

Tom bowed his head. "Sorry . . . But you have to admit it's creative."

Heather turned her attention back to the now bubbling marshmallow. "Sorry, I'm too pissed to find it funny."

"You have the right to be ticked off, considering what they did." With a steady motion, he led her stick toward him, slid the marshmallow onto a graham cracker, topped it with chocolate, and pressed another cracker down. The sticky mess oozed onto his fingers as he handed her the dessert.

White and brown goo stuck to her hands as she bit down. "This is disgustingly sweet." She licked her fingers as marshmallow dripped into the sand.

"You gotta love s'mores. It's campfire tradition to get sick on these things. Drink your wine. It'll cut the sweetness," he said.

"I've never had a s'mores wine pairing before," she said, wiping marshmallow from her mouth.

"Then you've been hanging with the wrong people." He smiled.

She drank the wine, which tasted bitter when combined with the decadent sandwich.

"If you think what they've done to you this week is bad, you should've seen the mess I picked up when they tried to sabotage your home inspection."

"Why would they do that?"

He pushed marshmallows onto two sticks and handed her one. "It's fun just to roast them. You don't have to eat them."

"Are you going to answer my question?"

He sighed. "You've walked into a century's worth of history. This place is all they have left. The world they grew up in—hard work, family traditions, and a sense of community—no longer exists. They're bombarded with technology and their kids barely have time for them. Their grandchildren don't bother to visit. The parties that have been held since the nineteen twenties are now obligations for their children who stop in on their way to something else. You were able to buy your place because Aaron stole his mother-in-law's house and moved her into a nursing home. They're just trying to preserve the life they built. They're afraid that their time has passed and you got caught in the middle."

She pulled her knees to her chest and wrapped her arms around her legs, the wineglass tucked into the crook of her elbow. "I get it. If I had what they had or grew up the way you did, I would fight to keep it too."

"You do have it," he said. "Molly and Victoria adore you."

"Yes, but the rest of them hate me. You grew up around all this, so you don't know what it's like *not* to have a place to call home. How would you feel if your neighbors sabotaged your house?"

He looked at her and she turned to stare at the fire. His hand turned her chin to look at him. "It would suck. I promise I'll put an end to it."

The fire was reflected in his eyes; her hurt and anger softened as she realized he genuinely felt bad for what happened. He moved his hand away and she shook her head. "No, this is my battle. If you get involved, they'll just continue to hate my presence. I'll figure it out." Heather took a sip of wine, stretched her legs, and began to roast another marshmallow directly in the flames. "Can I ask you something about Evelyn?"

"About the mailbox?" he said as he lifted his wineglass and drank.

"How did you know?"

"I thought they would've told you, but I should've known better. Their generation doesn't air private matters." He paused and focused on rotating his stick. "During World War II . . ."

"No! Not another war story. I think I'll go mad if I hear one more!" Heather said.

"Just be quiet and listen." He smiled at her impatience. "Evelyn was engaged to Maryland's brother, James. While he was at war, he bundled his love notes to Evelyn with his letters to his family. Every day she checked the mailbox to see if he'd written."

Heather took a sip of wine and put a new marshmallow into the flames. To her astonishment, it exploded into a bright orange fire and wouldn't go out. She waved the stick until the burning mass fell into the sand.

"You really haven't done this before," he said.

She grabbed a chocolate bar, broke off a piece, and stuck it in her mouth. "Just finish your story."

"James's platoon came under heavy fire and he was never found.

Evelyn married Roger three years later. They had a good marriage: five kids, twelve grandchildren, and who knows how many great-grandchildren. But Evelyn never forgot her first love. Every year, on his birthday, she wore his promise ring . . ." Tom paused.

"Heather, Evelyn has Alzheimer's. She can't remember Roger or any of her kids. All she knows anymore is that James is coming home someday to marry her."

Heather stared at the fire. "Poor Roger. I assumed she had dementia of some kind. I even thought she might have lived in my house growing up and was simply confused. But to have all this"—Heather spread her arms to indicate the community—"and she can't remember it. Does she at least know that these people are her friends?"

Tom shook his head. "No, they've aged. Most days she doesn't recognize them. Grandpa says Roger barely comes out of his house to socialize. There's talk about putting her in a home, but he doesn't want to take her away from the one place she does remember, her home and this neighborhood."

"Speaking of your grandfather, did you meet Geraldine?"

Tom laughed. "Yes, I hear you had something to do with that. Leave it to my grandfather to use the computer I bought him to pick up women. I told you he was a Casanova."

"I think you might have to keep him in check. I hear those sights are for serial daters. Should I call you if he starts having multiple women over at the same time?"

He laughed. "Like I could do anything about it." He stretched his arm across the log behind Heather's head and they both looked to the sky. The full moon dimmed the starlight.

"When I traveled to Peru, this Incan woman told me that the goddess of fertility looked down from the full moon and watched her daughters. Fertility wasn't just about babies; the ripeness of a woman's spirit rose during this time of month. Creativity heightened, and the feminine energy could drive any man to his knees."

He looked into her eyes. "Oh, really, any man to his knees."

"Don't worry, I'm not flirting with you. I used that information to write my column, but I never understood what the Incan woman meant."

"I think you understand more than you know just by being female," he said. "I like when you tell stories of your travels. You light up."

Heather stared at him: the fine chiseled lines of his face accentuated by the firelight, the wavy blond hair that made him almost too pretty, and the body that made her flush. She shivered and looked away.

"Are you cold? Come here." He pulled her into his arms and rubbed her bare shoulders with his large hands. "I told you to grab a sweatshirt."

The goose bumps on her skin weren't from the cold. She pressed her back against his chest, pretending she needed warmth. His heart beat against her body and she curled closer to him, feeling safe. His breathing changed and the air became alive with energy. She assumed her own attraction had her imagining the shift, but her heart began to race as his touch on her arm became softer, more intimate.

The world stopped when she looked up; their eyes searched each other. Her lips moved toward his, and the firmness of his mouth melted hers as they connected. She experienced a strange mix of warmth, comfort, nerves, and excitement. His hand brushed against her jaw and she whimpered from the depth of her longing to be touched this way. A tear dripped down her cheek and he pulled away.

"I'm sorry," she said as she jerked back, ashamed of her emotion.

"No . . ." He paused to catch his breath and looked away.

"I gotta go." She ran for her house, embarrassed. She was such an idiot.

"Heather!" He caught the door before it closed, but she continued to move up the stairs. She kept her back to him as she stood by the window in her bedroom. "Heather, please, look at me."

She froze, refusing to turn. He stepped within inches of her body. "You smell like chocolate, sugar, and wine mixed with the scent of your perfume. It's a little intoxicating and I lost myself."

"You don't have to explain why you kissed me. It's no big deal. You felt bad for what I was going through and . . ."

"I didn't kiss you because I felt bad." He brushed his hand along her shoulders and slowed his words. "I saw you in your pajamas and pigtails and I thought you were sexy as hell."

Her breathing quickened as he moved closer. With a slow caress, he ran his fingers down the sides of her arms. "I'm sorry I pulled back. It's been a long time since I've let anyone in. And God knows you should walk away after I've been such a jerk."

Heather crossed her arms over her chest.

The moonlight illuminated his skin as he turned her to face him. "I don't want to go." His fingers found paths along Heather's shoulders. Arousal flushed her body. Breath against the nape of her neck brought a soft moan. Fingertips down her spine sent shivering spasms up her back. He slipped off her tank top. His arms wrapped around her and she soaked in the touch of his skin— the companionship of another's body. She leaned her head against his shoulder, and his fingers traced the curve of her arm; her skin seemed to leap to his touch. He removed his shirt and then slowly slid the straps of her bra down her biceps. Her arms jerked in reaction, protecting the undergarment from falling. She wasn't ready to be naked in front of him.

"Let me see you," he whispered. He angled her in front of the old standing mirror and placed her back against his bare stomach, her black lace bra still in place.

With a gentle touch he traced the curve of her abs. The flow of her hips. The edge of her low-rise jeans that revealed the top of black lace underwear. She felt the pressure of his attraction against her lower back and he stepped away.

"You're staring," she whispered.

"You're beautiful."

She looked down, embarrassed by his compliment.

He picked her up, cradled her in his arms, and carried her to bed. He laid her head on the pillows. He unzipped her jeans and slid them down her thighs. His large hands caressed and massaged her waist with firm squeezes that made her breath catch. His mouth was warm on her shoulder, his muscles firm and strong over her body. Her hands felt the encasement of his abs and the dip at his hip bone as she pulled him closer.

Need began to tear at her and sensations flowed everywhere as he kissed her mouth, this time deeper. She couldn't catch her breath, and she rolled away to find a sense of self. She allowed his fingertips to trace her spine, and when he began to nip with feathery bites at her shoulders, she felt as if her flesh was entirely under his control. His mouth caressed the curves of her body, then he turned her onto her back. Her breath came faster and she felt exposed in her need for him. His kiss against the inside of her hip sent her over the edge, and her body shook in a wave of release.

"Wow," he said, pulling her onto her side and against his body.

～◦～

Tom's fingertip drew circles around her nose, cheek, and chin, rousing Heather from sleep. He kissed her lips, teasing her mouth open with his tongue, as he pulled her closer into the nook of his arm.

"Did I sleep in your arms all night?" She squirmed away from his hold, realizing she was naked except for her underwear in the morning light.

"Does that surprise you?" He grabbed the sheet as she tried to cover her body. "I like looking at you. Stop trying to cover up." He nuzzled his cheek along her neck, and the stubble on his chin sent tingling sensations racing down her back and arms.

"It's just . . . I have a hard time sleeping." Her feet squirmed as she tried to relax, but here in the daylight, the night before seemed like a dream, a beautiful fantasy that she didn't understand. There had been no intercourse, no complaints that she couldn't leave him in an excited state, unsatisfied. Instead, his mouth traced her body with gentle, fiery sensations.

She tried to pull the sheet around her and slide away, but he held her close.

"Can I put some clothes on?"

He kissed her eyelids and propped his head on his hand. He pulled the blankets and sheets out of her reach. "Your clothes are on the other side of the room."

"Has anyone ever told you that you're a child?" She sucked in her stomach and walked across the room in the bra and panties that had never come off. The footboard provided cover as she threw on the tank top and looked for her jeans.

Tom sat at the end of the bed grinning at her and grabbed her waist.

"My body is not your plaything!" She laughed as he wrestled her back to bed, pulled off her tank top and tickled her.

"Get something through your head." One arm pinned her under his body while the other hand caressed her face. "I hope I proved to you last night that I think you're beautiful and sexy. So, when you're around me, my personal request . . . be naked."

"You mean, when you're visiting your grandfather I should walk the beach without clothing?" Heather said with mock innocence.

The cleft in his chin deepened as he smiled. His warm lips traced her neck and she could feel his long eyelashes against her skin. "Now, that would give them something to talk about. I think Carl would vote for you to stay and he'd do your yard work for free." His hand tickled her belly. "It would definitely stop the abuse."

She twisted and laughed, then caught him looking at the clock. "Someplace you'd rather be?"

Muscular legs straddled her hips. "What's it going to take for me to lose conceited ass status? Romantic date? Flowers? Another root beer float? Though that's what started the nickname."

She wriggled away from him. A flash of how things had ended up with Charlie created fear of letting him in. "I don't need romance."

In the bathroom she pulled her silk bathrobe around her shoulders and grabbed her toothbrush. He followed, wearing the boxers that hadn't come off the night before. In the mirror she could see him leaning against the doorframe. In black boxer briefs, his large, muscular frame looked like Michelangelo's *David*. He made her want to spend the day in bed exploring every curve of muscle, but this couldn't be taken too fast.

Heather put toothpaste on the brush. "Look, you don't have to do anything for me."

Tom crossed his arms and waited while she brushed her teeth.

She rinsed her mouth, then turned. "I don't need a white knight bringing me flowers, taking me to dinner, and making my dreams come true. Romance is something guys do to hook women. Then when the relationship changes, we spend the rest of our lives wondering what the hell is wrong with us that we no longer inspire that kind of devotion. We never bother to look at what the guy has become."

He nodded. "So with your travel and my crazy work schedule, it's going to take about a year for you to trust me. I can work with that."

He walked toward her and kissed the top of her shoulder, once again sending tingles up and down her spine.

"You have plans today?" He walked to the bedroom and tugged on his jeans.

She followed him. "Are you listening to me?"

The T-shirt went over his head and hid the thick ripples of abdominal muscles. "Heather, I don't play games. Whatever I do for you isn't manipulation. If you don't want more than friendship, I won't push." He stood and cupped her face in his hand. "But last night, I felt something I haven't been able to experience in a long time. I'd like to explore it, but only if you want it too."

"Do you realize that I spend most of my life on the road?" Heather asked.

"Really? I thought you wrote your columns from looking at picture books." He checked the time. "It sucks that I have to leave. I remembered this morning that I have to be at a site in New Hampshire by noon. Come with me and let me show you what I do."

Heather looked at his beautiful smile and big eyes the color of tropical seas. She wanted to say yes, but she needed to work. There were travel plans to be made and pages to be rewritten, another column due. "I wish I could, but I'm swamped."

They went downstairs and onto the deck. A manila envelope sat on the railing. "Oh, I wonder whom this could be from?" she said with sarcasm. A small handwritten note had been taped to the front of the church bulletin: *The body is not meant for sexual immorality, but for the Lord, and the Lord for the body (1 Corinthians 6:13).*

Heather handed the paper to Tommy. "If Sarah knows you spent the night with me, everyone else is certain to hear the news."

"Maybe we should pass this message to Grandpa." He laughed. "I'm certain after all of his adventures he could use some saving."

Heather giggled. "So you don't care if your family knows about last night?"

"First of all, it's none of their business and second of all, I plan to repeat our immorality as much as possible." He bent and kissed her lips with a soft touch. "I'll call you later."

Victoria passed him as she walked toward Heather's home. She gave him a quick hug and then raced to Heather's side. "Did I just see him kiss you? Did he spend the night?"

"Maybe, but unlike you, I don't share my personal escapades." Heather walked toward her door. "Want some coffee?"

CHAPTER 22

Four days passed, and though Tommy called, their schedules kept them apart. The first night, something had gone wrong at a construction site and he couldn't make it back to Nagog. The next day his meetings ran late. The last two she had writer's block and had finally found her rhythm about the time he was free. With only a few weeks before she needed to leave for a monthlong trip to India and Nepal, she didn't know how they were going to get their relationship off the ground. They'd fallen into a rhythm of talking at midnight as they both curled into bed and said good night.

Their conversations were like bedtime stories to her. He spoke about woodworking and how he loved the smell of sawdust. She told him about her travel plans and each night he asked her to tell him a story of a trip she'd taken. In exchange, he told her memories of growing up in Nagog. Through these talks, she felt she could reach out and touch him and his love for this place.

Of course, her desire to live in Nagog was challenged anew with each passing day. The aerobic queens had started at six this morning, and Heather had been too tired to join them. With a blanket and pillow, she tried to make her bathtub into a bed, since it was the only place to avoid the noise. Her kitchen still smelled like dog poop, urine, and rotten eggs. This morning everyone's trash seemed to have found its way to her yard: banana peels, orange slices, meat hunks and bones, toilet paper, and aluminum foil covered her grass. She spent an hour cleaning up the mess and digging out smelly containers from under her porch.

As she was finishing, Carl walked up and said, "When you don't keep the lids tight on the garbage cans, the raccoons get in."

"I have a feeling it was a rather large raccoon that did this," she said, and gave him a meaningful look to let him know that she was on to him. Then Bill and Daniel joined him for their latest project that never seemed to be finished or take shape. As Heather went into her house, they were hollering over the sound of saws, drills, and nail guns.

Heather stepped into the shower, and the hot water turned ice cold within seconds. She yelped, jumped from the shower, and wrapped herself in a towel. The bastards must have turned off her hot water heater again. She dressed in jeans and T-shirt and went downstairs. In the kitchen, a small red ant crawled along her thumb when she opened the silverware drawer. She flicked it to the floor and stepped on it. The bugs had returned too.

After talking with Tommy that night by the fire, her solution to the men's abuse had been to let them get it out of their system. In two weeks, she'd be on the road again, only home intermittently. The hope was that by Halloween, they would've made peace with the fact that she lived here.

Suddenly, an old woman's screams came from her neighbor's driveway. As she raced across the backyard, Sarah came up behind her, and Heather slowed, not wanting to interfere.

Evelyn was fighting with Roger as he tried to seat her in the car. "No, I don't know you. My mother told me to never go anywhere with strangers."

Sarah took hold of Evelyn's flailing arms. "Honey, it's Sarah. Why don't I take you to the doctor's office?"

Tears streamed down Evelyn's face. "You're not Sarah. Sarah always wears a scarf to match her dress. You're an old woman. Will someone please take me to my mother?"

"Okay, dear." Sarah looked to Roger. "Another day?"

He nodded.

Sarah took Evelyn's arm and led her up the walk.

Evelyn moved away from Sarah and headed toward Heather's house. "I need to check the mailbox. My love is sending me a letter today."

Heather's heart went out to her neighbors. If only there was something she could do to help them, but for now she needed to help herself by getting her work done.

For three hours she sat in front of her computer, the sound of saws and hammers her constant companion. Her brain felt like an electronic appliance as the batteries ran low—it continued to work, but its progress was slow.

Outside on her deck, she stretched in the sunlight and thought about taking a dip in the lake. The warm air was thick with humidity and the cool embrace of the water might revive her senses. But for now she had to keep going. Maybe tonight Tommy would visit. The thought of seeing him in a bathing suit made her squirm. They could swim together, their wet bodies close as they kissed. The image gave her the strength to return to work, knowing that there might be a break in sight.

Under the oak tree, Sarah sat at the picnic table reading the Bible. Her voice floated on the breeze as she started to read the scripture aloud. "Love is patient; love is kind and envies no one. Love is never boastful, nor conceited, nor rude; never selfish, not quick to take offense. There is nothing love cannot face; there is no limit to its faith, its hope, and endurance."

"Sarah, why do you think I need saving?" Heather asked.

"You can't find love outside yourself; you must find it within and through the Lord. Then everything else falls into place."

"To be honest, I would really appreciate it if you'd stop giving me sermons. I'm not religious."

"Neither was Victoria. She felt fame would bring her happiness; in the end it didn't."

"She seems happy to me," Heather said.

"Looks can be deceiving, especially with Victoria." Sarah closed her Bible and walked away.

Heather shook off the conversation and went upstairs to her office. Where to start?

The phone rang and she picked it up. "Heather, it's George."

"How's my favorite boss these days?" She leaned back in her chair and tapped her pen against her leg.

"Not so good right now," he said in a sad tone.

Heather froze, panic rising in her body. "What is it?"

"The executives have decided to go with the television star for the Sunday column. Most of your syndicates will follow."

"So I'm out?" Heather said trying to control the fear that filled her lungs instead of air.

"You still have two years on your contract, and they plan to use you somewhere, they just haven't decided where yet. I'm sorry, Heather. I fought for you, but—"

"No, it's okay. I know, it's the industry," she said. "I should call Charlie and tell him. Should I cancel my trip?"

"I would put it on hold for now. I don't know if they're going to change your travel budget."

"Okay, thanks. I'll talk to you later."

Heather looked at the stacks of papers on her desk: flight itineraries, hotel options, this week's column. All the work she'd done in the last few months had been for nothing. Panic constricted her lungs and she opened her windows for fresh air. The smell of cigars filled the room. "It was so cold in Russia . . ." How many times could they tell the same tale? Their cigar smoke was ruining her furniture. Her new couch smelled like a men's club, and her beautiful home was being terrorized. She couldn't control anything else in her life, and if she wasn't going to be traveling, this had to stop.

She marched downstairs and out to the table where Bill, Carl, Daniel, and Joseph sat. "Do you mind moving? Your smoke is coming into my living room and your conversation isn't allowing me to work."

Bill puffed on his cigar and blew smoke into the sky. "We've been meeting at this table for over fifty years."

"So you've told me. Maybe it's time for a new place. Like your own yard," she snapped.

"You're being rude and I suggest that you take a different tone," Daniel boomed.

"Don't yell at me. I'm not one of your grandchildren. I own this property and I want you off it."

"Heather, try to calm down," Joseph said. He stood and placed a hand on her arm.

"No. I'm tired of your smoke coming into my house. It's time to move," she said.

"Now, that's a good idea," Carl said. "Everyone in agreement that Heather should move out of the community raise their hands." He lifted his hand into the air and smiled at her.

"What's going on?" Agatha barked as she walked toward them.

"We're voting Heather out of the community," Carl said.

"Sounds good to me," Agatha said.

"Why? What have I done?" Heather yelled. "Nothing except host *two* parties in the three and a half months that I've lived here."

Sarah emerged once again from her house. "Young lady, stop your screaming right now. The Bible says, 'Children obey your parents in the Lord: for this is right. Honor thy father and mother . . .'"

A volcano of emotions erupted in angry red sparks. "You're not my mother, and will you cut the 'saving me' crap? I'm sick of it. Your little notes about my sexual escapades and your Bible on my deck aren't going to convert me." Somewhere in the back of her mind, Heather knew she wasn't upset with her neighbors, but a monster had awakened—the stress from the last few months was taking on a life of its own.

"I know all about your little pranks. I get that you don't want me here, but this is my home. Do you understand?"

"Heather!" Sarah loomed over her. "You will stop this tantrum this minute."

The word *tantrum* set her off further. "I'm a grown woman. I expect a little more respect."

"Then act like it," Bill said.

"I don't care about planes overhead, about your feet being cold, or listening to your damn health problems. None of you knows what it's like to try and succeed in this day and age. So leave me the hell alone." She stormed into her house and slammed the front door.

Upstairs, her breath caught in her throat as she collapsed onto the chaise. A cloud of anger emanated from her trembling body. *They had it coming,* she thought. They'd stunk up her home and shut off her hot water heater. As she began to calm, the realization hit. She'd yelled at her neighbors and created a scene. Told them that she didn't care about their lives.

How was she going to face Tommy and explain how ugly she'd been? He'd hate her. Guilt sat in her stomach like oily pizza as she finally faced the real reason she'd been upset: her conversation with George. The career she'd spent six years building was on the line, and she needed to solve that problem first, or in two years she wouldn't have the money to pay for this place—that's if they didn't break the contract earlier.

She went into the office and picked up the phone. "Hi, Charlie. We need to meet. The *Globe* just took away the Sunday column."

"I'm at the apartment. Come over," he said. "I knew this was going to happen."

"Meet me at Gina's place instead. I'm going to be staying with her for a few days while I try to sort this out."

A half hour later, Heather was trying to force a suitcase into the back of her car. "They don't call you Mini for nothing," she grumbled. Tom's truck turned into the drive and her head fell forward onto the roof of the car. *Damn. Now he shows up.*

He stepped down from the truck. "Where you headed?"

"I need to get away," she said without looking at him.

"My thoughts exactly. I was hoping you might come to my place tonight. I'd like to cook you dinner." He smiled hopefully. "Unless you're leaving on a trip?"

"I can't have dinner with you." She tried to ram the suitcase into the car with her hip. He moved her aside, took the suitcase, and slid it into the front seat. Dirt and grease smudged his T-shirt and grimed his fingernails. He wiped at his clothing. "I'm a mess. I rushed here from work. On the way I blew a tire."

"That stinks. I'm sorry you had a rough day," she said curtly and walked around the car to the driver's side.

He kicked at the dirt, hands in his pockets. "Heather, I don't mean to be forward. I know I should've called first, but I'd really like to spend time with you. What's wrong?" He walked toward her and brushed a strand of hair away from her downturned face.

If she looked into his beautiful eyes, if she continued to let him touch her, she might break in half. She knew he'd reject her the moment he knew what she'd done.

"I can't do this right now," she said, and she turned to open the driver's side door when Victoria walked up and stopped at Tommy's truck.

No, Heather thought, *I can't face her too. I have to get out of here.*

"Heather, what's going on? Did something else happen with the men?" He stroked her arm. When she didn't respond, he leaned in to hold her.

"Please, just leave me alone," she whispered.

"Wait a minute. What happened since our phone call last night?" He moved closer and grabbed her hand.

"I don't think you and I fit. You visit your grandfather on weekends and are happy to sit home on a Friday night in an elderly community. I travel the world. Nagog isn't where I belong, and we both know it."

"You could fit here if you tried."

"No"—she shook her head—"I've been living someone else's life. I need to make my dreams come true, and I can't do that if I stay. I can't even write here. It's time for me to be realistic and return to Boston and get my career on track. I can't be distracted right now. Please, just let me go."

Tom stared at her, his face searching hers. "Okay. I don't understand, but if that's what you want, I'll back off." He took a step backward. "The sad part, Heather, is that I'm sure you'll get everything you want. I just hope when you get there, you're actually happy and don't regret the family you lost." He turned and walked toward his grandfather's house.

You can't lose what you never had, she thought. She got in the car and started the engine. As she backed up, she glanced at Victoria and gave a small wave, then looked away. The word *home* echoed in her heart, but she boxed up her emotions and didn't look back.

❧

Victoria stormed into Molly's kitchen. Her best friend sat at the table, her head in her hands. A half-mixed bowl of brownies had spilled on the floor and the thick brown batter was splattered against the cabinets, but Victoria didn't notice.

"You won't believe what I just heard," she said urgently.

"What?" Molly said in a soft voice.

"I was walking over to see Heather and I overheard her conversation with Tommy. She's going back to Boston! She practically told Tommy he wasn't good enough. That he's too simple. She obviously doesn't know anything about him! What he's accomplished. What it took for him to get there." Victoria paced. "All she does is push people away when they try to help her. I'm so mad."

"That's because she's you."

Victoria stopped. "Excuse me?"

"You're angry with her because she's you." Molly laid her aching head down again.

"That's crazy. I'm angry because she's making the wrong choices."

"No. You're angry because Heather forces you to face the mistakes you feel you've made." Molly rubbed her temples.

Victoria threw her hands up and rolled her eyes.

"I've watched you our entire lives," Molly went on. "You're my best friend. And there were times when I was jealous. All you had to do was walk into a room to be noticed. Your face was plastered on ads and billboards across America. You traveled the world, and when you decided to grace us with your presence I fell down like the queen was coming to visit. Everyone saw what you wanted them to see, your jet-setting and your fancy clothing. See any parallels yet?"

"I don't need to listen to this." Victoria walked toward the door.

"Stop right there! You *will* hear this, and at seventy-four it's about time you do," Molly yelled.

Shocked Victoria froze with her hand on the doorknob and turned.

"You want to know why I didn't get angry like the rest of them? I saw *you*. When no one else looked for the truth, beyond the glamour I saw the pain in your eyes—the fear of a lost lamb who also needed somplace to call home. Heather has that same look, and she doesn't have anyone to turn to like you did.

"Victoria, she's you. She fears that if she doesn't achieve fame and success, she's worth nothing. That was you after Joseph left for the war. All you ever heard was how beautiful and important you were. If you let yourself be weak or normal, if you showed people how afraid you were, then everyone would be let down. That fear got you an amazing life, a tremendous amount of heartache, and over fifty years lost with the man you love and the people who care about you."

Victoria opened her mouth and Molly pointed her finger at her. "Don't you interrupt me. I've listened to your opinion our whole lives and now you will hear mine. You're angry at Heather, not because of her, but because of what you lost."

Molly stood and held the sides of the chair for support. Then she walked to Victoria and took her friend's hand. "Heather is not Annabelle. Let her go. You can't show her that she's going down the wrong path, just like I couldn't show you."

Victoria looked away.

"You don't think that every time I saw you or heard your voice, I didn't want to race in? That when you came to me battered and broken, I didn't want to grab you and hold you in my arms until I knew you'd be safe from Devon?" Molly's eyes watered and a tear dripped down her cheek. "You were so afraid of a normal life—somehow being a mother and a wife here in Nagog was failure. You don't think I wanted to knock sense into that thick skull of yours, tell you that what you needed and wanted was to come home? You could've had both! Why do you think I ran to your rescue every time you fell? . . . Victoria, I couldn't stop you because it was your choice. Just like you can't help Heather unless it's what she wants."

Victoria shook her head. "Why?"

"Because it's her life. If you want to help her"—Molly stared into Victoria's silver eyes—"tell her the truth. Stop trying to impress her with stories of Hollywood, like the two of you have so much in common because you lived grandly once, and tell her what really happened. The good, the bad, and the very ugly."

"I don't want to talk about this." Victoria looked away.

"You never do. No one has been able to talk to you about any of it . . . especially not about Annabelle. You think that your example is what led Annabelle to do what she did." She put her hand on Victoria's shoulder. "You were an incredible mother and grandmother. That girl chose her path.

"Let Heather go. She's a scared girl determined to make her mark. Only she can decide when to stop running. It took you over fifty years. Do you really think your friendship can change it for Heather?"

Victoria opened the door and ran across the beach, so entrenched in her own pain she didn't notice Molly grabbing onto the chair as she lost her balance and fell to the floor. Victoria ran past Joseph's house and onto the road. She hit the main street and continued to run, stumbling over roots as she cut through the woods. Moist leaves caused her feet to stumble and she fell, ripping her pants. Her heart raced, but it was the pain of past regret that tightened her chest. "You were supposed to take me," she screamed to the sky. "Why didn't you take me instead?"

CHAPTER 23

Heather climbed the three winding flights of stairs to Gina's, and now Michard's, apartment. As she reached the door, her purse slid from her shoulder and splashed her coffee cup, the brown liquid sloshing onto her jeans and burning her hand. "That gives new meaning to Starbucks going to your hips," Gina said from the landing. "Come on in, I'll get you a towel."

Through the floor-to-ceiling windows of the living room in Gina's North End apartment, Heather could see the yachts lit up in Boston Harbor. Overhead track lighting, placed to accent the colorful, modern paintings that graced the brick wall, gave the room the feel of a gallery. Red curtains met black couches, and a bar had been built into the back corner of the midsized room.

The scent of garlic filled the kitchen where Michard chopped and diced. He kissed Gina's cheek and then nipped her neck as she wet a towel at the sink. She giggled and swatted at him with the towel before handing it to Heather. Heather tried to blot the coffee stain. She had a change of clothing in her suitcase, but it was in the car.

"Just borrow something of mine," Gina said as she grabbed Heather's hand and rushed her toward the bedroom.

When Gina bought her apartment, she'd built a dressing room in her large bedroom. The space included drawers, hanging racks, and inner compartments filled with silk, cashmere, designer denim, and leather. In a rainbow of colors, beads, and crystals, her shoes filled an entire wall.

"Grab anything you like," Gina said.

"Your closet is the place of dreams," Heather said.

"I thought I would hate sharing it with Michard, but there's something comforting about seeing his clothing next to mine. I love living with him. I was so scared to do it, but now that he's moved in, I'm just ready."

"Ready for what?" Heather asked as she pulled on a simple green jersey dress.

"That looks amazing on you. You should keep it. I never wear it because it makes my butt look huge." Gina fluffed Heather's hair. "Charlie's going to want you back when he sees you in that dress."

"You know you look fabulous in everything," Heather said as she stared in the mirror. "And Charlie and I are done romantically. This is a business meeting that needs to be done on neutral turf."

"I know, but there's nothing wrong with making a man want you." Gina grabbed Heather's hand. "I need to ask you something really important." She paused. "I know you're stressed and that this isn't the time to bring it up, but . . ."

"Gina, what's up?"

"It's been hard not to tell you, but I didn't want to upset you any more than you were—seeing that you were going through a breakup and hadn't found anyone."

"Gina, just tell me," Heather said.

"Michard and I are talking about marriage. I don't have a ring or anything yet, but he wants to travel to Italy next April to see his family. We've discussed getting married in Tuscany. I want you to be my maid of honor."

Heather squeezed Gina's hand. Her friend looked radiant with love. "Of course."

Heather hugged her friend and heard the front door open, then Charlie's voice. *Let the games begin,* she thought. Gina practically bounced out of the room as Heather took a deep breath and found herself biting the inside of her lip. In the kitchen, the table had been set and Michard was placing bowls of steaming food onto hot plates. "Hi," Heather said to Charlie. "Thanks for coming."

"We eat first and then you discuss business," Michard said. "Full bellies make any work easier."

They sat and passed the food, piling large portions of vegetables and pasta on their plates. Michard and Gina fed each other in the sickeningly sweet way of the newly in love.

"I spoke with Steven this afternoon. It turns out losing the Sunday column is going to be good for us," Charlie said as he ate pasta.

Heather finished her bite of food and then spoke, "What are you talking about?"

"It seems that your column has been holding you back. It's too touchy-feely. That's why I wanted the book to have more edge. You're too young to appeal to an older crowd, but that's what your writing is doing. Your main demographic is women in their thirties and forties who are college educated and single. The Travel Channel has plenty of shows geared to that demographic already. They want someone fun and sexy yet wholesome."

"Well, that's Heather," Gina said.

"It could be Heather, with a few tweaks," Charlie said as he drank his wine. "I'm going to hire a stylist. By the way, I do like the new haircut, but you'll need a whole new image. Something younger and hotter."

Heather pushed the pasta around her plate as she listened. Her foot tapped against the wood floor.

"You'll stay in boutique hotels or take ecotours: adventures in the jungle, kayaking with crocodiles, rafting the big rivers, bungee jumping. No more art galleries and restaurants. Instead you'll hang glide and scuba dive."

"Ooh, that sounds fun," Gina said.

"And how would this work into my contract with the *Globe*?"

"Well, if they like the idea, you would continue to write for them; if not, they will probably let you out of your contract."

"You mean I wouldn't be a writer anymore?"

"Heather, we're talking television. It's ten times the money and the fame. Who cares if you write your column?"

"He's right, Heather," Gina said. "Hasn't this always been your goal?"

"I guess," she said. As they ate, she tried to remember when her dreams had changed from wanting to be a writer to a television star. Was this really what *she* wanted?

~~❧~~

Heather shifted the blanket and slipped from the couch in Gina's living room. The clock read 4:00 in the morning. A dream of Nagog had woken her. She and Tommy were sitting on her deck staring at the stars. Heather thought about brownies with Victoria and Molly, and a smile played on her lips.

Her memories of the summer spilled out like the contents of a suitcase at the end of a vacation. No matter how well she packed the souvenirs, everything couldn't fit. The bag overflowed, and the only way she could close the zipper was to leave something behind. Heather began to wonder if she'd changed more than she thought over the summer. She couldn't decide whether to release the old or the new. Strangely, she realized Charlie and his ideas for her career were the old, and the new was the life she'd seen through Victoria's eyes. She wanted to be like Victoria, strong and independent.

For three hours she paced the apartment, trying to convince herself that Charlie's plan for her career was right. As she watched the sun rise over Boston Harbor, she opened her phone and called George's answering machine. "I know it's early, but I have an idea. I was wondering if you had time to talk with me today? Please call me back as soon as you get this message." She hung up and stared at the phone. The next call would change everything, but it was time.

"Hi, Charlie," she said when he answered. "I know you like to get an early start." She thought about the number of times he'd opened the curtains while she tried to sleep. "Listen, I've been up all night thinking about your plans for my career, and to be honest, I don't agree. I'm not a brand that can be changed by a stylist. I don't want to bungee jump off a bridge in New Zealand nor do I want to spend the rest of my life with you telling me I'm not good enough. So, before you say anything, you're fired. I'll have my lawyer draw up the official letter ending our contract. Good-bye."

CHAPTER 24

The afternoon air in Nagog smelled of pine and earth as a storm moved in. Fog rose from the lake and covered the woods' mossy floor. Root beer foamed between the vanilla scoops as Heather poured it into the glass, then spilled over the frosted mug and onto the patio table Molly and Victoria had bought her. Heather sucked at the light brown bubbles and licked the sides of the glass.

The days had grown shorter over the two weeks she'd been gone. Hues of yellow spread from the leaves' stems; autumn was creeping into Nagog's landscape. Soon the maples would be painted orange and red. Muggy heat would become a distant memory as blustery cold days forced people to wear sweaters. Heather wouldn't be here for the foliage this year. She had a new assignment and she'd be leaving in three weeks.

Daniel came out of his house and made his way across the street with chip bags in hand. Music could be heard over the community center's speakers. Heather watched Molly and Victoria fuss with balloons and streamers as they got out of Molly's car. Heather had returned this afternoon and hadn't heard anything about a special occasion.

Amends needed to be made with her neighbors, but they were busy planning a party. There was no need to interfere. There'd be time later to ease her conscience. Sarah walked across the road, a large platter in hand. More cars drove in and parked in front of the building as people hugged and greeted one another.

"No! Let me go. I don't know you!" Evelyn's screams came from the road.

"Evelyn, it's your birthday. Everyone's waiting for you." Roger tugged Evelyn's arm, but her feet remained stuck to the ground in front of Thomas's house.

"No. I don't know you." Evelyn wore a beret and a yellow organza dress.

"All your friends will be disappointed," Roger said.

"I won't celebrate without James," Eveyln said as she tugged away.

"Okay, darling." Roger hung his head and started to lead her home.

"I need to check the mail." Evelyn's face brightened. "I hope there's a letter from James telling me when he'll be home on leave."

Heather looked at the small, stooped couple. What had their marriage been like? Had Evelyn ever been in love with Roger, or had she pined every day for what she'd lost?

Evelyn approached Heather's deck and waved. "Oh, Maryland, have you heard from James?"

In shock, Heather looked to Roger. His eyes pleaded for help.

"I've been away and haven't checked the mail," Heather said as she walked toward Evelyn. "Why don't we look together?"

"Oh, I've been so worried. It's been a few weeks since we've heard from him." Evelyn linked her arm in Heather's as they walked toward the mailbox. "Soon we'll be sisters. I chose the lace napkins. I think lace is appropriate for a wedding, don't you? And my mother says that my grandmother's pearls will be my something old."

Heather went to the mailbox and pulled out an airmail envelope that didn't have a stamp. She handed it to Evelyn and the woman's eyes lit. She held it as if it were a fragile bird. "Will you open it?" she asked.

Heather took the letter and worked it open with her fingernail. "Do you want me to read it?"

Evelyn nodded with an eager smile.

Dear Evelyn,

I miss you. I think about you every day and dream of our wedding. I'll be home soon. Know that I love you.

James

It hadn't been Heather's best work, but since she hadn't known the couple, she didn't want to embellish too much. Tears touched Evelyn's eyes as she took the letter from Heather and held it to her heart.

"Are you going to the party tonight?" Heather asked.

"Oh, no, not without James." Evelyn shook her head.

"But Molly spent the whole day baking a cake. She'll be disappointed."

Evelyn paused and put her finger against her lip. "I couldn't upset her. Not when she went through all that trouble. I think we should go."

They linked arms as they crossed the street and Roger mouthed "Thank you" to Heather. She smiled as she led Evelyn into the building.

Everyone turned and screamed, "Happy birthday!"

"I got a letter today from James. It was in Maryland's box," Evelyn announced. "He's coming home soon." With that she patted Heather's arm. People lined up to give Evelyn hugs and Heather stepped away.

The people of the community turned to Heather as they realized what she'd done. Nods of approval came from her neighbors, and even Sarah smiled. Victoria came up and gave her a hug. "Why didn't any of us think to do that?" she said.

"You can take over while I'm traveling," Heather said. "I have to leave in three weeks."

"Where are you headed?"

"On a round-the-world trip for three months."

"So long? Is it for the book or the television show?" Victoria asked as she handed Heather a cup of punch.

"No. I lost both of those, but I gave my editor the idea for an online video column as well as a written one to show what it's really like living on the road as a solo female traveler. He loved it and he pitched it to our parent company, *The New York Times*. Now I'm going to be writing on their travel page as well as having an online presence."

Victoria hugged her. "Heather, that's incredible. I'm so proud of you. Have you told Tommy?"

She sighed. "You heard our conversation that day, and I'm certain by now he knows that I yelled at everyone. I don't think he'll care."

"You might be wrong. He's coming later—why don't you stick around and see what happens?"

"Hey, Heather," Carl said. "Mighty nice thing you did for Evelyn."

"It was nothing." Heather looked around the room. No one grimaced at her. Instead, they smiled. Maybe she had found a way into the community by caring about *their* lives.

"So how's your house smelling?" He laughed and patted her on the back. "We missed you around here. There was no one to pick on."

"Well, you better watch out or I'll figure out how to make those stink bombs and I'll leave them in your car," she teased.

Molly came bustling over and hugged Heather. "I forgot a few things back at my house. Heather, can you help me grab them?"

"Of course.

The wind kicked up as Heather and Molly walked along the road. Dark gray clouds blotted out the sun. The sand blew off the beach and pelted Heather's exposed calves. She needed to close her windows, but first she'd help Molly.

A new blue truck imprinted with *Woodward Architecture, Ltd.,* pulled into her driveway. Tom stepped down from the cab. He grabbed a present wrapped with a pink bow from the front seat along with large rolls of paper that look like construction documents.

"You know, I don't think I really need any help," Molly said to Heather. "Why don't you go say hello?"

Tommy put his things down on the hood of his truck and walked to join them. He pulled Molly into a hug and then stepped back.

"I've got to run and grab something," Molly said. "I'll be right back."

"Hi," Heather said as Molly hustled away.

"Hey," Tom said.

"How's life?" She looked into his eyes and was surprised to see that they reflected sadness.

"Fine. Didn't expect to see you here." He looked at the drawings on the hood.

"I fixed the problems I needed to work out," she said.

"That's good." The wind blew hard, and he ran to the truck

to grab the papers before they hit the ground. "Look, I need to put this stuff inside and probably wake Grandpa from a nap so he doesn't miss the party. I'll talk to you later."

"Yeah, sure."

The wind continued to grow stronger as she waited for Molly, wondering if she should walk to her house. Branches creaked and the electricity in the air raised the hair on her arms. Molly waved from the Jacobses' driveway. Her long sundress swished as she waddled across the road with three Tupperware containers in hand. *Oh, please let those be brownies*. Molly had done so much for her this summer—it was the first time Heather had been mothered—and she realized how much she'd come to love this woman.

Molly stopped in the middle of the street. The wind blew her white curls as she placed a hand to her eyes. Suddenly, the world went into slow motion. Molly's knees gave way. Her body crumpled. The Tupperware crashed to the road as her face hit the black pavement.

"Molly!" Only twenty feet away, Molly lay limp, a bright red puddle seeping from under her white hair. Heather sprinted toward her, but like the dreams where running felt like slogging through quicksand, her legs were leaden, and it seemed to take forever to reach Molly.

"Tommy! Victoria! Someone!" Heather dropped to her knees; the stones scraped bare skin. She felt for Molly's pulse. "Come on. Where are you?"

The rosy coloring of her cheeks turned white as she continued to bleed. Heather pressed against Molly's neck and found a faint pulse. The rock she'd struck her head on lay next to her face.

"Tommy!" The wind took her voice and sent it over the trees. "Tommy!"

The screen door slammed and Tom came running.

"She collapsed. I need to call 911. Stay with her." Heather ran toward the community center. Her pulse and breath quickened. With every stride she willed her heartbeat into Molly's chest. She stormed into the room. "Victoria, come quick!"

Everyone turned and watched her as she grabbed the phone on the wall and dialed the emergency number. "I need an ambulance. My friend collapsed."

A female voice came through the receiver. "I need you to stay calm so I can get some information. Are you in a residential home?"

"I'm at Nagog Drive in Littleton. She's in the street bleeding. I need you to hurry."

Victoria rushed to her. "Heather?"

"Molly collapsed and this operator wants to know if I'm in a residence."

Victoria turned and hit a button against the wall.

"Strong Security. What's your emergency?" a voice said through the intercom.

"I need an ambulance. An elderly woman has collapsed," Victoria said.

"I'm contacting EMS now and sending them to your address."

Victoria grabbed Heather. "Where is she?"

"The street. She fell. Her head's bleeding."

"Grab ice," Victoria yelled as she and the others ran outside. Police sirens and the wail of an ambulance could be heard in the distance. Heather grabbed a towel and filled it with ice.

The community had gathered in a circle around Molly. The ambulance made its way down the road and the crowd parted. Bill sat on the ground, Molly's hand in his, as he petted her hair. His huge body looked crumpled.

"You're okay. I'm here. I won't let anything happen." He kissed her forehead.

Carl knelt beside him and Joseph kept his hand on Bill's back. Two men jumped from the ambulance. A stretcher came from the back of the vehicle. Policemen moved the crowd toward Heather's yard.

Bill refused to release Molly's hand. Victoria lifted him and held his bearlike body to her chest. Heather watched his shoulders shake as he sobbed. "I can't lose her. Not yet."

"Stop this talk right now. Molly knows we can't take care of ourselves. She won't leave us," Victoria said.

As thunder rolled overhead, windows rattled. Darkness fell like a shadow over the scene.

Sarah fell to her knees and grasped her cross. With bowed head and closed eyes, she rocked and prayed.

The EMTs lifted Molly onto the gurney and loaded her into the ambulance. Bill tried to follow, but the man stopped him. "Sorry, sir. There's no room. You'll need to meet us at Emerson Hospital."

"Bill, my keys are in the truck. Get in," Tom said.

The truck pulled away. Everyone moved to their cars. One by one they left, a parade of teary-eyed family members following their kin. Heather walked up to the bloodstain and closed her eyes. Then the tears came, matching the storm as the lake rose and puddles collected on the beach.

◈

The emergency waiting room reminded Heather of Logan Airport: dull blue walls, flecked floors, and the ambiance of an asylum. A young man held an ice pack to his head, his face bruised and swollen. A teenage boy hugged a crying girl. Bright red, blue, and green children's toys had been scattered across the floor.

Heather walked to the reception desk, her wet clothing leaving a trail of water along the floor. "I need to find Molly Jacobs. She came in an ambulance. An elderly group followed."

"Miss, you're soaked to the bone." The woman had a round face and black unruly hair showing the first signs of gray. She wore a pink scrub top with a Scooby-Doo pin above a name tag that read *Millie*. Heather looked into the woman's brown eyes and wondered if the nurse came to work every day so she could put food on the table or because, like Molly, she lived to help others.

"I need to know about my friend," Heather said.

Millie walked away. She came back with a wool blanket and a towel, and handed them to Heather. Her fingers clicked across the keyboard and she picked up a chart. "She's on the third floor. There's a waiting room for family and friends up there. The elevators are around the corner."

Heather hesitated.

Millie pulled the towel from Heather's arms and wrapped it around her shoulders. The blanket went around Heather's body, and Millie rubbed her arms. "It's hard when someone we love is sick. But I'm sure Molly will feel better knowing you are here."

Heather hadn't realized how cold she'd been. How long had she been in the rain? "Thanks, Millie."

"If you need a cup of coffee or some food, the cafeteria is on the second floor," Millie said.

Heather stood outside the waiting room and peeked through the window. Molly's friends sat on leather couches and chairs. Evelyn, in her party clothing, looked lost as she listened to Agatha and Sarah talk. The two women kept their hands busy with knitting needles. The women never seemed to be without their yarn.

Tom's hand touched her shoulder. "Stalking?"

Fireflies danced along her skin. "I needed . . . worried . . . I don't want to be in the way."

"She's having an MRI. They think it's an aneurysm." He handed her a coffee from the tray he carried. The black liquid smelled stale. "Come in. It's going to be a long night." He opened the door.

Bill walked over to Heather and pulled her into a hug. She sank into his flesh. The scent of Molly's cookies was in his shirt.

"Thank you for acting as quickly as you did. Molly will be happy to know you're here," Bill said.

Tom pulled a folding chair from a closet and placed it behind Heather.

"Where's Victoria?" she asked.

"She went home," Tom said.

Joseph looked up. "I thought she was in the cafeteria."

Tom looked at his coffee. "She decided Molly would want her own robe and nightgown."

Joseph looked at Bill and then at the door. Deep creases appeared on his forehead.

"Why don't I check on Victoria?" Heather turned to Tom. "If you hear anything, you'll call?"

Tom nodded. Heather dropped the towel and blanket on the chair. As she walked toward the door, he grabbed her hand. "Stay with her, okay?"

Heather noticed the look of fear in Tom's eyes. "Of course. I promise."

CHAPTER 25

❧

The rain had stopped. Mist lifted off the ground in ghostly swirls and a faint rainbow, more pastel than primary, faded behind puffy white clouds as Victoria walked along Nagog Drive. Directors hunger for this scene, Victoria thought, as she stopped and looked at the lake.

As an actress, she'd spent hours in full makeup and wardrobe, fans blowing against her face to keep her look fresh, while the director waited to see what the sunset would bring. More often than not, darkness came without one line spoken for the camera. All those hours wasted when she could've been here in Nagog with Molly.

Victoria walked across the sand and onto the grass by Molly's house. At the tree house she climbed the ladder. Dirt and moss covered the wet wood. The low doorframe made her duck her head as she went inside the fort. Leaves had taken up residence in the rooms, and birds had left white marks on the window-sills. The kitchen table her father bought had scratches on its face and had lost its luster. The chair's vinyl had ripped, but the small metal legs still held Victoria's weight.

Dust covered the teacups and saucers that had been left on the table. Victoria lifted a cup and pretended she was eight again, playing house with Molly. "Yes, dear, I'd love more of your delectable tea. And would you pass me a scone?" Victoria grabbed a stick from the floor. She held it between her pointer and middle finger, brought it to her lips, and breathed in the imaginary smoke. "I think we should spend the day shopping in the city and then go for dinner." She would've been wearing her mother's cape and hat, both too big for her little body.

Molly, in her mother's flowered housecoat and high heels, would've said, "That would be delightful. And then we'll ride the carriage through the park and eat warm chestnuts."

Victoria placed the cup on the table. Her finger traced the once golden rim.

Two sleeping bags had been stored on the small bunks in the next room. Victoria grabbed the musty-smelling blankets and headed to the porch. The shiny blue material covered the wet planks protecting her as she sat with her feet dangling over the edge.

"On the good ship, Lollipop. It's a sweet trip to a candy shop. Where bonbons play . . . on the sunny beach of Peppermint Bay."

Victoria rubbed the pink pearl ring. Tears dripped down her cheeks as the memories from five years ago returned.

～☙～

The temperature outside had topped 100 that day and the humidity drenched the leaves until they dripped tears of sweat. The sunlight streamed through the windows of the sunroom and illuminated Annabelle's golden locks. She sat on the couch wearing Tommy's Harvard T-shirt, looking as if angels had lit a halo around her face. The wedding binder, filled with order slips, menus, seating charts, flower arrangements, and color swatches, sat open on the ottoman.

Armed with yellow, pink, and green sticky notes, Annabelle chose a different color for each category: yellow for details she worried still needed to be attended to; pink for notes to the wedding planner; green for the things that were too hideous—now that she'd really thought about them—to be part of her special day.

Victoria placed a tray on the end table and handed a glass of iced tea to Annabelle, who guzzled the drink and then placed the glass on the tray next to the turkey sandwich. She took a bite of the food and then put it down.

"Is the sandwich okay? I can make you something different," Victoria said.

"No, it's fine. Just the heat has taken my appetite," Annabelle said as she stuck another note in the binder.

"I think your loss of appetite has more to do with nerves about the wedding than the heat, and my cooking would make anyone lose their appetite. I'm calling Molly and having her fix something your stomach will appreciate. We'll sit and enjoy a barbecue and you can relax."

The child needed rest before the big day. Excitement had kept her up the last five nights as she continued to plan well after midnight. It didn't help that she'd just finished six grueling weeks traveling and performing, and was now jet-lagged.

She needed time with Tommy. He could relax her to sleep, but their hectic schedules had kept them apart.

"Why don't I make you a milk shake? It will cool you off," Victoria said.

"Thanks, Grandma, but I'm okay. I think I'm going to go for a run."

"In this heat?"

"Please, I dance and sing all night under the spotlights. I'll be fine and it will relax me. I think the lack of exercise is what's keeping me up at night." Annabelle placed the binder down and took another long drink of the iced tea.

Victoria pulled the heavy binder onto her lap and flipped through the pages. Pictures of the wedding site made her smile. Annabelle and Tommy would marry at a seaside mansion in Newport, Rhode Island. Two hundred fifty chairs, covered in white silk, would be decorated with pale silver roses. As Annabelle walked down the aisle, a string quartet would play with the sound of the ocean in the background.

The search for the perfect wedding gown had taken Victoria and Annabelle on three shopping trips to New York, one to Paris, and another to London, but they finally found the dress at Priscilla's of Boston, a local institution. Annabelle's golden hair would flow around the fitted silk top, which had small Swarovski crystals sewn along the bust. Pearl-colored material would drape along her curves and sway when she moved.

"I forgot one more thing. Can I see the binder?" Annabelle said as she wrote on a yellow sticky note.

"I don't know why you're stressed," Victoria said. "The wedding planner has everything under control."

"It has to be perfect. I feel like I've waited forever for this day." Annabelle took the binder and placed the note on the front cover.

"Well, it won't be perfect if the bride collapses from exhaustion." Victoria pulled the pen from Annabelle's hand. "Go for your run. I'll call the wedding planner and give her all your notes."

"No, I have to do this." Annabelle tried to grab the pen.

"You don't. Your jobs are to rest, get a tan, and make certain you glow. Tomorrow you're going to sleep late and then spend the day relaxing at the spa. It's non-negotiable. I'm laying down the law," Victoria said.

Annabelle stared at the pens and the binder. "Okay."

"And I think you should call Tommy and invite him to dinner."

Annabelle twirled the curl behind her ear. "He doesn't have time. He needs to finish three sets of drawings and he wants to paint the downstairs bedrooms tonight. Trust me . . . I've been getting more sleep than he has."

Annabelle went to her room and returned with headphones and tennis shoes. "I'll see you in an hour."

"You can't run in this heat for an hour. At most twenty minutes and then I expect you to cool off in the lake, sit in the shade, and take a nap."

"Okay, I promise." Annabelle waved and was out the door running up the road without taking the time to stretch.

Victoria spent the next hour on the phone with the wedding coordinator getting her assurance that everything was under tight control. If the night air became too hot, misters were in place to cool things down. Refrigerator trucks would keep the floral arrangements looking fresh in the intense heat. The chef had begun the food preparation. Marinades were done; the meat would be soaked in vacuum-sealed containers. The hair and makeup artists knew the exact designs the girls wanted. No detail had been left to chance.

Victoria hung up the phone and drank the tea, now watered down by the melted ice. The heat felt like a brick oven. Victoria pulled her hair off her neck and fanned herself.

The air outside felt thick. Fragrant barbecue smells came from the Jacobses' home as Victoria walked toward the beach in search of Annabelle. Molly had gone to work creating her magic in the kitchen. A good meal of potato salad, roasted chicken, corn bread, and fruit salad would give Annabelle's cheeks color. The child looked pale today.

A hot breeze blew across the sand. Where was Annabelle? She shouldn't be running in this heat for this long. Victoria turned and saw Annabelle walk up the road and then stop at the beach. She shook her head and Victoria could see her eyes shut as if they were being forced closed. "Honey, are you okay?" Victoria called.

Annabelle's body crumpled like she was a rag doll. She fell to the sand and Victoria ran to her side. "Annabelle!" Victoria shook her but she didn't respond. "Annabelle!"

Someone called an ambulance and Victoria rode with the paramedics. She stared at Annabelle's face, at her purple lips slightly parted under the plastic oxygen mask, willing her to be okay.

At the hospital they'd taken her baby through dirty white double doors marked with black scuff marks. "She pushed too hard," Victoria said as she paced in the waiting room. "She's exhausted, and it was so hot. I should've paid attention . . . not allowed her to go for that run. Oh, God, they kept saying something about an irregular heart rhythm. She's a young woman, how can there be anything wrong with her heart?"

"We don't know anything. It could be as simple as dehydration." Molly patted Victoria's arm and forced her to sit.

"Did someone call Tommy?" Victoria looked around the room for a pay phone. "He needs to be here. She'll be okay if she sees Tommy. Nothing bad can happen when they're together."

"I left a message, but his secretary said he was out of the office," Bill said as he sat and held Victoria's hand.

"Bill, drive to Providence. Annabelle needs Tommy," Victoria pleaded.

A doctor in blue scrubs walked through the white doors. "Annabelle Rose's family?"

Victoria stood. "Here." The doctor had kind, soft, Asian features. His black hair had begun to gray around the temples, giving him the look of competence, and Victoria felt comforted that he was taking care of her baby. "What's wrong with my granddaughter? Is she okay?"

"Your granddaughter is in third degree heart block with an abnormal rhythm."

"I knew she shouldn't go for a run in this heat. Does she have heatstroke?" Victoria said in panic.

"We're uncertain. Heatstroke can cause abnormal rhythms, but we want to rule out an underlying condition. Do you know if she's ever been diagnosed with any kind of heart abnormality?"

Victoria clenched Molly's hand. "When she was a young child, something was mentioned about an arrhythmia, but we were told it was nothing to worry about and that she would grow out of it."

"Does your family have a history of heart disease?"

Victoria's pulse began to race as she tried to catch her breath. "My mother died of a heart attack in her late forties, my father at fifty. Is my granddaughter having a heart attack? She's in her twenties!"

"We need to run some tests before I can give you answers. We might have to put an external pacemaker in if we can't stabilize her."

"Can I see her?" Victoria pleaded.

"Not right now. I'll come and get you as soon as she's stable."

The doctor left and a nurse led Victoria and Molly to a private waiting room. "This can't be happening," Victoria said as she paced. "She's a young woman about to be married. She can't be having a heart attack."

"I'm going to call Tommy again," Bill said.

"Please, Bill, find him. She needs Tommy," Victoria said as she paced and tried to catch her breath.

"Victoria," Molly said as she took her hand, "why don't you sit? You need to breathe and try to relax. We don't need two people passing out today."

The minutes clicked past. People entered the room and sat in the chairs reading magazines. The doctor entered. The room's white noise seemed to be amplified to the level of a rock concert. As he spoke, she allowed her thoughts to drown out his voice until his muffled words sounded as if they came from underwater. Cardiac arrest, fatal arrhythmia, nothing they could do. Victoria fell to the floor, Molly's arms wrapped around her as she screamed.

❧

Victoria grabbed the railings of the tree house and tried to catch her breath. Her hands and arms quaked as her jaw clenched until her head ached. She thought of the big maple near the family plots. The roses Annabelle had chosen for her wedding now grew at her grave. "It's my fault."

"Victoria? What are you doing up there?" Heather stood at the base of the tree, her hair and clothing damp. She placed her feet on the rungs, tested her weight, and then climbed to the plat-form. "Why aren't you at the hospital?"

Victoria shook her head. "I couldn't be in that room."

"Victoria, you need to go back. Molly's probably going into surgery; you should be with her." Heather scooped up the extra sleeping bag and hugged it around her damp clothing.

Victoria closed her eyes and let the night air fill her lungs. In her mind, she heard the psychiatrist's words, *The only way out is through*.

"It's all my fault." Victoria's hands shook. "I didn't pay atten-tion. Molly was sick, but I was too self-absorbed trying to rec-tify my own guilt to do anything about it. I saw the signs, but I brushed them off. Every woman I love dies from my mistakes."

Heather sat and rubbed Victoria's back. She pulled the sleep-ing bag around Victoria's shoulders. "It's not your fault. They think it's an aneurysm. If Molly had symptoms, she should've called the doctor. Or Bill should've taken her." Heather placed her hand on top of Victoria's. "Let me take you back to the hos-pital."

"I can't." Victoria shook her head and the tears fell onto the old sleeping bag, making wet splotches on top of the moldy spots. Victoria's neck shook until she felt her head might come loose. "My granddaughter died in that hospital. I can't lose my best friend in the same place."

Victoria rocked and Heather tightened her grip around her.

A distant look glazed Victoria's eyes. "I wasted so much time. I focused on all the things that were unimportant. And every time I needed Molly, she was there. I could've been here the last five years, but I ran away like I always do." Victoria closed her eyes and stilled her body. "After my granddaughter died, life went on. I was supposed to eat, do laundry, and get dressed. People got together and played cards. I couldn't do those things. Emptiness had taken over my soul. I almost killed myself, but I couldn't tell anyone, so I left and checked myself into a psychiatric hospital. I couldn't admit to anyone that the perfect Victoria Rose needed help."

"Victoria, I didn't know." Heather rubbed her palm over Victoria's back. "You always seemed . . ."

"Elegant? Successful?" Victoria laughed. "I'm a master at hiding what I don't want people to see. Molly was the only one who saw the truth."

Heather put her hands in her lap and picked at a loose string on her shirt.

Victoria spoke in a strained whisper. "My granddaughter went into cardiac arrest because she decided to go for a run. When they did the autopsy they reviewed her medical records and found that eight months before, she'd been diagnosed with hypertrophic cardiomyopathy. It's a genetic disease that causes thickening of the cardiac walls. The doctor told her that she should avoid strenuous activities since she'd become symptomatic. Annabelle was a stage performer and I assume she didn't want to quit dancing, so she didn't tell anyone." Victoria was silent as she stared at the sky. "When I spoke to her friends, they confirmed that Annabelle had dizzy spells, but she explained them by saying she was dehydrated. All I do is create pain. It's my fault Annabelle died. I passed down that unquenchable ambition, that drive for success and absolute perfection in everyone's eyes . . . I couldn't show weakness or ever stop moving, and neither could she. Now Molly might die because she was so busy taking care of me that she didn't tell me she wasn't feeling well."

Heather looked at the indigo sky where the first star of the evening had appeared. "I'm going to say something and I hope it doesn't sound disrespectful." She bit her lip. "You're not God."

Victoria stared with a blank, confused look. "What?"

"Listen, I don't know if I even believe in God. For most of my life, I've never really thought about it. But I do know that there are things beyond our control. I can't change how I grew up. You aren't the master of the universe. People don't die so that you can be punished."

"I told Annabelle she was perfect and beautiful. I didn't let her know it was okay to be anything else."

Heather shook her head in disbelief. "Wow, you're a horrible person. You made certain your granddaughter knew you were proud of her and that she was loved." Heather closed her eyes. "We all make mistakes. We all have crap happen in our lives. Yours didn't happen because of who you are." Heather paused. "You have a choice . . . be there for your family or hide away and sulk about the past. You may never know why Annabelle did what she did, but *she* chose to go on that run."

"She was an angel."

Heather softened her tone. "She was human. I was a stranger, and you cared for me more than anyone ever has. I can't imagine how much you would've given your own flesh and blood."

A meteor shot across the sky, its red tail streaked with orange.

Victoria heard her father's voice: "When a star dies, it puts on its final and greatest show." She was eight years old again, curled into her daddy's arms, watching the meteor shower. In her heart, she knew that the angels had created the brilliant display of shooting stars just for her. But now Victoria understood that the world didn't revolve around her. Angels didn't make the stars die for her entertainment.

Annabelle's smile flashed through her thoughts, and rage filled Victoria. It bubbled from her gut and grew into her throat. "You had everything. You were about to marry Tommy. Why did you hurt yourself? Why did you leave me?"

Heather jumped away, but when Victoria bent over, sobs racking her body, Heather wrapped her arms around her shoulders and laid her head on Victoria's back.

"She had everything," Victoria cried. "I don't understand why she took that chance."

Heather rocked her. "I don't know if you ever will. But you have to let her go. She can't come back, and you have people who need you right now."

Victoria's sobs echoed through the woods and then there was silence. Occasionally, Victoria whimpered and Heather squeezed tighter. She petted Victoria's soft hair and brushed the tears from her smooth cheeks. "You know," Heather whispered, "without you, I don't think I would've made it through this summer."

Victoria took Heather's hand and held it to her heart. "Thank you."

The two women sat in silence holding hands. They listened to the sound of the lake lapping against the shore, the crickets in the woods, and the wind tickling the leaves. Molly had always lived her life for the present moment, Victoria thought. She didn't need more than to love her family and take care of her house. No matter what went wrong, she was content. And if she died tonight, Molly would leave this life without regrets.

"Molly told me once, 'I don't pray for perfection in my life. I ask for the humor and courage to see everything I receive as the way it's supposed to be,'" Victoria said.

Heather laughed. "God, I'm not even close to that point."

Victoria patted Heather's arm. "I know, baby. I'm an old woman and I'm still working on it. So you have something to look forward to."

"Besides wrinkles, aches and pains, prolapsed bladders, and hanging breasts?" Heather said.

"Don't forget about the gas from peppers. You can use that one as a weapon against uninvited guests." She bumped Heather, and they laughed.

The stars twinkled in the night sky. Victoria pictured Annabelle, in her silver dress, dancing among the angels. The smile that had lit up a room, in Victoria's mind, now gave the stars their ability to shine. Heather was right. Victoria would never understand why Annabelle did what she did. The guilt Victoria carried might never subside, but it had been Annabelle's choice, and Victoria couldn't change what had happened. She placed her hands over her heart. *Good-bye, baby girl. Grandma loves you.* She opened her hands and let Annabelle go.

Victoria stood. "I'm going to gather a few things and head back to the hospital. Would you like to join me?"

Heather brushed the dirt from her shorts. "Let me change and I'll drive."

They climbed down from the tree house and Victoria went into the Jacobses' home. She packed a bag with personal items: toothbrush, Pond's cold cream, deodorant, bobby pins. As she opened the dresser drawers to gather nightgowns and underwear, she noticed the Bible next to Molly's jewelry box. Victoria picked up the old leather book and turned the gold-tipped pages. Victoria found a yellowed booklet inside. The cover read:

A Prayer Book for Soldiers and Sailors
PUBLISHED FOR THE ARMY AND NAVY COMMISSION
OF THE PROTESTANT EPISCOPAL CHURCH
BY THE CHURCH PENSION FUND
20 Exchange Place—New York
1941

Victoria cradled the booklet to her heart. So long ago, she'd been a girl who prayed for the sailor she loved and then left when he returned. After all these years, she'd found her way home.

∽◦∾

The lights in the waiting room were dimmed. Empty doughnut boxes lined the tables along with half-filled coffee cups and creamers. The irregular rumble of snores came from blanket-covered figures. Sarah sat awake, her hands working the yarn.

Joseph stood and rushed to Victoria as she walked through the door. He placed his hands on her arms and face, like a father checking for broken bones after his child has fallen from her bike. "You're okay?"

Victoria touched his face. Her fingers ran along the fan of wrinkles around his eyes. "I'm okay. Any news?"

"She's still in surgery; it will be a few more hours as they close, but the prognosis is good. The doctor said she'll be in the ICU for at least a week. He's upbeat about her recovery, but she'll need to go to a rehabilitation center. Bill and the kids are making arrangements now," Joseph said.

"But she's alive." Victoria placed her hand to her lips and said a silent thank-you.

Sarah looked up, frowned at Victoria, and then focused her attention back on her knitting. Victoria released Joseph's embrace, walked to Sarah, and sat beside her.

"Friend," she said, and placed her hand over Sarah's work. Victoria lifted the Bible from the bag of clothing. "I thought you might take comfort in this."

Sarah looked at Victoria.

"I'm sorry it's taken me this long to be there for you."

Tom hadn't been in the room. Heather walked through the empty halls looking for his tall frame. The waiting area downstairs had emptied; only one person remained, an ice pack covering his swollen ankle. Heather walked outside and found the blue truck, but Tom wasn't in the cab.

On the fourth floor, she found him. He stood by a large window, looking into a room that held five new bundled babies. Each child wore a pink or blue knitted cap.

"So this is where all that yarn goes. Do you think Sarah snuck up here and placed them on their heads as they were delivered?" Heather asked.

Tom faked a smile. "Yeah, knowing Sarah, she probably did."

His shoulders slumped, and his eyes looked tired. Heather realized what Victoria had said. Tom had been engaged to Annabelle. He'd lost the love of his life. It must've been hard for him to open himself to Heather, and she'd rejected him.

"You look exhausted. Why don't you go back to Nagog and get some sleep? I'll watch over them," Heather said.

He didn't look at her, but he nodded. "I think I could use a few hours of rest, but I'll wait until she's out of surgery."

He walked toward the elevator and pressed the button. The doors opened and he stepped inside.

Her foot stopped the doors before they shut. "Tommy, for what it's worth, I'm sorry I hurt you. I know this isn't the time, but I was ashamed of something I did that day. I couldn't face you. I know I can't change what I did, but if you need anything, I want you to know that I'll be there."

"Thanks, Heather." Tommy looked at the floor and stuck his hands in his pockets.

The door shut and Heather walked to the window. A baby boy had opened his bright blue eyes. He stared at her as he scrunched his nose and wiggled in his blanket. Heather pressed her fingertips to the glass.

New life. All possibilities open to him. Nothing has been decided or predetermined.

Heather thought about her situation. She had a new beginning. She might succeed at her new job, and then again she might not. As for a romantic relationship, she was alone, but for the first time in her life she had family and a home.

CHAPTER 26

❦

Click. Once again the staple gun jammed as Heather shot it against the green wire.

She had returned from her round-the-world trip to snow-trimmed roofs lit with colorful Christmas bulbs. Small pine trees were decorated with garlands of tinsel, and sparrows balanced on the evergreens' branches while they pecked at popcorn and cranberries that had been strung. The neighborhood had been transformed into Santa's village.

Family members had come to visit today for the party later. Buzzed on sugar, the great-grandkids of the neighborhood bashed each other with snowballs until their clothing dripped with slush. Heather could smell apple cider mulling in Sarah's kitchen.

Victoria had given her a box of ornaments and lights. Heather planned to buy the biggest tree she could fit in her living room. A fire would crackle while she drank eggnog and hung ornaments. After she trimmed the branches with a thousand white lights, she'd crawl under the tree, take in the pine scent, and watch the twinkle in the colored balls.

She wanted a gingerbread house on her coffee table and a stocking hung from her mantel. On Christmas morning there'd be shiny packages with big bows under the tree that she'd bought for the people she loved.

With her feet balanced on the stepladder, she pressed with both hands against the tool's handle, but still the staple wouldn't release. Unsupported, the light string fell to the deck, the colorful bulbs illuminating the fresh snow. She swore as she shook the tool and squeezed with her mitten-covered thumbs. *Kerchunk*. A staple flew and bounced off her French doors.

"Problems?" Tom asked from behind.

Heather jumped, nearly falling off the ladder. "Tommy . . . you scared me. I didn't hear your truck."

"I put the rusted baby down." He patted the blue vehicle she'd seen the day Molly had gone into the hospital.

She shook the staple gun. "Nice upgrade, but I'll miss the rattle now that I'm home again."

He came onto the deck and grabbed the staple gun from her. "I heard you were coming home early. Were you tired of the heat in Egypt?"

"You've been reading my column. Or did you watch my video blog?" She stepped down from the ladder.

He opened the spring-fed compartment, removed the crooked staples, and closed the gun. He lifted the lights above his head and secured the strand to the wood. "It wasn't by choice."

"Of course not." Heather bent and grabbed the wreath that had been lying on ground. She placed the hook over her door and fluffed the greenery. "I finished my work ahead of time so I could come home early for Molly's party. My editor understood."

Tom grabbed a second light string and climbed the ladder. "Along the trim?"

"Please." Heather glanced at his strong backside. "So you visited the website under duress?"

"Victoria e-mailed it to me every day."

"Oh, and she forced you to read it?" Heather teased.

Tom stepped higher on the ladder and continued to attach the lights to the house. "Okay, I admit, I found your adventures interesting."

"And of course brilliant." She smiled mischievously.

He looked down at her. "Well, haven't we become conceited?"

"Well, at least I'm not a conceited ass." She flashed him a smile. "I just know when I work my tail off that the results are generally admirable."

He laughed. "Touché."

She adjusted the multicolored, knitted cap Sarah had left on Heather's kitchen table that morning. Heather looked to her neighbor's house. A Christmas tree had been placed in the sitting room and its white lights showed through the frosted window. Sarah and Heather would never have the closeness she shared with Victoria, they were too different, but the letters Heather had sent Evelyn had softened her neighbor.

Tom stepped down from the ladder.

Heather tried not to stare at his eyes. On lonely nights during her trip, she'd imagined his touch along her arm, the way his lips felt against her mouth, and the smile that deepened the cleft in his chin. "I hear your grandfather's getting married."

"Yep. That man has gotten more action this year than I have."

"I'm beginning to think that the lake has *Cocoon*-like powers that rev them up," she said.

"You could be right. We were near it the night that we made s'mores."

Heather kicked at the snow. "Must've been the lake. I think I found a new career. I'm going to bottle the water and sell it all over the world."

He smiled at her. She felt her cheeks flush with warmth, though the temperature was well below freezing.

White trucks rolled into the community, and men began to unload chairs, tables, and linens. Victoria and Joseph came out of the community center to meet the caterers.

"It's going to be one hell of a party in Molly's honor," Tom said.

"Nineteen twenties–style all the way," Heather said. "Victoria and Molly picked me up from the airport and took me straight to the dressmaker for a fitting. I have to admit, I can't wait to wear my outfit. It's a pretty cool flapper dress."

"I bet you'll look incredible," Tom said.

"I might even save you a dance," she teased.

"Well, with Grandpa taken, you might be stuck with me." The snow began to fall in perfect, soft flakes. Tom stuck out his tongue and let an icy drop fall into his mouth. "Go look in the back of my truck."

"Why?" she asked.

"Because I told you to," he said.

Heather skidded across the icy drive as she ran to the back of his truck. Inside the bed sat two large trees bundled in rope.

Tom came up behind her. She turned to him. "You got me a tree?"

Warmth radiated from his body. "Actually, two: one for your living room and another for the bedroom. I think I read somewhere that you couldn't wait to get home and decorate."

She threw her hands around his neck and kissed his cheek.

The smell of the cold air mingled with his aftershave. She lingered with her nose against his rough stubble; her heart pounded, and electricity fluttered her nerves. His face turned, and then his lips were against hers. Soft. Gentle. His tongue explored the curve of her bottom lip and she felt herself shudder as she melted into his arms.

"Woo-hoo!" Victoria yelled from across the street.

Heather and Tom jumped apart at the sound of Joseph and Victoria clapping. Heather hid her red face against Tom's chest.

He bowed his head to her ear. "Why don't we bring the trees inside?"

"Sounds like a plan."

He picked up the tree and carried it onto the deck. Heather smiled, looked to Victoria and Joseph, gave a tiny wave, and then ran to open the door for Tom.

In her living room, Tom placed the tree in the corner near the fireplace. The room filled with the fresh scent of pine. Heather looked at the framed pictures she'd placed on the mantel: photos from her travels; she and Gina in Boston; her grandmother and mother from when she was little. Heather looked at the unframed picture of Victoria and Molly that she'd carried throughout her travels. It reminded her that no matter how lonely she felt, she had family back in Nagog.

Tom wrapped his arms around her. "Do you like the tree?"

"I love it," she said. *Home,* she thought. *I am finally home.*

ACKNOWLEDGMENTS

Stories begin with a spark—an idea that grabs the writer and forces them to embark on the journey of their characters' lives. In the process, groceries aren't bought, meals are forgotten, and confidence can be shattered. It's friends and family who make the process much easier. Thank you for all your support David Klosen, Jasmin Lolani Hakes, James Lusardi, James Tennery, Mignon Foster, Marilyn Caldwell, Ticia Zuniga, Connie Buckles, Kelli McDaniel, Amy Kohlman, Amber Turner, my entire figure-skating family, and to everyone else who cheered me on. I love you all. A special thanks to Melissa Bilodeau, Julianna Grant, and Daniel Miller for being my first readers.

I'd like to express my deepest gratitude to my agent, Yfat Reiss Gendell, who continued to believe in this story and to protect it as if it were her own. I'm blessed to know and work with you. I'd like to thank the entire team at Foundry Literary and Media, especially Kendra Jenkins, Rebecca Serle, and Cecilia Campbell-Westlind. Your insights, questions, and love for everything Nagog helped to make this book what it is today.

Writers always hope to find the perfect editor and publishing house. I hit the jackpot with Gallery Books and my editor, Lauren McKenna. Lauren, your wisdom, insight, and killer instincts on how to bring out the best in my writing have been a gift, but it's your fun nature that makes working with you such a pleasure.

Thank you, Alexandra Lewis, for answering all my questions and keeping me on track in a way that makes me feel like I'm your only client.

Thank you to Jean Jenkins for her professional critique of the first draft that helped me to become a better writer. Thank you, Lisa Litwack, for the beautiful cover. You made my vision of Nagog come to life and brought me home to Massachusetts.

To my grandparents, Theresa and Vernon Miller, it's because of your love, the safety of your home, and all of your stories that I was able to create the warmth of Nagog. I love you both.

THE Lake House

SUMMARY

In *The Lake House,* Heather Bregman, a young travel writer who is reeling from ending her engagement to her fiancé and agent, purchases a quaint lakefront house in rural Nagog, Massachusetts, with hopes of creating a home for herself. Unbeknownst to Heather, her dream house is part of a tight-knit community of people all over the age of seventy who are none too happy about an outsider moving into their neighborhood. She finds comfort in Molly, a Nagog native who has spent her entire life living within the community, and in Victoria, a former movie star who is returning to Nagog to repair relationships damaged by a lifetime of leaving town whenever tragedy strikes. Bridging an almost fifty-year age difference, Heather and Victoria form an inseparable bond as they both attempt to overcome demons from their pasts and earn the community's trust and respect. And despite the reluctance of Heather's new neighbors and Victoria's childhood friends, the two women eventually find acceptance, love, and a true home.

QUESTIONS FOR DISCUSSION

1. Both Victoria and Heather are trying to earn the Nagog community's acceptance in order to make a home in the town. If you were Heather, would you need to make friends with your new neighbors before you truly felt at home? Do you think this is unique to a small town like Nagog?

2. When Victoria returns to Nagog, she is met with hostility from her childhood friends. Do you think their anger is justified? Does Victoria deserve a second chance from them? Explain why or why not.

3. As the story unfolds, we learn that Victoria's old friends are not only bitter about her infamous sudden departures from Nagog but also with her arrogant and aloof behavior when she actually was in town. What do you think upset each character more? If you were them, what would upset you the most?

4. Victoria describes Molly as "brown sugar, cinnamon, and vanilla [. . .] homemade bread cooling on the kitchen windowsill" (p. 2). Is this description accurate? How would you describe Molly? Have you met a Molly figure in your own life?

5. While Victoria and Heather had successful careers, both women are struggling to find fulfillment in their relationships and friendships. Do you think it's possible, as Molly tells Victoria, to have both a prolific career and a happy home life? How would you achieve that balance?

6. Molly takes it upon herself to reunite Victoria with her estranged group of friends, but her efforts only caused fighting and more tension. Do you think it was right of Molly to try to force reconciliation? What would it take for Agatha and Sarah to accept Victoria again?

7. During one of their arguments, Victoria tells Sarah that "life is a hassle only if you make it one" (p. 104). Given all Victoria has lived through and lost, do you think she believes her own statement? Do you agree with it?

8. Heather's new neighbors reject her arrival partly because it is indicative of a greater generational change. While their situation is unique to the novel, do you think that fear is universal for older generations? Why or why not?

9. After trying to ignore her new neighbors' sabotage efforts, Heather finally erupts at them—a response she later regrets. How would you have handled the situation? Was Heather's anger justified?

10. In an effort to earn the community's acceptance and make amends for her outburst, Heather starts planting love letters in her mailbox for Evelyn to find. This act earns her more respect than her previous attempts to ignore the negativity. Why? Do you think, as Heather wonders, that "she had found a way into the community by caring about *their* lives" (p. 356)?

11. Heather separates herself from her condescending and manipulative fiancé twice, first by ending the engagement and then by

firing him as her agent. Which decision seemed more difficult for her? Did you think Charlie would remain her agent after she ended their relationship?

12. It took almost the entire novel for romantic relationships to blossom for Victoria and Heather, and both the women and their men had to overcome personal obstacles in order to be happy. Despite those obstacles, did you suspect that Victoria and Joseph, and Heather and Tommy, would ultimately get together in the end?

13. When Victoria becomes irate at Heather's return to Boston, Molly responds by saying, "You're angry because Heather forces you to face the mistakes you feel you've made" (p. 344). Do you agree with Molly's assessment? Explain why or why not.

14. Molly's health crisis and subsequent recovery ultimately brings the community closer together, including Heather and Victoria. How different would the ending have been if Molly hadn't survived? Would it have drastically changed the other characters' relationships?

ENHANCE YOUR BOOK CLUB

1. Channel your inner Molly! Prepare your favorite comfort food or baked good to enjoy during your book club discussion.

2. Much of *The Lake House* is about revisiting past memories, good and bad. Take your own trip down memory lane by bringing a childhood relic to or sharing a favorite memory with your book club.

3. Finishing *The Lake House* was part of author Marci Nault's life project, 101 Dreams Come True. Learn more about Marci and her inspirational project by visiting the website at: www.101dreamscometrue.com.

4. While the Nagog in *The Lake House* is fictional, there is a Village of Nagog Woods in Acton, Massachusetts. Do a little research on Acton and the real Nagog, and have your book club discuss whether they share any similarities with the story's town.

A CONVERSATION WITH MARCI NAULT

The Lake House *primarily follows Victoria and Heather, two women in different stages of life who have successful careers but are ultimately searching for more. What was your inspiration for these characters? Did you always plan to have such a large generational gap between them?*

The idea for this novel came from a nighttime dream where I found the house I'd always wanted but when I moved in I realized everyone was over the age of seventy. When I woke, I knew I needed to write the story. So, yes, I always intended for the women to have a large generational gap.

I never really thought about what inspired me to write these characters. I think that some of the ideas came from my emotions and life, but for the most part the characters grabbed hold and took me on a journey. It's almost as if I met them in person (though they were only my imagination) and they told me their stories. Victoria had a way of waking me in the middle of the night to talk. I spent months writing her character at four in the morning. I loved hearing her story, but I hated those months of insomnia. I remember waking up at eleven in the morning with my head on my desk and I had typed pages of jjjjkkkkk.

Heather started off being a character I would never want to spend time with. This story was originally a comedy, but it turns out I'm not that funny. Heather was ultramodern and a party girl, and the elderly people, determined to get rid of her in order to keep their way of life, wreaked havoc on her home. As I matured as a writer, and as my characters spoke to me, a whole new plot came to life. The story became more about the demons Victoria faced. Then Heather showed herself to be a young woman who thinks she needs success more than anything but in reality she needs to find a way home. Their friendship became the pivotal healer in both their lives. I wanted to make these women strong and independent, but with a need for softness in their lives—a safe place to land where they found the love they've always needed.

The loneliness that you see Heather and Victoria experience was very similar to how I felt the first years I lived in California. I felt out of place and without a home, and in some ways, creating Nagog gave me comfort.

There is an array of characters in The Lake House, *from gentle Molly to womanizing Thomas. Which character was the most fun to create? Do you identify with one character in particular?*

Thomas was absolutely the most fun to write. Creating his scenes always made me laugh. I love Molly and she reminds me of my great-grandmother who always enveloped me in a soft hug of bosom and belly. But I created a special bond with Victoria.

I can't relate to Victoria's loss except through what she shared with me (and I know I'm talking about her as if she were real, but sometimes characters feel that way) though in some ways I relate to her need for a bigger life and her fear that if she went home she'd stay safe. Living in California, I've been torn between the life I've chosen and missing my family in Massachusetts. I get to travel the world and I choose to go after my biggest dreams instead of settling into family life. I have a distinct desire to explore everything this world has to offer and yet a need to be wrapped in the comfort of home. There are times when I wonder if I'll regret my choices later in life because I've spent so much time away from my family. Thank goodness for Skype, which allows me to feel like I'm at a family dinner every Wednesday night.

While Nagog is a fictional town, did you base it on a real-life counterpart, such as the Village of Nagog Woods in Acton, Massachusetts?

There's a wildlife sanctuary in Acton with a path that leads to Nagog Pond. When I lived in that area, I would walk through the woods until I reached the dock. It's a wonderful place to get lost in thought. In a place devoid of houses and roads, I found serenity sitting on the dock watching bright dragonflies flit around me while the fish jumped out of the lake to catch bugs. I was so excited when I saw the cover of the book because it replicated this place beautifully.

Littleton town center is exactly as I described in the book. When you drive through town you're transported back to a simpler time— well, except for the large Mobil station sign on the corner. When I was a child we'd drive out to Littleton and go to Kimball's Ice Cream. The lines were so long that sometimes it took an hour to get a sundae, but on a hot summer night it was worth the drive and the wait for the home-made treats. I think fond memories of eating ice cream under the stars in Littleton, Massachusetts, is why I chose this setting.

It took Molly's health issues for Victoria to finally face the loss of Annabelle. Did you always intend for Molly to have a cataclysmic collapse? Were there any other plot twists you considered to help Victoria to come to terms with her granddaughter's loss?

I was actually shocked when Molly collapsed. Writers are some-times just along for the ride and we don't know what's going to happen until it actually does. I was walking on a quiet country road in a snowstorm in Lenox, Massachusetts, when I saw Molly's collapse and I knew that it had to be part of the story. Molly was Victoria's only real touchstone to Nagog. As Victoria tried to move forward after Annabelle's death she was distraught with guilt. I think many times in life when we haven't dealt with an issue our lives seem to replay the same emotions no matter what the circumstances. Molly collapsing was a way to bring out Victoria's pain and the blame she felt for her granddaughter's death. This scene came to me in one of the first drafts, so I never considered another plot twist.

What is your favorite scene in the book, and why?

I cry every time I read the scene where Joseph and Victoria are on the beach having dinner. The tears always start when she gets up and sits in his lap, asking him to make love, knowing he's nervous, and says to him, "Relax, I'll wait." They're the same words he said to her as a teenager and I think it shows the tenderness, love, and desire they've had for each other their whole lives.

Another favorite is the one where Tommy and Heather are sitting on her front deck drinking root beer floats. I mean what woman hasn't fantasized about a nice summer evening, stargazing and flirting with an incredibly hot guy. But I also love this scene because it brings out these characters' personalities beyond their personal problems.

Victoria and Heather head to Nagog to find a sense of belonging, and all the characters in The Lake House *have spent their lives either searching for or nurturing their homes and families. Do you have a place like Nagog that you consider your true home?*

My grandfather built my grandparents' home when my mother was a young girl. When I was a kid, my family would go to their house every Sunday afternoon and on holidays. I would play with my brother and my eight cousins, racing up and down the hallway, playing wiffle ball in the backyard, and before we left getting hugs and kisses from everyone. Before I moved to California, I lived around the corner from my grandparents' house and many afternoons I would stop in unannounced. We'd sit at the kitchen table eating homemade cookies while my grandparents shared stories of their youth. My grandfather passed away before the publication of this book, but my grandmother still lives in the house with my mother as her caretaker. When I go home to Massachusetts I visit my grandfather's sugar shack in the backyard where he would make maple syrup, boiling the tree sap down to a dark amber color. I can still taste his blueberry pancakes drenched in maple syrup.

There are multiple motifs in The Lake House, *including loss, friendship, and acceptance. What do you consider to be the main theme(s) of the novel?*

I feel the main theme is the human need for a place to belong—for home. Our world is so fast-paced these days that it seems like time is slipping away as everything speeds up. I think with our technology and the ability to travel and communicate with the world through the web, we've lost a little of what Nagog represents. I wanted to create a story that brought people back to that need for human connection and a slower pace of life that has a deeper quality to it. I wanted to show that there's an intrinsic need to be part of a family, to feel accepted for exactly who you are, and that no matter the age, this need doesn't change.

If you could choose one message or lesson for your readers to take away from The Lake House, *what would it be?*

I want people to realize that our elders are important in our lives. We can learn from their stories and their life experience. We tend to care so much about youth and fear age that we don't want to see our elderly. When I was researching this book I spoke to women from the World War II generation, and I have to say that they told the best stories. I was surprised by their spunk and liveliness in spite of illnesses or injuries. I think we've lost something in our lives by dismissing older people because they might not keep up with modern technology or are possibly set in their ways. We have this idea that life is over after a certain age, but in truth many people fall in love, travel the world, or take up new sports in their final years.

Also, sometimes what we think we want in life is the exact opposite of what we really need. If Heather had moved into a community with all young people she probably would've continued to be uncertain of herself, always trying to keep up with what she believed she should be. By moving into a place where everyone was older, she was able to gain confidence and find what her heart desired.

The Lake House is your first published novel, and according to your 101 Dreams Come True website, it took years to complete. What was the most difficult part of the writing process for you? What was the most enjoyable?

I've never been a patient person. The saying, "God grant me patience now!" has always been my motto. Writing takes incredible patience. This book took many revisions, in part because there were so many characters and it spanned many years with numerous flashbacks, and also in part because I was a new writer learning the craft. Each time I did a revision I wanted to finish it as quickly as possible, but writing doesn't work that way. The characters speak when they're ready. Sometimes I have no choice but to work around the clock and at other times I stare at the television hoping my emotional and mental state will fire up.

Then there's the waiting while your agent or editor read what you've written. I signed with Foundry Literary and Media with Yfat Reiss Gendel and I thought that I would be published within months. But Yfat was only going to shop my book when she felt it was perfect and when she felt she could match me with the best house and editor. This took years and I woke most mornings wondering if my dream would ever come true.

But there's something magical about finding a storyline or figuring out a plot. I feel fulfilled when a story is buzzing in my brain. I love getting to know my characters and seeing the world through their eyes: I laugh, fall in love, cry, and get ticked off with them. I feel incredibly blessed to be able to write and share my stories with people.

Now that The Lake House is finished, what is next on your 101 dreams list? Do you have any plans for future novels?

I've already begun my second novel. It's going to be a busy year as *The Lake House* makes its way to publication and I try to pursue as many of the dreams on my list that I can. I'm already taking tango lessons, launching a new bridal company, and planning to play on a trapeze and bungee jump. I'm going to travel through the canyons of Nevada, Utah, and Arizona, and overseas. All the while I intend to keep writing, salsa dancing, and figure skating.